PRAISE FOR TARA JOHNSON

"What a triumph! I've long been a fan of Tara Johnson's writing and consider this her best work to date. With skill, grace, truth, and nuance, she has woven together a complex and satisfying story of captivity and freedom, love and fear, and of courage to act on conviction. The characters are robust and deftly drawn, bringing this important piece of little-known history to full-bodied life. *To Speak His Name* ranks among the best books I've read this year."

JOCELYN GREEN, CHRISTY AWARD-WINNING
AUTHOR OF *THE METROPOLITAN AFFAIR*

"A rare offering for historical fiction fans, To Speak His Name tells of the Irish slave trade in the Caribbean. Thrilling and chilling by turns, Avalina and Josiah's story is one of overcoming, conviction, and love against all odds. Beautifully written, researched, and highly recommended."

LAURA FRANTZ, CHRISTY AWARD-WINNING
AUTHOR OF *THE SEAMSTRESS OF ACADIE*

"A haunting tale of a horrific past that unfortunately is true in many respects, and yet the story of Avalina is so much more than that. From the depths of despair hope rises and ultimately overcomes. A

touching, tender yet very real read from the pen of Tara Johnson—
one you don't want to miss!"

MICHELLE GRIEP, CHRISTY AWARD-WINNING
AUTHOR OF MAN OF SHADOW AND MIST

"Avalina and Josiah's story in *To Speak His Name* had me turning
pages late into the night. Masterfully written, I loved watching their
spiritual journeys unfold. Add to that the romance and a nail-biting
uncertainty, and it had everything I've come to expect from a Tara
Johnson novel."

ANE MULLIGAN, AWARD-WINNING
AUTHOR OF BY THE SWEET GUM

"*All Through the Night* strikes all the right notes in a Civil War
drama. Principled yet flawed characters grow with every chapter, a
multifaceted setting brings the era's turmoil to life, and intrigue and
danger keep the pages turning. Inspired by a real woman, this novel
sings with spiritual truths sure to harmonize with any reader's life
story: Another winner from Tara Johnson."

JOCELYN GREEN, CHRISTY AWARD-
WINNING AUTHOR OF VEILED IN SMOKE

"A soul-satisfying story, peopled with characters who shine all the
brighter against the dark backdrop of the Civil War. *All Through the
Night* will leave you with a song in your heart and a deeper appreciation for the courageous men and women who endured and changed
the course of history by their stand for truth."

LAURA FRANTZ, CHRISTY-AWARD
WINNING AUTHOR OF THE LACEMAKER

"The tumult of the Civil War serves as a fitting backdrop for this
story of two wounded people searching for purpose and approval.

Cadence and Joshua are endearing characters, each seeking to do the right thing and bring healing to a broken world, no matter the cost. Tara Johnson has penned a romantic and touching tale that also highlights a little known and sinister aspect of Civil War history. All Through the Night is a memorable novel not to be missed!"

SARAH SUNDIN, BESTSELLING AND AWARD-WINNING AUTHOR OF *WHEN TWILIGHT BREAKS* AND THE SUNRISE AT NORMANDY SERIES

"Tara Johnson is one of those rare writers who can weave history and fiction so seamlessly the reader is never sure where one ends and the other begins. A true talent and author to watch."

ELIZBETH LUDWIG, *USA TODAY* BESTSELLING AUTHOR, ON *ALL THROUGH THE NIGHT*

"Johnson returns to the Civil War for another exciting inspirational romance featuring a dedicated, devout heroine ... Johnson embeds the story with her customary attention to historical detail, but the deeply wounded characters remain the focus of this ruminative investigation into the personal toll of war. Johnson's Christian elements are subtle, allowing Cassie and Gabe's perseverance to provide inspiration and hope. Fans of Lynn Austin will enjoy this."

PUBLISHERS WEEKLY ON *WHERE DANDELIONS BLOOM*

"Bringing facets of Civil War history to life, *Where Dandelions Bloom* is an engaging journey of hidden identity and of discovering what's most important in life—and in love."

TAMERA ALEXANDER, *USA TODAY* BESTSELLING AUTHOR

"In her sparkling debut...Johnson crafts an inspirational tale of love, fortitude, and what it means to do the right things when the very concept of 'right' is challenged."

PUBLISHERS WEEKLY, STARRED REVIEW
OF *ENGRAVED ON THE HEART*

"Blending realistic, relatable characters and the heartrending issue of slavery against a beautifully painted backdrop, Tara Johnson presents a debut novel that will leave you satisfied and yet still wanting more...I highly recommend this engaging and intriguing historical novel."

KIM VOGEL SAWYER, BESTSELLING
AUTHOR OF *BRINGING MAGGIE HOME*

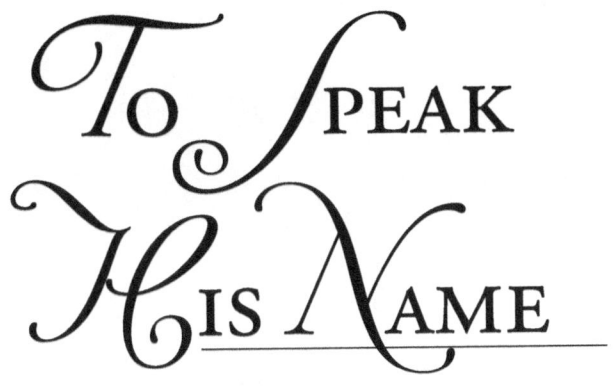

TARA JOHNSON

To Speak His Name, a Novel
© 2024 by Tara Johnson
Published in association with the Books & Such; Such Literary Management.
www.booksandsuch.com.

Paperback ISBN: 978-1-962845-03-8
Hardcover ISBN: 978-1-962845-04-5

Printed in the United States of America

For Dyllan Scout
You are my hero.

$\mathcal{P}$ROLOGUE

They tell me I was sold on a Thursday but being only a wee one, I have no recollection.

As I search through the dark recesses of my earliest years, I find only shards of images and snippets of color. And a melody. A sweet caressing song that haunts my dreams at night and calls to me during the waking hours. The words yet elude me but the song—the beautiful melody carried by the voice of a faceless woman—remains locked in my heart.

I recall small fragments: a woman's blue eyes, bright as a robin's egg, yet shadowed with a darkness I can't understand. Dirt-stained fingers wrapping around my arm to yank me from my bed. Spitting out salty, briny sea water onto sugary sand. Digging my hands into that same strange sugar and having it cake my dress and skin. Seeing the strange, braided trunks of palms, with their plumy tops.

I wandered through thick foliage amid the buzz of bees and the odd chirping of limb-swinging furry creatures, and I called for my mother over the cacophony of a strange new world. And there were ruins of a splintered ship, bobbing like flotsam on the wild ocean.

And then there was Master Cyrene. Big. So big, his form eclipsed the sun.

Just like he has ever since.

The fuzzy shards of my mind recall the shuffle into the large house that lorded over rich fields of sugar cane. Each morning, I pressed my face against the glass windows, studying the rows of men and women, their backs hunched over green, fluffy tops of cane as they gathered stalks into large bags. Others swung machetes through the lush growth. I was not allowed to be with them.

I did not belong. My pale skin was strange compared to the rest of those who inhabited this new land. A few with the sun-burned peach skin worked the fields. And then there was Molly, with her large bosom, freckled face, and lilting voice, as she stirred pots of stewed chicken in the kitchen and snuck me pinches of sweet confections such as sugar cakes or tamarind balls. Something about her reminded me of home, though I could not remember where home was. I often found myself staying close to her side until one of the servants shooed me away.

I was told my work was to scrub pots, clean out fireplaces, run errands for those in the kitchen, and entertain when the rich folk came to visit Master Cyrene. I remember little of it... only snatches of those early days, like the tiniest fabric remnants sown into a monstrous quilt. By day, my heart twisted for my mother. At night, I cried myself to sleep, the far side of my bed cold.

Yet the memory forever etched in my mind is quivering before Master Cyrene, whose tongue could bludgeon worse than a hundred clubs. His fists curled as he stared down at me. His roar was as fearsome as the wild animals who screeched through the night hours and lurked in murky shadows of the jungle.

"Baara promised me this child can sing. She heard her humming a melody, did she not? I want a songbird, a girl who can entertain and soothe my guests. This child does nothing but squeak like a mouse."

A woman placed a bracing hand on my back, her fingers digging through my thin dress to pinch my skin.

"Sir, she's only jus' arrived. She's frightened. Perhaps she needs time to adjust."

Master Cyrene's face contorted like the wooden masks he kept in his library. "Bah! My whip will help her adjust, and loosen her tongue as well!"

After my first beating, I rarely spoke again.

CHAPTER I

April 8, 1816
St. John Parish, Barbados

"Get to it, girl."

The slightest whoosh greeted my ears before a bone-jarring crack reverberated against my skull. Pain exploded in my head. With my ears ringing, it took long moments to register Baara's hand hovering, waiting to strike again. Sucking air through my teeth, I rose from the hearth, the bucket of ashes bumping my hip.

"You are much too hard on her, Baara," Tabia scolded. A surprising ally, since the woman was usually found whispering about me. *"A witch, that one is."* She'd said it often enough. "Da girl is simple. Striking her will not make her smarter."

I braved a glance at Baara, glaring at me with her crossed arms, dark eyes flashing.

She turned her focus to Tabia, brows lowered. "What do we do when we want a horse to move? If she is seen slacking, da Master will be rid of her. Do we want her tossed out on da street like the rest of da Redlegs?"

"No, but—"

Enough of your insolence. Or must I strike you too?"

Tabia tucked her chin and scurried away. I averted my gaze but stole another glance at the harsh woman. Her face was stern and

1

unbending, and I wondered if she had ever smiled, ever spoke with anything other than garlicky displeasure.

And then, afterward, the faintest light flickered in her eyes—not sympathy, for the woman had too much sense for such a base, useless emotion—but perhaps a kind of understanding, as if she too had been the lowest in the house and remembered the toil and chapped fingers, the loneliness such work birthed in relative isolation.

And if Baara had felt isolated, how much more for a white, freckled, mute slip of a young woman.

Or perhaps I had only imagined the glimmer of empathy before the shutter to the housekeeper's soul slammed shut once more.

I shivered and darted toward the kitchen door. I must cause no trouble.

The Redlegs... Would Master Cyrene cast me out, dooming me to a life with such a forsaken group?

Swallowing the dread settling like a noose around my throat, I hurried out the door, ignoring the bustle of servants and the scents of the midday meal preparations. I tossed the cold ashes onto the heap outside the pig pen, barely hearing their grunts as they rooted in the mud. Heat warmed my shoulders and danced across my cheeks. I raised my face to the sun, longing for... what? Something elusive. Something I had no words to describe.

"Ah, there she is. The Red Bird of Paradise."

My smile grew at the mention of my old nickname. Dear Matias. His white teeth flashed and he stopped next to the sty, taking a moment to wipe his stained shirtsleeve against his sweaty forehead. Gray peppered his springy curls.

"It'll be a hot one today, eh, Red Bird?"

I nodded and smiled at the old nickname. Matias had called me Red Bird of Paradise ever since I had been brought to the island, declaring that my red hair reminded him of the tropical bloom. Only

Molly and Master Cyrene remembered my real name. To everyone else, I was *that girl.*

I didn't mind being invisible. Invisible was safe.

"I have something for you." Digging into his pocket, he pulled out a bright blue feather. "Here."

I gasped at its beauty and gently ran my finger over its downy softness, marveling at the exquisite color. Aqua, like the dazzling water of the ocean when it roared in the morning. The feather melted down into a deep sapphire blue at its tip.

Matias returned my grin with a toothy one of his own.

"I knew you'd like it, what with watching the birds like you do. This feather is from a violetear. One of those beautiful hummingbirds that fancy the hibiscus blooms near the south side of the garden. Their feathers are a rare find."

I ran my finger down the plumy spine, delighting in the ticklish sensation. A work of art.

Matias wiped his forehead once more. "I better get back to work but I thought you'd like it. Just another gift of beauty from our Creator. Bye, Red Bird."

I watched him stroll away, machete perched on his shoulder as he whistled a jaunty tune. His simple comment troubled me.

This feather, a gift from our Creator? Who was he? Where was he?

Yet my questions could not be voiced, locked behind a door of silence.

The big house was lit up like a bonfire, light spilling through every window as dancers shrilled their excitement and laughed as couples stepped to the traditional songs of the season across the back lawn. Lanterns hung from every post. Bright panels of blue, crimson, and violet waved through the night air as the steady thump from the *boleadoras* blended with the soft strum of guitars and the gentle rattles of the maracas.

I held the platter of sweet cakes, waiting for an opportune moment to weave through the guests—powerful land owners shadowed by their elegant wives in glittering jewels and brightly colored silks, politicians, and those bestowed with the good fortune of Master Cyrene's favor—some ravenous from appetites that would not be sated, and others inebriated from the constant flow of rum.

This jubilee was much like all the others that had come before it. It was a festival of sorts to kick off the summer months before work consumed all the land owners, as well as a kind of supplication to the gods for fertile crops and an abundant harvest. The only one who soured under such talk of the gods and their fickle blessings was Matias. The man's lips would pinch hearing the servants' prattle. He skirted the activities with a wide berth, choosing instead to rest in his cabin with a block of wood and a knife while he carved trinkets for the slave children.

I managed to watch some of the festivities between serving drinks of mauby and rum punch, and offering delicacies such as tamarind balls, *conkies*, and rum cake. The elaborate dances and teasing expressions between the men and the women delighted my heart. If only every day was so joyful.

As I carried an empty platter across the lawn, the musicians struck up the music to "Jean and Johnnie" and I stopped, nerves buzzing as wild cheers rose up from the crowd. I all but forgot about the tray in my hands, entranced as brazen, buxom women stepped forward and danced with wild abandon for the cheering men. Heat crawled up my back and nestled in my cheeks, yet I could not look away from their swaying hips and suggestive smiles. A dance celebrating fertility could include nothing less.

I pulled my gaze away to gauge the reaction of the crowd, scanning the faces looking down from the big house's balcony. Some laughed, others, mainly women, looked away, their lips pinched in disapproval. When my gaze collided with Master Cyrene, my breath snagged in my chest. He was staring openly at me, his expression revealing nothing.

Had I done something wrong?

I swallowed the sour sensation coating my tongue and hastened away from the ribald music, seeking the busyness and stuffy heat of the kitchen.

Padding inside, I set the platter on the worktable, where Molly was quick to refill it with slices of coconut bread.

"How goes the festival? Are the guests having a good time?" Her normally fair skin was flushed red with the heat of the kitchen.

I nodded and averted my eyes, my former excitement doused. Molly appeared not to notice and she artfully arranged the delicacies on the platter.

"Aye, 'tis good. Master Cyrene will be in a buoyant mood, then." She tsked under her breath. "Unhappy masters make for unhappy servants."

I looked away and something in my expression must have given her pause.

She stopped and brushed the crumbs from her fingers before watching me through narrowed lids. "What is it, child?"

Child. She always called me that. Had ever since I had been carried inside the big house. But I was a child no longer. By my best count, at least half a score had passed since I'd arrived, ten years at the least. Perhaps even longer ... at least, by measuring time according to the seasons.

The images of the fertility dance and the Master's odd stare caused me to shiver. I used my right hand to buff my left arm.

Molly continued to peruse my face and I bit my lip. The words wouldn't come for anyone but her.

"It's Master," I whispered, pointing past the kitchen to the balcony. "I don't like the way he looks at me."

Understanding dawned on the matron's round face. She stepped close, her voice dropping to a whisper, russet brows pinching. "Has he done something?"

How to respond? He hadn't done a thing, not really. Yet his gaze had caused me to recoil. And even if he did, there was nothing that could be done. This was his world. His plantation. No one could stop him from taking what he wanted. I shook my head.

Molly's lips pursed. "Don't find yourself alone with him, you hear?"

Before I could nod, Baara rounded the corner, her scowl deep. "Girl! Where are da refreshments? Da last thing you want is Master shaming you before da guests. Get to it!"

I nodded and grabbed the now-full platter of bread before scooting out the door. When I returned to the festival, Master Cyrene was nowhere to be seen.

CHAPTER 2

Josiah Holland stood on the bow of the ship and inhaled deeply of the briny ocean air. The deck canted and he braced his feet as the first mate called out rigging instructions to scurrying crewmen. Salt spray sprinkled his face as he watched clouds slowly creep across the sunny sky.

Footfalls pounded behind him just before a hand slapped his back.

"Well, son, what do you think?"

Josiah glanced sidelong at his father and smiled as he gazed over the endless horizon of rolling waves. "The power. It's immense."

George Holland nodded, a sprig of his thick gray hair lifting with the wind. "It is, at that. The sailing master believes we'll be in Barbados within two days' time."

Josiah nodded. "What's it like?"

Father plucked a pipe from his pocket and made short work of stuffing the bowl full of tobacco. "Beautiful. Full of exotic flora and fauna. Strange fruit. The other slave holders are quite hospitable." He chuckled, striking a match against the rail of the ship. The pipe was soon smoking. "They seem to enjoy showing off their opulence."

"Do they have so much?"

The soft *p-p-p* of Father puffing his pipe was the only sound for a long moment.

"Do you see the size of the ship we sail aboard, son?" His barreled chest puffed out as he widened his stance.

Josiah grated under the conceit coloring his words.

"You've benefited from my hard work for years, content to reap the plantation's rewards while you frittered away your time at Willington Academy."

Josiah chuckled, but the sting of his words nettled. "You begrudge an education?"

"From a tutor, no. Willington was your mother's idea. And now, after eight years away, you have no idea how the family's operations run. How old are you now? Three and a score? Four?"

Josiah gritted his teeth. "I'm twenty-five."

"Long past time to learn." The smoke Father exhaled was snatched by the wind, tossed by the rising gales. Josiah frowned as he stared out across the expanse of water. The sky was swiftly darkening to lead. What did such bobbing and rocking feel like to those crammed below?

"Was it necessary to bring so many slaves aboard? Three hundred and fifty-seven seems excessive."

"And I'll sell every one of them." The deck tipped again, causing them to clutch the railing as a wave splashed against the hull, tossing up white foam that peppered their skin. "Think of the riches we'll gather from just one run to Barbados, Josiah. And I travel there once a year. How else do you think I keep your mother and sister fitted in their finery?" His laugh was cast away with careless ease. "Besides, the plantation owners of Barbados need more slaves to work their fields. They are practically begging us to help them. We're providing a service."

Josiah inhaled a courageous breath and turned to face his father... a man so similar to Josiah's own height and build, save for the generous gray that streaked his brown hair and beard.

"I've been wanting to talk with you about that. The profit, I mean. If we are to gain as much as you say, I wondered if it might be feasible to let me attend South Carolina College this fall."

"The university?" Father's brows lifted and he snorted a gust of white smoke from his nostrils. "Whatever for?"

Josiah swallowed. "To study. To learn."

A glower followed the pronouncement. "Willington Academy has taught you all you need to run the plantation. I will finish what they began in matters of business. What more would you need?"

Josiah's lips thinned into a hard line, hope slipping through his fingers like sand through a sieve. "I thought the study of law would be beneficial."

"Bah! A waste of time and money." Father waved away the notion with a sweep of his large hand and glanced across the expanse of churning sea. "What you need has been passed down from my father, and his father before him." He grunted and stroked the bowl of his pipe. "I thought when the South Carolina General Assembly founded the university several years ago, it would be an experiment in frivolity." He shook his head, even as a tug of briny wind blew the pipe smoke away. "Productive lives are learned through the old ways."

Josiah opened his mouth to reply when footsteps pounded across the deck. He turned to see sailors carrying emaciated bodies from the cargo hold below. One by one, the seamen tossed the rigid corpses into the ocean with a resounding splash.

"What's going on?" Josiah curled his fists and moved to stop the sailors as more bodies continued to be hauled up, each form gaunter than the next. Father placed a staying hand on his arm.

"Calm down. They didn't survive the voyage. That's all. It's to be expected."

Josiah blinked. "So you toss them overboard? Like refuse? No ceremony? No prayers spoken on their behalf?"

Father puffed, not a speck perturbed by the morbid loss of life being paraded before his eyes. "It's not ideal but it happens every voyage. Sometimes we lose a crew member too." He shrugged. "A pity, but there's naught to be done for it. Travel by sea claims many lives."

Swallowing, Josiah watched as thirty-two corpses plunged into watery graves... unmarked, unsung. A knot formed in the pit of his stomach, even as nausea bubbled up his throat.

He had been aware of his father's callousness at home among their own slaves on the South Carolina plantation, but when a professor at Willington challenged the boys to read Aphra Behn's *The Royal Slave*, Josiah's eyes had been opened to a new ideology... and it had haunted him ever since. When he eventually stepped into the role of owner and manager, he would be able to right many of his father's wrongs. Make sure each man and woman was treated fairly.

Why had he not considered how his father's actions spilled across his other business endeavors... rippling across an ocean?

"Master Holland?"

Josiah looked down. A wide-eyed slave boy of no more than seven stood staring up at him, his large, dark eyes solemn. He held a rectangular box in his hands.

"Captain Mayfield wants to know if you'd like a cigar."

Josiah smiled and squeezed the boy's shoulder, trying to ease some of the seriousness from his face. "What a kind offering. And what is your name?"

"Toby, sir."

"A good name for a strong boy." Josiah took the humidor and selected a cigar, lifting it to his nose to inhale the aroma of cherry. He was not overly fond of smoking, but the cigar might prove beneficial in sweetening the disposition of their host in Barbados. "Please tell the captain he is most generous."

Toby carefully took the wooden box back into his possession and offered a tremulous smile, as if afraid revealing a bit of happiness might not be tolerated.

"How long have you served the captain, Toby?"

The lad scrunched his brow as he thought. "Less than a year, sir, best I can recollect."

"Only a year?" George Holland frowned. "Not long, but I suppose you've got your sea legs by now."

"Yes, sir." Toby swallowed, returning his attention back to Josiah. "When my momma died on the ship, the captain kept me."

Josiah stared into his small, earnest face. "Your mother is gone?"

"Yes, sir. Died on the voyage. Got the sickness down in the hold."

George grunted. "Likely typhus."

Josiah swallowed the lump rising in his throat. Typhus? What went on below deck? Such diseases were often brought about by waste and unclean conditions, whether through food, water, or some other way miasmas traveled.

"Where were you and your momma originally headed?"

Toby looked down, shifting his weight. "Don't know, sir. The slave catchers, they captured us and chained us up aboard ship. Couldn't understand what they was saying." He swallowed. "Captain Mayfield, he taught me to speak in English."

A sudden pang twisted Josiah's chest. What would it be like to enjoy a normal day's work with family and suddenly find yourself chained and shoved into the hold of a ship by strange faces, crude men, and foreign speech?

"Go on now, boy." George waved his hand impatiently. "Attend to your duties."

"Yes, sir." Toby scurried away, head bent as he lugged the humidor away.

But something about the silent shouts in his mahogany eyes refused to leave Josiah be.

Hours later, when he laid his head upon his bed, sleep would not come. Watery graves flooded his thoughts.

Sometime in the wee hours of morning, Josiah pushed aside the blanket covering his body and sat up. Enough! Why couldn't his mind let go of the poor souls tossed overboard? Perhaps Father was right... he was being overly emotional. The sea was treacherous... or was it only an excuse to mask oppression?

The only way to know for sure was to visit the bowels of the ship that held the enslaved. He would find no peace until he did.

Pulling the glowing lantern from the hook on the wall, he held it high as he opened his berth door and crept down the narrow passageway, following it as he descended deeper in the heart of the massive ship. With each new set of stairs, the air grew damper. When he finally stumbled into the cargo hold, he gasped for breath. The massive space choked the air from his lungs. The odor was thick and fetid, a nauseating blend of human waste and sweat. Pulling a handkerchief from his pocket, he used it to cover his nose and mouth.

The lantern clanked in his hand as he lifted it, its piercing light illuminating half-naked men, women, and children. The chains clinked as they pushed up from the sticky floor, staring at him with fear etched into their gaunt faces. A little girl to his right shrank back at seeing him, her voice emitting the softest of squeaks.

Swallowing down the bile climbing his throat, he swung the light over the room, turning in a slow circle. No food. Buckets of fetid water. A couple of chamber pots running over with waste. His gaze fastened on an old man curled in the corner. Josiah approached, noting the protruding ribs of the man's chest. His eyes were closed but there was no rise and fall in his chest. Dead.

All these poor souls were forced to sit with their own excrement and sleep with the dead?

He'd seen enough.

With leaden steps, he climbed the stairs and found his way to the deck, sucking in deep draughts of the briny air that slapped his cheeks.

He'd never seen something so vile. And he was helpless to know how to stop it.

Sunday morning dawned with calm waters, a blessed respite after the evening's stormy tumult. The ship's rigging creaked with the gentle sway of the waves, like a mother's lullaby, but Josiah felt no comfort. Only a nagging queasiness in his middle with the images of the dead slaves, and the starving people below who refused to leave him be.

He ground the toe of his boot into the slick wood of the deck, weary of the stiff chairs, and even more fatigued by the droning voice of the minister addressing the group of sailors and officers. His gaze kept straying to Toby's thin form, who stood at attention to the side, his expression blank, eyes empty.

Did he miss his mother? What life would he have aboard ship with a crew of crass men and foul language, watching men and women die the same way his mother had?

Josiah swallowed and blinked heavily.

He attempted to focus on the potbellied, pockmarked minister, but the man sounded as if he were reading from a grade-school primer instead of the Scriptures.

He stood before the small congregation gathered on deck, his voice dreadfully stale.

"'Woe unto them that decree unrighteous decrees, and that write grievousness which they have prescribed; To turn aside the needy from judgment, and to take away the right from the poor of my people, that widows may be their prey, and that they may rob the fatherless ... '"

Josiah squirmed. The words, though lacking conviction, needled. Why?

His gaze strayed once more to the little boy silently standing at attention. Where was his father? Josiah could almost hear the screams of pain that must have ensued as he was ripped away from his loved ones.

Blowing out a breath, he tried to distract himself, watching a flock of birds fly overhead, their destination somewhere beyond.

The minister let the Bible fall shut. "And now, a hymn."

He gestured toward one of the sailors, who stood and cleared his voice.

> *"O for a thousand tongues to sing*
> *My great Redeemer's praise*
> *The glories of my God and King*
> *The triumphs of His grace."*

The man's rich baritone rang across the waves, sending shivers down Josiah's spine. Powerful. Others lifted their voices to join the song.

> *"Jesus! The name that charms our fears*
> *That bids our sorrows cease*
> *'Tis music in the sinner's ears*
> *'Tis life and health and peace.*
> *He breaks the power of cancelled sin*
> *He sets the prisoner free;*
> *His blood can make the foulest clean;*
> *His blood availed for me."*

Josiah's breath snagged in his chest, awareness trickling through him like dripping water.

He sets the prisoner free . . .

Those corpses had all been prisoners. Father had been their captor. And he, Josiah, had played a part in their bondage.

Trembling, he looked down at his hands. Not crimson with blood, but somehow, he felt as if he'd plunged a dagger into each of their hearts. His tongue was thick as he glanced to his father.

The old man sat like a toad. Bored. Unaffected.

Josiah looked down, scarcely able to draw a breath. Why was this bothering him so? He'd been raised knowing the necessity of slavery as a means for a productive plantation. He'd watched the newest slaves arrive fresh from the auction block, some of their faces defiant and hostile. Others were resigned, yet Josiah had not empathized one way or another. It was a way of life. Nothing more. No different than the changing of the seasons, the crimson leaves of autumn, or the swelling river after April rains.

Or was it?

He'd heard the rantings of the impassioned Quakers, had read snippets of their circulated pamphlets. When his father spied the traitorous material, he'd raged, labeling them nothing more than addlepated zealots before tossing the pamphlets in the fire. Josiah had assumed the Quakers were merely ignorant of plantation systems.

Perhaps he'd been wrong.

He looked up and found Toby watching him, his mouth tugged downward, eyes flooded with an emotion Josiah couldn't define. As if . . .

He was trapped and desperate to be released.

The men ended the hymn and the worshipers dispersed, yet Josiah sat, his thoughts rumbling like a thunderclap.

What if everything he believed about his life, his values, his inheritance, was a lie?

CHAPTER 3

I breathed deeply, inhaling thick pulls of damp air as I pressed my back into the flowing fronds of the bearded fig tree. Here in the field, at least, no one could see me. The chirrups of crickets filled the air, assuring me I was far away from Baara's calls or Master's knowing gaze.

Hands quivering, I reached into the basket and held up the book. I studied the markings etched into its dark green cover. I let the basket drop at my feet and held the precious object reverently. It was brave to smuggle it from Master's library. Tracing my finger over the odd curves and lines, I frowned.

No. Not brave. Foolish. Reckless. Risking the lash for an object I could make no sense of. My throat clamped as I slumped against the tree trunk, letting my body slide to the sandy soil.

Ever since I had seen Tabia studying a small book behind the henhouse one cool spring morning, my curiosity had grown. Where had she found the slim volume? Master Cyrene strictly forbade any slaves reading or owning these sorts of materials. But Tabia wasn't just glancing over the print... she was studying it, absorbing every word. When she heard my approach, she hastily shoved the book into her apron pocket and scurried back to work.

What mysteries had Tabia uncovered that I had yet to learn?

A monkey chattered overhead, taunting me. As I stared through the thick foliage hugging my seclusion, some wordless need clawed at my heart.

16

I was trapped. Forever bound to Master Cyrene and this land. I yearned for something I couldn't name. Couldn't grasp.

My breath seized as I focused on the volume resting on my lap. I picked it up, marveling at the crackling pop it emitted when I forced its pages open. Had no one read it? How many other books filled Master's library that lay unexplored?

My gaze roamed over the black figures, the bends, lines, and juts. I stared hard, willing their meaning to become clear. The longer I sat, the greater my frustration. Slamming the volume shut, I tossed it into the basket, ignoring the sudden flutter of a warbler from a bush behind me as my outburst startled it into flight.

Understanding the strange symbols was key. It must be. The key to unlocking the fear that stole my voice. My past. My questions. But how could I unlock their meanings without someone to show me?

Letting my head tip back, I allowed the sluggish warmth of the afternoon to dull my senses and seep into my bones. The roar of the ocean beckoned beyond the lush vegetation of flowers and trees. A bee buzzed near my ear and I swatted it away. Monkeys hopped from branch to branch, scavenging for mangos, nuts, and papayas, tossing away the remnants with a plop on the dense forest floor.

And not too far off, a melody drifted from somewhere beyond the trees. A masculine voice. Old. Curious, I craned my neck to discover the source.

"When I survey the wond'rous cross ... "

Rising, I grabbed the basket and tiptoed through the brush, careful of each snap of fallen palm that littered the jungle floor.

"On which the Prince of Glory died ... "

I crept closer to the voice as it grew stronger. Bending, I peered through the brush to see Matias sitting cross-legged on the ground, eyes closed, face lifted as he held his palms open to the sky. His springy, black curls were frayed with the humidity, and his mahogany skin glistened with moisture, but his expression was perfectly peaceful. Had I ever experienced the rapture I beheld on his face?

"My richest gain I count but loss, and pour contempt on all my pride."

I frowned, confused. He must have heard my footfalls in the sandy soil, for he turned and smiled upon spying me hiding among the foliage.

"Ah, Red Bird. Come. Sit with me as I worship."

I wouldn't hurt the sweet old man for anything so I obeyed, setting the basket near the base of a tree before easing down next to him. Deep lines crinkled around his eyes.

"Today is a day to worship. It's the day the Almighty One has made. I sing His praises, yes?"

I nodded but watched him carefully as he resumed his earlier stance of upraised palms and face. His voice broke as more words poured past his cracked lips.

"Forbid it, Lord, that I should boast, save in the death of Christ my God. All the vain things that charm me most, I sacrifice them to His blood."

I didn't understand. He called his god Christ yet said he was dead. Why worship a dead god?

The song drifted away and Matias's eyes closed as the melody shifted to words . . . words spoken as if this god could hear him.

"I thank Thee, most Holy One, that You hear my humble cries. Give me this day my bread. Keep my tongue from evil and my feet from mischief. Bless Master Cyrene and help me to serve him faithfully, not as unto a man but as serving You. Bless Red Bird and draw her to You. Amen."

I stared through the entire ritual, watching my friend carefully. There was naught but earnest pleading in his expression. A kind of devotion I didn't understand. Who did he think could hear him, save for myself?

He reopened his eyes and drew in a cleansing breath before turning to me with a white-toothed smile. "You think I'm crazy, Red Bird, no?"

I shrugged but puzzled all the more when he threw back his head and laughed. "I worship the Almighty, taught by my mother when she was enslaved in Dominica. I find few here on this plantation that share my beliefs so I come the first day of the week to commune with my God alone." His dark eyes twinkled. "Save for today, when you blessed me with your presence."

He stood and offered me a helping hand up. "You come back next week and we will worship again, yes?"

I nodded dumbly, unsure of what I had agreed to.

Spying my basket, he crossed under the small canopy of the trees and retrieved it but frowned when he saw the book I had tucked inside. Lines deepened between his brows. "Where did you find this?"

I swallowed. I dared not admit I had taken it from Master Cyrene's library. But Matias was not simple. He knew. He must.

He thumbed through the book, lines tightening around his mouth. He looked up and speared me with a reprimand. "You must hide this. Never let anyone see it."

Breath catching in my throat, I nodded. He was right. My foolishness would not only affect me, but the lives of all other slaves on the plantation if the theft were discovered.

He sighed and dropped the book in my basket. "Come, Red Bird. I'll walk you back."

"Ach! Girl, where have you been?"

Baara slapped my fingers as she yanked the empty basket from my hands. I sucked a breath through my teeth. I had earned her wrath by sneaking away for a respite. I made no cry, but bore the shame with downcast eyes, my hands throbbing with pain-filled pulses.

At least the book was now safely hidden away under my mattress.

"Don't you know what is going on?"

I lifted my gaze and shook my head. She heaved a thick sigh and adjusted the orange fabric wrapped around the crown of her dark hair.

"Two men from da states have arrived. Slave traders, and Master wants to entertain them. Give them housing for da night. Go to da east wing. You will prepare da guest bedrooms."

I nodded and scurried away to do her bidding lest the scowling matron strike me again.

As I padded down the corridors to the guest rooms, my thoughts tumbled and crashed like the waves at high tide.

Slave traders? Was Master Cyrene looking to purchase more slaves? I swallowed. Weren't the many in the fields and the dozens who filled this house enough? My pulse slammed to a crawl. Or perhaps he thought to sell those he already had.

Throat dry, I hastened into the first room—smoothing bedding, scrubbing down every piece of furniture until it shined. I must please Master Cyrene.

Life on the island was difficult. How much worse would a new master be?

Josiah walked slowly through the plantation's parlor, his hands behind his back, as he drank in the stunning details. Cyrene Harding had made quite a home for himself, surpassing even the most lavish houses in South Carolina.

Stopping in front of the massive windows, he gazed out, admiring the sweeping grounds and tropical plants growing in lush decadence around the home. Palms, ferns, fig and cherry trees dotted the landscape. Flowers boasting the brightest blooms of red, purple, buttery yellow, and even sapphire mingled through vine and trellis. He smiled to himself. The gardeners back home would be green with envy at the beauty.

Footfalls approached. Josiah turned to see Father entering the parlor, his shipman's clothing now changed to the attire of a man of means.

"Well, Josiah, my boy, what do you think?"

"It's captivating." He gestured toward the massive windows lining the large room. "The windows are especially impressive. The use of light is stunning."

"Mm." Father grunted, plucking his handkerchief from his pocket and mopping his neck. "Too much light for me. Draw the curtains, I always say." He frowned and tucked the fabric away. "Blasted humidity. It's thick enough to cut."

Another set of footfalls approached, followed by a booming baritone voice.

"Gentlemen!"

A swarthy man entered the room. His eyes and hair and goatee were dark, with only the thinnest threads of silver snaking throughout. He smiled widely, but it did nothing to mask an underlying danger in his gait and manner. Like a mountain lion. Watching, calculating. Far too shrewd.

"I am Cyrene Harding." He tugged on his blue silk vest, his lips twitching into a smile. "Welcome to the Azaka Mede Plantation." His voice was cultured and clipped, bearing little of the Caribbean accent that colored most language in Barbados.

Father bowed low. "We thank you for your most generous hospitality."

"Of course." Harding nodded. "I can do nothing less for our western neighbors."

Josiah's gaze drifted from the traditional furnishings—Turkish rugs, crystal chandeliers, and Chippendale furniture—to their host. "That's an interesting name. Azaka Mede. Where does it come from?"

"Ah." Harding strolled to a small table filled with decanters holding amber liquid. Pulling the stopper from the top of the largest, he poured a glassful and held it out to Father, who took it with eager hands. "That is a good question." He gestured toward the remaining glasses. "Would you care to imbibe?"

Josiah waved the offer away. "Thank you, no."

Nodding, Harding poured himself a generous amount and smiled. "This plantation is a tribute to the god of agriculture. The natives worship Azaka Mede at the time of harvest when the granaries are full." He sipped from his glass and smiled. "Nothing better than our rum."

Josiah arched a brow. "You said the natives worship this god. Who do you worship, sir?"

"Josiah..." Father murmured, his voice rippling a quiet warning.

Harding merely smiled. "I worship nothing, Mr. Holland, save, perhaps, the glorious companionship of a woman from time to time."

Heat flushed Josiah's collar at the lewd insinuation. Father's chuckle only served to widen Harding's grin.

"Come now. Enough of all that." Moving to the fireplace, Cyrene Harding pulled a cord hanging from the ceiling. "Let us get you settled and comfortable, yes? Tonight, we will dine and be entertained. Tomorrow, we shall discuss business."

Father finished his rum and placed the empty glass on the table. "We thank you."

A dark-skinned woman entered, her bearing erect, hair wrapped in a bright orange strip of silk, her gaze trained on the floor. Harding turned.

"Baara, show these men to their rooms. See to their every comfort."

The servant dipped her head. "Yes, sir. Come dis way, gentlemen." The soft lilt of her accent was like a gentle breeze.

They followed her down the winding corridors, marveling at the architecture of the plantation—marble accents and intricately carved wood trim and banisters. She showed Josiah to his quarters first, pushing the door open with grandiose relish.

"Here, sir. Will dis suit your needs?"

The room was decorated in shades of blue, complete with massive windows, a gold damask lounging couch, and a wide walnut bed. His trunk waited at its foot.

"This is more than adequate. Thank you."

The servant nodded. "You have your own lavatory in da adjoining room. A servant will arrive momentarily to unpack your trunk."

He shook his head. "There is no need. I can see to it."

Her brows lifted. "As you wish, sir."

She left to attend to Father, leaving Josiah in the quiet of the massive bedroom. A personal lavatory? He moved to explore such a phenomenon.

Josiah swung the door wide. A gasp startled him, propelling him backward. There inside the small room stood a trembling girl. No, not a girl. A woman. Lithe of form, with hair the color of copper. Her curls had escaped their pins and cascaded down her slim shoulders. Smoky blue eyes blinked wide in her face. Her full lips rounded, revealing her shock. She clutched a rag and bucket in her hands.

"Pardon me, miss. I only thought to see what lay beyond the door."

The beauty merely licked her lips, her gaze darting around the cramped space for escape. Josiah puzzled. Did she fear him?

"I mean you no harm."

Her chest heaved, breath quick. She spoke not a word. From alarm? How to help her understand she was safe? He stepped farther back into the bedroom.

"See? I've only just arrived. My trunk is here." He smiled gently. "Forgive me for intruding."

The young woman blinked, her breathing now slower. She shook her head, lifting the rag and bucket as if trying to show him. His brows lifted.

"You were cleaning?"

She nodded, the faintest traces of a smile hovering around her lips. He returned her smile.

"For that I am most grateful. Forgive me for startling you."

Nodding once more, she padded from the lavatory and crossed the bedroom toward the door. Josiah was overcome with the urge to keep her with him a bit longer.

"Wait!"

She turned.

"What is your name?"

The maid merely smiled shyly and slipped from the room.

CHAPTER 4

I awoke from a dreamless sleep, my small quarters above the kitchen shrouded in shadows. Morning's rays had yet to paint the sky. The air was sticky with humidity but cool. I stretched, curling my toes into the worn quilt that I had been given as a child when I arrived on the island. The patchwork had long ago faded into dull hues of red, green, and light blue but there was a strange kind of comfort in its presence. It was one thing I could call my own. Nothing could ever make me part with its thin warmth.

Pushing up to a sitting position, I leaned over and struck a match to light the lone candle next to my bed. Its light pierced the darkness as the acrid odor curled in my nose. Reaching under my pillow, I pulled out the book I had taken only yesterday from Master's library. Guilt tasted bitter on my tongue. I must find a way to return it.

I traced my finger over the shimmering gold border engraved deep into the mossy cover. Entrancing. Sighing, I hugged it to my chest. Perhaps what I found irresistible was the mystery that lay inside. What did it say? How could I learn?

I'd believed none of the slaves on Azaka Mede could read ... until I watched Tabia hungrily drinking in the words. How many others had acquired the skill yet kept the secret hidden? And why should station be the difference between ignorance and knowing what lay between the pages of a book?

Master Cyrene said he provided all we needed. We ought not long for anything more than our food and provisions. Yet something in me rebelled at his words.

My gaze shifted to the colorless walls and dropped to the floor. Something small and dark moved near the baseboards. Tucking the book under my pillow, I watched a line of ants parading down the wood trim where the dingy walls met the floor. They moved with order, precision, and a haste the plantation overseers would envy. No doubt last evening's rain had driven them inside to seek sustenance and shelter.

My eyes pricked. Was this all there was to life? Work, preparing food, exhaustion, and death? And then what? Nothing? The bleakness of it washed over me with a cold I wished I could erase. I shivered and buffed my arms beneath my thin white muslin gown.

Or perhaps the ants were working for something I couldn't understand.

How did they come to be? How did I? All I knew of my own existence was the scattered memories of being cast from the sea upon sand.

Some thought me a witch. I'd heard the children of the field slaves say so. Maybe I was. Birthed by the ocean and cursed upon earth. My voice often stolen away by some kind of strange magic. Whenever someone stared at me, the cold fear would rise through my middle, choking off sound and thought.

For one who longed for nothing more than the power of speech, and for the icy terror to leave me be, my powers were few indeed.

"Did you hear the news?"

I looked up from chopping a mound of pecans to see Molly's round face near mine, her words soft as a summer gale, brows lifted. Wisps of faded red curls framed her brow.

I shook my head and she leaned closer, casting a quick look over her shoulder to make sure we were still alone in the large kitchen.

"A slave in the Saint George Parish was accused of poisoning his master."

I gasped and watched Molly's lips compress into a thin line, my hands pausing from their work.

"'Tis truth I speak. Philip brought news of it just this morn. He overheard Master Cyrene discussing it with his guests. Happened on the Green Hope plantation, so's I was told. A house slave slipped oleander into his drink." She shook her head. "Aye, trouble's brewin', for sure and certain."

Such a horrid turn. But would the trouble miles away come to touch us here at Azaka Mede? I bit my lip and resumed chopping.

Molly sighed. "I suppose it's no worse than the trouble that found us in Ireland, aye?"

The woman often spoke of her homeland, but how she had come to be a slave at Azaka Mede, I did not know. The few times I had broached the subject, her sorrow had overwhelmed her to the point she could not speak, her words locked away almost as thoroughly as my own.

Phebah scurried into the kitchen, brown eyes wide. "Girl! You dere!" I looked up from the pecans and met Phebah's worried stare as she twisted her fingers. "Come. Baara is looking for you. A dark mood she's in today, too."

I set the knife down on the cutting board and shot Molly a worried look. What had I done?

Molly shooed me away. "Go on, then. I can finish this up in a wink. Best not keep her waiting."

I followed Phebah through the kitchen and into the back hallway where Baara stood, her dark eyes glinting like broken glass, her hands propped on her skirted hips.

"Are you deaf as well as dumb? I have been calling for you."

I dropped my head, heat scouring my neck, and prepared for the blow that was sure to come. Instead, Baara sighed.

"Master Cyrene requests to see you in his private quarters."

The Master? My mouth turned to cotton as trembling started in my middle and spread through my limbs. No good came of seeing the Master any time or place.

"Take heart. He only requests his chambers be cleaned. Nothing more."

A rock lodged in my throat, but I nodded and moved down the hallway to collect the needed supplies from the closet tucked behind the kitchen. I tossed rags, a jar of water, and a small bottle of lemon oil into a bucket, as my mind attempted to unknot the strange turn of events. Master Cyrene spent his days overseeing the work of the plantation, or was gone attending to business matters I had no privilege to understand. Surely his current guests would keep him busy this day and I could work undisturbed.

I trudged up the stairs, lugging the bucket. How many years ago had I been taken and the ship carrying me away had battered its timbers upon this island? Ten? Twelve? The seasons blurred, their sharp edges melting into vague memories. I had no idea of my age but since my initial failure to sing, Master Cyrene had ignored me, save for the occasional kick or slap to flee his presence.

Memories of his odd gaze upon me during the festival assaulted my heart once again.

I attempted to push down my clacking nerves and crossed the large house, up the stairs to the Master's room.

He only bids you clean. Nothing more. Don't anger him. Be invisible.

I stared at the dark mahogany of the forbidding door and willed my hands to cease their trembling. Lifting my fingers, I knocked.

"Enter."

The masculine voice rang with authority. My heart beat wildly against my ribs.

Easing the door open with a squeak, I let it shut behind me with a soft click and gripped the handles of the bucket until my fingers ached, waiting. Master Cyrene turned in his seat at the writing desk.

"Come to clean, I see. Good, good." Waving his hand toward the massive fireplace on the opposite wall, he mumbled, "You can start over there."

The tight knot in my middle unfurled by small measures. Perhaps he would be too busy attending to his writing to pay me any mind. I placed the bucket on the floor and tugged a cloth free. I ran the rag over the cherry wood of the mantel gently, admiring the sheen. Nary a *scafar*, as Molly was prone to say. Colorful Irish brogue often peppered her speech, and though I had no memories before coming to the island, the words often felt like home.

The scratch of the Master's pen against parchment filled the silence. I cleaned the mantel, emptied the fireplace of ashes, washed the windows, and rubbed lemon oil into the massive wardrobe.

The citrusy scent of the oil always soothed me, no matter how long the day or how vexed I was in spirit. I inhaled the intoxicating scent with a satisfied sigh when an odd sensation prickled between my shoulders. Pure silence. The sound of the Master's pen had ceased. A dark presence hovered over me.

"Your hair . . ."

I whirled, pressing my back into the wardrobe, its curves and contours poking my ribs in painful jabs. Master Cyrene stood far too close. I could smell his skin . . . the mingled odor of ink and soap. I pressed farther into the unforgiving furniture, ignoring the stabs of pain.

He curled a tendril of my hair around his finger, studying it carefully. My throat turned to ash.

"What color would you say this is?" His voice was low. His question both frightened and confused me. I swallowed. There was a strange gleam in his expression. My stomach curdled like neglected cream.

"Not purely red but spun with gold." He smiled, but it wasn't pleasant. "Sunrise." His gaze lifted to meet mine. "Yes, that's it. It's the color of the sunrise."

My breath thinned, pulse erratic. I waited for his temper to twitch. Instead, he watched me like the sleek black cat who stalked mice and birds behind the house. Waiting.

Master Cyrene tilted his head. "How old are you now, Avalina? Seventeen? Eighteen?"

I shook my head. Awareness dawned in his expression.

"Of course. I forgot for a moment. You can't speak. Some would find it unfortunate." His lips curved into a smirk. "I'm starting to wonder if it might be quite advantageous."

A shiver coursed down my spine, rattling my limbs as he let his gaze roam my face, my neck. His finger pulled my coil of hair tighter until pain punctured my scalp.

"Master Cyrene! There's trouble in da south field!" A masculine voice called from the hallway. Amos? The old gardener sounded frantic.

With a growl, the Master released my hair and turned, pausing only to toss an ominous farewell over his shoulder. "Until later."

He stalked from the room, and I stood in place for long moments, my stomach convulsing.

A beating would have been preferable to what I had just witnessed in his expression.

CHAPTER 5

Josiah swatted his neck, slapping at another mosquito as he, Father, and Cyrene stomped across the grounds toward the sugar cane fields. Their host tossed a smile over his shoulder. "If it's not the mosquitoes, it's the sand flies. Yes?"

"Which is worse?"

His wide shoulders lifted in a shrug. "Both are annoying but some of the mosquitoes carry dengue fever." He frowned. "Not a pleasant malady."

Father groused, rubbing his neck with a handkerchief. "Visitors stew about our South Carolina heat and humidity. They've yet to taste the bite and swelter of Barbados."

Josiah chose to ignore his complaints and instead focused on the beauty around them. Palms and bearded figs, red and pink hibiscus blooming along the pathway, the chattering monkeys overhead as they searched for bananas and coco plums—all of it was an exotic kind of wild beauty. Why, last night, after a delectable meal of strange but delicious foods, Josiah had retired to his room and been lulled to sleep by the gentle *gleep, gleep* of whistling frogs. Surely the Garden of Eden couldn't have been more ideal.

Except for the tumult that had erupted in the fields less than an hour ago.

Harding had said nothing to them, but Josiah had watched the ruckus behind the house. The overseer had come running, bellowing for the master. As Harding rushed out of the house, his overseer met him halfway across the lawn. Some of their words drifted on the air.

"Rebellion..."

"The fellow must pay..."

Harding had given the overseer swift instructions and stomped back into the house, his body tense. All was not as it seemed at Azaka Mede.

Josiah's thoughts tugged back to the present as they rounded a corner and the path opened to reveal a field full of bodies hunched over tall, green stalks of sugar cane. Sweat glistened off the men's bare backs. Women wove between them, their shoulders rounded as they lugged sacks full of stalks from one end of the field to the other. Many of the slaves were dark. A handful were white, their skin burned red from the glare of the sun.

Father stopped, chest heaving. "Harvesting cane already?"

Cyrene pursed his lips. "Only this field. The others aren't ready." He pointed to the east. "The men over there chop the ready stalks with their machetes and the women haul them to the huts over there." He swung his hand to the west, where several ramshackle cabins squatted in the blistering sun. "We press the cane inside. Some of the harvest is kept as a syrup, and with some, the slaves boil it down until it turns into a solid mass." The owner smiled, his dark eyes flashing. "You can thank us for the sugar cubes you enjoy in your coffee and tea."

Watching the hard labor of the workers spoiled both for Josiah. The same sour nausea that had bubbled up his throat on the ship revived itself again. He clenched his jaw, nodding toward the field. "What of the disparity in skin color among your slaves?"

"Ah." Cyrene chuckled. "The Redlegs." He propped his foot on a nearby stump. "King James the First helped us with that." His teeth flashed but there was no warmth in his expression. "The story goes that in the 1600s, his majesty was disgusted by all the poor Irish filling his streets after the Battle of Kinsale. The English killed thousands of them and sold thousands more as slaves, sending them to the New World, as well as islands like Barbados." He winked. "We've found the Irish still fetch a tidy sum, though most work as indentured servants now. Either way"—he shrugged—"it's cheaper than paying a full day's wage to a hired hand."

Josiah frowned. Father had not mentioned any of this to him before they sailed. Why?

"How does their work compare to that of the Africans?" Father scowled at a bee that hummed too close to his ear and waved it away.

Cyrene shrugged. "A slave is a slave. I work them until they are of no more use to me."

And then what? Their unspoken fate lingered in Josiah's mind. Stomach curdling, he started to turn away but Father's sharp question caused him to freeze.

"Where are you going?"

"I've seen enough."

"You'll not learn to run the plantation properly without absorbing all you can here." Father braced his legs shoulder-width apart and crossed his arms. "Isn't that what you want?"

Words tripped on Josiah's tongue. Was that what he wanted? His shoulders sagged. No. He wanted to study law, but his wishes did not matter. He had been born to take his father's place as head of the family someday. To wield his power and influence with naught but a simple command. That was the way of it. What was expected.

Shouts erupted from the right side of the field. A beefy man wearing a sweat-soaked neckerchief charged forward, his face mottled red as he clutched the thin arm of a slave child. The boy's eyes were wide with terror as the man threw him down at Cyrene Harding's feet.

Harding arched a single brow. "What's all this about, Bixby?"

The large fellow, apparently the overseer, wiped a large hand against his sweaty forehead and nodded his head toward the child quivering at Harding's feet. "Found this one stealing eggs from the henhouse when he was supposed to be pressing syrup."

The child looked up, a single tear falling from his eye and dribbling down his smudged cheek. "I's sorry, sir. I won't never do it again." He couldn't have been more than eight or nine.

Cyrene Harding knelt to stare at the child, his head tilted. "You understand that I'm the master here, yes?"

The boy nodded, sniffling back his tears. "Yes, sir."

"You understand those chickens and their eggs are mine?"

"Yes, sir." His chest heaved with shuddering sobs. "I was just hungry, sir. I won't never do it again. And Mr. Bixby here caught me before I could even take one."

"Mm." Harding nodded calmly and rose, before staring down the boy with a hard glint in his eyes. "Three lashes while tied to a post."

The child cried out but Bixby yanked him up by the back of his dirty collar. "You heard the master, boy."

Lashes . . . on one so young? Josiah's middle pinched once again as he stepped forward. "Harding, I really must protest. He's naught but a child!"

Harding's lips thinned into a hard line. "A child who must learn not to steal from his master's hand."

Father nodded. "Quite so."

Josiah watched, helpless, as they stripped the thin shirt from the boy's back and tied his hands to a post. All the slaves stopped to watch, their faces solemn. The little lad sobbed as his torso hugged the wooden support. Harding looked over the field of enslaved and raised his voice.

"Doesn't matter the age ... anyone caught stealing will be punished!"

At the pronouncement, Bixby unfurled a thin whip from his belt and flung it overhead. The ribbon of leather sliced through the boy's back with a deafening crack. The child's body jerked as he cried out in pain.

Josiah gripped his father's arm. "Is there nothing we can do?" He murmured the words through gritted teeth. His father shrugged away from Josiah's touch, eyes narrowing.

"A man can do with his property as he sees fit."

Disgusted, Josiah turned away, desperate to blot out the screams, the images now engraved in his mind. He could not stomach this or be party to it. Turning on his heel, he stalked away but froze when his father's voice called at his back.

"Where do you think you're going, Josiah?"

A spark of rebellion welled in his chest. He whirled to meet his father's steely gaze. "Anywhere but here."

As he stalked through the vegetation hugging the sugar cane field, and the boy's cries drifted through the air, the weight of Josiah's future hung like a noose around his neck, tightening with each second that passed.

Josiah wandered through the lush garden, trying to admire the grounds, but turbulent thoughts rolled through his mind. What was wrong with him? Watching their own slaves work the plantation back home had never unsettled him the way the workers in Barbados had done.

Yet he had never witnessed one so young being whipped.

He strolled between plumy palms, stopping to study the large red blooms Cyrene had called hibiscus. After fingering a large waxy petal, he sighed. How different this trip was from what he'd imagined. He'd prayed the voyage would allow him and Father to forge a stronger relationship... one built on mutual respect. Even make headway in getting Father to agree to send him to college, but his father had shot down the plea with a single puff of his pipe.

Josiah kicked a pebble near his shoe. What had he expected? Heaven knew, George Holland was a difficult man to please. Hadn't Josiah been trying to earn one word of praise from him since his youth?

He had yet to achieve such an impossible feat.

Climbing the steps to the door of the sprawling plantation home, he let himself in through the sunny conservatory and meandered down the hallway. The aroma of cherry pipe tobacco tickled his nose. Turning to his right, he peeked past the carved walnut door. Rows of book-lined shelves. The library.

He stepped inside to study the titles and a soft gasp snagged his attention. He startled to see the lovely russet-haired maid that had cleaned his room standing near the back of the library, a green-and-gold-engraved book in her hands.

"Oh, pardon me, miss. Just perusing the collection." Josiah smiled and nodded to the large shelves. "Quite a library, I must say."

The lady merely stood frozen, blinking at him with her stormy eyes. Why did she not speak? Was it fear that rendered her mute or something more?

Stepping close, he tilted his head to read the title clutched between her white fingers. "Shakespearean sonnets." He lifted his gaze to hers, wondering what thoughts lay behind her solemn gaze. "One of my favorites. A brilliant man."

She bit the full curve of her lower lip before hesitantly offering it to him. He lifted his brows. Understanding dawned. If she was a slave at Azaka Mede, she could not read. Was this the reason for the fear he witnessed in her expression?

"Would you like me to read it to you?"

Her blue-gray eyes shone with a stunning light as a bright smile curved her lips. She nodded enthusiastically, a red curl bobbing against her shoulder with the movement.

"I'd be happy to." He flipped through the sonnets, skimming through each before settling on one. "Here we are. Sonnet 18. 'Shall I compare thee to a summer's day? Thou art more lovely and more temperate. Rough winds do shake the darling buds of May, and summer's lease hath all too short a date.'"

He glanced up from the text. She had stepped close, watching him in breathless anticipation, her gaze never straying from his face. Some kind of invisible pull stretched between them, taut as the ropes tightening the sails of a ship in a gale-force wind.

Swallowing, he forced his eyes back to the page. "'But thy eternal summer shall not fade, nor lose possession of that fair thou ow'st, nor shall death brag thou wand'rest in his shade, when in eternal lines to time thou grow'st. So long as men can breathe, or eyes can see, so long lives this, and this gives life to thee.'"

His own breath was suspended as he finished and studied the long sweep of her lashes, the smooth curve of her cheek. Was her skin as soft as it looked?

A noise from down the hallway caused her to startle. A little woman with a round face and graying red curls peeking from under a mobcap leaned around the library door.

"Avalina?" The new woman's eyes lifted in surprise as she spied Josiah in the study. "Oh, pardon the interruption, sir. I need the maid's help in the kitchen."

Avalina? Was that her name? He turned to ask, but she had already moved to obey. The book in his fingers suddenly seemed awkward and heavy. Before leaving, she turned back slightly, the ghost of a smile on her lips, and slipped from the room.

"Ah, rubbish! It'll never happen."

Josiah shifted his weight in the dining room chair as his father speared the flaky fish on his plate with a scowl. Cyrene smiled at Father's blustery ire, calmly sipping madeira from a large glass as he reclined against his chair with lazy ease. He arched a single brow and set down his wine.

"Ah, but since the Slave Trade Act of 1807, the British Empire is snuffing out the practice of slavery." Cyrene plucked a grape from his plate and chewed slowly. "Surely you must believe America will soon follow."

"Bah! All William Wilberforce and his Quaker friends accomplished was giving the Americas a monopoly on the slave trade." Father glowered and reached for the bread on his plate. "They were naught but troublemakers who did not understand the unique problems inherited with a producing plantation."

Josiah toyed with the flavorful rice on his plate. This evening's dinner conversation left him uneasy. He'd heard Father's argument a hundred times. Had agreed with it to a certain extent. There was considerable cost in running a profitable piece of land. But what if the abolitionists were right? What if there was a better way to operate?

"The Quakers." A snort of derision huffed from Harding's nose "We are not immune from their wiles here in Barbados. One in particular has made quite a nuisance of himself in Saint John's Parish."

"A pity, that." Father bent his gray head as he thought, lips puckered into a frown. "Is there nothing that can be done to rid the island of him?"

Cyrene chuckled and picked up his napkin to wipe his mouth. "Nothing short of murder. Don't think I haven't considered such a thing."

Surely the man spoke in jest. At Josiah's frown, Cyrene turned his head and studied him with a cool, assessing gaze. "Do my words displease you, Mr. Holland?"

Josiah caught his father's alarmed look from the corner of his vision. "Displease? No. But I have yet to see why both opinions cannot share space. This abolitionist surely feels he is in the right, just as you do."

A small sneer lifted the corner of Cyrene's lip. "Spoken like an American. Freedom to speak, freedom of ideas." He met Josiah's gaze with a hard stare. "Yet for all the talk, blood is still spilled over such clashes, is it not?"

Josiah lifted a brow. "Do you fear blood will be shed in Barbados?" The morning's concern over some sort of rebellion murmured about between his host and the overseer drifted through his mind once again.

"No." Harding's gaze dropped to his glass of wine and he fingered the stem absently. "We have control over our slaves."

"Interesting." Josiah leaned in. "Wasn't it just this morning that we were told of a slave in another parish poisoning his master?"

A muscle ticked in Cyrene's cheek. Father's harsh whisper sliced the air. "Josiah . . ."

Cyrene waved his concern away with a flick of his wrist. "I do not mind the question, Mr. Holland. Your son is merely expressing his thoughts, as Americans are wont to do." A cold smile curved his mouth. "I fear when opinions differ, there is no other recourse than for the strong to dominate the weak."

Josiah's lips flattened. "So in the matter of this slave who poisoned his master, was he the strong or the weak?"

Cyrene's nostrils flared but his smile never wavered. "His master was weak." Lifting his glass in a mock toast, he smirked. "You will find that for Azaka Mede, I am the strong one. Always."

Josiah lifted his chin but dared not risk his father's displeasure by challenging Harding again. There was something altogether unsettling about the man. A kind of repressed violence, held in a vessel of manners and polish. Josiah's gaze drifted to his father, who was staring at him through narrowed eyes.

Pushing away from the table, Josiah rose and nodded to his host. "This was a delicious dinner. I thank you."

Cyrene nodded and took another slow sip of his wine. "The pleasure is mine. Feel free to roam about and explore while your father and I retire to my study for cigars."

He'd been dismissed—and found nothing but relief at the prospect. "Thank you. Good evening, Mr. Harding. Father." He nodded at both of the men.

His father waved him away and Josiah gritted his teeth as he exited the large dining room. He needed a distraction. Something other than the grating company of the plantation's owner.

He stepped through the back doors to stand on the balcony overlooking the gardens. A large silvery moon cast pewter light over the yard. The intoxicating aroma of plumeria filled the air. Josiah walked down the steps and fingered the bright pink blooms of bougainvillea draped over the balustrades.

A soft melody drifted from somewhere deep in the garden's lush growth. A lyrical hum that reminded him of the sweetest violin. The sound…it was magical. Hitching his breath as the song slipped from compressed lips to soft words, he padded deeper into the tall stalks of the palms and red ginger lilies.

"I 'twas a fault, alas! I'm guilty still…"

He walked closer to the angelic voice. It drew him, called for him to capture the ethereal song in his heart.

"For still I love, and while I live, I will…"

In the depths of the garden's shadows, he pushed back a palm and sucked in a breath.

Avalina stood in a patch of pale moonlight, her fiery hair unbound, and she padded barefoot in the soft grass and tenderly caressed the clustered blossoms of white hanging down from a trellis.

"A song of love I sing…" The melody spilling from her lips tapered into a soft hum, rising and falling like the swells of the sea. He swallowed and stepped closer.

At his approach, she gasped and turned away from the flowers before pressing herself more closely to the shadows of the palms. Even in the splattered moonglow, the wide fright in her eyes shone plainly.

"Please"—he lifted a hand in entreaty—"don't be afraid. I—I just heard you singing and thought…" What did he think? He lowered his hand and took a deep breath. "Your voice is glorious."

He watched her fingers tremble as she shifted away to escape. He forced himself to stay still, as if calming the inclinations of a startled doe. A sudden realization caused his mouth to curve.

"You can speak, can't you?"

She licked her lips and tensed to bolt, but he reached out and gently wrapped his fingers around her wrist, stopping her flight.

"Please, I mean you no harm."

She looked down at his fingers, then slowly lifted her gaze to his. He released her as the tension in her muscles relaxed, then offered her a smile. "The song… what is it about?"

Avalina looked away, her face half hidden in the shadows. He waited so long for her to answer, he feared she wouldn't until her soft whisper broke through the darkness.

"Yarico."

At the murmured reply, she fled. Josiah watched her slip between the palms, feeling the loss of her presence, but he dared not pursue. Such an action would scare the poor thing witless. What was it she had said? Yarico? What did that mean?

He turned to walk back to the house, his thoughts in a knot. Barbados was nothing like he'd imagined … including the mysterious maid with the golden voice who would not speak.

But why?

I slipped upstairs to my room and shut the door behind me with a soft click before resting my back against it, heart pounding in my ribs.

What had happened in the garden? One moment I'd enjoyed the only respite I'd had for days and the next, the tall, dark-headed stranger with the handsome smile had once again appeared, his expression stunned. I ought not to have noticed the width of his strong shoulders, nor the dark stubble lining his jaw, but it was the look in his eyes that caused my stomach to flip in such an odd way. Admiration shone in their depths.

Such a thing had shaken me to my core.

Another thought invaded, this one much more ominous. What if the man told Master Cyrene he had heard me singing? What would I do?

Icy dread snaked through my chest. I'd stayed invisible for years. And now, with one moment of foolishness, I may have thrown it all—my safety, my peace—away.

I shook my head, my trembling fingers plunging into my hair as I kneaded my temple. And what had freed my tongue to answer his question? Never before had I been able to answer without words stalling in my mouth, save for the sweet moments I shared alone with Molly. Language, answers, thoughts would flood my mind yet none of them could break past my lips.

It reminded me of old Mari, the elderly slave woman who was struck down with a strange illness one day. For weeks, her movements had been stiff and halted, her tongue unable to move before she was taken in death.

Baara would say the slave owner's son had spoken an incantation over me, some kind of black magic. Yet there was a kindness in his eyes. A goodness I had yet to witness in most men, save for Matias, Amos, and a handful of others around the plantation.

And that scared me far more than anything else.

CHAPTER 6

The morning dawned and Josiah had no interest in sitting in Cyrene and Father's oppressive company. The night before, Father had cornered him before bed and scalded his tongue over Josiah's pointed questions to Harding during dinner.

"What possessed you to speak so to our host? A wealthy host, I might add. The man whose whims might determine our own success in the coming year?"

Josiah had flushed warm under his father's spittle-flung words but offered no rebuttal. He wasn't sure what had possessed him to speak his thoughts so freely. No, that wasn't true. Something about seeing the small slave boy whipped for attempting to sate his hunger had unleashed a thousand questions in Josiah's mind. Not just questions... anger.

Yet he had remained silent as his father fumed and, after a harsh admonition to never repeat such behavior again, retired for the evening.

He ought to seek out Master Harding and play the part of a repentant young man. Instead, he requested a carriage to carry him into town. He longed to see this strange land with his own eyes, make his own opinions about the customs and people surrounding him.

Though the humidity was suffocating, the slight breeze stirred by the ocean currents brought a breath of relief as the horse clopped down the road leading into the bustling parts of Barbados.

And away from the scarred backs of the laborers in the field.

Josiah rubbed his temple, wishing the strange new torment would leave him be. He glanced up, staring at the hunched back and stooped shoulders of his driver. His body silently swayed with the rhythm of the carriage. Aged fingers loosely held the reins. He said nothing and requested nothing.

His silence shouted today.

As fields melted into buildings, Josiah drank in the sights of the island. Craftsmen selling woven baskets, farmers calling out for shoppers to buy their fruit. On the opposite side of the road, a fisherman loaded his latest catch onto a table as a woman fanned the flies away with a large palm, beckoning people to buy while the fish were yet fresh. Small children held bouquets of tropical blooms boasting vibrant colors, shyly asking passing men to purchase the blossoms for a coin. A small cart loaded with hanging strands of dried chilis and herbs rolled by. The thick, tantalizing aroma of thyme tickled his nose.

Josiah smiled at the people's honest work. Their productivity.

A loud voice boomed farther up the road, causing a small crowd to part.

"'Tis a shame, and nothing less! These be our brothers, our sisters, me friends! We must rise up! Fight for what is true and just. God shall thus shed the blood of those persons who enslave their fellow creatures."

Shouts and boos followed the loud pronouncement. Josiah frowned and looked up at the driver. "Please, sir, if you could pull over here, I'd like to explore this area."

The driver nodded and urged the horses to a stop. Josiah emerged from the carriage and wove through the clogged street to the gathering just beyond the throng of shops. Pushing through the murmuring bodies, he stopped short, surprised to see a small man, barely four feet in height, his eyes narrowed into slits. The man's visage was altogether humorous. His arms were as long as his legs, and a large hump malformed his back, but perhaps it was his long, snowy white beard scraping the ground that made him appear even shorter than he was. Still, there was no mistaking the fire in the diminutive fellow's countenance.

He shook his bony finger as he turned in a small circle to the mob pressing around him.

"Slave-keeping is a soul sin."

One man in the crowd scoffed, waving his hand in dismissal. "Ach! Little Benjamin, you're cracked in the head."

The tiny man pierced him with a knowing look. "Better the head than a cracked heart and a seared conscience."

Josiah swallowed.

The small fellow held up a handful of pamphlets. "Take one if ye have a thirst for knowledge. Such things are free for those who have a heart to seek her."

The crowd dispersed, some muttering about the foolish man. Two or three requested a pamphlet. The man offered them one with a smile. "God bless ye."

Josiah stood before him, mouth dry, unsure what to say. The dwarf stared up into his face, eyes pinched.

"Have ye a request, me brother? Or do ye only mean to stand and gawk?"

"I—I would like a pamphlet, please."

He pushed the missive into Josiah's hand. *ON SLAVEHOLD-ERS: THE APOSTATES* was printed in bold font across the top. Josiah released a tight breath. The little man turned to take his leave.

"Wait!"

He turned back, eyes sharp. "Aye?"

"Would you allow me to buy you a drink? Perhaps ask you some questions?"

Stroking his long, gray beard, he pursed his lips. "I've no taste for spirits."

"Neither do I."

"Nor do I eat meat. Flesh is God's creation."

Mischief sparked in Josiah's chest. He grinned. "As are fruits and vegetables."

The strange man threw back his head and bellowed a laugh. "I shall enjoy a visit with ye."

Josiah wrapped his fingers around a chipped cup of tepid water as he stared at his companion across the scarred table of the ramshackle tavern. The pub was a far cry from the establishments back home. Sweat-soaked bodies crammed into the sweltering room to get a plate of stewed chicken, rice, and beans. Some laughed in the corner, happily drowning their sorrows in rum.

The tiny orator, Josiah had learned, was named Benjamin Magee. Despite Benjamin's early vehemence, and his piercing stares, Josiah found himself at ease with the fellow's lilting brogue, his Quaker-influenced speech, and the gentle way he moved through conversation. By measures, he found his muscles relaxing, his interest in his companion far more stimulating than the pub's fare.

"So I says, says I, I must sail for open waters. See what lies beyond this land. And here I be." Benjamin grinned and scooped up another spoonful of rice before chewing with abandon. He jabbed his utensil in the direction of Josiah's plate. "Best eat, lad. I can jaw all day but the matron'll be comin' 'round quick enough to take our plates."

Josiah speared another piece of the savory chicken and smiled. "Have you always abstained from meat?"

Benjamin shrugged. "Ach, not always. But for as long as I've been old enough to fix me own plate, aye. Me poor mither swears that's why I didn't grow as I ought." He chuckled long, blue eyes dancing. "But me da says the world could not handle me in any bigger package than the one I have."

Leaning forward, Josiah toyed with the rim of his cup. "Have you always been a passionate sort?"

Benjamin stroked his white beard. "Mm...I suppose I have, at that. I was forever taking up the cause for some poor soul or the other. The child in school who had a tough go of it. Or bringing home stray animals, much to me mither's dismay." He smiled. "But what's the use of having a heart if we choose not to let it feel for others, eh?"

Indeed. And that was the crux of Josiah's problem. He'd been living life blind to the horrors around him, deaf to the cries of the suffering.

Benjamin watched him carefully. Josiah averted his gaze.

"Ach, what's troubling ye, lad?"

Taking a sip of water, Josiah set the cup back down slowly. "What makes you think I'm troubled?"

A smile quirked Benjamin's lips. "'Tis not often a rabble-rouser like me is asked to sup with a fine gentleman like you. Nor have you said much of yourself." His eyes narrowed. "How's your heart?"

Josiah met his gaze, his pulse tripping. Odd question, but one that stripped away the façade he'd hoped to keep in place. Instead, he sucked in a deep breath and released his reply in a whoosh.

"I'm a slave holder. An apostate. One of the very men you condemn."

"Aye. I figured as much."

Josiah blinked. "But you said nothing. Sat down to eat with me."

"And so I will again."

Josiah dropped his head in his hands. "I don't understand."

Benjamin shook his head. "'Tis not I that condemns ye, Josiah. 'Tis the Holy Spirit and your own heart."

"My own heart..."

Resting one elbow on the table, Benjamin leaned forward and jabbed a gnarled finger into his shoulder. "Tell me, what has changed within ye?"

Josiah swallowed, running his fingers through his hair. "I—I don't know. My family has always owned slaves. My father—the plantation, I am expected to take over the running of it when he passes. It's all I've ever known."

Benjamin leaned forward and curled his fingers around Josiah's arm. "Then what happened?"

"We sailed here." Josiah's jaw tightened. "And I saw what they were enduring below deck. Watched them sold off to Cyrene Harding. Saw a child whipped yesterday for daring to eat. And now"—fire burned in his chest—"it's all I can see everywhere I go." Josiah looked up, his gaze colliding with Benjamin's, vision blurring as hot tears swam to the surface. "You ask how my heart is? It's calloused. Maybe it's dead. I'm not sure. All I know is that I'm guilty because I had a hand in their suffering."

Josiah dropped his head back in his hands. Benjamin offered a gentle pat on his back. "Ach, your heart is not dead. Otherwise, it would not be tormented. God's dealing with you, lad. It was the same for me years ago when I first came to Barbados. I had no idea of the brutality or misery so many of our brothers endured, and still must bear up under today, but I felt as if I'd awakened from a deep sleep."

Releasing a sigh, Josiah straightened. "Yes. That's how it feels."

Benjamin nodded. "The calling on each man's life is different. Mine is to proclaim the truth wherever I be. Soon, I'll be moving."

Josiah frowned. "Moving where?"

Benjamin took up his spoon. "To Philadelphia. There is a powerful move of abolitionists there who are working to see slavery destroyed in the States." His blue gaze widened and narrowed in that shrewd way he had. "But what of ye? What will you do now that yer heart has been awakened?"

"I don't know." Josiah shook his head, pulse beating an erratic rhythm through his veins. "What I do know is that it cannot remain as it has been."

"Mm." Benjamin squinted a single eye and studied him carefully. "I foresee a bright future for ye, young Holland. The Almighty shall use ye."

How he prayed it be so. Yet how could God possibly use someone with such a tainted past? A slaveholder … a man of God?

And how could he escape the future his family had planned?

"Here, me love. Take the batter and beat it a mite for me. My arms are stiffer than the eggs."

I took the bowl from Molly and whisked the eggs in small circles as quickly as I could, watching the sugar and eggs foam into small peaks. Naomi scurried around us in the kitchen, carrying steaming pots of *cou-cou* and rice. Tabia rolled out dough for pastries or poured coconut rum batter into pans. Though Master's dance this evening would be small, it would be lavish.

Molly eased into the chair beside me with a soft grunt and fanned her red cheeks with the end of her apron. "Too old for such goings-on, I am."

I smiled at her theatrics. Molly always declared she was too old for whatever task was at hand. She was one of those creatures who seemed to have no age, and was neither old nor young, but an eternal fixture on the plantation.

Molly studied Baara, who walked swiftly past, watching the preparations with a jaundiced eye. When the head maid left, Molly leaned forward, her voice naught but a whisper.

"Have you heard the scuttlebutt coming from St. Philip's Parish, lass?"

My interest piqued. I slowed, searching her face, and shook my head.

Molly glanced from side to side, as if afraid someone might overhear her muted whispers. "Word has it a group of slaves are planning an uprising. They can taste freedom."

My breath snagged. Was such a thing possible? And how did Molly ever hear of it? I frowned.

"Now, don't give me such a look, lass. I have my ways of knowin', you ken. Things are a-changin'." Her eyes rounded. "Freedom is but a breath away."

Freedom? The idea both excited and terrified me. What would it be like to go where I wanted? To do what I wanted? No one's whims or needs to see to.

But where would I go? I could do nothing but clean and cook a little. I shivered and buffed my arms. How would I live? Eat? Such thoughts snaked through me like cold tentacles. I didn't like thinking of it.

The slaves of St. Philip's Parish ... what if their coup was unsuccessful? Retaliation would be swift and complete. Trembling started in my middle and spanned outward.

Molly must have seen the fear awash on my face, for her own features relaxed. "Ah, don't go frettin' now, lass. It may come to naught, leastwise if England has her way. I overheard Master talking with his guest just this morning. Parliament is working to abolish slavery here in the islands. If it passes, there won't be need for uprisings or bloodshed." Molly's eyes shone. "We'll walk out these doors with our heads held high."

My hands shook. I dropped the whisk into the batter. Walk out the doors to ... where? Where would we go? What kind of life could I possibly have outside these walls? I had no way to earn a living. No family.

Molly stood and squeezed my shoulders. "I can see you're overcome. 'Tis excitin' but until the time comes, we best keep our heads down and act as if we know nothin'."

I nodded slowly and returned the bowl to Molly's hands.

Though my lips were silent, my mind screamed louder than it ever had before.

CHAPTER 7

Josiah stood next to his father, watching the dancers dip and sway in the warm spring air. Servants scurried between the spectators, offering wine, rum, meat pies, and confections as the music of strumming guitars and drums drifted through the night. Lanterns spilled streams of light across the lawn and even the back gardens were aglow with the celebration this evening.

He had no interest in the dance. The whole thing was soured for him—a once fascinating event now demonized in his mind by all he had witnessed among the slave quarters. How could anyone dance and laugh and play in the face of such oppression?

Walking through slave row this afternoon with his father had only solidified all Benjamin Magee had told him. Their living quarters were sparser than any he'd seen at home in South Carolina. Thin children spilled out of each shanty, their rations little more than corn meal and beans. How long since the little ones had tasted game or fruit? At least in Barbados, fruit was plentiful in the loaded trees, but when he'd commented on such, Harding had huffed.

"The children know they dare not take a piece of fruit from my groves, or else they suffer the lash."

The only comfort Josiah found was knowing the slaves at their own plantation was be treated with more dignity than they enjoyed in this forbidding land.

A small comfort, indeed.

Lifting the cup of punch to his lips, he let the tang of gooseberry and rum linger on his tongue. Father elbowed him gently.

"Lots of lovely ladies, are there not?"

Josiah merely grunted. Father shot him a sidelong glance.

"You ought to ask one or two to dance."

"Father..."

"Come now, Josiah." His father turned to eye him more fully, a cup of rum punch in one hand and a cigar in the other. "You are a handsome young fellow. Why not think of making your mother happy with a suitable match? There are many wealthy plantation owners' daughters here."

"Mm. And I'm sure they're dying to move all the way to the States and leave their families behind."

"That's the way of it. I would be happy to discuss doweries with any you take a fancy to."

Unbidden, a fiery-haired, silent beauty danced through his thoughts. He shook the image away. What was he doing? How could he consider wedding a servant?

Still, there was no other who so intrigued him.

He laughed mirthlessly. Such a social breach would send his mother to an early grave and his father into fits of apoplexy.

Shoving his free hand into his pocket, he fingered the small piece of paper he'd tucked inside. Something he would show her if they ever met again.

"I don't think I'm ready to consider such things." Speaking with Benjamin Magee had upended all he'd ever believed. A burning passion ignited his soul now. A passion to right the wrongs of his family. But what to do about it? Could he really reject all his family believed and forge a new path? He shuddered at the thought, yet it would not leave him be. How to find the courage to do what would be required for such a change? His father would disown him and his mother's heart would break.

He was in no position to court anyone.

"Bah! You're young. An ideal time to wed."

Josiah turned to his father and met his blue-eyed gaze with his own. "Focus on Isabelle. She will be coming out soon."

"Your sister?" Father's gray brows lifted. "Not for another two years."

"It will come soon enough. If you'll pardon me, I would like to stroll the grounds."

Father's lips pinched. "Take care to observe the young ladies as you do. Your future hinges on your obedience in this."

Josiah turned away, irritation mounting. When would he be given the freedom to make his own decisions?

Never. His father never yielded to another's ideas and plans. Josiah was trapped. The future was laid out before him, as rigid as iron.

Placing the punch cup on a tray, he moved across the lawn, studying the movements of the dancers. Their steps were not altogether different from the waltzes at home. The instruments were a bit of a change, but not an unwelcome one. The drums mimicked heartbeats, their patterns changing with the tempo of each song.

He moved away from the dancers to slip into a more secluded space. Somewhere beyond the cheerful melee, he could hear childlike giggles. Stepping carefully across the lush lawn, he moved to a circle of palms tucked in the back of the property. He sidled closer as the laughter increased. Young Caribbean accents blended with mirth.

"Here! Dance with dis!"

He stopped when he noticed the source of the joy.

Avalina stood in the circle of slave children, grinning as she danced with a broom. The children held their sides, laughing at her comical expressions. She dipped and swayed, acting as if the broom were her knight in shining armor . . . and the children couldn't get enough.

He stepped close to their circle. When some of the little ones spied him, they gasped and ran for cover. Avalina froze, her eyes wide, movements stilled at his arrival.

Josiah's pulse thrummed a heady staccato. She was here, and only moments ago she had been dancing. Smiling. Would she do the same if he held her in his arms? Spun her in slow circles? Dare he try?

Inhaling deeply, he stepped forward and held out his hand.

"I believe I can make a better partner, although I might be just as stiff as your current beau."

She looked between his outstretched fingers and the broom and gently dropped the tool on the grass. He waited, breath still lest he cause her to bolt once again.

Slowly, she slipped her hand into his. He drew her closer, cupping his fingers against her slim waist and moving both of them in small circles while the musicians played across the expansive lawn.

The top of her head stood just under his jaw. A perfect fit. The scent of plumeria flooded his nose as he breathed in her fragrance. She lifted her gaze to his and his chest pounded. Perhaps it was the moonlight, or the beauty of the island, but his gaze dropped to her lips. All he needed to do was lean in...

The music stopped, followed by distant applause as the guests clapped their appreciation. The spell was broken. They stepped apart and he found himself suddenly tongue-tied. A deep blush dusted her cheeks.

"I—ah, I'm sorry to have interrupted your previous dance." He gestured to the fallen broom. "And that I scared off your many admirers."

She shrugged, a ghost of a smile teasing around her mouth. He shoved his hand in his pocket, his attention snagged by a sharp crinkle.

"Oh, here! This is for you." Her brows lifted as she watched him tug the slip of paper free. He held it out to her and she took it reverently. "I know you have not been taught to read, but I wanted to make sure you had this. It's a scripture. From the Bible."

A small furrow marred her brow as she looked at the note.

"I know. It seems silly to give you something you can't read, but..." He was bungling this. "I mean, I know you have a desire to learn, and I wish I were staying here long enough to teach you, but this is a start to memorizing the Scriptures."

She lifted it and shrugged slightly, eyes expressing confusion. He understood the question.

"Ah, of course. I should tell you what it says, yes? 'In the beginning, God created the heavens and the earth.'"

A slow smile spread across her face. She clutched the scrap to her chest and nodded.

His own heart soared at her response. "You're welcome."

Harding's voice could be heard just beyond the trees. Stark terror replaced the joy on her face. Josiah stepped closer, dropping his voice to a whisper. "You fear him, don't you?"

She nodded and bit her lip before slipping into the shadows.

Josiah clenched his jaw and moved away from the circle of trees, his thoughts a tumult.

Harding was a devil. What had the odious man done to her?

CHAPTER 8

There was a comforting cadence in the morning routine of the house—the hiss of the scullery maids' brushes against the stone hearths, the clicking of boots through the corridors, the aroma of cinnamon sweet breads baking in the heat of the kitchen. It was the rhythm of my life, of security. Even the scowls on Baara's dark face held a comforting sameness, like the rising of the sun or the cyclical pattern of moon glow in its silver splendors.

Or perhaps the peace that filled me was due to the handsome guest who had waltzed with me in the garden the evening before.

The thicket of trees, our shroud. The glow of the stars, our light. I wished the moment had never ended.

But it had. The spell was quenched at music's end and Master's voice. I inwardly cringed as I chopped carrots in the kitchen, the orange color staining my fingertips. His dark presence hovered over everything ... my thoughts, my rare moments of pleasure, my future.

Shivering, I dropped a handful of carrots into the waiting pot of broth. What was I thinking? I had no future. Nothing beyond bowing to Master's whims and working until I drew my last breath.

Ever since Molly's whispered secret the day before, the thought of freedom itched like a burr between my shoulder blades. Perhaps that was the yearning my soul had been crying for.

Something crinkled in my pocket as I bumped against the worktable. The stranger's note. A flicker of hope. What was it he had said? It was a scripture. The only one who ever spoke of such things was Matias.

In the beginning, God created the heavens and the earth. But who was God? Where was He? He must be too large, too infinite to be seen. After all, if He was the one who made the stars, the sun, and the moon, He would be too big to be a human like me. Wouldn't He?

The rhythmic chopping left my mind free to wander. A dangerous pursuit . . . especially since I had no answers. It seemed the more I picked at these strange yearnings—the thirst for freedom and the knowledge of God—the more elusive they became.

Sighing, I moved the large pot onto the stove and opened the oven door below before throwing another log into the glowing red embers. The heat prickled my skin. The stew would be a hearty meal for the servants, despite the Master and his guests dining on roast fowl and cilantro rice. As I shut the oven door, light footsteps sounded behind me. I turned to see a young slave boy standing in the frame of the back door, his eyes large and breathing heavy.

"You are the witch, yes?"

I frowned, well aware of the moniker but helpless as to how to eliminate it.

The little lad took a step forward. "Help me, miss. My mum is ailing. Failing fast. Baara, Naomi . . . all of them servants say you have the power of healing with herbs. Maybe the powers of a witch." His dark eyes searched my face. "My mum needs your magic."

I shook my head. I had no powers. No special abilities, but I *had* paid close attention when Molly taught me about healing herbs. She had said often enough that she wanted me to have a special skill. Such abilities would make me more valuable to Aza-ka Mede. Though, with my tied tongue, the only people who ever called for me were those on slave row. At least I could be of use to them.

Moving to the pantry, I gathered an empty basket and quickly filled it with the pouches of herbs I kept drying at the top of the shelves—cerasee, gully root, conga-lala, cow-itch, rice bitters—I threw it all in. I turned back to eye the broth barely beginning to bubble on the stove. Who would see to it?

Naomi walked through the back door, a dead, plucked chicken in her hand. I pointed to the pot and lifted questioning eyes. She frowned.

"You want me to keep an eye on it?"

I nodded. She sighed.

"Fine. But no lollygagging, you hear? Baara will have both our heads."

Nodding again, I followed the little boy from the back of the kitchen as we made our way toward slave row. I struggled to keep up with his anxious stride and thick chatter.

"My name is Jovani. My mother is Esme."

I nodded as we scurried past the lawn and the gardens to the line of palms and trees just ahead. Sweat beaded my temples as I breathed the sticky air.

"She's been sick for a while. Can't stop coughing. Feels low all da time. Bixby has whipped her twice already for laziness." Jovani swatted away a wide-leafed plant and plowed through the shade, his small body easily dipping between vegetation. He shot me a side-long glance, eyes narrowed. "You really a witch?"

I shook my head and stepped over a fallen log. He nodded with satisfaction. "Some of da other children said you weren't but da adults believe you are. How come you don't talk?"

Shrugging, I shadowed his steps. Words wouldn't come when I wanted. The cold fear choked them off. What good would it do to try? It seemed every time I was stared at with expectation, and watched with a questioning arch of a brow, my tongue glued itself shut. The only time I uttered a word was in quiet conversation with

Molly, and the new stranger who had discovered me singing. The very same who led me in a dance and tucked the strange, beautiful words into my hand. My cheeks still burned at the memory of his touch, the gentle warmth in his eyes. Why did my lips loosen for him?

"Dere!" Jovani pointed as the palms dropped away to reveal the green stalks, fields of sugar cane. "Momma is over dere, on the far side."

Instead of skirting the edges of the field, Jovani plowed right through the green-topped rows. I hastened to keep stride with his scurrying steps. Sweat glued my bodice to my skin as I inhaled the loamy scent of earth and the sweet, woodsy aroma of the cane looming overhead. Several times I almost lost the boy but my ears sharpened to the sound of his rustling.

In long moments, we were through the maze and a row of shanties appeared. I looked over my shoulder. No workers or overseers could be seen. They must be working the other fields this day.

Esme's rattling cough reached us long before I walked through the door. Jovani pushed it open with a dry squeak. The dim light drifting through the small, square hole in the wall illuminated a thin woman curled on her side on a lumpy rope bed. Her fingers clenched as she coughed into her fist, each movement strained. I approached her side and knelt on the floor, letting the basket rest beside me. When her eyes slid open and she saw me studying her, her dark gaze widened.

"Jovani!" Another cough rattled. "You bring da witch?"

"She's not a witch, Momma." He lowered his head and scuffed his bare toes against the dirt floor. "She heals."

This sickly woman did not trust me. Her suspicion cut through my marrow as I studied her face. Color was poor. Reaching over, I gently pinched the skin of her hand. The skin remained in place and did not bounce back to its shape.

"You hurt me!" She coughed again and clutched her hand to her chest. I shook my head. How to explain? It would better serve to treat her than to waste words that would not come.

I pulled the cloth pouch filled with bay leaves from the basket and quickly rose to stir the embers of the small fireplace. A pot was already filled with water, hanging over the waning coals. Good. I dropped in several leaves and stirred.

"What ya going to do to me?"

"Momma, please ... "

I held up a calming hand to Jovani and smiled to let him know her words did not trouble me. She was only scared. Scared and weary.

When enough of the bay leaf had seeped into the water, I dipped a clean cloth into the tea and let it soak before wringing it out and moving back to Esme. I mimed placing the damp cloth on my own chest and waited. She watched me through narrowed eyes for long moments before answering with a curt nod. I gently slipped the cloth between her thin shift and the skin of her chest. Her rattled breathing quickly eased.

Jovani approached and pressed close to my side. "She gonna be well, miss?"

Was she? I hoped so.

I emptied the dredges of the bay tea onto the grass outside the hut and moved to refill the pot with water from the bucket sitting by a rickety worktable in the corner. Leaning to peer into my basket of herbs, I pulled out the pouch of soursop leaves and waited for the water to come to a boil. Jovani made himself useful by gathering more wood from outside to stoke up the fire. Sweat trickled down my neck and I wiped it away with a grimace. Perhaps we could sweat the fever from Esme's body.

When the water boiled, I took four of the leaves, tore them into small pieces, and added them in, shooting Esme glances from time to time. Her cough had eased, her breathing settled, but she watched me as if afraid I might poison her.

Turning back to the boiling tea, I sighed. What more could I possibly do to earn her favor?

I shook the musing away. Better to be invisible and ignored than be the focus of suspicion. I had never earned anyone's favor anyway, save for Molly.

When the leaves had been strained, I poured the tea into a dented metal cup and handed it to Jovani, motioning for him to serve it to his mother. He nodded and approached her side cautiously, as if afraid the slightest movement would upset her already frail condition. She frowned but sipped it slowly, grimacing between times.

Gathering the herbs back into the basket, I rose to depart. Jovani turned from his mother and grasped my hand. I startled. So rarely had I been touched. After a moment, I curled my fingers around his and looked down into his upturned face.

"Thank you, miss."

Smiling, I touched his cheek and made my way back to the big house. Stepping inside the kitchen, I froze when I saw Baara waiting for me, her face a dark cloud of fury. A burning smell lingered in the air. She turned and pierced me with a withering stare.

"Girl, what did you do?"

I blinked and licked my lips, glancing around the room now crowded with servants. In the corner, Molly twisted her fingers together, her expression fretful. The others ... Cuffy, Phebah, and Tabia stared silently, their eyes wide. And then there was Naomi, her chin lifted, expression triumphant.

Baara stepped close, lips pinched. "You are supposed to make da stew and instead you leave to do ... what?" She eyed my basket of herbs with a cold stare. "And now we have no food for our midday meal!"

Naomi had betrayed me, purposely let the meal burn. But why?

Baara stared at me for a long moment.

She lashed out, wrapping her hand around my wrist, and yanked me toward the back door. "You must be punished."

No! I knew what the fated words meant. The lash. I had spent my entire existence avoiding such a dreadful thing. Behind me, Molly cried out but Baara ignored her, dragging me outside. Terror snaked through my middle but I dared not struggle, dared not make the punishment worse. Baara whistled for one of the male servants. She threw me to the ground, where I landed with a painful thud, dirt puffing up around me and coating my tongue.

"Sam! Come here!" Baara's piercing yell did not make the groomsman rush in haste. Instead, he shot me a pitying stare from across the expanse of lawn and trudged to her side. Where the whip had come from, I did not know, but she shoved it in his hands.

"Five lashes."

Five? I cringed and buried my head in my arms, curling up into a ball. Panic pounded my ears, my chest.

"Wait!" Baara's harsh call gave me hope. Perhaps she would grant mercy. I sat up and watched her approach but she knelt and unbuttoned the front of my shirt before yanking the fabric down to my waist. Her gaze held mine for a long moment, her lips pinched, but there was something in her eyes ... compassion? Empathy?

And I knew then ... she had experienced the same.

She leaned over, her voice a stern whisper.

"Better punishment from me than da Master. It will go easier on you."

Her whispered words brought little solace. She rose again, leaving me alone in the dirt.

Mortification burned deep as I tucked myself into a ball. At least my long hair covered my chest from the servants' eyes.

I heard the whip whistle through the air a split second before a slicing, unbreathable pain ripped across my back. Something warm and wet slicked my skin. Blood?

Another lash and my voice found freedom. I cried out at the next crippling sting. Sobs tore from my chest as I pressed myself into the earth.

Invisible, invisible ...

A whistling crack and my body jerked. I squeezed my eyes shut, sobs tearing at my throat.

Maybe someday, we'll find freedom ...

Invisible ...

Pounding footsteps ran toward me and I heard a masculine voice shout, "Enough!"

I trembled as I lay on the ground, my head tucked into the crook of my arm. The whip landed on the ground next to my prostrate body and I stared at the hated object, salt filling my mouth.

"I shall take up this action with your Master. Now all of you, leave!"

Skirts rustled and steps faded before I heard more fabric shuffling. Braving a glance over my shoulder, I gasped through my bleary-eyed gaze.

The handsome stranger, the one who had given me the scripture, called for a blanket. I curled in on myself even more. Hiding.

He approached cautiously. "Shh. I'm not going to hurt you."

His voice was as calming as a gentle rain. A blanket was gently draped over my back but I sucked in a breath at the sting. I reached as far as I dared to snag the fabric before tugging it to cover my chest and wrapping it around my torso. I froze when his fingers tugged bloody, wet tendrils of hair away from my neck.

"Avalina ... " He breathed my name, half sorrowful, half a whisper. Emotion clogged my throat. "Can you stand? I would carry you but ... "

But my back was torn to pieces. The pain would be unbearable. I nodded slightly, clutching the blanket with tight fingers.

As tenderly as cradling a newborn colt, he cupped my elbows and assisted me to my feet. I squeezed my eyes shut as the world shifted, my feet shaking with unsteady steps. My rescuer guided me carefully across the yard. Humiliation burned my cheeks as fiery pain danced across my shoulders. With each step, my skin stretched, causing fresh stings to ripple across my back.

"Where is your room?"

I looked up into his face, my gaze colliding with the depths of his coffee-colored eyes, and I swallowed, pointing to the space above the kitchen. He nodded ever so slightly and led me into the house and up the stairs. I pointed again at the door that housed my only sanctuary. He turned the knob before gingerly guiding me inside. Keeping the blanket wrapped around me, I slid onto the bed on my stomach. Each movement was fire.

When the fabric brushed my face, I sobbed anew. My quilt. My only treasure would now be stained with blood.

"I'll be back in a moment."

His footfalls faded and my cries settled into a soft mewling. I must have fallen asleep—or perhaps I passed out—before I heard him, or someone, again. Water dribbled in a bowl, perhaps being rung from a cloth, before the same damp cloth was pressed to the burning skin of my neck. If the flesh above the cuts was tender, how miserable would the lash marks in my back be?

"This should be enough water for da time, sir." Tabia. I recognized her voice. "I'll fetch Molly for you. She needs to treat da girl, not you."

"I'll not tend to her back. That is best saved for someone she knows and trusts, but I'll stay until Molly arrives. Leave the door open."

Tabia's footfalls disappeared.

"I don't think I ever told you my name."

It was him, the stranger. I stilled, staring at the wall, my eyes averted from his, waiting to hear the words that slipped from his lips.

"It's Josiah. Josiah Holland. I hail from South Carolina. Have you ever heard of it?"

I shook my head no, body relaxing while clutching the blanket to my front. Blessed shelter, though he had done nothing untoward. Nothing but keep me company. Protect me.

"It's a lovely land, yet not as beautiful as Barbados, that is for certain. Why, the trees and flowers, the fruit... everything here on the island is exquisite."

His voice was a soothing balm, a caress.

"My father is intent on buying and selling slaves with your master, but I am learning that perhaps such things are not for me."

I blinked as I stared at the gray wall. Why was he telling me this? And why did he come to my rescue?

Josiah chuckled softly, a light laugh that siphoned into a sigh. "I imagine your master and I will have quite a row later."

I squeezed my eyes shut again. Master Cyrene. Trembling formed in my middle and spread to my limbs. What would he do? He would not like his authority being usurped, especially by a foreigner.

Josiah's voice gentled. "I promise, I will do whatever I can for you."

Tears burned my eyes as a large lump swelled in my throat. Why? Why would he trouble himself over a slave?

More footsteps approached and I heard a soft gasp. "Oh, the poor lamb."

Molly. A fresh sob scraped my chest. The only woman I'd ever considered dear enough to be my mother.

"Ach, how I wish I could have prevented it. A curse be upon Naomi! She knew what she was about."

"Naomi?" I heard the frown in Josiah's voice. "Is that who is to blame for this grievous offense?"

"Aye." I heard Molly shuffle closer, her plump fingers roving through my hair. "Jealous, she is."

Jealous? Why was Naomi jealous of me? Such a thing made no sense.

"Why?" Josiah's voice was low, a deep baritone that resonated like distant thunder.

Molly hesitated. "I think it best if I tell you later, sir. Go on. 'Tisn't proper, having you here in her room, pardon me for saying so, sir."

"I know." I felt his gaze settle over me. "I just wanted to make sure..."

"I shall see to a salve for her back." Molly swallowed. "And see that Master is made aware of her condition."

The icy dread seized me again. His reaction would be fierce... but would it be directed at me? The utter humiliation of being whipped in front of the others was crippling enough. I could scarcely breathe at the thought of it. But to have such a punishment yet again at the Master's hands...

I squeezed my eyes shut.

Fingers rested atop my head and Josiah's voice filled the room.

"I ask, Thee, Almighty God, to ease her suffering. Heal her by Thy great power..."

More words. None of them made sense but a strange kind of peace settled around me anyway. Josiah lifted his hands from my head. Before he could leave, I turned ever so slightly and grabbed his hand, imparting a squeeze as my gaze met his.

A thank-you. The only thing I had to offer.

He bowed low and pressed a kiss to my fingers.

I didn't understand this strange man. The son of a slave holder who concerned himself with my punishment. Such a thing was not done.

He turned to Molly, his brows raised. "May I speak with you outside before I leave?"

Molly bit her lip and nodded before her gaze flicked to mine. "I shall return with medicine in a minute, lamb."

I nodded and settled my chest against the thin fabric of my quilt.

And then I was left alone, with naught but the echo of his prayer to offer solace.

CHAPTER 9

Josiah stepped into the hallway to face the plump woman who barely rose to his shoulder. What to ask? She stood before him, blue eyes wide...honest. Only the slight twisting of her fingers betrayed her nervousness.

He ran his hands through his hair before scrubbing the back of his neck. "I thank you for seeing to Avalina's needs."

"'Tis the least I can do." She dipped a small curtsy, head bowed with respect.

"What is her story?" He crossed his arms.

"Her story, sir?"

"How did she come to be here?"

The diminutive woman pursed her lips. "'Twas a wild day, that. Surely ye know of King James the First's edict to clear the streets of Ireland?"

He frowned. "Yes, I heard of that horrible act."

She sighed and looked away. "Police rounded up the poor in droves. Pushed them onto ships and sold them as slaves to the islands. Though the practice is not what it once was, unscrupulous men yet steal women and children from their beds in the poorest parts of Ireland."

He gentled his tone. "Is that how you came to be here?"

"Aye." Her eyes glassed but after a moment's struggle, she blinked the tears away. "Fought like a banshee, I did, but no good came of it. Sold to Master Cyrene over twenty years ago."

"I'm sorry." He swallowed. Such cruelty he could not fathom.

She shrugged her soft shoulders. "I have learned to make the best of it. Took my oath of marriage to a man in Ireland when I was but a score." A muscle bobbed in her neck. "He died before I was taken, so at least we did not have to deal with the pain of being physically separated this side of eternity. I have learned contentment, though this would not be the life I'd chosen."

"Clearly. Is that what happened to Avalina?"

"Best I can figure. She wandered onto the plantation as naught but a wee sprite of six or so, calling for her mother. Would sing herself lullabies to soothe her battered heart. Poor lamb." The woman sniffed as she relived the troubling memories. "We later learned she was the sole survivor of a shipwreck...likely a slave ship intended for another island, but no one knows for certain."

Josiah inhaled a shaky breath. "How terrible."

"Aye." The woman bit her lip. "When Master Cyrene was told she could sing, he took her as his slave to entertain guests. When she refused the first time, he beat her until she was nearly broken. The little thing has rarely spoken a word since, save to me on occasion." Her spine straightened, chin jutting forward. "She trusts me."

He curled his fists, Harding's cruelty igniting a fury deep inside. Yet was he any better? The son of a slave owner, destined to become all his father was? "I heard her sing once."

The woman's eyes rounded. "Did you? A miracle, that."

"It was beautiful. When I asked her about the song, she merely said, 'Yarico.' What does that mean?"

The woman shifted her weight. "'Tis a native song about a slave named Yarico and a slave holder who fell madly in love with her. Inkle was his name. He swept her away to save her from her master yet later sold her again, burdened by the guilt of their class differences."

"Mm." Josiah grunted and frowned. "Not a happy tale."

"Not much of Avalina's life has been happy, sir."

How he longed to change her fate. To even change the destiny of the woman before him. To change life for all of them.

An idea niggled. His father would think him mad, but once the thought took root, hope flamed anew in his chest.

"Thank you..." Realizing he had already forgotten the woman's name, he quirked an eyebrow.

"Molly, sir." She dipped another curtsy. "Thank you for your kindness."

The muscles in his neck tensed. "One more thing." He held up a staying hand, lips pursed. "Why does this Naomi woman dislike Avalina?"

Molly reddened, her gaze dropping to the floor. "'Tis not fit to speak of in mixed company, sir."

"Please."

Biting her lip, the little woman met his gaze, eyes troubled. "I can't say for sure, mind you, but some of us have noticed Master watching Avalina of late, if you know what I mean." Deep scarlet burnished her round cheeks.

His nostrils flared. He did know. Too well.

"Naomi... she is the one Master usually seeks out for... such things."

Heat scorched his neck at the thought of the vile man touching Avalina. "I see."

"I'm sorry, sir." Molly bowed her head meekly. "I cannot say more. And I wish there was something I could do to remedy such goings-on."

Molly was helpless in the situation, but he was not. Perhaps there was something to be done, after all.

But it would hinge on the agreeability of Cyrene Harding.

Josiah stood in Harding's ornate parlor late that afternoon, the sun streaming through the tall glass windows. He prayed the owner of the plantation was as cheerful this day as the room he'd built.

Wiping sweaty palms down his trousers, he paced the length of the space, absently pausing before a small shelf filled with classic literature. Faust, Shakespeare, Machiavelli ... the latter caused him to inhale a fortifying breath. Did Harding subscribe to such ideals?

He feared such was the case.

The object of his thoughts strolled into the parlor and headed straight for the amber-filled decanter on the serving table.

"Young Holland." He looked up from pouring and arched a brow. "I am told you wish to speak with me." Harding took a swig of spirits before eyeing Josiah with a straight stare. Josiah squared his shoulders.

"Yes, sir. I confess to some interference on my part with one of your servants and wanted to make sure you were told of my involvement from my own lips."

Harding's dark brows dipped. "Pray tell."

Josiah lifted his chin. "This very afternoon, I witnessed one of your servants whipping another, and I stepped in to stop it."

Harding's tongue probed the inside of his cheek. "I see." Taking another swig, he placed the glass on the table and crossed his arms. "And you feel justified in this?"

"Yes, sir, I do. The punishment was severe. When I arrived, a female kitchen slave had been given at least four lashes to the back."

Harding's eyes narrowed. "And who decides what is severe on this plantation?"

Though the words were softly spoken, his tone held a bite.

"I apologize for overstepping my bounds, sir, but I do not apologize for protecting an innocent."

Harding chuckled and moved to stare out of one of the large windows. "And who says this woman is innocent?"

"The woman cannot speak in her own defense."

Cyrene turned then, his brows lifted. "Avalina?"

Nodding, Josiah waited.

Harding cast him a sidelong glance and moved around the room, walking slowly, absently touching knickknacks and books, though Josiah knew his mind was not at ease. "Avalina... she pleases you, yes?"

Josiah frowned. "Pleases me?"

Harding stopped and chuckled, eyeing Josiah with a smirk. "You wish to keep her for yourself."

Heat slithered up his neck and bloomed in his cheeks. "Sir, you are out of line."

Pursing his lips, Harding arched a single brow. "Am I? Such things are not so strange. Your own father knows of what I speak."

His father? No, such a thing was not done on their plantation. Josiah clenched his fists and took a step closer, longing to smash his knuckles into the smug man's face. "You will not speak of my father in such a manner."

Harding's stance stayed relaxed. Maddeningly so. "Forgive me, young Holland. Clearly, you and your father are much more virtuous than I."

"I want to buy Avalina from you, sir."

He blurted the words, then wished he'd waited when he saw the flicker of irritation spark in the man's eyes. "Out of the question."

"But, Mr. Harding, surely you have no need for such a slave. I—"

"I have no need?" Harding growled, eyes narrowing to slits. "You have no idea what I need. You dared to interfere with the running of my plantation and then have the audacity to come seeking my favor."

"But I—"

"I'll not hear another word on the matter." Harding stalked past him to leave the room but paused at the door and tossed a sleek smile over his shoulder.

"Perhaps when I tire of her, we shall speak again, but for now"—he arched a dark brow—"I have my own punishment to mete out."

Punishment? Josiah's breath thinned. "No, sir, I beg you—"

Harding left the room without another word, slamming the door with a bang. Worry clawed up Josiah's throat as he funneled his fingers through his hair.

Speaking to Harding had only made matters worse. What had he done?

I blinked in the darkness, shifting carefully against the bed. My sleep was fretful. Perhaps I should have taken a sleeping draught after all. My back was raw, a throbbing swath of agony.

What time was it? Angling my head, I studied the pewter light coming through the small window. The moon was high. The night stretched on endlessly.

I sighed and clutched the quilt in my fingers when a sound outside my door snagged my attention. The knob turned and the door opened with a dry squeak. A man's shadow filled the doorway. I gasped and scooted to the wall, ignoring the stabbing pain in my flesh.

"Avalina."

Master Cyrene. Cold dread coiled around my heart. Why was he here?

"I have been told of your disobedience."

My mouth turned to ash. What would he do?

He closed the door behind him and stepped into the shaft of moonlight illuminating a square in the middle of my floor. His body was an eerie sight, half shrouded, half alight. Like a specter.

"And now I learn young Holland has taken a fancy to you."

Josiah? Confusion mingled with the terror clamping my stomach.

"You will not leave me, do you understand?"

He reached out and stroked my cheek with his fingers. I drew back at his touch and he growled before clamping his hands around my wrists.

"You are mine, and you will never leave." His sour breath warmed my cheek before he turned, slamming the door behind him.

CHAPTER 10

Morning sun prodded my puffy eyes open and I winced, first at the onslaught of light coming through the single window of my room and second, from the pinch of pain that burst across my back when I attempted to stretch.

Yesterday's nightmare invaded, evaporating the blissful ignorance of dreamless sleep from the edges of my mind. Whipped. Exposed. Shamed... then cradled.

My eyes stung with the sudden rush of tears I'd believed all but extinguished after yesterday. My nose tingled as fresh emotion welled once again. Josiah Holland, my rescuer. Molly's soft ministrations to my raw, bleeding body. Master's terrifying midnight visit. I shivered. Comfort mingled with pain. Hope slamming against despair. My throat clamped shut as hot tears coursed down my cheeks.

Invisible. It had worked for so long. But never again.

Swiping the moisture from my face, I slowly shifted against the lumpy mattress and moved my hand under my pillow. The small slip of paper crinkled. It wouldn't make noise much longer, as I had fingered it incessantly since being gifted with the message... a string of words I couldn't even read. Yet they called to my heart all the same.

In the beginning, God created the heavens and the earth.

I drank in the bit of knowledge like a parched man sucking in rain. Created by God. The heavens and earth. But what of man?

Of fowl? Of the sweet nectar that housed itself inside the stem of each flower? Of the ants that kept their vigil with the precision of a soldier? What of me and Molly and Matias? What of Josiah?

What did God see?

I fisted the message, crumpling the words in my palm. The tiny drop of knowledge only increased my thirst for more. More words. More questions. More confusion. What I needed was answers.

Sighing, I fell back against the pillow. What kind of God allowed the cruelty of the lash? Of masters and overseers who struck down those who wanted nothing but freedom?

A ribbon of guilt snaked through my middle. Such thoughts would lead to nothing but pain. This was my life, my destiny. There would never be another.

The door creaked open and I shoved the message back under my pillow, angling my head to see who might be braving a visit. A cold stone sank in my stomach until Molly's plump body filled the doorway, a tray in her hands. Though teary-eyed, I forced a smile.

"Ach, love. Good to see a wee bit of cheer on your face." She set down the tray and moved to examine my still-exposed back, her tongue clucking. "Though I could say different about your poor skin. Puckered and raw, it is."

I nodded against the pillow and shoved a tendril of hair away from my lips. Time would be my healer.

"I brought you a bit of breakfast. Medicine too. And Master says you are to rest today." She pulled a small container from the tray and dabbed the salve on her fingertips before posing the greasy appendages near my skin. "Brace yourself, lamb. Pain before scars."

I sucked in a breath to ready my body. A sting, then blessed relief. The two sensations tumbled over each other until my lash marks were covered in the healing balm.

"There now." Molly wiped her fingers on a rag and moved around the bed, the tray traveling with her as she set a plate of eggs and bread before me. I shifted to my side, moving slowly. "Eat up. Sleep. Need you a draught for pain?"

I shook my head. I had never liked the groggy effects of the sleep draughts some of the slaves concocted. A bit of black magic, that, leaving one with the sensation of overly large arms and limbs that refused to work correctly.

"You wouldn't take any last night either." Molly cupped soft fingers around my cheek, her eyes sad. "Would that I could take this from you, lamb."

I turned my head and pressed a kiss into her palm. With a sigh, Molly dropped her hand away but her eyes sharpened at something near my pillow. She plucked the scrap of paper from my bed. I gasped, too late realizing it was the crumpled verse Josiah had given me.

Her eyes rounded as she drank in the script before her gaze shifted to mine and held fast. "What is this? Who gave this to you?"

I licked my lips, shrinking back.

"Avalina." Her expression flooded with fear. "Burn this. You must. If Master, or even Baara, were to discover it..." She swallowed, not daring to say what I knew already to be true.

A far harsher punishment than the one I'd endured. Perhaps even death. Everyone knew the punishment awaiting a slave who dared learn to read.

I snatched it from her fingers and nodded. Doubt filled her eyes.

"Girl, tell me..." She looked over her shoulder to ensure we were still alone. "Can you read?"

I bit my lip and shook my head.

"Then how do you come to have it?"

I hesitated, then swallowed. "From the son of the slave trader." I turned my gaze away, fixing my eyes on the wall, fearing I had betrayed his kindness and mercy.

"You play a dangerous game, love. What are you thinking?"

That was the problem. I thought. Far too much. I pressed my lips together as Molly's shoulders slumped. "He cares for you, doesn't he?"

Did he? I had no idea. The ways between a man and a woman were a mystery to me. Still, Josiah had been naught but kind. Is that what a wretched creature I was? That simple kindness would be mistaken for something more?

I curled in on myself, pushing out the image of Molly's probing stare at my back. The thought of burning the only gift I'd been given flooded my heart with a pain that exceeded the lashes etched into my skin.

But why? I couldn't read it anyway.

With a sigh, my friend shuffled to the door and paused. "Be careful with your heart, lamb. If you give it to this man, it will be broken."

Then she left, the click of the door following behind. My fate was sealed with the same finality.

Josiah stood in the middle of the sweltering field, the green tops of sugar cane swaying slightly with every life-giving breath that scattered the sticky humidity, watching as Father and Cyrene haggled. . George Holland had brought hundreds of women and children to sell but wanted a couple of Harding's big bucks for his own fields— large men who could work hard. The Holland Plantation's slaves were getting older. Tired. The two men seemed not to notice the furtive glances from the sweat-slicked workers who labored over the cane, hacking the stalks down with machetes. Their hasty looks held remnants of fear . . . a thinly veined terror at the possibilities awaiting them.

Father pointed to a particularly large man who boasted thick ripples of muscles across his back. "What do you think of that one, Josiah? A bull of a fellow, isn't he?"

Cyrene smiled and rocked back on his heels. "Ah, one of my best workers. I'll not lie to you, Holland. He'll cost you a much higher sum."

Father grunted and turned to study Josiah. "What say you?"

He swallowed and swatted a fly away that buzzed near his ear. "There is much to consider. Is this man promised to a woman here? How many children has he sired? I think it best not to tear him away from his family."

Cyrene laughed dryly. "A funny one you are, young Holland. Ezra breeds with who I tell him to breed."

Prickling at the haughty tone, Josiah shot him a hard stare. "You speak as if he were nothing more than a prize stallion."

"So he is." Cyrene shoved his hands in his pockets. "He's worth three of most of the other field hands."

Father stroked his graying beard. "You drive a hard bargain, Harding, but I can see his worth well enough."

And what of the worth of the child he'd whipped only a few days before? The boy's screams yet muddled Josiah's ears. Images of Avalina's ribboned, bloody back invaded. The strange unease crawled once again through Josiah's belly. He didn't know what to do with this foreign feeling. Was it guilt? It felt more like sickening disgust. An empathetic pain. He winced and shook his head. What he'd witnessed on Barbados and the frank conversation with quirky Benjamin Magee had altered everything. And it wasn't as if he hadn't heard similar arguments from abolitionists before. Why couldn't he shake the man's words from his heart?

He knew why. Seeing the dead slaves thrown off the ship had scarred his mind more than he'd thought possible. Avalina, the child, the fear in the field hands' eyes … how had he lived so long in such ignorance?

A long-ago memory invaded. He had been nothing more than a boy of seven. Eight, perhaps. A neighbor had come to call, a Mr. Rutledge. Josiah had crept down the hallway and pressed his ear to the door of Father's study, where the heady scent of tobacco squeezed its way from under the door. How much longer until he would be old enough to join the men? Speaking of manly things, smoking cigars, and drinking the amber liquid Father so readily poured whenever company arrived?

Mr. Rutledge had sighed heavily. "There's not much else to be done, George. My son has scoffed at his inheritance. Everything I've built—all my father built—and he's chosen to cast it aside like a worn boot."

Father had grunted, the leather chair squeaking as he shifted his weight. "It's a crime, that's what, Rutledge. A son who shows such ingratitude to his family and his Maker is no better than a reprobate. No mistaking that. And the Good Book makes it plain what happens to those who dishonor their parents."

Josiah had peeked through the crack where the door had opened from the jamb. Mr. Rutledge took a sip of liquor from his glass, his lips pinched and thin. "You speak truth, as much as it pains me to agree."

Father's brows pinched. "If Josiah is ever so foolish to try such a thing, I'll take the lash to him myself. A son who will not receive his destiny is not a son at all."

Rutledge nodded, his expression pained and voice soft. "A child of the devil … "

Josiah blinked, his focus returning to the present as he shifted his weight and crossed his arms. Here he stood, at an impasse, unable to move, unable to change a thing about this whole mess.

Father cast him a sidelong look and murmured, the lines deepening around his eyes. "Focus, Josiah. Someday I'll be gone and this entire process will fall on your shoulders. You must be wise and shrewd in these dealings."

Again, dread crept through his chest. Shrugging it away, he pointed across the field to the palms beyond. "Is there not another field that lies beyond this one?"

Cyrene nodded. "Indeed. Take a walk and explore it. You may find more slaves that suit your fancy in the north lot." His dark eyes gleamed knowingly. "Perhaps a female or two if you long for a bit of companionship."

Father chuckled and Josiah gritted his teeth. He had no interest in such things. Harding's comment was no doubt a mocking stab at his request to purchase Avalina. Worse still, Father's laughter picked at his heart like a vulture scavenging for meat.

Surely his father had never engaged in such crass, demeaning relations with their own slaves. Although Barbados was a veritable paradise, he was thankful to soon be returning home to South Carolina, where tyrants like Cyrene Harding had no place.

Leaving the two men to their haggling, he skirted the edge of the field until the heat of the day gave way to the blessed relief of shade from the thick canopy of palms and brush. He plunged deeper into the thicket of vegetation, watching for snakes that might be lurking underfoot. He walked long minutes more, thankful for the reprieve.

Soft masculine chatter drifted by, causing his ears to perk up. The fellow had a thick Caribbean accent like most here on the island and he paused to listen.

"Do you like it, Redbird?"

Josiah frowned. Redbird? Was the fellow talking to birds? Odd, that. He crept closer to the sounds and startled when the voice launched into song.

"All creatures worship God most high, lift up your voice in earth and sky. Alleluia!"

Pushing beside a large palm, Josiah froze. An elderly slave lifted his hands to the heavens in a small clearing, his song rising and falling like the waves of the sea. And at his side was Avalina, who watched him with pure admiration, if a bit of puzzlement, a bright blue feather held between her fingers.

Josiah's chest squeezed. She was pale, no doubt yet bearing the pain of her shredded back, but she was here, out of her bed and watching the elderly slave with rapt attention.

The man stopped his song and moved to grip her fingers, the feather still held in her hands. His dark skin contrasted starkly with her pale skin but the gesture seemed right... like the comforting touch of a grandfather to a child.

"Redbird, I thank you for meeting me now in this moment of worship. Yet we cannot truly worship the God of creation with bitterness in our hearts." His eyes narrowed with a discretion only the aged possessed. "Have you forgiven Baara for the pain she inflicted upon you?"

Avalina sucked in a breath, her eyes wide. The man offered a gentle smile.

"Yes, I saw it all. And how my heart ached. It was unfair and unjust but the Almighty, the God of Light, cannot coexist with darkness. Unforgiveness is a bitter brew, consuming all it touches. You must forgive Baara."

Avalina looked away and the old man sighed. "The same hymn I learned from my first master, the one I sing to you now, also says this." He cleared his throat and launched into the melody once more. "And ev'ryone, with tender heart, forgiving others, take your part. Alleluia! Ye who long pain and sorrow bear, sing praise and cast on God your care. O sing Alleluia!"

Josiah watched Avalina bite her lip, her shoulders sagging with the invisible struggle. Oh, how he longed to come to her defense! The old slave asked too much. She yet bore the cuts of the whip. But making his presence known would somehow shatter the sacredness of the moment.

No worship service back home had every been so poignant, so deep.

The old man patted her hands and released her. She sucked in a tremulous breath and looked down at her fingers.

This woman, who held all her mysteries in silence, gently stroked the tip of the brilliant sapphire feather with reverence. Her creamy skin was dotted with a spray of freckles. The fan of her eyelashes told a thousand stories ... downcast, a blushing maid's embarrassment, lifted, a frank curiosity.

An odd thunder pounded Josiah's chest. If only she would look at him in such a way.

He shoved the wayward thought down. They were worlds apart. Doomed to be nothing more than slave and master. How he longed for it to be different.

She was kept captive in a strange world, like a rare bird watching those who passed from the confines of its cage. And Cyrene Harding, her captor.

Josiah turned away, sick at heart, and left the two of them to whatever worship ritual this was.

Why had this young woman entranced him so?

Perhaps it was the knowledge that some birds, long imprisoned, were unaware of freedom when the cage door was finally thrown open.

Did not all caged creatures need someone willing to lift the door of their prison to offer the gift of flight? Coax them out if fear held them tucked inside?

It was that very thought that refused to leave him be.

Josiah scanned the crowded markets in town, his eyes searching for one man. In two days, he and his father would leave Barbados behind.

He must find Benjamin Magee.

Filing past the crowded bartering square, Josiah turned in a slow circle. Faces blurred, the calls of hawkers buzzing in his ears like the dreary drone of flies. Had the fiery man already fled to the States?

Pressing past the crush of shoppers, he turned left and followed the flow of rickety wagons and people strolling through town. A piercing voice bellowed beyond the normal hum of activity.

"All ye masters, who are contentedly holding your fellow-creatures in slavery, well knowing the cruel sufferings those innocent captives undergo ... ye who profess to do unto all men as ye would they should do unto ye ... "

Benjamin. Pulse thrumming, Josiah pushed past two men haggling over the price of chickens and jogged farther down the street, looking to the right, then left.

Ahead a crowd had formed in front of the produce market. Benjamin's calls grew stronger. Josiah slowed to a walk and wiped his sweaty forehead with his arm.

"Ye must throw off the coat of tyranny as I do!"

Josiah pushed his way through the crowd to see the diminutive man in the center of the commotion, one eye squinted as he yanked off his coat to reveal a military uniform underneath. People gasped as he tossed the cloak into the dusty street.

"Ye who are treating your fellow man in such a way"—Benjamin pointed, turning in a slow circle—"may as well plunge a dagger into each of their hearts."

The old man pulled a dagger from his side and plunged it into his own stomach.

Josiah gasped as blood gushed from the wound. Women screamed and fainted. Men shielded them from the horrid spectacle, yet Benjamin stood upright, unaffected. When his piercing gaze landed on Josiah, a wide grin split his face.

"Josiah! 'Tis good to see ye."

Josiah blinked, unable to comprehend the specter before him. Blood yet dribbled down the front of his uniform and pooled beneath his feet. Women sobbed into their hands as men yelled out obscene epithets at the Quaker. Shaking his head, Josiah stepped close.

"What—what have you done?"

Benjamin looked down at his clothes and cackled, blue eyes twinkling. "'Tis no matter, young Holland. I filled a bladder with pokeberry juice and tucked it under me uniform." The audacious man then winked, and Josiah took a cleansing breath.

Crazy, he was.

An angry man stormed toward Benjamin and yanked the lapel of his uniform, pulling him off his feet. Spittle flew from the enraged stranger's mouth as he snarled.

"Be gone! You do nothing but torment and terrorize those who come to market."

Josiah stepped between them, trying to shield the Quaker from the stranger's fury. "He is naught but an elderly man."

But the fellow's anger was not yet sated. He pulled back his fist and plowed it into Josiah's jaw.

Pain exploded as he staggered backward and smashed into a melon cart. Fruit spilled into the street. The shouts of the crowd barely registered before Josiah lunged at the muscled stranger, smashing his fist into the man's nose. Blood squirted.

Everything was a blur afterward. People shouted. Fists and bodies flew. Dust rose up, choking the air with a thick haze. Josiah dodged a punch and rammed his body into a man's middle, slamming him into a group of men who had circled around Benjamin once more.

As the melee grew, Josiah whirled to Benjamin. "Let's get you out of here!" Another fist hurtled toward him but he dodged to the left and answered with a punch of his own.

Benjamin nodded. "Follow me!"

The two men scurried down a nearby alley. Josiah glanced over his shoulder, panting as he watched the fighting crowd melt into the distance. Light shifted into shadows as Benjamin took him down one alley and then another. For an elderly gent, the old Quaker could make a quick escape.

Finally, they slowed near a battered door. The old man unbuttoned his uniform coat and tossed it aside. Sure enough, a sliced, empty bladder fell onto the street. Only a few speckles of pokeberry juice marred his shirtwaist.

"Come inside. Najaf will provide us sanctuary."

Benjamin pushed the creaky wood door open and slipped inside. Tossing one final glance over his shoulder, Josiah followed and cupped his aching jaw. He winced. When his father saw the repercussions of the exchange, he would be livid.

They walked into a kitchen where a large Negro man stood over a pot, stirring swiftly. He looked up with a smirk, one eyebrow arched.

"Trouble again, my friend?"

Benjamin chuckled. "Always." He waved toward Josiah. "Meet a new companion, Josiah Holland."

Josiah lifted a hand in greeting and Najaf nodded. "Welcome." He jerked his head beyond the kitchen. "Go. Sit. I will bring you food in a moment."

"I'm obliged." Benjamin pushed through the door and led them into a shadowed tavern. The room was empty save for a single man staring out the open window, absently sipping a drink.

As they settled into chairs at a table, Josiah whispered, "Are you sure we'll be safe here?"

"Safe?" Benjamin's white brows lifted. "No. Nothing in this world is safe. But yes, I believe the Almighty will protect us. Najaf is an abolitionist and has given much to the cause."

"Like what?"

Benjamin's lips pressed into a hard line, his white beard moving with the action. "That is his story to tell. Not mine."

The kitchen door swung open and Najaf entered, steam rising from the two plates he carried. He set the fare before them without a word and left them on their own. Josiah sniffed as his mouth watered. The aroma of stewed chicken, rice and fried tortillas wafted into his nostrils.

Benjamin sighed. "Stubborn man. He always insists on serving me meat. Says it will give me strength." He winked while grabbing his spoon. "Just one of a few areas where we disagree."

After a hasty grace, the men dug in. The savory fare was spicy but filling. Najaf appeared once more to bring them a fruity juice. Dragon fruit, he called it. Delicious. Nothing at Cyrene Harding's table could compare with this.

Scooping up a spoonful of buttery rice, Benjamin chewed slowly, eyeing Josiah with an inquisitive stare. "What led ye to seek me out today, young Holland?"

Setting down his cup, Josiah sighed. "I am at . . . an impasse. I have no other way to describe it."

"About?"

He swallowed and lowered his voice. "My father's business. Soon to be mine."

Benjamin chuckled dryly and tore off a piece of tortilla. "If ye've come to me for a balanced discussion, I'm afraid ye will be disappointed."

"No, it's not that. I well understand your beliefs and am discovering that I share many of them. But how do I pull myself away from my father's way of life without dishonoring him?"

"Ah, I see." Benjamin leaned back and swiped the back of his sleeve across his mouth, one eye squinting as he thought. "Let all things be done in love."

"Pardon?"

The old man leaned forward, resting his forearms on the scarred, wooden table. "When it comes to loyalty, we owe all to the One who ransomed our souls, do we not?"

"Yes, of course, but—"

"So allegiance can never be given to two parties. It's incompatible." He tore off another piece of tortilla and popped it in his mouth, causing his beard to bob up and down with the motion. "Yet the love of Christ compels us to treat all men with dignity and honor. That includes yer father." He leaned forward. "Ye must be firm, but gentle."

"You didn't seem gentle in the market moments ago."

"I was honest. Not violent. The assault came from those who long to shut up their ears from the truth."

Josiah sighed and fell against his chair, rubbing the back of his neck. "Father will be furious."

"Just so. But the most loving thing ye can do is tell him the truth."

Josiah frowned. How could shredding apart his family legacy be loving? "What do you mean?"

The Quaker chuckled. "I suspect ye come from a family that teaches love is compliance. Love is obedience to God, yes, but not always the whims of man. Love is truth. Love confronts. It encourages and teaches. The most loving thing we can do is to walk and speak in truth."

Josiah toyed with his tine and pondered the thought. Had he been instructed with a warped view of love? Perhaps. Obedience to Father was prized and failure was punished. Love was withdrawn until compliance was gained. Wasn't that the way of it in all families?

"I see I have much to consider. But there is one other thing." He swallowed, unsure why daring to speak of Avalina caused his stomach to clench in pain. "There is a woman. A slave on Harding's plantation. I long to see her freed."

Benjamin's shrewd blue gaze narrowed to slits. "You care for this woman?"

Did he? Certainly with the kindness and affection given to all God's creatures, but there was something about her. Something that called to him.

"Never mind." Benjamin shook his head. "I can see the answer on yer face."

Josiah glanced around the room and whispered, "I sought to purchase her from Harding but he refused."

A scowl marred the old man's brow. "Ye offered to purchase her, as if she were nothing more than an animal at market?"

The question stung. Heat warmed Josiah's neck. "No, of course not. I only—"

Benjamin's nostrils flared. "Much of yer father still resides in yer mind, young Holland. This woman is made in the image of God. She is His daughter, not property to be haggled over."

Shame curled cold in his gut. "Of—of course. But I only long to give her a better life. A new start. Surely such a thing is not wrong."

Benjamin pursed his lips. "Yer intention is honorable but ye devalue her by attempting such."

Frustration growled at Josiah's core. He dropped the tine onto the plate with a clatter. "Then what do I do? How can I help?"

Benjamin calmly chewed a mouthful of rice. Quietly. Slowly. Josiah longed to lash out at the man's thoughtful pause.

"Ye cannot be her Savior, Josiah. There is only One who can do that."

A slap across the face would have been gentler, but the words settled through his heart like sand slipping through a sieve. Benjamin was right. Josiah had longed to step into her life and be the one to rescue her from a dismal future.

"So I do nothing?" Josiah dropped his head in his hands and massaged his temples.

"No, son. There is much ye can do." Old Benjamin smiled. "Teach her about the One who can redeem her while ye have the opportunity. Then leave the rest to the Almighty."

Najaf reappeared and hunkered over Benjamin, stooping to murmur something low in his ear. The old man nodded and rose swiftly, wiping his mouth once more with his sleeve.

"Me friend bids me go. Many are searching for me. I depart Barbados soon on a ship bound for the States." Benjamin rested his gnarled fingers on Josiah's shoulder and squeezed. "I will see ye in Philadelphia."

Josiah shook his head. "But I'll be returning to our plantation in South Carolina."

The old man turned and smiled over his shoulder, eyes twinkling. "God is doing much in ye, young Holland. And when the time is right, ye will seek me once again."

CHAPTER 11

I lugged the slop bucket out the back door of the kitchen, my back screaming with the strain. Though I had been able to work throughout the day, each movement was agony. Yesterday's rest had not healed me as much as I'd hoped. Each pull of muscle threatened to tear the skin Molly had tried so delicately to soothe into compliance. Walking on bare feet to the hog pen, I tossed the scraps into the trough and watched the fat creatures amble to fight over the sustenance.

A smile tugged at their eager grunting, their speckled, hairy ears flopping as they rooted through the mess. A simple life, they had.

Footfalls—boots crunching against gravel—approached. On instinct I tensed and turned, hoping it would be only Matias or even Amos.

Naomi stood staring at me, a basket clutched in her hands, dark eyes slitted. My blood thickened like pudding at the poison in her expression. The old, cold fear rose swiftly through my chest, choking my throat, killing the one question I longed to ask. *Why did you betray me?*

"You think you're so special. You who are so different than da rest of us." Her nostrils flared as she took a step closer. "Master wants me. Do you hear?" She grabbed my chin between her fingers and squeezed, nails digging into my flesh. "I mean to be the lady of dis house someday and I won't let you get in my way." She released my face with a small shove. A smirk twisted her lips. "Can't talk. Can't think. You are a witch, and I've made sure everybody knows it."

Heat billowed in my chest, like smoke rising from a chimney. It was her? This vile vixen . . . all this time, spreading lies about me. Poisoning the others to believe I carried some kind of dark evil inside. And my back . . . the shame, pain, and humiliation of the whipping rolled over me like an ocean wave.

With a guttural scream in my throat, I drew back my hand and slapped her across the face. My hand smarted as her head snapped to the side. Her eyes widened and she threw the basket to the ground before lunging.

I didn't care. Didn't think. I clawed and slapped, years of torment and hate bubbling up as we fell to the ground, tearing at each other the way the animals of the island attacked when provoked.

"Witch! An evil god lives in you. You are cursed!" Her teeth bared.

Strong arms pulled me away from Naomi's punishing hands. I panted, hair in my eyes as Amos yanked Naomi back, his arm snaked around her waist as she shouted and writhed.

"Curse! You are a curse!"

I attempted to lunge toward her once again, to silence her vile shouts, but the wiry arms surrounding mine held me fast. "Be at peace, Redbird. Be at peace." Matias's voice murmured near my ear. "Naomi speaks lies. Let it go."

Every black thought, every emotion I'd quelled through the years rose up like a great bird inside. My silence was not stupidity. Nor was it indifference. I had seen every snarl of derision, every huff of exasperation. Heard every word spoken against me.

And my heart screamed to cry out against it. To be heard.

"I know." Matias gentled his hold as Amos pulled Naomi away. I sucked in deep draughts of air. His gnarled fingers stroked my hair, smoothing it back into submission. "I see the pain you carry inside. The God of heaven does too."

The old man whispered words of comfort as my pulse calmed, my fury melting into confusion and pain. Tears spilled down my cheeks and dripped from my nose.

"You must forgive, Redbird."

Forgive? Forgive Naomi? Forgive Master Cyrene? Never. They had shredded my soul. Taken all that remained of my hope and crushed it beneath their feet.

I yanked myself from Matias's grasp and vehemently shook my head. I would never forgive them. My old friend's shoulders sagged.

"You're only doubling your pain, Redbird. But it's your choice to make."

He shuffled away then, leaving me alone by the pig pen. I hastened to smooth my hair, anger blanching my heart white-hot.

Matias was right. It was *my* choice to make. The only freedom I'd ever been given.

And at that moment, my choice was to hate.

The hues of twilight had painted the sky lavender, orange, and pink. I stopped for only a moment to admire the fleeting beauty on my way to see Henry, who tended to the animals. Molly had need of goat's milk and requested I fetch it. I cast my gaze side to side, nearly tiptoeing. It would not do to run into Naomi. Not so soon after our disastrous meeting earlier that day. I had spoken of it to Molly, who had swallowed me in a hug and told me not to concern myself with the likes of Naomi anymore.

But I had already witnessed the worry in her eyes. The fear that trouble lurked at the door.

"Pssst!"

I looked up from my walk, the metal pail banging into my leg. The sound came from behind the smokehouse. I searched through the lengthening shadows, eager to find the source of the summons. A child from the shanties, perhaps?

A dark face peered around the edge of the small building, but this was no child. It was a man. A large figure I had never seen before at Azaka Mede. Prickles of warning danced up my neck.

The man caught my stare and motioned for me with his large hand, an invitation to approach. His face held no malice.

With bated breath, I glanced around the lawn. I tiptoed to the smokehouse and slipped to the back, where the only protection was a line of palms overhead. The big man stared down at me.

"You a slave here at Azaka Mede?"

I nodded. White teeth flashed in his face.

"I'm Bussa, a ranger at the Bayley estate in this parish."

I blinked. A ranger? This man had the freedom to move between plantations, all under the orders of his master.

Looking over his shoulder, he stepped close and lowered his voice. I longed to retreat, but something in his eyes held me fast. "An uprising is planned. We will no longer yield our bodies and souls to the tyrant. Many here know this is coming. Those who can will gather tonight outside the boundaries of Bayley Plantation when the moon is high. Tell Cain."

Bussa then slipped into the canopy of trees, his body melting into the shadows. A cold stone sank in my middle. What did he mean? An uprising ... how? When?

"Tell Cain." The only man I knew named Cain was a large fellow who lived in the third shanty from the left on slave row. Was he part of all this?

I buffed the gooseflesh prickling my arms and moved back to the hog pen to gather the discarded bucket. The old fear rose swiftly to my throat. If I could somehow push past the terror that stole my words, what would the outcome be? War? Blood? Death? If I remained silent, the fleeting opportunity for freedom would pass by Azaka Mede—a freedom that beckoned me ever more since my whipping. Its long fingers held out in invitation when my heart had given way to the anger inside.

I bit my lip until I tasted metallic blood. Bussa erred in telling me of this dark premonition, for who could I share the news with? My tongue was locked, as stiff and unyielding as a reed.

And the only one who had been able to break the barrier was Molly and the young Master Holland. And I had only spoken a single word to him.

Molly. She would know what to do.

Slipping my fingers around the bucket handle, I hurried back to the kitchen, my thoughts as tangled as a wad of yarn. A breeze tugged tendrils of my hair across my face and I flicked them away with my fingers. The final brushes of light faded into darkness as night descended. In the distance, thunder rumbled. A storm approached, though its power seemed pale in the face of open rebellion. Another crash boomed beyond the rolling skies and I looked up, the stars appearing and disappearing as inky clouds rolled across the expanse of heaven.

My limbs trembled from much more than the approaching gale.

I glanced up at the thick sky, my lips anxious to beg for help, but who would come to my rescue?

I was alone, and the only answer was a dark grumbling in the heavens.

Sleep was long in coming. My back was tender, so all I could do was stretch out on my stomach. Yet it wasn't pain that kept my mind spinning, but the thought of a group of slaves huddled mere miles away, planning open rebellion. I had shared all Bussa had told me with Molly. A strange gleam shuttered her eyes but she merely patted my hands and told me all would be well. But would it?

When the dark strings of sleepiness finally tugged at my eyes, a soft knock issued upon my door. I frowned and eased from the bed. Had Molly forgotten some task in the kitchen? Fear niggled. Or perhaps it was Master returning. Bile choked my throat.

"Avalina?"

The terse whisper leaching in didn't sound like Master Cyrene. Propelled by curiosity, I wrapped a gray shawl around my shoulders before opening the door a crack. Young Master Holland stood just outside.

I sucked in a surprised breath and his handsome face winced. He held up his hands in apology.

"Forgive me. I know the hour is late and it is not proper for me to be here."

I started to shut the door to block out his words but something held me rooted in place, my fingers frozen on the knob. He looked down at his feet and glanced back up, his gaze roaming over my face.

"We are departing soon, in only another day. I—I have something to give you."

A deep melancholy pervaded my heart at the news. How short a time he had been here yet I felt something—like a silken thread—that bound his heart to mine.

I glanced away. Foolishness. I was naught but a slave girl, forever tied to Azaka Mede. And he? He would become a powerful land owner like his father. Our destinies were not to be entwined.

And yet, he had still come to seek me out this night just before his departure.

"Step outside for a moment with me?"

His dark eyes were hopeful. Gentle. How could I refuse? Nodding slightly, I held up a hand, asking him to wait as I closed the door and slipped back into my single dress hanging from a hook on the wall. In moments, I was following his tall form through the corridor, down the stairs, and out the back door.

I breathed in the sticky, cool air of evening. The storm had passed, though an occasional breeze carried slivers of feathery rain. The clouds had parted, leaving the stars to glow once again. Though I supposed they had never really stopped shining. They had only been obscured by darkness.

He led me to the gardens near the back of the house and reached into his pocket. The silver moon illuminated his every move. I held my breath as he pulled out an object and offered it to me. Moonglow glinted off the shiny circular metal.

I sucked in a breath. A pocket watch?

He reached for me, his firm fingers grazing the inside of my wrist as he dropped the cool metal into my outstretched hand. My skin warmed at his touch but he pulled away quickly. My thumb rubbed the engraved circle, noting the etched flowers and leaves branded into the metal.

"It's a compass." He showed me how to open it with a small press of a button near the lock. The lid sprang open and a needle quivered in the center. I smiled and turned in a slow circle, watching the spindle shift and twirl. I looked into his face and he was smiling.

"Do you like it?"

I nodded and bit my lip. No one had ever been so kind to me. But why? Why did he care?

"I wish—I wish there was something I could do to ease your suffering here. Something I could say . . . " He swallowed and looked away before angling his body closer and gazing up at the night sky, scattered with stars. "Beautiful, isn't it?"

I nodded, unsure about what might be going through his mind. He glanced back and met my eyes. "Do you know how to find the North Star?"

I shook my head no and he cupped my hand holding the compass, guiding it carefully in a small arc. "It's one of the brightest stars, always due north." My gaze bounced between the wobbling compass needle and the diamonds twinkling overhead. After studying the compass for a moment, he pointed overhead. "There. There it is."

My focus landed on a single star burning brighter than all the others. Entrancing. Whether it was from the heavenly body or the man at my side, I couldn't say. He glanced down into my upturned face, expression unreadable.

"The same God who made the stars is watching over you. He knows your name, Avalina." Josiah exhaled a tremulous breath, his gaze fixed on mine. "And though we may be far apart, know that when you're looking up at the stars, seeking that same God, I will be too."

I swallowed as he reached up and stroked my jaw with his thumb. How I longed to lean into his touch, to drink in the sensation, but he dropped his hand and sighed.

"May the Almighty watch over you."

And then he was gone.

CHAPTER 12

April 14, 1816
Barbados

Easter Sunday dawned with sunshine and a scattering of thick clouds as Josiah, his father, and Cyrene Harding rode in Harding's sleek black carriage on their way to worship. Josiah smiled wistfully as he blinked against the dust stirred up by the horses' hooves as they moved down the road. Easter had always been a happy time in South Carolina. No doubt Mother and Isabelle were dressed up in their best finery, worshiping on the family pew of St. Mark's before going home to feast on a succulent dinner of roast, buttery breads, and sweet pastries. He missed them.

Harding pursed his lips and tugged the cuffs of his starched white shirt into perfect order, drawing Josiah's gaze from the passing scenery. "Do you hear it?" A dark brow rose. "We approach the ocean." He fixed his focus on Josiah's father. "Mr. Holland, you'll find our church at St. John's Parish to be an astounding work of art. A marvel of architecture, complete with winding staircases and fixtures made of rare wood."

Father's lips quirked into a smile. "I can't wait to see it."

"Not only that"—Harding's eyes flashed—"the great Fernando Paleologus is entombed onsite." Harding studied his fingernails as if he hadn't a care in the world. "Paleologus, of course, was the descendant of the second brother of Constantine, the last Christian emperor of Constantinople."

The man's condescension grated, but Josiah merely smiled. "And what of the sermons at this church? Do you find them intriguing?"

"Religion bores me." Harding waved his hand dismissively. "I find far greater benefit in mingling with the parishioners. We must keep up appearances. Our friends close and enemies closer, yes?"

Josiah pressed his lips tight. Best not vent his opinions lest he anger both of his companions.

A lone figure appeared, walking down the road toward Azaka Mede. The man was dark and burly, and as the carriage rolled closer, Josiah straightened. He knew this fellow ... why, the scowling traveler was none other than Najaf, the man who had sheltered him and Benjamin from the mob only yesterday. A knapsack was slung over his wide back. What was Najaf doing?

As the carriage passed him, Josiah caught his unwavering stare and nodded ever so slightly but he looked across the carriage to see Harding sneering.

Father's brows lifted. "You know that man?"

"No. Likely a slave bent on mischief." Harding pursed his lips. "I shall mention his appearance to those at St. John's. We shall learn what we can."

Najaf was a free man. This much, Josiah had gleaned from their visit to his tavern yesterday. Why cause him trouble?

As they left Najaf in the distance, the smell of salt air intensified and the screech of gulls increased as the carriage brought them to a cathedral nestled at the top of a rise. Blue, sparkling waters of the Atlantic glittered beyond the clearing, and a gentle breeze lifted locks of hair from Josiah's brow as the driver pulled the carriage to a stop and engaged the brake. Dozens of other carriages milled around the tall cathedral. Men wearing dark suits and women boasting colorful silks, parasols, and fans filled the lawn, chatting as they converged for worship. Josiah descended from the carriage and glanced up at the tall turret nestled in the middle of the building. Grand and intimidating.

Unease ribboned through his middle. A far different place of worship than the one he'd witnessed between the elderly slave and Avalina in the midst of ferns and palms. Yet somehow, he preferred the jungle to this cold building.

Harding turned back to wave him forward as he approached a cluster of well-dressed men. All of them plantation owners. All of them stiff as broom handles. Josiah found his focus returning to the dark-skinned drivers sitting quietly in each of the carriages. Their faces were serene, almost hollow, except for one...a young man who glanced side to side, as if searching for someone. Something. The reins were clutched tightly in his fingers even though the brake had been set.

Josiah sucked in a breath when another driver met the young man's eyes and motioned him to calm. The young man nodded and released a pent-up breath.

The antsy driver, and the men's unspoken communication, reminded him of the steadfast pull of Najaf's gaze as they'd passed on the road. Josiah's spine prickled.

Something odd was afoot.

I blew out a breath and swiped the filthy rag one final time over the side of the kitchen stove. Blacking the iron beast was my least favorite chore but at least it was done. I glanced through the kitchen window to see all the day's light had plunged into the inky darkness of night. Dropping the rag in a bucket, I wrinkled my nose as I glanced down at my fingers. Each one was stained black. Sighing, I rose and dunked my hands into the tepid water basin before grabbing a bar of lye to scrub my skin clean. I heard Molly's footfalls approach, but she said nothing—merely glanced out the kitchen window and returned to the table, where she picked up her sewing once more.

She had done the same thing all evening... check the window and sew, all without uttering a word. Something wasn't right. Swallowing, I wiped my hands on a rag and faced her.

"Molly?" My voice cracked and I cleared it softly. "Is there something going on?" I could think of little else but Bussa's sudden visit the day before. Dark musings had flooded my thoughts all day.

Looking up from the needle and thread in her hands, Molly blinked rapidly, as if trying to focus on my question. "Going on?" She laughed but it was brittle. "Whatever do you mean?"

"You've done nothing but stare out the window all evening." I nodded my head toward the fabric in her lap. "And you've pulled out more stitches than you've kept."

Her bright blue eyes held mine a second before her shoulders slumped. "You always could read me thoughts, lamb." She bit her lip. "Freedom is coming. The truth of it is—"

"Girl!" Baara pushed through the kitchen door and speared me with a sour look. "Da Master is calling for you. Go, lest you anger him."

My tongue turned to cotton. Not again. My gaze sought Molly, who winced and looked away.

Foolish of me to look to her for rescue. What could she possibly do? She was as helpless as I.

Nodding slowly, I left the kitchen and crossed the parlor but an orange glow outside caught my attention through the massive windows. I pressed my hands against the glass, eyes narrowing to comprehend what I saw in the distance.

Demonic hues of red and orange glowed over the silhouetted tree line. I flung open the French doors and the acrid stench of smoke assaulted my nostrils.

"Avalina!"

I whirled to see Master Cyrene glowering at me from the top of the stairs, his eyes narrowed. "I called for you. Why have you not come?"

Swallowing, I backed up a step and gripped the knob of the door before pointing to show him the horizon. Dark eyes widening, he stomped down the stairs, his movements leaden as he blinked at the sight. A corner of his nose curled in disgust.

"Fire." He straightened. "Not ours. Too far away. Still, we ought to prepare."

I swallowed and glanced back to the eerie sight through the window. A red glow lightened the night sky. That looked like no small fire. If it was not already on the property, it would be massive to be seen at Azaka Mede.

I glanced at his profile. A muscle twitched in his jaw. He turned away but whirled back to latch his hand around my wrist, tugging me behind him. My arm burned but I dared not fight. Instead, I fumbled along as he bellowed to the house.

"Fire! Everyone gather outside and bring whatever buckets we have. Hurry! Form a line around the plantation."

The household flew into a frenzy as men and women appeared, anxious to do his bidding. I glanced down at his white fingers wrapped around my wrist. Why wouldn't he let me go to help?

He tugged hard and I cried out at the stab of pain as he pulled me down the hallway to his study. Flinging open the door, he shoved me inside. I staggered but remained upright as he stalked to his desk and pulled a revolver from his bottom drawer. Breath thinning, I moved to press my body against the nearest bookshelf.

Invisible, invisible…

Master Cyrene muttered to himself. "All this local babble about a skirmish and it's naught but a fire. Either way, I'll be prepared." He shoved a handful of bullets into the chamber and locked it with a click before placing it on the desk. He lifted his gaze to mine and stepped close ... so close I could smell the brandy on his breath. My fingers groped along the books lined at my back, searching for something, anything I could use to keep him from me as he plunged his right hand into my hair, pulling me toward him. He slammed his lips onto mine and I froze, revulsion crawling up my throat.

"Freedom is coming ... "

The memory of the lash slicing into my still-tender back arose like a taunting specter. I could see the compassion in Josiah Holland's eyes as he hovered over me. Naomi's accusations. Then, the nightmare that had haunted me since I was small of Master screaming as he whipped my legs, my arms, my back. And his horrid visit mere days ago.

Invisible ...

Freedom ...

I could not succumb. Something fierce and wild rose up in me. I would not simply lay down and accept my fate. I bit down hard on his lip ... so hard, he leaped back with a scream of pain, wiping his hand across his mouth.

"Why, you vile witch!"

The back of his hand connected with my face. The sharp crack was followed by searing pain in my temple as I slammed onto the wooden floor. I scarcely had time to draw a breath before he was on top of me ... clawing at my bodice, shaking me into submission.

The study ceiling bobbed and swayed, blurring in odd lines as he pressed his weight into mine. Tears blurred my vision. If I could only be free of him. I squirmed. Just a bit more ...

I flung my hand over my head and searched for a weapon. My fingertips snagged a thick volume wedged into the lowest bookshelf and I yanked it free with a grunt before slamming it into his face. He howled with rage and I scrambled to rise, my dress torn.

He loomed over me, a trickle of blood at the corner of his lip. He snarled as I rounded the edge of his desk.

"You went too far, Avalina."

Heart thrumming, I lunged for the gun resting on the desk and pointed it at him, hands shaking against the cold metal. The barrel wobbled under my grip. I cocked back the hammer as my pulse pounded in my ears. He sneered.

"Do you really think to shoot me?" He shook his head slowly, his gaze never leaving mine. "You are nothing. I am your master," he shouted. "I am everything!"

He lunged.

Heart fluttering, I squeezed the trigger. My body jerked backward at the explosion.

Master's body jolted too, his eyes rounding as he slumped to the floor. Time slowed, each second an hour as he crumpled near my feet. Salt filled my mouth as I stared at the crimson pool spreading under his body. Dropping the revolver into my apron pocket, I fled. Each footfall echoed. Time and space, noise and color fell away. The hallway swam in my eyes, my legs as wobbly as a newborn colt's.

What had I done?

CHAPTER 13

Cyrene Harding's shouts of "Fire!" pulled Josiah from the book he was reading within the confines of his guest bedroom. He tossed the volume aside and rushed to the window. Sure enough, angry crimson streaks danced over the tree line. He sucked in a breath and stepped back. The sight filled the entire window, from east to west. That was no small blaze. His pulse tripped.

It would take every man, woman, and child in the area to squelch such an inferno.

He raced through the room and flung the door open wide, only to see his father doing the same from across the hall. George Holland's shirt was rumpled and his normally smooth, pomaded hair was in disarray.

Father frowned. "Did I hear someone shout fire? What should we do?"

"Help gather water, I assume." Footsteps pounded throughout the house, each attendant and guest anxious to be outside to stop the blaze.

Bristling, his father straightened. "Working…alongside the slaves?" He frowned. "How would that look?"

Josiah gritted his teeth. "Now is not the time for power struggles, Father. If you won't help, I will."

He turned to leave his father behind but quickly heard his footsteps padding down the stairs behind him. Josiah flung open the parlor doors overlooking Azaka Mede's lush land, and the thick odor of smoke choked him. Pulling a handkerchief from his pocket, he pressed it against his nose as he hastened toward a group of slaves gathered on the lawn. Father coughed behind him.

As he approached, Josiah paused. The crowd was doing nothing. No buckets. No anxious hastening to extinguish the flames growing ever closer. Awareness raised the hairs on the back of his neck.

A large field hand stared at him, a pitchfork clutched in his fingers. He gave Josiah a measured look, his free hand opening and closing in a fist. Josiah's mouth turned to cotton. What was going on? Why weren't they moving?

Father shouted, seemingly unaware of the malice coiled through the man's body. "What is the meaning of this? All of you ... gather water at once!"

The man took a heavy step forward, his white teeth flashing in the semi-darkness. "We ain't got to do nothin' you say no more."

Josiah moved to shield his father from the cluster of men gathering around. He held up his hands for peace. "We have nothing to do with any of this. We only want to help extinguish the fire."

The slave roared a laugh but quickly sobered. "We rising up." He took another step and Josiah shuffled backward, muscles tensed. "We casting off the chains. And it's happening all over the island. What you see there"—he gestured toward the fire glowing ever brighter in the distance—"that's us screaming 'no more.'"

A gunshot boomed in the distance followed by shouts. A cluster of slaves burst from the trees, pushing a bloody and beaten Bixby in front of them. The overseer screamed as a man yanked the coiled whip from his belt loop and lashed his legs.

The fire was planned. It was rebellion.

Josiah whirled back to his father and yelled, "Run!"

Before he could escape, the slave lunged, stabbing the air between them with the pitchfork. Josiah jumped aside, his gaze shifting between the man and the crowd of the enslaved gathering around him. "I have no quarrel with you."

"You're one of them!" The mob descended.

Josiah fell, swinging his fists wildly. His knuckles smashed into thick jaws, but there were too many. He curled in on himself as hard blows to his head and back rained down. He cried out when booted feet slammed into his middle. A punishing crack to the head came next, then merciful nothingness.

Tremors wracked my body but I had no idea what to do as I hid in the kitchen pantry.

Dead. Master Cyrene was dead and it was my fault.

Images of his blood pooling on the Turkish carpet filled my mind. I clutched fistfuls of my hair and squeezed my eyes shut. The memory of his fingers scraping my skin rose afresh and I whimpered in the darkness.

What should I do? Where was everyone? Molly? Baara? I couldn't think. Couldn't focus amid the screams pummeling my brain.

The fire. I sucked in a breath and opened my eyes. Outside. Everyone was outside. What would happen when they discovered Master's body?

Nausea bubbled up my middle and I lurched from the pantry, hastening to the sink, where I cast up my accounts. I wiped my mouth with the back of my hand and sucked in shallow breaths. If the others learned I had killed Master Cyrene, I would be hanged.

Dread mingled with panic. No. I couldn't let them find out. Not ever.

I rubbed shaking hands down my face. The others would surely suspect me of killing him if I remained by myself inside. I had to join them. Blend in.

Crossing the kitchen on quivering legs, I threw open the back door and winced against the stench of burning wood and the sickly-sweet scent of sugar cane being licked by the approaching flames.

Breathe.

But it was difficult to calm my frantic breathing with smoke hanging so thick in the air. I coughed. Soot coated my tongue and filled my lungs. The acrid fog pricked my eyes until tears gathered as I walked on wooden legs across the yard. Shouts rang. Bodies scurried across the lawn. Some carried weapons and farm tools. Others lugged fabric, candlesticks, and China plates. My thoughts scrambled. This was no orderly system of preservation. This was a revolt.

Bussa's word stabbed my mind with fresh awareness. I swallowed, turning in a slow circle. I could see it now. The slaves were stealing, looting, and destroying anyone who stood in their way.

What to do? Where to go? A gunshot cracked in the distance. I cringed and ducked, creeping along the shadows of the house. Men and women waved sharpened sticks and machetes in the air as they shouted, "Freedom!" I placed a hand over my mouth to muffle my scream as a group of men dragged Mr. Bixby's lifeless body behind them. More gunshots popped. A group gathered beyond the gardens. From somewhere inside Azaka Mede, the sound of shattering glass punctured the air. I hunkered low, creeping along the edge of the building, hiding.

Invisible…

A dozen or so men on horseback broke through the clearing, firing guns at the slaves. Near the garden entrance, Tabia screamed as she lunged for the nearest horse, waving a pitchfork over her head. The rider pointed his gun and pulled the trigger, a bright burst sizzling from the end.

Tabia fell to the ground. Unmoving.

Had I done this? Relaying the information to Molly that Bussa had given me? I knelt in the dirt and covered my head as more glass shattered. A stray bullet slapped the house, splintering wood above my head. Particles drifted down, peppering my hair and skin.

Slaves shouted and fought the horsemen. I stumbled farther down the edge of the building until my foot tripped over a body. Gasping, I dropped to the ground, rolling over the still form with a grunt. When I saw his face, blood siphoned from my own.

Josiah.

Bruises and blood marred his skin. A deep gash near his temple was sticky with blood. No! Not this man who had shown me such tenderness. I gulped back a sob, letting my fingers rove over the handsome planes of his face.

"Josiah." I hunkered near his ear and murmured his name. "Please don't leave."

A groan burst past his lips and I found my breath. He was still alive.

Another groan and his body shifted. Even in the darkness, I could see his eyes peek open. He blinked slowly. "A-Avalina?"

I nodded and winced as another shot thudded into the wood over our heads. He would be killed in the tumult. No one would care that he wasn't like Master Cyrene or his father. They would see him as nothing more than the son of a slaveholder.

I had to get him out of here.

He rolled over slowly, each movement heavy as he winced and scooted onto his knees. Gripping his middle, he moaned. "My ribs."

I offered my hand. He grasped it, his eyes narrowing as he rose in the shadows. "Your clothes... what happened?"

My fingers gripped the torn fabric of my bodice as I attempted to smooth it back into place. A useless attempt. My sleeve was torn beyond repair, and the rest of the fabric was a disheveled mess. I could never tell Josiah what had transpired in the study. Nausea bubbled once again but I forced it down and ignored his probing look. "It doesn't matter."

Another gunshot. I gasped as he shielded me from splintering wood overhead. We shuffled along the shadows of the house. Hoof-beats pounded across Azaka Mede. Arriving soldiers fighting the en-slaved. Metal clanged, and shouts intensified as the fire roared ever closer. I coughed and Josiah wrapped his arm around me, fumbling our way to the kitchen door. We slipped inside and hunkered down.

It was then that I saw. A scream split the air and it took my ears a moment to realize the sound was mine.

Molly lay in the middle of the kitchen floor, eyes sightlessly staring up into the ceiling, a blot of crimson spreading across her chest.

CHAPTER 14

Josiah pressed Avalina's head to his chest, barring her quivering body from the gruesome scene. A man walked into the kitchen, a gun in his hands. Soot marred his face and deep lines furrowed his brow. His vest, shirt, and pants were rumpled and filthy, bearing the scars of a night of fighting. Instinctively, Josiah tightened his hold on Avalina. If this stranger thought to take her from him, he'd have to use that gun to do so.

"I'm James Scott, owner of the Bailey Plantation." He shoved his gun down into his holster and nodded at Molly's body. "I barely escaped my place." He cursed and frowned as he moved to watch the melee unfolding past the window. "Never seen such a night as this. Where is Cyrene Harding?"

Josiah swallowed, still holding the sobbing woman in his arms. "I don't know. Last I heard, he alerted the house to the fire. I've not seen hide nor hair of him since." Avalina flinched within his arms.

Scott grunted. "Doesn't bode well." He straightened and fixed Josiah with a knowing look. "The other plantation owners are making haste to Bridgetown. We'll have protection there."

"I'm not a plantation owner, sir." Josiah shifted and winced, carefully hugging Avalina to his chest to continue shielding her from the sight of her beloved friend lying prostrate on the floor. "I'm only here as a guest of Harding's."

Scott grimaced. "Terrible time for a visit." A muscle ticked in his jaw. "Best come to Bridgetown anyway. Those bloodthirsty men out there won't care about you"—he nodded toward Avalina—"or your missus."

Missus? Josiah sucked in a breath. Of course. Avalina was white. And he was holding her. The man naturally assumed the two of them were married. An idea niggled. Dare he?

He nodded. "I—I thank you for the invitation."

Scott gestured toward Molly's still form. "Sorry you walked in on this." His nostrils flared as he stared at the dead woman. "I entered and she screamed. Half crazy, she was."

Josiah frowned. "Was she scared?"

Scott shrugged. "Don't matter. She was hysterical. I killed her. Had to." He nodded toward the tumult beyond the window. "See what happens when we don't stamp out disobedience?"

Fury burned like a pillar in Josiah's chest. Did Scott really believe this diminutive woman had the means or capability to end his life? Such an idea was ludicrous. And his actions? Senseless. Cruel.

There was no undoing it now. Any of it. Avalina gripped his shirt with white knuckles. He glanced down and a new resolve siphoned through his middle. He couldn't fix any of this horrid night, but he could fight to make sure it never happened again. Fight for the safety of the innocent. Fight for a better way.

God, show me how.

He led Avalina away from the kitchen, his gaze drinking in every shadow. Every imagined foe lurking in the shadows. Glancing up at the stairs, he straightened.

They must leave Barbados. Tonight.

After tucking Avalina safely inside his own room, Josiah opened the door to his father's suite and found him cowering in the chifforobe, a nasty cut on his cheek.

"Father!" He offered him a hand as the older man crawled out. Josiah winced, his own ribs aching at the strain. He released him and gestured to the cut. "That looks deep."

Grunting, his father gingerly patted the now-dried blood on his face. "The fools were breaking in windows as I passed through downstairs. A shard caught my cheek."

Josiah turned and hauled Father's suitcase onto the bed with a grunt. "We must leave tonight. It's not safe. I met another plantation owner downstairs who said revolt is erupting all over the island. Owners are fleeing to Bridgetown."

"Leave?" Father's eyes bulged as he stopped Josiah from opening his suitcase with a grip on his wrist. "We can't leave! I haven't finished business with Harding yet."

"Look around you! It's over. If we stay, we take our lives in our hands. That in and of itself does not give me reason to fear, but you can't abandon Mother and Isabelle this way. Especially over something as fleeting as a business transaction."

"This *business* is our livelihood, Josiah." Father glared, releasing him with a huff. "Are you saying our family's future isn't worth it?"

"That's exactly what I'm saying." He opened his arms wide, even as the chaos outside pounded the walls and wobbled knick-knacks placed around the room. "Is all this worth it? Is making money really more important to you than human life? Than war? Than peace?"

"Vengeance will be swift on those who took part in this." Father walked the length of the room and paused, rubbing his hand across his temple. "It's Barbados. They don't have control of their property the way we do."

Was the man blind? Or merely choosing to ignore the reality before him? Josiah narrowed his eyes. "Pack if you want to come with me. Stay hiding in the chifforobe if you don't." His jaw tightened. "But I'm leaving on a ship tonight."

"Josiah!" His father's shouts pounded his back as he stalked from the room. Swallowing, he crossed the hallway and heaved a thick sigh. Now the final question remained ... how to steal away?

I paced the length of Josiah's room, every nerve buzzing, my thoughts a knotted tangle. My heart was sore and bleeding at the thought of Molly being cruelly struck down with such cold indifference. She must have been terrified to shriek so at Mr. Scott. I had rarely heard her shoo away flies with frustration.

And what would Master Cyrene do?

I shook my head, rubbing my temples with quaking fingers. No, Master was dead. I had seen to it. Cold shudders wracked my body, starting in my middle and extending to my limbs. I could yet feel his hands on me. My chest constricted and I slammed my eyes shut.

The door creaked open and I gasped in surprise that melted to relief when Josiah Holland stood in the doorway. His expression was hesitant as he shut the door and moved to stand before me.

"We must leave."

I nodded. Yes, leave. Away from the fire. From the blood. From Master's body growing cold downstairs.

He opened his mouth and closed it again before swallowing. "I mean to America."

America? The States? Such a thing had never entered my mind. "How?"

His hand covered mine, his roughened, bloody knuckles pressing warmth into my cold fingers. "There will be questions. Conscription concerns. You are a white woman." His eyes darkened. "It will not be safe for you alone. But I can protect you if ... " He swallowed, breath turning shallow. "If we were to marry."

Spots danced in my eyes. Marry this man? Practically a stranger until naught but days ago? But more than that. He had shielded me from the lash. Had carried me to safety. Had shown kindness and understanding. And he was offering refuge even now.

His gaze dropped to our hands. He rubbed his thumbs over the backs of my fingers. "I can see you safely to South Carolina. Give you a new start. Freedom." His gaze lifted to mine. "Would you like that, Avalina? Freedom?"

Yes. No. I didn't know what to think. What to feel. I was terrified and dizzy and scared and—

But if the truth of Master's death was discovered, I would swing from a rope. Wincing, I exhaled a thick breath, pushing away the fear that tried to keep me silent. "Why?"

"Why?" His dark brows lifted.

"Why help me? I am nothing to you."

A muscle ticked in his jaw as he looked down. "All my life, I have lived in foolish oblivion, not really seeing the truth of my family's choices." His gaze locked onto mine. "No more. I want no more of it. And I'll spend the rest of my life trying to blot out the stain of my family's sin."

He meant it. Calm resolution straightened his wide shoulders and lifted his chin. I could trust this man ... couldn't I?

But what of affection? Of love? A small, foolish part of me longed for what Molly and her husband had enjoyed.

"Is that the only reason?"

His Adam's apple bobbed as he swallowed. "There are many reasons."

There was something he wasn't saying. But in truth, it didn't matter. I couldn't stay. Master's dead body yet screamed at me from the library.

"I'll go with you."

He heaved a sigh of relief and nodded. "Good, good." He released my hands and offered a wobbly smile as he rubbed the back of his neck. "I can't pack my trunk. Too much weight will make it difficult to travel to the docks." His expression brightened. "Ah. Here!" He pulled open the chifforobe and yanked a knapsack from the inside. "Take this and put your belongings inside. We'll share until we have the opportunity to shop for more."

I stared at the satchel, my focus unblinking. My belongings? Understanding dawned on his face.

"You have no belongings?"

I shook my head. My quilt was the only thing of value and it could not be stowed in a simple bag. Sorrow drifted across his eyes like a cloud but quickly cleared. "No matter. We will purchase your necessities later." He stalked to the desk and pulled valuables from the drawers, shoving in money, a comb, a handful of papers, and a book before moving to the bureau to grab an extra shirt and trousers. "There now." He glanced around the room. "We'll get some food on the way out."

Wait! I did have something of value. I motioned for him to follow me from the room. We padded as silently as we dared and crossed the house to my room in the servants' wing. I held up my hand to ask him to wait in the hallway before slipping inside. Everything was still. A lump grew in my throat. What madness was this, that I was leaving all I'd ever known to find freedom? I knew nothing of such things.

Shoving the dark thought aside, I knelt and ran my hand under the lumpy mattress. When my fingers grazed the cool metal of the compass, I smiled. One more tug, and I pulled the scrap of verse he had given me from its hiding place. That was all. Two small items to link me to the island.

I stepped back into the hallway and held up the compass and verse for his inspection. A warm smile broke across his handsome face. "You want to take them?"

I nodded and slipped them inside the haversack. With a grunt, he swung the bag across his shoulders and grabbed my hand. "Come on. Let's go."

We tiptoed down the stairs. Another gunshot boomed outside. I cringed and pressed my face against his arm as we padded across the parlor, passing open doors on the left.

"What the devil?"

Josiah's soft oath caused me to look up. Blood leached from my face as I realized we stood in the open doorway of Master's study. Josiah released my hand and stepped inside, wincing at the pool of crimson beneath Master's still form. Shaking his head, he stepped back and reclaimed my hand. "A slave must have shot him." His jaw hardened. "Come on. We've got to get out of here."

Only when the front door clicked shut behind us and we were safely concealed in the dark shroud of the jungle, did my heart commence to beat again.

And then stopped at the sight before me.

CHAPTER 15

Josiah studied Harding's livery from the dark refuge of the jungle. The looming fire had coated the air, the plants, all of Azaka Mede with a layer of ash. Shouts burst in the distance. The fighting was all around them. A horse whinnied from somewhere inside. No doubt the animals were as anxious to flee as he was.

He glanced down at the slim woman near his side. If she were hurt because of his foolish decisions...

Another whinny followed the sharp crack of gunshots near the house. The skirmish was just far enough away. They could make it. They had to.

Smoke thickened and he blinked away the burning in his eyes as he leaned close to whisper in Avalina's ear. "Can you ride?"

She nodded and murmured, "A little."

His lips thinned. "That will have to do, then. Follow me. We each grab a horse and head for the docks." He studied the contours of her face in the hazy moonlight. "If we get separated, look for a ship called *The Dauntless*."

Licking her lips, she nodded and released a breath. Brave girl. He tucked her hand in his and darted across the clearing before easing the livery door open with a soft squeak. He cringed. How could a door be so loud on a night drunk with the blood of war?

They slipped inside, the odor of smoke mingling with hay and animal dung. A horse in the corner snorted. Another pawed the ground, anxious to be free. He stepped into the first stall and murmured sweet words to the stallion huffing with impatience. His velvety coat was sleek as oil.

"There, there. Good boy. Easy."

He offered a final pat and glanced to see Avalina calming a paint pony in the next stall. He handed her the haversack. "Here. Hold this while I grab their tack."

Josiah turned to the wall when pain exploded across his back. He slammed to the floor, every bone in his body burning with the impact. Avalina screamed and the horses reared, shrieking in fear.

Flipping onto his back, Josiah had half a second to prepare. A large man lunged at him, a massive board in his hands. Josiah kicked his middle, sending him sprawling against the back wall with a loud crack.

He scrambled to his feet as fast as he could, ribs aching as he fumbled for a weapon. The worktables were stripped bare. He grabbed a can of leather oil and flung it toward the stranger, who roared in outrage, pawing the moisture from his face. Josiah moved to protect Avalina as another figure emerged, cracking a glass jug over the attacker's head. The villain wobbled, then slumped to the floor. Their hero shuffled forward, dark face wreathed in concern.

Why, it was the man he'd seen worshiping with Avalina in the jungle. A sob escaped her lips and she rushed to hug the man's neck.

"There, there, Redbird. All's well." He patted her back and released her before sizing up Josiah with a squint. "What you doing with her, sir?"

Josiah straightened, watching the man carefully. "I plan to get her out of here. Give her freedom."

The man pressed his lips into a hard line and swiveled to study Avalina. "This what you want, Redbird?"

Biting her lip, she nodded slowly. A sad smile tugged the aged man's mouth.

"Then go. Take Ephraim and Manasseh." The man pointed to the sleek black stallion and the chestnut farther down the stalls. "They's good horses. Raised 'em myself. Get you where you need to go in no time."

Josiah stepped forward and offered his hand. The slave's eyes widened but he took it and squeezed.

"Take care of Redbird now, you hear?"

"Yes, sir."

"Just Matias. Ain't no sir." He smiled and tugged Avalina into a hug. "Be safe. Go with God, Redbird."

Avalina's smile wobbled as she embraced the old man. Josiah made quick work of getting the horses' tack on and the saddle cinched. He lifted Avalina onto Manasseh's back and glanced back at Matias. "You want to come with us?"

The old man shuffled his feet but frowned and shook his head. "The good Lord told me my place is here, sir."

Nodding, Josiah swung up into the saddle, shifting his weight to feel the horse's strength beneath his legs. "May God be with you, Matias."

"Always." He smiled and patted his chest with gnarled fingers. "He always here."

Matias swung the barn doors open and Josiah kicked the stallion into motion.

"Yah!"

Josiah pulled Ephraim to a stop as Avalina slowed her own mount. Sultry smoke hung low near the crowded docks. Crowds clamored where the road ended. Soldiers on horseback guarded the loading bays. Josiah squinted in the darkness. The large ship to the left looked like *The Dauntless*. But was it? And how to get on board?

"Please let us leave. I must gather my family to safety before our slaves run us through!"

Josiah turned to watch a soldier sneer at an older gentleman, a displaced plantation owner from the looks of him. The man's wife sniffled at his side, quietly dabbing her nose with a handkerchief. The soldier's eyes narrowed.

"I cannot help you, sir. Got my commands. Governor Leith himself has ordered the docks closed for ship travel until the unrest dissipates."

No ship travel. Josiah glanced down into Avalina's face. She was biting her lip, clearly sorting through the implications of such a maneuver. What could they possibly do now?

"How many plantations are affected?" Worried lines marred the older man's brow.

The soldier straightened. "Last I heard, there were at least fifty uprisings reported, with numbers climbing."

The older woman wailed anew and pressed her mouth to her useless lace hankie. Her husband patted her back absently.

"There, there, Varina."

Another howl of anguish. Irritation flickered in the soldier's eyes at the woman's caterwauling.

"Try not to fret, madam. Imperial troops are on their way to quell the rebellion."

"But what shall we do in the meantime?" The older woman sniffed again, her eyes red and glassy from the constant weeping.

"All those trying to flee the violence should make haste to Bridgetown."

The crowd roared in protest as the soldier held up his hands for quiet. Josiah tugged Avalina's arm and tilted his head in the direction of the shadowed buildings lining the docks. They scurried to press against the closest storefront, Josiah's jaw ticking as he mulled the possibilities.

Avalina licked her lips. "Where will we go?"

"I'm not sure." He frowned. If only he knew where Benjamin resided. Surely his friend hadn't already left for the States.

He sucked in a breath and snapped his fingers. Najaf! He would know what to do.

Josiah met Avalina's anxious gaze. "Stay close to my side. I think I know someone who can help."

Josiah pounded harder on Najaf's door. Where was he? Perhaps among those calling for revolution. Wincing internally, he scoured his hands across the back of his neck until the door was flung open. The African glared from inside the darkness of his pub.

"Fool!" Najaf peered out into the street. "Do ya think to alert everyone dat you've arrived at my door?"

"No, I just—"

Najaf cut off his words with a growl and hastily ushered them inside. Avalina tucked herself behind Josiah. He cleared his throat.

"I'm sorry to inconvenience you, my friend. I need help."

"You're lucky you caught me here. I've been gone all day." Najaf's eyes narrowed. "And why would a white man and woman be needin' my help?"

"I need to get us out of here. Tonight."

"And go where?"

Josiah hesitated. "To the States."

Najaf shook his head. "It's nigh impossible. The governor has closed da ports. No one in or out."

Josiah straightened. "Please. I'll never breath your name to a soul. Benjamin already told me you have contacts. Ways to get things done."

Najaf snorted and ran his fingers down his face. "Dat crazy old man. Is dere no end to da trouble he'll cause me?" Looking up, he fixed Josiah with a hard stare. "And why should I be helping you?"

"Don't do it for me." Josiah stepped aside and slipped his hand down to gently press the small of Avalina's back as she stepped into the sparse light. "Do it for another slave who longs to be free."

His eyes widened. "You, miss?"

She swallowed and nodded. Najaf sighed and rolled his shoulders as he turned to pace the length of the room. After long moments of silence, he whirled to face them, his expression fierce.

"All right. I know someone who can help. But you and I?" He slashed his hand through the air. "We've never met. Understand?"

"Perfectly." Josiah heaved a relieved sigh. "I owe you one."

"Nah, man." For the first time, the hint of a smile cracked Najaf's lips. "Dat's two you owe me."

I panted in the sticky night air as I followed Josiah and our large rescuer past the crowded docks to a different part of the city . . . where men and women no longer railed against the unmoving soldiers. My lungs and legs burned at the fast pace, but at least we had left the melee far behind. I should have been trembling like a palm frond in a storm, but the warmth of Josiah's hand around mine steadied my frayed nerves.

Through the darkness, I could hear waves lapping against the deserted stretch of docks on the far side of the village. As we slowed our pace, Josiah frowned, still babying his ribs with his free hand.

"Why are there no soldiers posted here?"

Najaf chuckled softly, his voice a whisper as he paused to study the docks with a sharp eye. "Soldiers gather to control people, but here? Dere is nothing but a shallow bay."

"Then how will we leave?"

Najaf pointed to something in the inky blackness. "I have a small boat anchored dere. Nothing more than a rowboat, but it will carry you to a waitin' ship. A large vessel dat has been avoiding the British navy." Najaf grinned, his white teeth flashing in the pale moonlight. "Dey help me from time to time."

"Smugglers."

"Yes. Here." Najaf pulled something from his pocket and shoved it into Josiah's hands. I tried to suppress my gasp as Josiah stared at the wad of money clutched in his fingers. He shook his head.

"No, my friend. I cannot take this. It's too much."

Najaf held up his hands when Josiah tried to give it back. "Consider it a loan." He pulled an envelope from his pocket and thrust it toward Josiah. "Or consider it payment for work done."

A cold stone sank in my stomach. What had we become involved with? Josiah must have the same dismay, for his brows dipped low. "What work?"

"I need you to take dis to a man in Charleston." He shoved the wrinkled envelope into Josiah's hands. "An Edward Pickering. He works at Charleston Shipping and Freight."

What choice did we have? I blinked back the sting of tears. I had cost Josiah much. Too much. His father's company, his possessions...I opened my mouth to protest but he was already nodding in agreement.

"It will be done."

Najaf smiled. "Thank you, friend. Now you shall only owe me one favor."

We crouched low in the darkness as Najaf silently slid into the water. My stomach cramped with hunger. Exhaustion warred with shock as I waited, breathless. In moments, a small rowboat appeared. The large man held out his hand, waiting expectantly to assist me. Moonlight glinted off the ripples of water. I blinked and hesitated. Could I really do this? Could I really leave Azaka Mede and everything I'd ever known?

The memory of Master Cyrene lying in crimson eclipsed my sudden doubts. Nausea bubbled. I had to flee. There was no other choice.

Sucking in shallow breaths, I slid my fingers into Najaf's waiting palm and eased into the boat. It bobbed and swayed beneath my weight. My pulse hammered. When I'd finally settled into the middle seat, Josiah eased down. Najaf handed him an oar and they rowed silently into the inky night.

Each slap of the oar slicing through water caused my heart to bleed a little more.

CHAPTER 16

Josiah's arm muscles screamed from the long stretch of rowing but the pain couldn't compare to the nagging ache in his ribs. He grimaced and paused, glancing through the inky waters. The lights burning along the docks of Barbados were far behind, mere pinpoints and flickers now. Save for the light slap of waves against the oars, all was silent.

Avalina sat across from him in the boat, her arms wrapped tightly around her torso. Would that he could have spared her from the horror she had witnessed this night.

A cool breeze tugged, lifting strands of his hair from his forehead. Najaf's instructions had been scant. In the darkness, how could he tell if he'd missed the smugglers completely?

"Raise your hands in the air, nice and slow."

The masculine voice bounced off the water. Josiah whirled and the glint of a revolver winked in the moonlight. Avalina gasped and slowly lifted her hands in the air. Josiah frowned and followed suit, squinting into the darkness. In moments, a small boat edged alongside their skiff. A muscled man rowed while another held a gun in his hand.

"Who are you?" The gun-wielding giant glared.

Josiah had no recourse but to speak the truth. "I am Josiah Holland, sent by a man named Najaf."

The two strangers glanced at each other, silence stretching as taut as taffy. The man's gaze swung back to Josiah as he cocked the hammer on the gun and narrowed his eyes. "Why?"

Josiah swallowed. Perhaps these were not Najaf's friends. "He bids us go to South Carolina to deliver a letter."

"To whom?"

Should he tell them? It would do no good to lie. He had no idea what situation they had inadvertently delved into. "An Edward Pickering."

A smile broke across the man's face. Tucking away the gun, he lifted his brows. "Then I suppose you'll be needing our help."

I gripped the callused hand of the man lifting me over the banister of the massive ship. My feet settled on the wet, wooden deck and I sucked in a breath as the entire ship canted to one side and then the other. I didn't know if the darkness made the sensation worse or if morning's light would further tilt my perception. Shifting out of Josiah's way, I clutched the slick wooden railing, bracing my weight from the sway of the creaking ship as he crawled over the side.

Sailors quickly gathered around me, their movements sleek as cats. Even in night's shadows, I could see the guarded skepticism marring some of their brows. Others pinched their lips with disdain. One fellow, a thick hulk of a man, smiled, his goatee tipping in at the corners, though the expression held no warmth. I swallowed, grateful when Josiah stepped in front of me, blocking me from their stares. For once, I was thankful for the lack of lantern light.

A tall, bearded man approached, his bearing erect as he tucked his hands behind him.

"Welcome aboard *Neptune's Tide*. I am Captain Blackthorne." He jutted his chin in the direction of the two large men who had found us amid the waves. "Bones and Erasmus tell me you are friends of Najaf's."

"Yes, sir." Josiah's shoulders squared, a show of bravado, yet as I clutched his arm in my cold fingers, I could feel the tension coiling the muscles in his forearms. "He helped us escape the madness taking over the island."

"Madness?" Blackthorne frowned, dark brows furrowing. "Explain."

Josiah reached for my hand and squeezed, as if to ease my fears. "Slaves all over Barbados are rising up, sir. Burning, stealing, and murdering their masters."

I tucked myself closer to Josiah's side, the image of Master Cyrene's lifeless body invading once again. My stomach tightened into a knot.

"Mm." The captain looked toward Barbados. "We could smell the smoke but had yet to learn the reason why."

"Soldiers have been dispersed to quell the uprising and Governor Leith has ordered the docks closed. Plantation owners are being evacuated to Bridgetown."

The captain's brows lifted high. "And why are you not with them?"

I glanced up at Josiah's strong profile. He held the captain's gaze with unswerving confidence. "I am not a plantation owner, sir. My father and I were merely visiting from the States."

"And where is your father now?"

Josiah's lips flattened into a hard line. "He chose not to flee."

Captain Blackthorne grunted. "Admirable? Or perhaps foolish." He turned to the crew and grinned. "Guess we'll not be sneaking to the docks this night, men."

One of the sailors frowned and stepped forward. "Why not, sir? There are still goods to be had."

"Ah, but with the docks closed, our presence will easily be noted." The captain smirked. "Unless you take a fancy to being shot by Imperial soldiers, I suggest we head for safer waters."

The sailor nodded. "Aye, sir."

"Would you be willing to let us sail with you, Captain Black-thorne?" Josiah pulled the wad of bills he'd been given by Najaf from his pocket and held them toward the captain. "We can pay for any expense we may cause you."

Captain Blackthorne's eyes widened before reaching for the currency. "Aye. That's a fair trade, Holland."

I heaved a sigh of relief.

"But, Captain"—a lanky fellow with a shock of hair that stuck out like straw lunged forward and pointed at me—"'tis bad luck to have a female aboard ship!"

The captain chuckled and stepped closer to study me. I longed to cower at his wide shoulders, authoritative presence, and shrewd gaze but forced my eyes up to meet his. The corner of his mouth quirked. "Tell me, are you bad luck, miss?"

My tongue stalled. The words wouldn't come. Instead, I shook my head.

"See there, men!" The captain laughed and turned back to his crew. "The damsel confesses she is of no threat to us." He snort-ed and slowly walked the length of the deck. "Never did abide all the blather about female curses aboard ship. Why, wasn't it Posei-don that married Amphitrite, goddess of the sea? Besides"—he winked—"this maid is a lovelier sight to behold than the lot of you."

Some of the sailors barked a laugh but others grumbled un-der their breath. Heat scorched my cheeks. Josiah's hold tightened around my fingers.

Captain Blackthorne pointed at the thick sailor with the leering grin. "Slocum, show our guests their sleeping quarters."

"Aye, sir."

"For the rest of you, prepare to set sail."

The sailors murmured and turned to begin their work, but be-fore we could follow Slocum, Josiah stepped forward.

"Captain, I forgot to ask," he called out, "you *are* sailing for South Carolina, are you not?"

Captain Blackthorne tossed a smile over his shoulder as he turned away. "Yes. Eventually."

Eventually? Where were they going? Josiah glanced down into my face, his brows knit. "Don't worry. I'll keep you safe."

I swallowed and nodded as Slocum approached. The man licked his lips, watching me with a hard stare. Josiah stepped in front to block me from his view. The sailor frowned.

"Follow me."

We traipsed across the tilting deck, down a set of stairs to a corridor that was pitch black. My fingers skimmed the walls as I pressed closer to Josiah's strong presence. Another turn and honeyed lantern light illuminated a row of doors. Slocum pointed to the first one. "Here. For you, sir." He eyed me, a smile tilting his mouth as he stepped to the next door and opened it slowly. The hinges squeaked. "And this one's for you, miss."

Josiah frowned, eyes narrowing. "We will only need one room, sir."

The man's dark brows deepened. "One room?" A scowl marred his expression. "There, then. Take the first one."

Josiah nodded curtly and pulled me inside behind him. "Thank you." He then shut the door in the sailor's face with a soft click. He whirled to me, his expression apologetic, and released my hand. "I'm sorry, Avalina. I don't trust that fellow. Better he think us married." He scrubbed the back of his neck. "I should have asked you first. If you prefer—"

He should have asked me? No one had ever given consideration to my wishes before this night. I shook my head. He stepped close and placed his warm hands on my shoulders. "I can't protect you in a separate room but I fear for your reputation."

I cleared my throat. "I have no reputation."

A small smile tugged his mouth. "In my eyes, you do."

My thoughts tripped. Why did Josiah see the worth of a slave? No one else in my acquaintance ever had. Perhaps he was playing me for a fool. Or maybe...

I rubbed my temple with shaking fingers. I couldn't think.

"Today has been too much for you." He nodded toward the narrow bed tucked against the wall. "You take the bed. I'll sleep on the floor near the door, and I promise, you'll come to no harm."

I swallowed and nodded. What other choice did I have? My mind was muddled, my body aching from fatigue. My muscles yet throbbed from Master's earlier cruelty. All I longed for was sleep. And peace.

Josiah forced a small smile. "We can talk more tomorrow. It's been a hard day for both of us."

Was he worried about the bargain he'd struck with Najaf? Unease slithered through my middle once again.

He set his knapsack against the wall and grabbed an extra blanket from the bed before moving to the door, where he eased onto the floor, sucking in a gasp at the pain in his ribs. Looking at me from across the berth, he offered a small smile, a dark brow arched high.

"Do you plan to sleep standing up?"

Heat scorched my neck but the twinkling in his eyes caused the knot to unfurl in my stomach. I slid between the scratchy covers, gingerly testing the weight of the lumpy cot.

I lay in the bed, my mind numb. Heart sore. The ship's timbers groaned as it swayed back and forth, back and forth, the motion a lullaby.

As sleepiness tugged my heavy eyelids, the creaking ship carried me away from Barbados, my prison.

It was then I realized some prisons are their own strange comfort.

CHAPTER 17

"Remember the song of home."

Mother's voice called to him across the sun-dappled yard. Fortressing oaks, with their gnarled branches stretched overhead like arthritic fingers, blocked the worst of the shimmering heat from Josiah's eyes. He looked up, winking against the light bursting through the foliage.

"Come, Master Josiah! We will race."

Josiah glanced sideways at Fountain's wide grin. White teeth flashed in his playmate's dark face.

Footsteps rustled the grass. Old Moses appeared, a smile cracking his whiskered lips. "Winner gets an aggie. No joshin' from me. I gots the marble to prove it." The gardener held up a bright blue agate suspended between his dark fingers.

A race for a new aggie? Josiah nodded at Fountain. The boys loved to play marbles in the gardens and Old Moses knew it.

The elderly slave's brows lifted. "When I say go, you-ins run now, you hear? Race around the roses and Miss Virginia's prize azaleas. First one back wins the aggie."

They nodded and tensed for the call.

"All right now . . . run!"

They took off. Wind whipped Josiah's face. He could hear Fountain's laughter. His own squeals of joy bubbled up as they reached the edge of the roses. Their feet pounded, stirring up clouds of dust. Heat scorched his legs and chest. It was so hot . . .

They turned another corner and Fountain slipped a pace ahead. Josiah's arms and legs pumped harder... the distance stretched... just out of reach.

They raced past Old Moses, who cackled a mighty laugh and declared Fountain the winner by only a step. Josiah grinned at his friend, who marveled at the blue orb now held in his hand.

Then Josiah was yanked away from the merriment. Faces sobered as they blurred past. He was being dragged backward, his legs kicking as the world shrank. Mother's knit brow faded as he was carried inside. Pain exploded through his head as the floor rose up to meet him.

"Shame! That's what you are, boy. A shame. Do you hear me?"

Father towered over Josiah, his face mottled crimson and veins bulging in his neck. What had he done? Josiah scrambled away, each movement a squeak as his skin rubbed against the polished floor. But Father yanked him up by the shirt collar. His feet dangled in the air as he whimpered, staring into his father's bloodshot eyes.

"No son of mine is bested by a slave child." Father's teeth clamped down, his lips pulled back as he shook Josiah's collar. His head swam. Spittle flew from his mouth. And then the ground rose up to meet him once more as he slammed into the floor. Father's long finger stabbed him in the chest.

"Never again. You hear me? Never again will my son show such weakness in front of the slaves." Josiah trembled and winced as Father stooped down, his face inching closer. "Or you'll no longer be my son."

In the distance, Mother was calling, her voice rising and fading like a breeze. "Remember the song of home, Josiah. Remember the song of home... "

Father raised his hand to strike once more, and—

Josiah gasped, startling awake with a jerk. His head slammed into the door of Avalina's cabin. Murmuring through a grunt of pain, he rubbed the side of his skull and willed his heart to ease its rapid thrumming. Darkness cloaked the room, save for the thin light of a lantern hung on the wall, its glass clinking ever so softly with the bobbing of the ship.

Sweat dampened his skin as he panted and eased back on the floor. The old memory oft bloomed into a recurring nightmare, twisting and writhing as time passed, but never before had his mother's soft admonition been present. *"Remember the song of home."*

Mother had uttered the phrase when anyone in the house departed for trips ... business dealings, visiting relatives, or even things as simple as dances. She, in her own way, tried to remind the lot of them to see each choice as a reflection of whose family they belonged to.

He blinked in the darkness, ribs aching. Josiah remembered but it was not the sweet memories his mother had intended. No doubt, she imagined him remembering the chirp of mockingbirds, the roar of the ocean, the strength of his father, and her voice praising him for the little accolades that lit a child's life. No. Now his mind churned up the songs of the slaves in the fields—their glistening backs hunched in toil as their mournful cadence rose and fell like breakers during high tide. The crack of a whip. The overseer handing them thin bags of rice, cornmeal, and beans each month, an allotment that his own family would never dream of consuming. Dark-headed Miles, enslaved since his birth, drooping, his hands gripping a large fan as he waved it back and forth in the heat so Mother might not perspire.

Hattie, Fountain, Isabelle, Mother, Father ... he winced. What would they say when he arrived home with a woman? Memories were cruel phantoms. Punishing specters that pointed the soul to things it had deigned to ignore.

He sat up and raked his hands through his damp hair. Even the memory of his sister's sunny, dimpled smile was shadowed, darkened by the plight of those around him. Was there anything for him there anymore?

Avalina sighed in her sleep and shifted, the soft sound reminding him of the coo of a dove. What was he thinking, dragging her to his family's plantation? She knew nothing of his world ... how to dress or behave among pampered Southern women. She could not even hold a conversation, a grievance that would cause all the tongues in Charleston to wag. And while he cared little for nuances of the societal elite, his heart twisted in pain at the rejection that was sure to come. The circles his family moved in were known for their sweet-as-sugar tongues and poisonous bites.

The only thing that could protect her was him. A legal alliance. Father and Mother would have little say if they were married before arriving. He swallowed and glanced again to her sleeping form. Would he be a good husband? Did he even know where to begin?

Heart thumping in painful rhythm, he eased back down onto the unforgiving floor.

He feared he had taken Avalina from one torture into another.

I blinked against the darkness encircling my foggy mind. The cot beneath me shifted to and fro, like the swing of a cradle. Timbers creaked. Where was I?

Easing up on one elbow, I glanced through the shadowed room, my gaze landing on Josiah sleeping near the door. One arm was flung over his eyes, a blanket tangled around his feet.

The events of the previous day rushed back with dizzying clarity. The rebellion, hastening from Azaka Mede, and worst of all, Master Cyrene lying in a pool of blood.

I fell back against the cot, my stomach twisting. I pinched my eyes shut to erase the memory of Master's fingers grabbing, the glint of evil and lust in his expression, but nothing could blot out the torment already embedded in my mind. I was ... filthy. As if a hundred baths couldn't begin to cleanse the odor of him from my skin.

Josiah blinked and stretched but hissed a breath and grabbed at his ribs. "Ow."

He had taken a beating yesterday. For me. For his father. And what did he have to show for it? Cracked ribs and sleeping on a hard slab of floor. Despite the pain he must be in, he blinked at me and offered a sleepy, "G' morning."

Was he never ill-tempered? I moved to his side and knelt before tugging up the bottom of his shirt. His eyes widened. "What are you doing?"

I tilted my head, confused at his protest. "I can help, but I must see your wounds first."

Was that a flash of crimson streaking up his neck? He blew out a breath and gritted his teeth before carefully inching up his shirt. Red and purple bruises mottled his ribs. As tenderly as possible, I ran my fingers over his skin, pulling away when he sucked in a breath between his teeth.

"There is swelling. You need a poultice of feverfew and garlic."

Easing up on one elbow, Josiah arched a brow. "Too bad I'm fresh out." His pursed lips ghosted into a lopsided smile. "How do you know about feverfew and garlic?"

"Molly taught me about healing herbs since I was a wee one. She thought such a skill would come in handy with the Master." Rocking back on my heels, I sat and tucked my knees to my chest, making sure the rumpled skirts covered my legs. "She feared I would be sent to the sugar cane fields otherwise." Dear Molly. An ache expanded in my chest, the hollow space where my heart had once been. A heart Molly had nurtured despite her own limitations. What was I to do without her?

The backs of my eyes stung. Josiah studied me, his expression sad. "You loved her much, didn't you?"

My throat clogged so I merely nodded. Pushing up to sit, Josiah lowered his brows. "Tell me how you came to be in Barbados, Avalina."

I shook my head. "I—I don't know." I looked down and picked threads of my frayed hemline. "I only have vague memories. Snatches, Molly would call them." I sorted through the images in my mind, every face, every color and hue like small squares of a patchwork quilt that refused to be sewn together. "I remember a ship, much like this one." I peered around the small cabin, reaching for anything familiar that might trigger more thoughts. "And I remember waking up on the shore, wet sand stuck to my hands and dress." I shrugged. "I suppose someone from Azaka Mede found me and brought me to Master. And I—" I trembled, shutting out the black memories swarming to be released.

"What is it?" Josiah leaned slightly forward, his gaze fixed on my face.

"I remember standing before Master Cyrene. He screamed when I refused to sing." I shook my head, breath growing shallow. "I tried, but I couldn't. It was like the words, the melodies were stuck. He had wanted me to entertain his guests, but when I failed, he..." I dropped my gaze and stared at the floor. "He beat me, almost to death, Molly said."

Josiah groaned. From my downcast gaze, I watched his fists flex and release, over and over again, as if he wished he could use them.

"I was relegated to work as a maid after that."

Warm fingers cupped my chin and Josiah lifted my face to his. I saw only concern in his expression. "What else did Cyrene Harding do to you, Avalina?"

I couldn't tell him. I wouldn't. My skin itched again. I needed a bath.

Before I could formulate a reply, something banged against our door.

"Captain requests your presence in his quarters." The bark from the other side was not gentle, but a harsh command. Josiah's gaze fastened on mine, but I merely nodded. What choice did we have? We were at the mercy of Captain Blackthorne ... and we had yet to see if the man was an angel or a demon.

Easing up from the floor, Josiah straightened and grimaced. "Coming."

The voice from the other side sounded as if wet rocks were lodged in the fellow's throat. "Be quick about it."

Josiah ran his fingers through his tousled hair and swung the door open wide. Slocum stared from the doorway, his beady eyes narrowing. I instinctively moved behind Josiah. Something about the sailor's expression reminded me too much of Master Cyrene, despite his stocky build and thick neck.

"I'm ready." Josiah took a step forward but the sailor's snarl curled one side of his stubbled lips.

"Captain said to bring the girl."

CHAPTER 18

After hearing a bellowed "Enter!" Josiah stepped into Captain Blackthorne's cabin in the aft portion of *Neptune's Tide*, ducking low to avoid bumping his head on the short threshold. Avalina shadowed his steps, her breath shallow near his ear. Her breathing matched his own.

He narrowed his eyes to peer through the shadowed quarters. Curtains of red velvet and gold tassels hung from ceiling to floor. A wide bed was situated to the left of the room. To the right, an ornately carved dresser of mahogany and in the center a modest table boasting six chairs upholstered with the same red velvet that hung from the ceiling. Behind the dining table, a low desk. Two tallow candles were lit, their lumpy wax dripping down the sides. The buttery wax had already puddled around the holders. Captain Blackthorne sat behind the desk, hastily scribbling on parchment with a quill. Josiah looked back to ask Slocum if they should wait to address the captain but the sailor had already fled.

Offering Avalina a hesitant smile, he stepped forward. "Captain, you summoned us?"

Captain Blackthorne held up a finger for silence and finished his transcription. With a huff of satisfaction, he pushed back from the desk and stood, eyeing both of them with a sharp stare.

"How did you sleep?"

Josiah hesitated, his ribs yet aching. It had been a long, miserable night but none of that had anything to do with the quarters and everything to do with their circumstances. "Well enough, thank you, sir."

The captain's dark eyes swung to Avalina and held. "And you, miss?"

Ducking her gaze, Avalina nodded.

The captain took uneven steps toward them, his beard bobbing as his lips pinched into a frown. "What's the matter? Cat got yer tongue?"

Avalina swallowed, her gaze never straying from the floor. Josiah cleared his throat. "Speaking is difficult for her, sir. Most times, she can't."

"Mm." The captain took another swaggering step in their direction, limp pronounced, and his gaze fixed hard on Avalina. His head tilted. "Can't or won't?"

Josiah winced. The man had little graciousness in his manner. But instead of cowering, Avalina lifted her chin and met the captain's gaze with a steely one of her own. Captain Blackthorne chuckled.

"A bit of spirit, I see. I like it, I do." He waved them toward his table, his limp creating a *thump, THUMP, thump, THUMP* against the floor. "Come and eat with me. The boys will be bringing a bit of food to break the fast momentarily."

Josiah obeyed, pulling out Avalina's chair and seeing her settled before sitting in the straight-backed wooden chair. At least the velvet cushioning lent him a bit of comfort, however small.

"Now then, tell me, how did you meet Najaf?"

Josiah frowned, wondering how much to share. He had no idea of the relationship between the two men, only that at the mention of Najaf's name, passage had been granted. Was it an alliance of mutual benefits or of friendship?

"I was listening to a man speak to a crowd in St. John's Parish. He was waxing eloquent, and somewhat fiery, on the evils of slavery.

In only minutes, he had riled the crowd into such a frenzy, a mob formed and fighting ensued. Being the man was of a more elderly age, I took it upon myself to see him to safety." He felt Avalina's gaze bore into him as he shared. No doubt, she considered him a strange man. Son of a slaveholder, protecting an abolitionist. "We ducked into Najaf's tavern for safety."

Blackthorne cackled and pounded his fist on the scarred wooden table. "Benjamin Magee, I bet. I'd wager my last piece of gold on it."

A smile tugged Josiah's mouth. "Right you are, Captain."

Captain Blackthorne grinned, revealing a row of yellowed teeth, as crooked as warped piano keys. "I've met him on several occasions. Gave him passage once. I believe the Almighty made him so short in stature because the world could not handle him in a grander form."

A soft knock issued on the door before a thin young man, more child than teenager, entered carrying a large platter filled with food ... fluffy biscuits, a variety of fruit, wedges of cheese. He set it down before the captain and bowed slightly. "Anything else for your morning meal, sir?"

"Aye. Coffee and three cups."

"Yes, sir." The lad straightened and blushed to the roots of his hair when he saw Avalina. He scampered from the cabin, nearly tripping over his own feet. Blackthorne chuckled.

"Ain't seen a pretty miss in far too long. Forgive his clumsiness."

She nodded, a soft pink dusting her cheeks. Josiah's mouth watered looking at the food before them. How long since they'd eaten? His stomach cramped with hunger.

The captain waved toward the food. "Help yourselves. I'll not eat 'til my coffee arrives. Seems a sin until a bit of warmth hits my middle."

Nodding, Josiah hesitantly reached for a biscuit. There was no plate and he held the sustenance in his hand, unsure what the protocol was on this ship. The captain studied him and smiled.

"No plates here, lad. At least not in the mornings. We save heavier fare for evenings." He arched a dark brow, eyes twinkling. "And with naught but a bunch of smelly men, we've found it does no good to practice the social graces."

Josiah nodded and bowed to offer a silent thanks before taking his first bite and grabbing a plump apple. Avalina sampled a biscuit, a wedge of cheese, and timidly plucked a cluster of grapes from the platter, setting them on the bare table. The red-faced boy returned, bearing three steaming cups, before disappearing once more.

"Ah, good lad." The captain took a sip and settled back into his chair with a smile. "Much better. Now, since we share a common friend, I wondered if we might not have common interests."

"Common interests, sir?" Josiah arched a brow high as Captain Blackthorne leaned forward, ignoring the food, his gaze steady on Josiah's.

"What do you know of Edward Pickering?"

"Pickering? Nothing, sir. Just that the letter Najaf gave me should be delivered to the same."

"But you've no knowledge of the contents?"

"None."

Blackthorne stroked his dark beard and leaned back in his seat before absently buffing an apple against his shirt. "I wanted to cut you in on a deal, young Holland."

Across the table, Avalina frowned, chewing slowly and watching the captain as if she feared he might sprout wings. Josiah's gaze flicked back to the captain's. "What deal?"

"I suspect if you were listening to the good Benjamin wax long about abolition, you are a supporter, are you not?"

"Well, I—" Warmth crept up his neck. Was he? He'd been taught all his life that slavery was a necessary part of farming, of growing and producing goods for the country. But seeing those bodies thrown overboard on the trip to Barbados had pummeled his conscience with bitter regret. And after meeting Avalina . . .

His jaw firmed and he offered a curt nod. "I am."

"Good, good." The captain smiled and reclined a degree in his chair. "I propose an alliance of sorts. You scratch my back, and I scratch yours."

Josiah pursed his lips. "What if I have nothing causing me to itch?"

The captain threw back his head and laughed. "I like you, Holland. Take ease. This is nothing of a nefarious nature. Merely"—he pursed his lips—"tricky."

"You mean dangerous."

Captain Blackthorne shrugged a thick shoulder. "Perhaps. But I can reward you handsomely for your trouble." Reaching into his pocket, he pulled out a small bag and tossed it onto the table. Josiah frowned and untied the leather strap binding it together. The bag opened to reveal a handful of gold coins winking back in the soft glow of candlelight.

"What's this?"

The captain bit into his apple, droplets of juice peppering his beard. "Doubloons. Spanish gold. All yours if you add a bit of extra to your Edward Pickering delivery."

"What? Another letter? A package?"

"Of a sort." The captain chewed on another chunk of apple. "A person."

Josiah felt his brows lift into his hairline. "A—what?"

Blackthorne smirked. "Surely you must know by now what Najaf, and your friend, the good Quaker Benjamin Magee, are involved in. Human smuggling. Freedom. Abolition."

146

Josiah sucked in a breath. Human smuggling? Perhaps in philosophy, but were they really involved in actually smuggling people like chattel? This was much more than he'd bargained for when he'd promised to deliver Najaf's letter.

Instead of answering, he thrust out his chin and narrowed his eyes. "What makes you think I would take part in this? It's illegal."

Captain Blackthorne nodded calmly. "As is stealing a maiden slave from a plantation and transporting her to the States."

Avalina sucked in a harsh breath, the wedge of cheese in her fingers dropping to the table with a light *thunk*. Her gaze sought his and she licked her lips, complexion ashen. Josiah's gaze swung back to the captain. "Why do you say that?"

Blackthorne chuckled and reached for a biscuit as if enjoying light banter at a garden party. "Come now, Holland, I'm not blind. Nor am I ignorant of the ways of Barbados. The Redlegs...the poor Irish who were brought to the island years ago under the edict of King James, working as indentured servants...the unfortunate ones, slaves." His crooked teeth flashed before he bit into the biscuit. White crumbs dotted his beard. "And you arrive with her in tow the same night an uprising overtakes the island?" He shook his head. "One plus one equals two, brother."

Josiah's mouth turned to cotton. "What do you plan to do with her?"

The captain's dark eyes widened. "Do with her? Nothing, man. You misunderstand. I'm not threatening you. Just making you aware I know where your heart's convictions truly lie." He offered Avalina a smile. "Sorry to give you such a start, miss. I meant no harm."

She nodded and dropped her gaze to the table. Josiah's jaw tightened. The captain left him in a pickle, for sure and certain. How could he refuse? The man was right. The moment he had broken bread with Benjamin Magee, his heart had rejected the ways of his father, of his family, his heritage. Nor would he be able to live with himself if he turned away a person in need.

Leaning forward, he rested his forearms on the table. "Tell me about the person you need me to deliver."

My heart thrummed like a hummingbird's wings. The food in my mouth turned to ash. The captain had seen through our pretense. Through me. He'd pegged me as a runaway slave, though my tongue had remained silent. How many others would see? How many others would know?

I resisted the urge to cover my upper right arm where Master had branded me when I was naught but a child. I was his property, he had said, before pressing the red-tipped end of a metal brand into my flesh. I had screamed with the agony, vomited at the stench of my own burning flesh before awakening in my bedroom, where Molly had treated the wound with tender ministrations. Cold bitterness engulfed me. Master Cyrene had made sure I would never truly be free.

I wasn't free at Azaka Mede and I wasn't free here aboard *Neptune's Tide*.

What was Josiah taking on, not only delivering a mysterious letter to an unknown man, but now a fugitive? Yet, I bore the escaped slave no malice. Wasn't I in the same condition as he, desperate for one taste of freedom, yet dependent on the charity of others to claim it?

The captain's gravelly voice bit into my musings. "It's the perfect cover, you see. What with our other smuggled goods below deck. It's true we've broken our fair share of laws, but the way I see it, we are offering up our own kind of penance to the Almighty every time we help free one of the enslaved."

Josiah grunted, his expression unreadable. My stomach soured. He was in far too deep, and all because of me. If he hadn't rescued me from the island, he wouldn't now be faced with such dangerous choices. If he were caught...

I shuddered to think of the result.

Josiah rubbed his chin slowly, thoughtfully, the handsome planes of his face lined with a fierce gravity that took my breath away. He was going to do it. And my heart would break if he was discovered. He would hang, as surely as I lived and breathed.

Pushing away from the table, I rose. Josiah looked up at me. "Are you feeling unwell?"

I nodded and pointed to the door. A sympathetic smile tugged his mouth. "I will join you outside soon."

I pointed to his ribs and he chuckled. "Yes, I'll ask the captain for some bandages."

With a nod of satisfaction, I slipped through the door and let it shut behind me before moving to the railing and inhaling a deep draught of salt air. Waves splashed against the hull of the ship. Men scurried about, some adjusting the ropes, others washing fish netting. I felt more than one curious gaze upon me but kept my face toward the sea, relishing the feel of sunshine on my skin.

But something weighed heavy in my pocket. Slipping my hand into the folds of fabric, my fingertips brushed the cool metal of Master's revolver. He could not know. No one could.

Sea waves splashed against the side of the ship, and I swallowed. No one need know of my sin.

Yanking the burden from my pocket, I dropped it over the edge of the rail. It splashed into the depths with a satisfying plop. Buried. Gone.

A low, menacing voice whispered near my ear.

"All alone, little miss?"

I turned to see Slocum approach, a deadly glint sharpening his eyes.

CHAPTER 19

Josiah pulled a bite of cheese from a wedge and popped it in his mouth, chewing slowly. He considered every angle, all the things that might go wrong. But there was nothing for it. The captain knew he would help... could do anything but simply walk away from a person in need.

Captain Blackthorne stroked his beard, expression thoughtful. "I understand if you say nay, Holland. It's a dangerous business, smuggling people." He grunted. "Smuggling anything, truth be told. Been doing it for nigh unto ten years and the danger never dissipates."

Pursing his lips, Josiah probed. "Have you never been caught? I thought the British covered these waters."

"Aye, they do. And we've run into some close calls, that's for sure and certain."

"Yet you haven't stopped." The statement was more of an observation than a question.

"Nay, nor will we until we see this dreadful malady scourged from the land."

Josiah leaned back in his chair and tilted his head. "I wouldn't have taken you for an abolitionist, sir." He smiled. "Perhaps a pirate."

Blackthorne grunted and reached to pluck a grape from its stem. "Never judge a book by its cover, Holland." His eyes twinkled as he popped the fruit in his mouth. "Nevertheless, being oft misjudged does lend itself to be rather useful at times. Authorities seldom believe a pirate, as you say, could be working for a cause greater than himself, just like some men believe a woman has naught the intelligence to be a spy, or a child to carry a letter of great import."

"True enough." Josiah tucked that bit of information inside, intending to ruminate on it later. "Very well, I shall help your fugitive reach Pickering, but I'll need help from you on several matters."

The captain lifted a single dark brow. "And what are they?"

"The first is your men's help in smuggling the man off the boat when we dock."

"Done." The captain waved his hand in dismissal. "This is nothing new for them. Just tell the crew what you need."

Josiah nodded. "What is the fugitive's name?"

"Esco. Esco Pence. He's hiding in the bowels of the ship."

"I'll go below and introduce myself later. Perhaps between the three of us, we can form a plan to take him to safety." Josiah shifted. "Second, I would request some bandages and feverfew, if you have it. I believe I broke a rib in the fighting yesterday and Avalina is worried."

Captain Blackthorne plucked another grape and nodded. "I shall ask Cook what we have below. We've not a physician or medic on board, but one or two of the men make sure to keep a stock of medicinals at hand."

"Thank you."

The captain studied him for a long moment. "You know what folks will think, don't you, when you arrive with a woman in tow? You seem to be a well-bred gentleman, and traveling with a pretty young miss with no family to speak for her, well, tongues will wag."

He swallowed. "Which comes to my third request." He blew out a thick breath. "I need you to marry Avalina and me."

Pursing his lips, he nodded slowly. "Agreed. When?"

Josiah rubbed the back of his neck. "As soon as she agrees."

Blackthorne chuckled. "Skittish, is she?"

"Yes, no." He shook his head. "So much has happened just within the past day. I don't take such a commitment lightly, nor should she. I suppose I don't wish to overwhelm her."

"Seems to be overwhelmed already, if you don't mind me saying so. Hasn't spoken a word since setting foot on ship."

Josiah looked down and picked at his fingers. "She can't speak, sir. Not to others, anyway. Only to me."

"Strange malady, that." Blackthorne frowned. "What would cause such a problem?"

"I don't know but I suspect much of it has to do with the man she fled from."

Blackthorne leaned forward, eyes narrowed. "Abolition is personal for you, isn't it, Holland?"

Josiah's thoughts drifted to the nightmare of the previous evening, his father and mother's faces swimming in his vision. "Yes, and growing more personal all the time."

What would they do when they learned the truth? That their son not only sympathized with the abolitionist movement, but had helped lead not one, but two people to freedom?

He would be disowned. A cast-away, penniless, with no future to give Avalina. His chest constricted. There was only one solution.

They could never know.

He fisted the small bag of coins and shoved them into his pocket. A bit of insurance in case they ever learned the truth.

The captain stood. "I'll summon you later to meet Esco. Go on down to the galley now and tell them the captain said to let you survey the medicines we have tucked aside."

"Yes, sir. And thank you."

Blackthorne grunted and moved to his desk. Was it only last night Josiah feared they had boarded a ship filled with cutthroats?

Everything about his world had tipped on its side during the last fortnight.

He opened the door and stepped into the sunshine.

And immediately, his blood went cold.

A filthy sailor had his meaty paw wrapped around Avalina's arm and had shoved her against the railing.

Slocum's sour breath invaded my air and I cringed, looking away. His fingers dug into my flesh and I cried out.

"You and me, girlie, we were destined to be aboard *Neptune's Tide* together. Don't ye think?"

I longed to scream, to shout in his grimy face, but the words choked in my throat.

"Unhand her at once!"

Josiah's voice boomed through the air and Slocum released me, whirling to sneer.

"Who's asking?"

"Her husband." Josiah took a heavy step forward, eyeing the sailor as if he were a snake Josiah longed to crush with his boot.

Husband? They had made no pledge to one another, yet at Josiah's acid response, fear shuttered the sailor's eyes.

"And here I thought she desired me."

In a flash, Josiah's fist smashed into Slocum's nose. I jumped back, heart hammering as blood spurted. Sailors came running, eager to jump in the fray. Slocum spit blood from his mouth and lunged forward. Fists pounded against bone as a tumult erupted.

I skirted away from the railing, bumped and jostled in the chaos. A sailor's shoulder jammed into mine, nearly knocking me off my feet. When a huge bear of a man charged toward Josiah, I swallowed, scrambling for anything that might serve as a weapon. There! An empty rum bottle lay on a single crate.

Clutching it around the neck, I swung it against the back of the attacker's head with a sharp crack. The huge fellow paused, swayed on his feet, and crumpled to the ground.

Josiah looked up at me, a slight smile ghosting his mouth. "Thanks."

I nodded and held the jagged remnant of glass in my hand, waiting for another attack, when a boisterous shout split the air.

"Enough!"

The men froze and turned slowly. Captain Blackthorne stood in the open doorway of his quarters, teeth clenched and eyes ablaze. A sailor next to me visibly trembled at the sight.

"What is the meaning of this?"

Silence grew thick in the air. Josiah panted, holding his ribs, and pointed at Slocum. "I caught that man laying his hands on Avalina."

The captain's gaze swung to Slocum, his narrowed eyes darkening to charcoal. He took a menacing step forward. Then another. He eyed the sailor up and down, expression like flint. "Is this true?"

Slocum's nostrils flared, his mouth marred by blood trickling down his cheek and dripping off his chin. He offered no defense, merely smirked.

Captain Blackthorne's face mottled red. "I see the truth well enough." He glanced away, hard gaze roving over his men. "Hear me well. Any man who abuses our guest, or speaks unkindly or in an ungentlemanly way to her, will be punished." He nodded to the men at his left. "Take Slocum below deck. He will be released at the next port with no pay."

Slocum jerked, his defiant expression siphoning to terror. "But, Captain—"

Blackthorne lifted his chin, a breeze toying with the ends of his black beard. "Do it again, and I'll feed you to the sharks." His lips pinched as he stared over his crew. "That goes for the lot of you!"

Slocum slumped as two sailors grabbed him by the arms and pulled him below. I pressed my hand to my quaking stomach, my breakfast souring.

The captain stepped close to Josiah and murmured, "Best we be about your business quickly."

What did he mean? But Josiah merely nodded as Blackthorne issued orders to his men. Josiah turned to me, his hands cupping my shoulders, gaze roving my form. "Are you well?"

I nodded, my limbs still quaking at what might have transpired if he hadn't appeared when he did.

He offered a lopsided smile. "Where did you learn to fight like that?"

I shrugged. I couldn't tell him how my heart had frozen at the thought of him injured. How my soul shredded thinking of him bleeding and dying. How had he come to mean so much in such a short time?

"You're a very brave woman." Josiah released me and pursed his lips. "Come, we best leave the crew in peace until feelings have calmed. The captain told me we can make use of the medicines in the galley."

I sensed the now-sullen sailors watching me as I followed Josiah below deck. Fresh air was soon eclipsed by a stale odor of unwashed bodies, alcohol, and mold. I shivered in the darkened corridor, even though the air here was warmer than on deck. Josiah paused at one spot, no doubt at an impasse on which direction to turn.

I tugged his sleeve. "Follow the smell of food."

We traversed a passage to the right that opened into a large room filled with an oven, large tables, and open crates brimming with vegetables, fruit, and uncooked grain. Two large hams hung from hooks on the wooden ceiling. A lanky fellow with hair the color of ginger looked up and swiped sweat from his temple with the sleeve of his shirt.

"'ello. An' what kin I do for ye?"

Josiah's gaze swept the space. "Captain sent us to find some medicine, as well as bandages."

"'appy to oblige. There now." The cook pointed to a large cabinet butted against the opposite wall. "Take what ye need."

I eased around Josiah, anxious to see what this ship had in the way of herbs. I knew little of doctorin', save what could be foraged in the wild. Pulling out the first drawer, I spied scissors, rolls of white bandages, and pliers. I shuddered to think what the pliers were intended to do. Extract teeth, perhaps. Running my tongue over my own teeth, I grabbed two rolls of bandages and the scissors before opening the next drawer. Small bottles of whiskey and rum filled the inside. Perfect for numbing pain but doing nothing to heal. I shook my head and closed the drawer softly.

Josiah stood behind me, watching while holding his ribs. The tussle on deck had done him no favors. What if he was bleeding internally? His complexion was ashen, a far different color than his usual sun-tanned skin.

I stooped to pull out the lower, larger drawers. Dried grasses and plants were tied in bundles. Small pouches filled the right side. I carefully rummaged through the assortment. No feverfew but I found white willow bark, lavender, and a small pouch that contained cat's claw. Though I had never used the herb before, I remembered Molly speaking of its benefits when a trader visited Azaka Mede one day.

Molly...

I swallowed, pushing away the knifing pain. My sweet friend, cut down as if she were nothing more than a threadbare garment to be discarded. A lump rose in my throat. My vision blurred. Sniffing,

I closed the drawer and clutched the items to my middle. I glanced toward the cook chopping onions nearby while whistling a jaunty tune. The room filled with the tangy smell.

Stepping close to Josiah, I whispered, "I need lard, a mortar and pestle, and a small bowl of water."

He nodded and requested the items from the cook, who cheerfully pushed the items into Josiah's hand. "Come back if you need more."

Offering a small smile, I followed Josiah back to the cabin. My head swam with all the turns. How would I ever find my way to the deck alone?

I squared my shoulders. I would have to. I was no longer a slave of Azaka Mede. I was a free woman.

The thought was strange. It left me hollow. Hopeful. Terrified. My fingers trembled and I clutched the herbs closer to my middle.

Upon entering the cabin, Josiah winced as he shuffled across the floor. He sank into the lumpy mattress and placed his arm around his ribs once again. My heart tugged.

"How are you faring?" It was as easy to talk with him as it had been with Molly.

"I'll live." But his face was far too pale, his normal good humor absent.

"Please, let me see to you."

Blowing out a breath, he nodded and unbuttoned his shirt. I looked away, far too aware of our small confinement. The strange vulnerability of us here, together. He tossed his shirt to the side of the bed and sat upright. I winced when I witnessed the purple bruises that had spread across his ribs. He had been bleeding internally, but how much?

I placed the mortar and pestle on the small table near the bed and sprinkled several leaves of cat's claw into the bowl before adding some lavender and crushing it with the pestle, grinding it into a fine

157

powder. After scooping a plop of lard into the bowl, I stirred the herbs into the fat before moving to Josiah's side. I held up the mess and offered a small smile.

"This will ease inflammation and pain."

He wrinkled his nose. "Smells ... interesting."

I smiled and carefully spread the liniment across his ribs. He sucked in a few breaths as I soothed the salve into his skin. I wiped my greasy hands on the hem of my skirt and reached for the bandages before looking up into Josiah's face with an apology in my expression.

"I'm sorry, but I need to bind your ribs. It may hurt."

He chuckled low in his throat. "They can't hurt any more than they do now."

"This should help once it's over." I unraveled the roll gingerly, pressing the fabric against his salve-covered flesh. I leaned in to work the bandage around his torso and I heard his soft inhale near my ear. I glanced up and my heart skidded to a stop. His gaze dropped to my lips. Space disappeared and time slowed to a crawl. My pulse pounded in my ears as he leaned forward ever so slowly and brushed his lips against mine.

I was falling, drowning. His fingers cupped my face as he deepened the kiss, his lips caressing my own. Never had I felt so cherished ... so treasured. I couldn't think. Couldn't breathe.

He groaned and pulled back, resting his forehead against mine. The bandages lay forgotten in my limp hand.

Running his fingers through my tousled curls, he whispered, "Marry me, Avalina. Marry me now."

CHAPTER 20

Josiah hadn't meant to ask her so suddenly, but he didn't regret it. He ran his fingers over her lips. Lips as soft as the slightest brush of a feather, velvety to the touch and sweet as nectar when tasted.

This was something he could do. Give her protection. And she, in turn, would provide a buffer between him and his father. If Josiah didn't act quickly, George Holland might arrange a marriage for him, thus entrenching him deeper into his family's stronghold.

A marriage would benefit them both, and, judging by their kiss, attraction would be no issue.

But was he doing this for Avalina ... or for himself?

He pushed the black thought away.

She opened her mouth to respond when a harsh pounding issued on the door.

Pitiful timing. He called across the berth. "Yes?"

A masculine voice answered. "Holland, Captain Blackthorne wanted me to alert you. A formidable gale is rising. A fierce storm lies just ahead."

He blew a breath from between his lips. "Thank you. I'll be on deck shortly."

As the footfalls padded away, Avalina's eyes rounded. "You ought not be on deck, not with your ribs so battered."

"I'll be fine." He winced and eased his arms into his shirt, hastily buttoning the length of it before rising. "The captain would not warn us if the storm weren't menacing. You need to stay in here until the worst has passed."

"But I—"

He shook his head. "I'll not see you tossed overboard."

She propped her hands on her slim hips. "Yet you take the same risk."

He smiled, enjoying the sassy arch of her brow. Who knew she held a pinch of vinegar inside?

"Just remain in here."

He shut the door behind him, offering a quick prayer for safety. This journey had been nothing but angst from the get-go. At least he knew Avalina would be safely tucked inside.

I paced the length of the small room yet again. I couldn't stay inside a moment longer.

My stomach rolled as the ship canted sharply to the right. Moving to the door, I gripped the handle as the massive boat tipped this time to the left. I stumbled through the passageway and climbed the stairs, clutching to any handhold I could find. I stepped onto the deck and my stomach sank.

Dark clouds had swallowed the sun. Wind whistled eerily through the rigging, causing the sails overhead to snap in protest. *Neptune's Tide* shuddered as waves swelled, lifting it up one moment and plunging it low the next.

Steadying myself by gripping the edge of a large crate, I sucked in deep draughts of briny air. A strange silence wrapped itself around me, even as an electric charge of lightning buzzed above. Silver flashed a second before thunder bellowed. I yelped and covered my head as the crew scurried into motion. Captain Blackthorne shouted over the crash of angry waves. "Secure the lines! Heave!"

The blurred faces of men rushed past—Bones, Erasmus, and a dozen others—as the men hastened to brace the ship for the storm's onslaught. Where was Josiah?

I took a hesitant step forward, scanning each body until my gaze snagged on him. There he was, in a line of sailors, gripping a length of rope leading to the foresail with white knuckles. Pain was etched into every line of his face.

I walked swiftly to his side, anxious to pull him away, lest he injure himself further, when the pewter clouds opened up and drenched us all. Water soaked my dress to my skin. I pushed away the thick ribbons of hair clinging to my face and neck when the deck tipped sideways. I flailed and slammed into the wooden planks. I grasped for anything I could, but the slippery moorings proved too much. My body smacked into the railing. I coughed against the rain flooding my nose and mouth and pulled myself upright despite the weight of my sodden clothes weighing down my limbs. I clung to the railing as the wind whipped the rain into a fury of lashes against my skin. The leaden sky was saturated with streaks of silver lightning. The cacophony of shouts, rain, the howl of wind, and sharp cracks of booming thunder rattled the wood beneath my feet. The sea was a salivating, breathing beast.

My heart crawled into my throat. This was no mere storm. This was punishment from the gods. They had seen me murder and now my sin had endangered the entire crew.

A spark skittered up my back as waves pounded the hull, unleashing furious gushes of water that rose over the railing and slammed into every breathing human on board. Water lifted me off the deck. I was tossed, my fingertips reaching to brush wood, steel, a rope, but the world fell away from my touch.

My body was plunged into the fury of the ocean, cold saltwater filling my nostrils and lungs. This was nothing less than I deserved.

I had doomed us all.

CHAPTER 21

Josiah gritted his teeth against the piercing pain in his ribs and pulled on the line, keeping rhythm with the sailors around him.

A man named Duffle climbed the mast and shouted at them from his perch above. "Hold, men! Don't let 'er go!"

Digging his boots into the floor, Josiah grunted, his arms burning. The thick gusts of wind strained against the sails, now bloating with the menacing current. In truth, Captain Blackthorne had waffled between two options: pull the sails down and let *Neptune's Tide* be led where it may, or keep the sails up to fight the tumult. If the men could withstand the strain, they might be able to skirt the widest path of the monster bearing down on them. But which choice was best? It would be best not to plunge into the depths of the squall.

Timbers creaked and groaned under the strain, mimicking the pinch in his side. The waves churned and foamed, the ocean's fury growing as the charcoal sky seeped with swirling chaos, like ribbons of cream in coffee. When a man called for them to release the length of rope, Josiah heaved a sigh and glanced over the tipping deck. A single raindrop splattered the smooth wood planks beneath his feet, each drop rolling as the deck lurched. A harsh gust of wind snapped the sail, the crack mimicking the sharp raps of thunder growing louder each second.

Blackthorne bellowed, "Secure the mainmast!"

Yet, Josiah could make no movement. His feet were frozen—immobile at the sight of Avalina staring out over the swelling sea. The wind tossed her fiery tresses like a whip. Her pale fingers gripped the slick railing, but instead of shuddering at the mounting torrent, she pressed closer to the edge, as if the rolling beast knocking the ship to and fro called to her. Was it wistful yearning for something beyond, or was she frozen in fear?

And why hadn't she stayed below as he'd insisted?

With his next breath, the heavens unleashed a torrent. Water ran in rivulets down his face, sliding under his collar, soaking him to the skin. Blackthorne shouted a string of commands, but his words drowned into a buzz in Josiah's ears as he moved to pull Avalina to shelter.

Before he could take two steps, the ship tilted to the right and the object of his concern lost her footing, slamming into the slick deck with a yelp. His pulse pounded in his ears when her slim body slammed into the railing as a large wave crashed over the side. The furious wind and water blinded him. When he cleared his vision, Avalina was gone.

His heart thudded painfully as he raced to the railing, screaming into the chaos. "Avalina!"

Lightning sliced the sky yet he could see nothing but swelling waves pounding the ship with unleashed fury. Where was she?

Captain Blackthorne shouted, "Holland! What are you doing?"

Josiah whirled back, blinking against the rain pelting his skin and lashes. "Avalina! She fell overboard!" He pointed over the side of the ship and swung his legs over the railing. *God, be merciful.*

After uttering the short prayer, he dove into the deep.

I coughed up saltwater and kicked against the torrent pulling me away from the ship. Another wave swept my soggy form to the left and flooded my nostrils as I panted, flailing in the current. I couldn't see, couldn't breathe. Another angry bellow from the heavens and I was sucked under. Leaden skirts tangled around my legs. The blurry ship dipped and swayed, shrinking from sight.

I would die here, drowned in the same water that carried me to Barbados. Naomi told me I had been cursed by Olokum, god of the sea, as evidenced by my arrival on the island so many years ago. What if she was right?

Rain blinded my eyes as I fought to stay afloat, muscles screaming. Terror snaked through my middle as old haunting nightmares assaulted my mind. A ship breaking apart, floating wood, bloated bodies, and blood...

The old memories were nothing more than an eerie foreboding of my own demise.

A strange coldness seeped into my bones. Breath squeezed my lungs as water flooded my nose and mouth. I had nothing left. Darkness invaded and the sound of thunder and shrieking wind was eclipsed by a strange hum in my ears. My lungs burned with need as I sank below the waves. An exhalation of breath and then...

A strong arm snaked around my waist, yanking me up. Air slapped my face but a foreign panic assaulted my heart. I couldn't breathe. Was I dead?

"Avalina!" Josiah shouted from somewhere behind me. "I'm here!"

Images and colors blurred. From somewhere beyond, another masculine voice yelled, "Holland, I'm tossing you planks. They are tied to the ship. Grab them and Bones and I will pull you in!"

Men or angels? I was too confused to care.

Josiah muttered something near my ear a split second before something pounded harshly on my back. Like a brick dislodged from a crumbling wall, water shifted in my chest. I sputtered and coughed, senses snapping to life.

"Avalina!"

Craning my head, I blinked against the rain and wind blinding me. Josiah held me in his arms, dark hair plastered to his head.

"I've got you. Bones and Hurley are going to pull us to safety. Do you understand?"

I nodded dumbly, body jumping as another crack of thunder reverberated through the air. From somewhere overhead, a clanking sound just before a large plank plopped against the foaming waves. Keeping one arm around my waist, Josiah pushed me toward the chained chunk of wood. He wrapped my half-frozen fingers around a chain and looked upward.

"We're ready!"

Slowly, inch by inch, the sailors pulled us up the side of the ship and over the railing. Josiah and I fell into an exhausted heap on the slick wood of the deck.

Alive, alive, alive . . .

My nose and mouth pressed against the unforgiving deck, breath heaving, and all I could think was that I should be dead at the bottom of the ocean. Why? Why had I been spared?

Blinking back hot tears mingling with the saltwater on my face, I rolled over and grasped Josiah's hand. He was pale, chest rising and falling with heavy pants, but he was alive. He blinked slowly and winced.

His ribs. My refusal to stay inside might have cost him his life.

What kind of miserable creature was I?

Captain Blackthorne thumped to our side and frowned. "Holland, take the young miss below deck and away from this squall! We want no more souls swept into this torrent." Looking at his men, his chin jutted out. "Let down the sails! We roll with the sea or we die!"

As the sailors scurried to obey, Josiah pushed himself to his feet. I followed suit but we struggled to keep our balance in the wind shrieking through the deck. Before I could slip once again, he grabbed my hand and tugged, silently begging me to follow.

I trembled as he led me to my berth. I coughed over and over again, as if my lungs would never be free of the ocean's grip. But I was no longer worried for myself. My concern was for Josiah. Had my disobedience caused him irreparable harm?

I should be dead. Yet my quaking limbs and chattering teeth told me I was very much alive.

Once we reached the room, Josiah yanked the scratchy blanket from my bed before wrapping it around my dripping, soggy form. Water puddled around both of our feet.

"Thank you." I nodded toward his blanket neatly folded in the corner. "You need to dry off too."

Walking slowly, he bent over with a grimace and grabbed the covering, rubbing it first against his hair before letting it settle around his shoulders. I watched his measured movements, throat clamping. What if he had died trying to save me? I wasn't worth it. If he only knew what I had done...

Tears scraped my chest and a sob escaped.

Josiah stilled as he stared at me. "What's wrong?"

"I'm so sorry." A lump lodged in my throat, choking off my words. "I almost died. And you..." Shuddering against the tears, I shook my head. "You almost perished too."

"Hey, easy now." He shuffled to my side and squeezed my shoulder. "The Almighty was looking over us."

Chin quivering, I looked away. His words made no sense. How could I make him understand?

"I should have obeyed."

An intense sadness swept over the handsome planes of his face. "I'm not your master, Avalina. You don't owe me obedience. I only wished to keep you safe."

"You say the Almighty was looking over us, but we nearly perished." I stared into his face, blinking rapidly. "Who is this Almighty you speak of? And it's not just that we almost perished. I deserved to die."

He frowned. "What do you mean?"

I let my eyes slide shut at his probing stare. "I'm not who you think I am."

A line pinched between his brows. "Come. Sit. We can figure this out."

"No." I shook my head, pulling away from his touch. "I—I ... " But the words wouldn't come. I couldn't tell him what I'd done to Master Cyrene. It was too horrid.

But Josiah stared at me, waiting. I must give some reason for my outburst. "Naomi always told me I was a witch, cursed by Olokum, god of the sea. That's the reason I arrived on Barbados, spit out on land and accursed with the inability to speak when required." I nodded my head toward the deck, bracing my feet when the ship canted sharply to the left. "My presence aboard *Neptune's Tide* has angered him. I've brought my curse down on all of you!"

True, but only partially. There was so much more I needed to say.

"Avalina"—Josiah cupped my blanket-covered shoulders with his hands—"there is no Olokum."

I swallowed. "How do you know?"

"Because of this." Josiah turned from me and reached for his knapsack, pulling a worn book from its insides. "The Bible teaches us what we need to know of such things." A gentle smile tugged his mouth. "There is no god of the sea, or of land, or the sun, or moon. There is only Jehovah, the Creator of all."

"You sound like Matias." Shivering, I tucked the blanket tighter around my shoulders. "He believed in only one god."

"Jehovah is not a figure made by man, and He's not one of many gods. He is *the* God."

Did it matter? Whether one all-powerful Creator, or Olokum, I had to pay for my crime. This storm was vengeance for the wrong I'd done.

"Remember the words I wrote for you?"

I let my eyes slide shut, trying to remember the phrase exactly. "'In the beginning, God created the heavens and the earth.'"

Josiah nodded. "Perfect. Those words came from this book. Let me show you." He flipped to the first page and pointed to squiggles on the top row. "Jehovah is another name for God."

"But this means nothing to me if I can't understand what the figures mean."

He stilled, blinking slowly. "Of course. I'd forgotten you can't read." He straightened, his dark eyes twinkling with mischief. "That's easy enough to remedy. I'll teach you."

I sucked in a breath. "Teach me?" He would show me the mysteries inside this book?

"Would you like to learn?"

"Oh yes!" I grasped his hand, then yanked my own away. In my excitement, I was too forward but he merely chuckled.

"We'll wait until this storm abates, then get to work. I have a feeling you'll run circles around me."

I scoffed and bit my lip. "I fear my mind will be too dull to be taught."

Josiah's smile dipped as he reached out to stroke my chin with his thumb. "That is something that could never be said about you. You hold the intelligence of a thousand libraries in your eyes." He let his fingers drop to his side. "And I can't wait to see you realize it."

CHAPTER 22

After the storm abated, leaving a weary crew in its wake, Josiah helped the men put the ship back to rights, each movement agony. If his ribs weren't broken before, they certainly were now. Standing in Captain Blackthorne's personal quarters, he rubbed his side and thanked the captain for the fresh, dry blankets he'd provided, as well as parchment paper, the stub of a pencil, and a new candle in a tin holder.

As he descended into the sleeping quarters of the ship, he berated himself for assuming Avalina viewed the world as he did. Foolish of him. Of course, she had little or no knowledge of the Scriptures, save whatever Matias had taught her. With no way to read, and inundated with the mystic beliefs of those on the island, the idea of the Almighty must be as foreign as snow in Barbados.

He blew out a tight breath as the ship creaked softly in the still waters. How could he have thought to marry her? Scripture was clear. *Be not unequally yoked.* Yet could Providence not yet work a miracle in her heart, despite a union born out of necessity?

Easy, Josiah. These were dangerous grounds he now tread. Purposely disobeying God and expecting His blessings would lead to nothing but heartache. But how to protect her and still maintain his distance? He had inadvertently thrust her into a strange new world with little thought of the repercussions.

And the responsibility weighed heavy on his shoulders.

Forgive me, Lord, for making a mess of this. I sought only to give her freedom.

And what would he do if he arrived home with a strange woman in tow, and no wife? He swallowed. If George Holland made it home at all, and survived the insurrection, his father would rage and no doubt force Josiah's marriage to a spoiled, pampered debutante. Mother and her friends would call Avalina a heathen, unfit for society. He cringed at the very thought. An imaginary noose tightened around his neck. He no longer wanted to be part of his family's world. Avalina was his way out of their choking hold.

Perhaps his motives in helping her escape were not completely as altruistic as he'd once imagined them to be.

Pushing the door open, he forced a smile he didn't feel as she looked up at his arrival. Sitting on the edge of the berth, her hair cascading in a riot of damp curls over her shoulder and wrapped in a dark blanket, she looked ... right.

He swallowed and shut the door behind him with a soft click. *Father, help me ...*

Setting the items on the edge of the berth, he straightened and wiped his hands down his damp trousers. "Captain Blackthorne gave us some dry blankets, as well as paper, pencil, and a fresh light."

"That was kind of him."

He grunted and looked around the small space. No chairs, no table. And it was *not* a good idea to sit on the bed. He tugged the collar of his shirt and eased onto the floor, sitting cross-legged before spreading the items around him. Using a fresh matchstick the captain had set in the cup of the candle holder, he struck it against the floorboard and tapped the flame against the candle wick. It flared to life with a sizzle. The room glowed with honey. Avalina's soggy skirts rustled ever so slightly as she slid from the bed and scooted to his side. When her shoulders brushed his, shivers of awareness shot through his arm. What a strange malady their relationship was. He both yearned for her presence and wanted to flee in terror at the same time.

Clearing his throat, he grabbed the pencil and sketched out the clean lines of an *A*. "It will take time and practice to learn how to read. I've never taught anyone before, so if I say something confusing, please let me know."

Avalina nodded but made no comment.

"This is an *A*. A short *A* makes an 'aah' sound. Like in the word *apple*."

Her brow furrowed. "What do you mean by a short *A*?"

"Ah." He smiled. "I got ahead of myself. Most vowels have both a long and short sound. I'll teach you more about that later. For now, it's best to learn *A* either sounds like 'aah,' or it says its own name."

"*A*." Avalina bit her lip and traced the lines with her finger.

"Here." He held the stub of a pencil toward her. "You try to write it."

She hesitantly took the pencil and copied the pattern with clean strokes before glancing up at him with excitement pooling in her expression. "I did it." Never had he seen such pure joy in another's eyes. How fortunate he was to have received an education…and how bereft Avalina's life.

"Excellent." He met her gaze and offered a smile. "And guess what? That's also the first letter of your name."

She sucked in a breath and her lips curved into a smile so wide, his chest ached. "Please teach me more."

He chuckled. "I doubt we'll get to all twenty-six letters today."

But he was wrong. Avalina proved to be extremely intelligent, digesting the information nearly as quickly as it came. In the space of an hour, she had learned the entire upper-case alphabet, how to write her name, and three other short words.

"I feel as if the entire world is laid out before me for the first time."

Josiah relaxed, propping one elbow on his knee. "That's what writing, reading, and books do. At first it seems nothing more than squiggles and random marks, but then you learn to read and you connect to the mind and heart of the author. Time disappears. We can read the philosophies of Aristotle, or climb into the thoughts of great inventors like DaVinci. It binds together people of all races, creeds, and ages."

"What a lovely thought." Avalina hugged her knees to her chest, the damp blanket sagging from her shoulders. "Ever since I was little, I would sneak into Master's library and thumb through the books, wondering how to unlock what was inside." A slight breath escaped from between her lips. "Standing on the precipice of knowing is exhilarating."

Josiah nodded and reached for his Bible. "And the best is yet to come."

"Jehovah's book?"

He smiled. "The wisdom of the ages is contained inside. It's a love letter from God Almighty to His creation. It's filled with history, mystery, love, adventure, intrigue, prophecy, and so much more."

Avalina leaned closer with a pleading glance. "Where does it speak of the angry seas? Where does this Jehovah mention Olokum, god of the sea?"

Was that a frisson of fear he detected in the timbre of her voice? "Olokum is never mentioned by name, but there are many accounts of the Almighty denouncing the gods created by man."

Her gaze dropped to her skirt-covered knees. "Are there any times when your God used a storm to destroy a person?"

What was she saying, or rather, *not* saying? Pushing the query aside, he nodded and flipped through the onion-skin pages. "Well, not *destroy* a person, but He does use natural disasters to work His will in the lives of men. Jonah comes to mind. He was a prophet and when God told him to travel to Nineveh and warn the people there about their need to turn away from the wrong they were do-ing, Jonah instead ran away."

Slowly, he read the entire book to her, running his finger over each word so she could catch the rhythm of the written language. The longer he read, the more she curled in on herself, shoulders slumping, head lowering. Strange, that.

When he closed the Bible, she looked away. "I think I've learned enough for one day. Thank you."

Something troubled her, that was for sure and certain. And un-doubtedly her body still suffered the fatigue of escape and battling the storm. Restlessness emanated from her form. The best thing he could do now was let her rest.

He slowly rose and held out the Bible to her. "Here. Feel free to take it. I know there's not much you can read yet, but you might be surprised. If nothing else, it will allow you to practice what you've learned."

Nodding, she grasped the volume, but as he turned away to leave, he witnessed her push the book as far away from herself as possible.

Condemned. Condemned. Condemned.

The words pounded my brain as relentlessly as a clock. How was it possible to swing from the greatest of elations to the deepest dread all in the space of an hour?

Drawing the strange markings, learning letter names, and mim-icking their sounds had dulled my mind to the danger lurking for me. I had angered Josiah's God. Indeed, it was not Olokum's venge-ance that had nearly lashed apart the ship, but Jehovah's.

In the silence of the berth, I swallowed loudly and crept to the bed, crawling between the covers, as if I could hide from the One who had captured the prophet Jonah by a great fish. Josiah had said his God had done so to capture Jonah's attention, not as some form of retribution, yet I found no solace in his insistence. Trapped in the innards of a sea monster—with no light, no sound but the gurgling of digestive juices—sounded like the worst kind of punishment.

And if this same God was willing to inflict pain on one of his own, how much more would He do to me...a murderer?

CHAPTER 23

April 24, 1816
San Juan, Puerto Rico

"Land ho!"

Bones shouted the sighting from his perch in the crow's nest. Josiah looked up from his work of untangling fishing nets to peer at the island growing closer with each minute. Captain Blackthorne swaggered across the deck and crossed his arms with a satisfied smile. "Ah, Puerto Rico. Land of delight."

Josiah frowned and dropped the nets near his feet. "Sir, why do we sail so close to the island?"

The captain smirked. "It's hard to gain its ports without nearing its shores, aye?"

"We're stopping in Puerto Rico?"

"For a day's span only. Enough time to do some trading, let the men enjoy a respite. Then we set our sights on South Carolina."

Josiah bit back a groan. The letter from Najaf burned his pocket. And the human he was to smuggle to Edward Pickering ... how was he to accomplish all these things with a journey that stretched on endlessly? He longed for nothing more than to arrive in the States and be done with his piece of ... well, whatever it was he was involved in.

As if the captain could read his troubled thoughts, Blackthorne motioned for Josiah to follow him below deck. "Come. It's past time you met someone."

Stepping lightly through the dark corridors, they skirted the crew's quarters and the capstan before plunging farther inside the belly of the ship. Slocum hurled epithets as they passed him locked inside a large cell. A plate of breakfast was overturned on the floor inside. The captain paid him no mind as he continued on toward a large room filled with cargo. Slocum's curses melted away as the two men crossed the large space, picking their way between barrels of spirits, rich Caribbean coffee, and flour. Crates were stacked in tall columns, some of them marked with stamps that read *silks*, others that bore the words *cinnamon, turmeric, tea,* and *cocoa".* Josiah's mouth watered at the rich smells permeating the dank space.

He ran his finger over the top of a hogshead of molasses. "If I were captain, I would be tempted to visit the stores often and sample the quality of the merchandise."

Captain Blackthorne patted a particularly fat barrel and chuckled. "Do not be fooled by some of the stamps. A smuggler's life is a series of illusions. This barrel of pickles actually contains Spanish wine."

Tucking the bit of information away, Josiah shadowed the captain to a deep shelf stuffed with baskets of potatoes, carrots, butternut squash, and beans. Flipping a latch to the right of the shelf, the captain tugged the storage shelf toward himself, revealing a hollowed room behind. Looking back at Josiah, he wordlessly nodded and ducked underneath the frame to enter, Josiah on his heels.

The hidden room was no bigger than a closet but a pallet covered with a tattered quilt was tucked in the corner. The soft glow of a lantern illuminated the space. A thick stack of books rested on the floor, along with a tin plate of half-eaten food and a bucket of water.

A tall, muscled man with gleaming mahogany skin stared at them from where he sat against the wall, the light from the flickering lantern casting oscillating shadows on his face. One knee was bent, his bare arms relaxed—one carelessly slung over his knee, the other resting on his lap.

Captain Blackthorne nodded. "How fair you, Esco?"

"Well enough." The Caribbean lilt of his baritone was both easy and intimidating. "Last night's storm was enough to make a grown man weep."

"Did you weep?" Josiah took his measure.

A muscle hardened in Esco's whiskered jaw. "I never weep."

Tough as nails, this fellow was. The captain widened his stance. "Esco, this is Josiah Holland. He will be taking you to Edward Pickering once we reach the States."

Esco looked Josiah up and down, doubt folding his brow. "Does he know what he's doing?"

Josiah grinned. He liked this Esco fellow. He knew his own mind.

"I have had very little experience but I did recently smuggle an enslaved woman from Azaka Mede onto this ship."

Esco grunted. "Easy enough to slip through the authorities' fingers during a rebellion. Much harder when there's no chaos to cover the sound of your running feet."

Josiah lifted his chin. "How did you escape?"

Esco pursed his lips, his accent a slow, rollicking drawl. "Najaf knows what he's doing. He set the plans in motion with Bussa and the rest. A master's primary concern is not keeping an eye on his people when he fears for his own life."

"True enough."

Esco narrowed his eyes. "And if there is no chaos to hide our path to Pickering?"

Josiah crossed his arms. "Then we make our own."

Silence stretched one second. Two. Esco burst into a melodic laugh and shook his finger in the air, white teeth flashing.

"You and I ... we will do just fine."

Blackthorne arched a brow. "We will soon stop in Puerto Rico for a day's time. I will be trading. Anything you'd like?"

"Maybe another book or two." He nodded toward the stack of volumes near his cot. "Read each of these three times through already."

Josiah startled. "You can read?"

"Taught by my mother. When she was child, she fanned the master's children as they were educated by their tutor. She listened, watched. Sharp, she is. Taught me everything she knew."

"I think you'll succeed as a free man."

The slightest hint of a smile tugged Esco's mouth. "I think so too."

Captain Blackthorne grunted. "Feel free to grab a bit of air tonight. The crew will be filling their cups in San Juan, enjoying the revelry of Festival de las Flores."

Glancing to the captain, Josiah frowned. "What is that?"

"Puerto Rico's flower festival. Tree farmers and growers from all over the island come together to celebrate the arrival of spring. Flowers are hung from every available post. There is music, dancing, and food."

Perhaps Avalina would enjoy the sights and sounds. If nothing else, it would enable her to see the traditions of a new place and get her mind off all she'd lost.

Captain Blackthorne tipped the edge of his hat to Esco. "I'll check on you later tonight, then."

Esco frowned. "I'll not be stepping foot on deck, sir. Not with that fool prisoner still in shackles. He sees me, and he'll tell everyone about how you smuggled me to the States."

Blackthorne harrumphed. "Most of the crew knows what we do. He cannot accuse me without implicating himself."

Esco leveled the captain with a hard stare. "I've heard his rants and curses for two days now. Take my advice, sir. Tell that prisoner nothing, or you'll soon see yourself dangling from a hangman's noose."

"Be thou my vision, O Lord of my heart. Naught be all else to me, save that Thou art…"

The soft voice crested and dipped like waves lapping the shore. The face was shrouded in shadows, nothing more than a mist, but she was so close, I could nearly touch the woman's cheek. I reached out and—

My eyes flew open.

Another dream. Another nameless voice, expressionless face, yet the recurring phantom never failed to soothe my heart. This mystery lady was my home. That was the only way to describe it.

Rubbing my bleary eyes, I clutched the scratchy blanket to my chest and lifted myself on one elbow.

Then startled.

Josiah was gone. His blanket was neatly folded into a square in the corner. The lantern hanging on the wall clicked softly with the creak of the ship, its flame flickering weakly. With no window, it was impossible to tell the time of day from inside the room. Where could he be?

My stomach growled with need and I swung my feet over the side of the berth, each muscle screaming in protest. The past few days had finally caught up with me.

I searched through Josiah's knapsack for a brush and hastily smoothed the snarls from my hair before plaiting it into a single braid.

Snatching the blanket from the berth, I wrapped it around my shoulders to serve as my warmth from the ocean's gale winds. Pushing the protesting door open, I made my way through the shadowy corridor, my steps uneven as the ship tilted to and fro. When bright light appeared, I hastened forward, my skin prickling. I never had cared for the dark.

Musty air gave way to the fresh brine of ocean life as I stepped onto the deck. The sun peeked high overhead amid clouds as fluffy as freshly brushed cotton. All traces of last night's terror were wiped clean. Puerto Rico loomed just ahead.

I moved to the rails and gripped the worn wood with one hand, tightening my makeshift shawl with the other.

Sailors scurried here and there, all of them engrossed in a job of some sort—winding rope, hauling supplies, scrubbing the deck. I sensed their curious stares but ignored them. Over the open mouth of sea, I waited, studying the waves. With no need to speak, there was naught to do but listen. The roars of thundering foam, the swish of waves breaking against the lumbering boat, the snap of sails—all of it like music, yet who was creating it?

A mystery. The same as the comforting cadence of the woman singing in my dreams night after night. The curiosity called to me, yet, just like the dream, it eluded my grasp.

Reaching for the compass tucked in my pocket, I pulled it out and held it aloft. The dial spun in dizzying circles just before the needle wobbled, its tip hovering over a marking. A growl ripped my throat as I snapped it shut and dropped it back in my pocket. Why was everything a practice in vexation?

Yesterday's joy at learning to read had been eclipsed by a fear I had yet to shake. Would that one horrid moment in the master's study forever ruin the freedom looming before me?

The pebbly voice of Captain Blackthorne pierced the morning quiet.

"Set sail for San Juan, mates. A night of trading and revelry await all who obey!"

A cheer rose from the men as the captain set their course. Sails were adjusted, and the men hustled to their tasks. As Blackthorne conferred with his first mate, I studied the deckhands unencumbered. A thick fellow with bulging arms coiled a length of rope over his shoulder and burst into song. "Haul on the bow'lin, the bow'lin haul, aye!"

The sailors responded as one to the call—the sailor in the crow's nest high above, even the deckhands unknotting rope—each movement filled with purpose, some kind of unspoken communication rippling between them.

In response, the crew sang, "Haul on! Haul on!" Each sailor pulled on the lines as if working as one, a machine of spirit and strength, adding their shouts to "Haul!"

"Boney was a warrior."

The crew called back, "Way, hey, ya!"

Straining, pulling, and tightening . . . a majestic dance between shanty man and crew, the crew and the ship, the ship and the sea.

It was a beautiful language all its own.

The rhythm, the melody . . . all of it lodged in my mind, begging to bubble past my lips as their song drifted by like a jaunty wind.

"Come all ye young fellows that follow the sea, hay-hay, blow the man down . . . "

A chuckle sounded behind me. I whirled, my pulse a staccato, but it eased by measures when I realized it was only the captain.

"Morning, lass. Bonny day, isn't it?"

I nodded and turned my focus to the sea. I wasn't sure if I trusted this grizzled man or not. I sensed a darkness in him, like a coiled snake, yet lines of kindness and wisdom framed his eyes. Wisdom only acquired through hard living.

"Master Holland is below deck, grabbing both of ye a bit of bread and cheese."

My stomach growled on cue and the old sailor smiled, revealing a row of crooked yellow teeth.

"We do not have the finest food on board, but there be plenty. Eat your fill, lass." He turned his gaze to mine and held fast, eyes narrowing ever so slightly. "Aye, it's a hard time of it ye've had, ain't so?" His voice was soft.

I fumbled for some kind of response. Oh, why did my tongue never break free when needed? Swallowing hard, I nodded.

Captain Blackthorne leaned close, his voice a whisper. "Ye're safe here, lass. No harm will come to ye. And I know. I was once enslaved too."

I sucked in a breath at his blunt admission. The captain awkwardly patted my shoulder and sauntered away. I pulled the blankets tighter around my neck. It was not from the cold breeze. For the first time in my recollection, it was as if someone could see me. The real me.

And I was terrified.

CHAPTER 24

April 24, 1816
San Juan, Puerto Rico

Only a storm the magnitude of the one that had nearly torn them apart could have expedited their journey to such an extent. Was it chance, or the hand of Providence?

Josiah gazed into the blue sky dotted with cotton clouds. *Neptune's Tide* had borne the strain of the tempest admirably, but the ship now had scars as its legacy. The two largest sails were torn, hastily patched by the sailors. A handful of tools had washed overboard in the same carnivorous wave that had swept Avalina from the deck. But Captain Blackthorne did not seem perturbed by the loss. Merely anxious to set foot on the approaching island.

The grizzled man squinted through a spyglass as land loomed larger. From this distance, Josiah could see the thick palms lining the shore, and the stone buildings rising above, crammed together like rows of fish at a market.

Captain Blackthorne sighed with a smile and tucked the spyglass into the pocket of his coat. "Puerto Rico. The Rich Port." He cast Josiah a sidelong glance. "That's what it means in Spanish."

"It is a lucrative island, then?"

"Some would say so." A gust of briny wind flapped the edge of the captain's hat. "Once valuable for its gold, though it was long ago mined away by governors like Ponce de Leon." The captain braced his roughened fingers around the railing and leaned forward, lips pursed. "Still, it boasts many resources: tobacco, coffee, and sugar. Not to mention its exquisite beauty."

"Indeed." Josiah crossed his arms, bracing his feet as a sailor shouted instructions behind him. "And what of the people?"

The captain's crooked teeth flashed from a space in his beard. "Kind and generous."

"You know some of them well?"

The captain chuckled. "Quite well. My wife is here, waiting just over there." He pointed to a spot on the western part of the shore. "Marta." His voice was soft when he spoke her name.

"I didn't know you were married."

"Ah, my Marta doesn't like the sea. Gets sick every time she sets foot on deck. We understand each other. She knows how the water beckons me, and I know how deeply the island calls her. With every passage, I make port in Puerto Rico to see her." He grunted and fixed Josiah with a hard stare. "Women have a way of getting into your blood, aye?"

Swallowing, Josiah nodded. That was certainly true of Avalina. Everything had changed the moment he laid eyes on her. Why?

"The only one I could give up the sea for is my wife. She has not asked it of me yet, but when she does, I'll acquiesce."

"What would you do instead?"

Shrugging, the captain turned his gaze back to the island. "Fish. Build small vessels for the locals. There is always something to do. Some new adventure to explore. A life of routine never did suit me. Too much wild in my blood, I reckon."

Is that why the thought of overseeing Father's plantation didn't suit? The sameness, the routine, the monotony? Josiah's life would be nothing but harvest and production, accounting ledgers and the perpetual changing of seasons.

His stomach knotted. Where was Father, anyway? Still hiding in the closet at Azaka Mede? Or was he even now racing his way in another vessel toward Charleston? Surely not dead. Josiah brushed aside the worry. George Holland was too stubborn to go down without a fight.

Either way, a reckoning was coming and Josiah must brace himself for the maelstrom that would ensue.

Arriving home with Avalina would be shock enough. Informing his father he wanted no part of running the plantation? Unthinkable.

Josiah jolted when the captain bellowed, "Prepare for arrival in San Juan! No slackers or I'll see you off *Neptune's Tide* once we reach port."

As the men scrambled to obey, Blackthorne grunted and spoke for Josiah's ears alone. "After I see to purchasing new material for sails, and replenish the sugar I had intended to buy in Barbados, I'll visit my wife." He narrowed his gaze at Josiah. "Buy some reading materials for Esco." Pulling some coinage from his pocket, he pushed it into Josiah's hands.

"Yes, sir." He looked down at his filthy clothes, grimy from days aboard ship. "I'll purchase some new clothes for Avalina and myself as well. It won't do to arrive home looking like we've been sailing with a bunch of pirates."

Blackthorne laughed heartily and slapped Josiah on the back. "Sorry I'll be to see you depart, young Holland. I could use a good sailor like you."

"I'm flattered, sir, but my destiny lies somewhere beyond."

Just where or what that destiny was, Josiah could not fathom.

How strange to be strolling through the markets, not as a slave, but as a free woman.

I tucked myself closer to Josiah's side as we picked our way past the hawkers and farmers crowding San Juan's local market. The odor of fish mingled with the scent of steamed *pasteles* in banana leaves, and the spicy aroma of peppers. Fruits and vegetables of every shape and size were crowded onto carts, waiting to be purchased, and traders called out to those in the street, holding out fabrics of crimson, purple, and deep blue for inspection. Both the wealthy and the poor haggled over prices with vendors. I gawked at a woman with skin the color of cinnamon who wore a white dress with sleeves so large and puffed, I was certain she might float away like a paper lantern.

"Pretty lady, pretty lady!"

A vendor to my right beckoned me, an orange piece of glazed pottery in his hands.

"Come see! Pottery handed down from Ponce de Leon himself! You need, yes?"

Biting my lip, I shook my head no. At the man's crestfallen expression, Josiah chuckled low near my ear.

"Good choice."

I looked into his face and he winked. My stomach fluttered. He nodded in the direction of the pushy vendor, who was now plying his wares to another woman.

"See his hands? They are covered with clay. No doubt he is the potter and is trying to sell his pieces for more than they're worth."

A bird squawked overhead, dipping low. A flash of sapphire caught my gaze as it flew away, reminding me of the last brilliant feather Matias had given me. A pang of sadness squeezed my chest. What was he doing at this moment? Had the fighting ceased? Surely nothing would be the same at Azaka Mede with Master Cyrene dead.

Shivering, I hugged my arms to my torso.

Witnessing my reaction, Josiah cupped my elbow, a concerned expression shadowing his face. "We need to get you better clothes."

"No." I shook my head. "I'm fine."

A smile tipped his mouth. "I'll not drag you to South Carolina wearing a single shabby gown."

Heat crept up the back of my neck and bloomed in my cheeks. Did I look so disreputable? He was ashamed of me. He must be. I wanted to make him proud, but how could I with no money to purchase something new?

"Come. Let's try that shop just ahead."

He pulled me along, his hand gentle but firm on my elbow, and I swallowed. Why did he not understand?

Before I could protest, a bell rang overhead as we pushed the door open. A woman with dark hair, and sleeves more puffed than the woman in the market, scolded a young girl in rapid-fire Spanish. Upon seeing us, she stopped and shooed the girl away before turning to Josiah with a smile. "You shop here, yes?"

"*Si* " Josiah smiled and tugged me forward. "We need some new dresses and"—his neck splotched crimson—"whatever other things ladies need."

The matron eyed my attire critically and clucked her tongue. "*Esto no esta bien.*" Shaking her head, she circled me, lifting the corner of my hem with a scowl. "*Puedo hacerlo mejor.*"

I wasn't sure what she meant, but judging by her rigid posture and dark glances at my tattered gown, it wasn't good.

"Come, come." She motioned me toward the back of the shop and pushed me into a small closet. What was going on? Before I could blink, three gowns were tossed over the top of the dressing screen. "You put on. Put on and I see."

Put them on? These dresses of silk and lace? I was far too dirty to even touch the delicate fabrics, much less slip them over my body. And I had no way to pay for them. Yet arguing with the intimidating woman would not be well received.

Wincing, I slipped off my old gown and it puddled around my feet. I could hear Josiah's masculine voice as he chatted with the matron, who alternated between broken English and a smattering of Spanish. When I donned the gown of blue silk, I stepped from behind the screen and cleared my throat.

Despite the hard fist tightening my middle, I couldn't help but finger the soft silk. It was…heaven. The neckline dipped lower than I was accustomed to, but it was not immodest with its high waistline and lace-trimmed hem.

Upon seeing me, the woman clapped her hands in delight. "*Es bueno! Muy bonita!* Now, go"—she shooed me into the closet once more—"you wear the green."

The green gown. I understood.

The afternoon passed in a rapid blur of fittings, colors, fabrics, slippers, brushes, combs, and white lacy undergarments. Never had I been so scolded, or had so many items shoved into my hands. I giggled to myself. Baara and this bossy woman could never have existed in the same house without a fight ensuing.

But how could I possibly help her understand I had no way to pay for the luxuries? Shame burned my cheeks. And Josiah would no longer want me to meet his family if I didn't find a way.

I could sell her the compass he'd given me but as soon as the thought flitted through my mind, I batted it away. I couldn't. For some reason, it meant too much.

After the woman unmercifully brushed my hair, she jabbed hairpins into the mass of curls, pulling them from my neck. I was now in a lavender gown of shimmering organza with short sleeves and small flowers embroidered around the hem. I stepped into the slippers she pushed in front of my feet and clapped her hands.

"Mister Yosiah!" She spoke his name with a strange lilt. "Come and see."

I held my breath as Josiah stepped into view. His expression was ...

Stunned.

I swallowed the lump in my throat but could not pull my gaze from his. A wide smile stretched his mouth and his eyes ... they burned with an intensity that caused heat to mount in my belly.

"Avalina, you are beautiful."

His whisper was hushed, almost reverent. I shook my head, eyes burning.

He turned to the matron. "I need to speak with her alone."

A frown deepened the lines around her mouth, but she nodded curtly and left us.

I blinked away the moisture stinging my eyes. "I can't do this."

He tilted his head. "Why not?"

"I have no way to pay. The prices, the amount of what she had me try on ... " I winced. "All I have of worth is the compass you gave me and I would rather dress in rags than give it away." I heaved a deep breath. There. I'd spoken my mind. If he was ashamed of me, so be it.

Instead of the anger I expected, he laughed. Did he think this was funny? Heat billowed, rising in my chest. "I don't think it's funny at all. Why, I—"

Forcing his mirth under control, he cupped my shoulders, but the grin didn't leave his face. "I'm paying for this. Not you. I don't expect you to sell what little you have. A gift is a gift. It should never be taken back and traded away."

Confusion tugged. "So you're doing all this because ... "

His gaze drifted to the floor before connecting with mine once again, and my toes curled. "Because I want to."

There was something he wasn't saying. In truth, I wasn't sure I wanted him to.

"I'll repay you."

His hands slid from mine as he sighed. "Gifts don't come with the intention of payment."

I fell silent. I couldn't speak a correct word in his presence. What man was this, who gave so generously without thought of recompense?

Strange, but then again, wasn't that why I'd trusted him enough to leave with him?

"I—thank you."

A muscle hardened in his jaw. "Harding should have provided all these things for you. I'm simply righting his abundance of wrongs."

Something about the admission rang hollow. I didn't understand the ache in my chest at his words. "Whatever the reason, I owe you much."

The matron bustled back and the pinched line between Josiah's brows eased. "Thank you for your help. We will purchase everything you chose."

I gasped. Everything?

A glint of greed lit her dark eyes but she smiled, much like a cat when cornering a mouse. "And for you, sir?"

He straightened. "I have already chosen clothes for myself. Along with a shaving kit." Turning to Avalina, he rubbed his shadowed jaw. "I suppose I'll have to make myself presentable again when we arrive in the States."

I looked away. In truth, I rather enjoyed the dark stubble. It gave him an untamed look that matched his adventurous heart.

But such things were not fit to say. He was not mine.

And why did such an admission nettle?

I straightened my shoulders, steeling my resolve. I needed no one. Hadn't Master Cyrene already taught me the folly of being controlled by another? Shuddering, I crossed my arms, hugging them to my chest.

Soon we would arrive in America and I would learn to stand on my own two feet. I would do it, or die trying.

CHAPTER 25

Josiah patted his stomach and groaned. Never had he eaten so much.

After purchasing their new clothes, and tossing the ratty ones into Senora Rosa's rubbish bin, Josiah had explored San Juan with Avalina, feasting on *rellenos de papas*, *arroz con gandules*, bananas, roasted coconut, and papaya. He was close to bursting.

All over San Juan, locals hung streamers and clusters of flowers from balconies and buildings. With dusk sweeping in, shrouding the city in the cloak of night, paper lanterns lined the streets, the soft glow from their honeyed light casting twinkling markers up and down the cobbled roads. Musicians plucked guitars and laughter peppered the night air as the city prepared to celebrate the Festival of Flowers. The sweet fragrance of purple camas, hooked spur violets, and chocolate lilies filled the air.

Despite the hum of excitement flooding the streets, Avalina seemed distant. Quiet, even for her. Had he shamed her by paying for her clothes? He'd not meant to make her feel awkward, but there was no help for it. She could not achieve a fresh start and a new life wearing the garb of a house slave.

Or was he merely using the excuse because he was embarrassed to bring her before his mother?

The thought nagged like a burr. Josiah stared absently over the throng of people gathering in the city square. Surely he wasn't so weak of virtue ... was he?

Avalina shifted near his side and he shot her a sideways glance. There was certainly no reason for shame in her appearance. Since she'd donned her new attire, it was all he could do to drag his eyes away. She was stunning... like a crimson hibiscus in bloom.

Be ye not unequally yoked...

The command was a constant reminder. He fisted his hands at his sides. He never should have suggested marriage. She'd said nothing of his offer and he would not bring it up. His job was to see her properly settled in the States. How that would come to be, he had no idea. There were few options for a woman alone with no education. She could always seek employment as a maid if he wrote her a reference, but after coming from such a demeaning existence only to be thrust into it once more, well, Josiah chafed at the thought. She deserved more than scrubbing fireplaces and emptying chamber pots.

Dash it all, why did he care so much anyway? Perhaps his father was right. He was too soft-hearted to be of good to anyone.

Cheers rose from the crowd as a broad-shouldered man with a loose white shirt stepped into the middle of the square. He carried a *guitarra* in his hand as his voice boomed over the gathered crowd.

"*Bienvenido a el Carnival de Flores!*"

Cheers erupted. Avalina leaned close to his ear and whispered, "What is he saying?"

Warmth tickled his neck from her soft exhalation. "Uh, something about the Festival of Flowers." His Spanish was rudimentary at best. "I'm sorry. I can only pick up a smattering of words in Spanish."

"That's all right." Her eyes glowed as she watched the boisterous man. "I can tell much just by watching."

Josiah inhaled her sweet scent of jasmine. Or was the fragrance from the blossoms hanging overhead? He couldn't tell. She slid her hand into the crook of his arm. His muscles tightened in response.

"*Tiempo para bailar!*"

At the raucous shouts rising, Josiah pulled Avalina over to the shelter of the nearest building as men and women, boys and girls whooped in delight. Musicians plucked the opening strains of a lively song. The thud of drums, the jingle of tambourines, the steady *SHH-shh, SHH-shh* of maracas ... even the brassy call of the *trumpetas* mingled into a glorious harmony. The crowd split into groups and danced in dizzying circles with laughter as they clapped to the beat.

Strain melted from Josiah's shoulders. The past week had been naught but a blur. Too much change. Too much danger. He would etch this moment in his mind as a reprieve from the chaos.

He glanced down to the girl at his side—no, *woman*—as she watched the people of San Juan celebrating. Avalina's beauty and spirit were equal to none. And despite her humble life in Barbados, she held herself with a quiet dignity that surpassed the debutantes and high-society matrons in Charleston. The only evidence of tension inside her was the way she bit her lower lip.

She turned to face him, eyes pleading. "Teach me."

He arched a brow. "Teach you what?"

"How to dance."

Josiah chuckled. "If you remember, you and I danced once before at Azaka Mede. The night of the harvest celebration."

She glanced away, her expression wistful as she studied a woman spinning in a tight circle, her flowing red skirt swirling around her ankles. "I only know how to take simple steps back and forth." Her gaze flicked back to Josiah's and held fast. "You know the dances and their steps, don't you?"

"I do, at least the ones from South Carolina, but—"

"Please?"

She had asked for so little. How could he deny her?

With a slow nod, he tugged her into the bevy of dancers, a strange dread constricting his chest. Why couldn't he shake the thought that this was a bad idea?

"For a fast song like this, we need only clasp hands like so." He grasped her slim fingers in his and sparks shot up his arm. Did she sense it too? Clearing his throat, he continued. "I—ah, then we dip low to the ground as we step to our right." She moved her body in the opposite direction and he chuckled. "Sorry. My right, your left."

Her brows knit in concentration. "Then we tilt back and rise as we shift our weight to the other foot." He held tight to her hands as they dipped and straightened, dipped and straightened. "Good."

Avalina beamed into his face and his mouth dried to cotton. *Concentrate...*

"Now step and repeat. Dip and rise. Step. Dip and rise."

Before he could count to ten, they were swept into the throng of revelers. After each count of eight, he grasped her right hand and spun her in a circle. A giggle burst from her lips and he startled. Such a pure, joyful sound. Like silver sleighbells on a snowy day.

Avalina's eyes sparkled as they grew breathless, laughing as they caught the nuances of the Puerto Rican dance. The steps were not so very different from the quadrilles back home. He spun her once more as the musicians struck the final notes. The crowd clapped but Josiah was frozen, his hand in the air as Avalina spun back to him, her face inches from his.

Their breathing was one, their gazes locked. It was as if some imaginary force was drawing them together, pulling, weaving...

Avalina licked her lips and his gaze fell to her mouth. From somewhere behind her, a body jostled into hers, thrusting her closer into his arms. She gasped and clasped his shoulders. Unbidden, his arms slipped around her waist. She was soft and perfect and—

Yes, this was a very bad idea indeed.

The trumpet blasted out a lone melody and Josiah released her. What was happening to him? He forced a smile he didn't feel. "There. You've learned your first official dance."

Avalina nodded and blew out a breath. He needed a distraction. Anything. Glancing around the square, he spied a booth of refreshments set up in the far corner. "Would you care for something to drink? It's a bit warm tonight."

She nodded again and he led her back to the protection of the building behind them. "Stay here and I'll return with something in a moment."

As he pushed his way through revelers and exuberant locals, he longed to kick himself.

Indeed, he was treading dangerous waters.

There was a strange light in Josiah's eyes as he held my arm high in the air. Something I hadn't noticed before. He'd stilled, watching me, waiting for... what? I wasn't sure. But the music around us faded, and I could no longer hear anything, save for my heartbeat thrumming in my ears.

In truth, I was glad he offered to fetch a drink. I was warm and for some reason, I couldn't think clearly in his presence. Not tonight anyway. What strange malady was this?

All I could think of was the one taste I'd had of his lips... and I wanted more.

Heaving a cleansing breath, I watched the villagers celebrate. A girl of no older than five danced clumsily with a chubby boy no taller than herself. Her brother? A sweetheart, perhaps? Their innocence brought a smile to my lips that was quickly replaced with a frown.

I suppose normal is whatever one grows up with, but I was quickly realizing my life at Azaka Mede had been anything but.

There was no innocence, no wonder. Only orders, obedience, and work. How different my life would be if I'd been raised as these little ones were—happy in their play, their joy, their families, and yes, even in their work.

Perhaps someday I would know what normal was.

I looked down and smoothed the lavender fabric, relishing its delicate folds. What would life be like in the States? Did all the women wear such dresses? What would be required of me? My feelings warred between elation and terror.

A hand clamped over my mouth and a thick arm snaked around my waist. Breath fled as I clawed at my faceless captor. A foul odor assaulted me as he pulled me backward. My slippered feet dug into the cobblestones but I could not break free. From somewhere behind, a door thunked open and was slammed again with a loud crack. I was thrust into a dark room. Cold alarm snaked through my middle as those same meaty fingers shoved me against a hard wall.

Strong arms pinned me in place. I opened my mouth to scream when a foul rag was shoved in my mouth.

"Ah, ah, ah, little princess."

I only managed a shrill squeak with my mouth full of the offensive fabric. A low chuckle sent shivers down my spine.

"You ruined my life, got me locked up aboard ship. Now you're going to pay."

Slocum. That vile pirate.

His enormous paws closed around my neck. I clawed at his face, his hands, my nails snagging bits of his skin, but he would not relinquish. My lungs burned. My head was thick, my neck seared with pain. The wall behind me offered no relief. I desperately grasped at my skirt, as if a weapon would materialize from thin air.

I had nothing. This would be my end.

I wheezed, my last breaths escaping as Slocum's fingers dug deeper into my flesh.

CHAPTER 26

Josiah returned to where he'd left Avalina, bearing two cups of rum punch, but she was gone. He frowned. Perhaps some fellow had asked her to dance. Jealousy seared his chest and he shoved the black thought away.

He sipped the stout drink, relishing the flavor of tart citrus on his tongue, as he scanned those in the thrum of the dance. After another minute passed without sign of Avalina, a stone lodged in his stomach.

Something was wrong.

He set the cups on the ground and half-walked, half-ran between laughing couples, children eating confections, and old people eyeing the festivities with toothless smiles. His heart pounded. It was as if she'd disappeared.

Running his fingers through his hair, he returned to their agreed-upon meeting spot and scanned the buildings behind him. *Lord, where is she?* The door to the two-story warehouse was ajar.

He shoved his way inside and his blood ran cold.

Scant moonlight from the open door illuminated a man choking a woman. Her muted scream tapered into a dull squeak as she clawed at his grip with no effect.

Avalina?

Rage enveloped him and he charged her assailant, wrenching the thick fellow backward. Avalina slumped to the ground. Josiah smashed his fist into the man's face. Something slick covered his fingers. Blood?

Yanking the stranger by his shirt collar, Josiah pounded his flesh over and over, bone against bone in the near darkness. His knuckles ached but it was nothing compared to the fury lashing his heart and numbing his mind. The attacker finally roused enough to release a bellowing shout. A fist smashed into Josiah's jaw. His head snapped backward as he fell to the ground. His ribs and head protested but he shook off the pain and pushed to his feet. The man dashed through the door and fled.

Panting, Josiah rushed after him but stopped when he saw the staggering size of the crowd that had grown over the past few minutes. There was no way he would find her attacker now.

Instead, he turned back and rushed to Avalina's side in the darkened space. As he leaned over her, she blinked rapidly, a feeble attempt to make sense of her surroundings. He cupped her face in his hands.

"Who was it, Avalina? Who attacked you?"

"Slocum." Her voice was nothing more than a croak. With tender ministrations, he cradled her in his arms and rose.

She squirmed in protest. "No, I can walk. Your ribs."

"I'm fine." He could hear the brittle tone of his own voice. White-hot anger simmered in his veins. If he got his hands on that vile scoundrel...

She slid from his grasp. "You'll draw more attention by carrying me." She winced and swallowed hard. If he'd entered a minute later...

He shuddered at the prospect.

Lifting her chin in the thin moonlight spilling through the doorway, he cringed when he spied dark red splotches marring her neck.

Slocum would pay.

He clasped her hand and led her from the dark building, the sounds of revelry now a grating dissonance in his ears.

The first order of business was to get her safely tucked inside the protection of *Neptune's Tide*.

A handful of men milled on deck of the ship as Josiah and Avalina walked aboard. One sailor rushed to Josiah, eyes wide as his gaze landed on Avalina's neck.

"What's wrong with your woman?"

Josiah didn't bother to correct his choice of words. "She was attacked during the carnival. Where is Captain Blackthorne?"

"That's what I need to tell you. He—"

But Josiah didn't wait for an explanation. He charged ahead, tossing a directive over his shoulder. "Tell him I need to speak with him immediately."

"But, Mr. Holland, the captain is—"

He was too agitated to listen or care. After leading Avalina to the berth, he shut her inside with strict instructions not to leave. When he arrived in the ship's hold, he muttered an oath under his breath.

Slocum's cell stood wide open, a bloodied sailor dabbing his head wounds with a wet rag as he sat on the floor across from the cell.

Josiah frowned. "Is that you, Erasmus?"

"Aye." The lanky fellow grimaced as he swiped at a nasty cut near his eyebrow. "The captain will have my hide, that's for sure and certain. He was going to leave Slocum at port tomorrow before we sailed." He shook his head and winced. "I can't believe he got the jump on me."

Spying a bucket of water nearby, Josiah knelt and offered to wash Erasmus's rag.

"Thank ye."

Josiah nodded and rung out the excess before gently cleaning a blotch of blood away from the sailor's ear. The ease of the chore calmed the tempest swirling in his gut. "You look like you crossed a mother bear."

Erasmus grunted. "Foolish, that's what I am. I came to bring Slocum his daily allotment of cheese and bread. Got too close. The blackguard lunged at me with a knife." He offered a one-shouldered shrug. "Guess we didn't check his boots before we locked him in. Cut the keys from my belt and made haste to escape. I went for my gun over there." He nodded toward a stack of crates to the right. "Slocum was too fast. Slashed me a couple more times and slammed me into the wall. When I woke up, he was gone. Took my weapon too."

Josiah clenched his jaw. "He attacked Avalina in San Juan."

Erasmus groaned. "All my fault, it is."

"No. Slocum chose the behavior that got him in this mess, and he chose to attack you."

The sailor's puffy features drained of color. "He didn't use my gun, did he?"

Dipping the bloody rag back into the bucket, Josiah tightened his jaw. "No. He choked her."

Erasmus winced as the rag rubbed against a particularly nasty cut.

"We fought and he escaped."

"I thought your jaw looked a bit worse for the wear."

Josiah grunted. "I need to talk with Blackthorne."

Erasmus snorted. "Don't we all? He's not here."

Marta...the captain's wife was in San Juan. Josiah had forgotten. Handing the rag back to the wounded man, he rose and scrubbed the back of his neck. They needed to set sail before Slocum caused any more trouble. Worse yet, the sailor knew all the clandestine activities on board. If he went to the authorities...

"Bones and Flapjack went to fetch him from his missus." Erasmus dabbed away blood near his temple, lips thinning. "I'm not sure what will make him angrier... that Slocum escaped or that we are taking him away from time with his wife."

"There's no help for it. The captain needs to know what's going on."

"Indeed, I do."

At the sound of Blackthorne's gravelly voice, Erasmus gasped and straightened to attention. The captain crossed his arms and glowered. "I could scarcely believe it when Bones told me. And the tongue-lashing he received from my wife when he and Flapjack showed up at our door." Blackthorne narrowed his eyes and tsked. "Marta was none too happy."

Erasmus cowered under his captain's thunderous stare. "Aye. 'Twas my fault, sir. He attacked when I fed him his dinner, and—"

"Enough!" The captain held up a silencing hand. "You'll be docked a week's pay. Clean up the mess and then find Bones. We set sail immediately. I want Bones, Jim, and Gibbs to round up the men in port. If Slocum tells the authorities what we've been up to, we'll have more than an escaped, disgruntled sailor to contend with."

"Aye, sir." Erasmus hastened to clean up the blood and scattered meal on the floor. Josiah breathed a sigh of relief. The captain could see the seriousness of the situation and had wasted no time in formulating a plan. Once they set sail, it would be mere days until they reached Charleston.

Before Josiah could relax, Captain Blackthorne spun to him with a fierce growl. "And you!" He jabbed a thick finger in Josiah's chest. "You will marry that girl immediately, or I'll throw you overboard myself."

Josiah's jaw dropped open. "Sir? What do you—"

Blackthorne scowled. "You took her from Barbados, no doubt plying her with sweet words about America, freedom, and hope."

His lips pursed. "You inadvertently thrust her into chaos with no ed-ucation, no skills, no plan, and no husband to see to her protection."

Wait. The captain was blaming *him*?

But he continued ranting, unconcerned. "You're not the first lad to have his head turned by a pretty face, but I'll be jiggered if you don't fix this."

"How was I to know Slocum had escaped?"

"It doesn't matter!" The captain took a step forward, eyeing Josiah with a glint in his eye that brooked no argument. "'Tis a coward who promises a young miss to take her from her problems only to leave her with double instead." The captain's hard stare sof-tened. "I speak from experience, young Holland. How do you think I found my Marta?"

Josiah studied him carefully. "Your wife was a slave?"

"Indentured servant, to be precise. I saw how hard her life was and whisked her away, yet for years I left her without the protection of my name, my presence, and any way to find a better life." A mus-cle twitched near his eye. "The Almighty came after me and correct-ed my poor behavior." He thrust his chin forward. "I'll not see ye make the same mistake I did. The lass has been through enough."

Stung in conscience, Josiah nodded slowly. He would ask Avali-na to marry him tonight. His pulse galloped as the situation washed over him in waves. This would change everything.

How could he possibly squirm from the grip of his family's power while providing for a wife?

I ran my fingers over the swollen flesh on my neck. It was sore to the touch, and when I attempted to clear my throat, a raspy squeak was the only sound that emerged. A bitter laugh snaked from my chest. I'd spent a lifetime trying to speak, and now I was physically unable.

TO SPEAK HIS NAME

Curling my fists through my hair, I yanked until the pain searing my scalp overshadowed the frustration welling in my chest. I was tired of feeling helpless, of having no voice, no say. Weary of being subject to the whims of frightening men. With a growl, I smashed my fist into the lumpy cot, pounding the scratchy pallet over and over.

How did a person achieve power? How did one reach beyond themselves to assert control?

A soft knock sounded on the door. I turned, forcing my erratic breathing to calm. The door creaked open and Josiah entered, his tall frame and wide shoulders filling the doorway. He glanced at the pummeled bedding before searching my face.

"Are you well?"

Was I? I didn't know anymore. In truth, I wasn't sure I cared. The past two weeks had been a terrifying blur.

I nodded, for the thought of forcing words past my throat was too much to bear at the moment. Josiah took a step closer and paused.

"I—uh, I wanted to see how you're feeling." His chocolate eyes missed nothing, not my marred neck or the tiny furrow that I'm sure now divided my brows.

Instead of replying, I shrugged. He sighed and moved to sit on the edge of the cot before grasping my hand.

"I've been remiss in my duty to you. In my haste to see you free, I whisked you away from all you've ever known and have twice left you to suffer under the hands of a deranged man."

Duty? Something about the word tasted like vinegar as I rolled it in my mouth. A chore. An obligation. The thought chafed.

"Captain Blackthorne thinks it best—I think it best—if we marry immediately."

Marry Josiah? I sucked air between my teeth. I could never have imagined this would be his response to the evening's chaos.

Seeing my hesitation, he rose swiftly to his feet and grasped both my hands. "At least for the time being. You will have my name, my protection legally and physically. I promise not to touch you in, well, the ways of marriage." Cheeks reddening, he looked away. "When we arrive in the States, if you are able to procure a new life that suits you, we can draw up an annulment." He winced ever so slightly.

The idea was both exciting and distasteful. This was not about love, or a marriage to be of mutual benefit to both parties, as were the ways of the aristocrats in Barbados. No, this was nothing more than gentlemanly duty.

I was a fool. All this time I had taken his kindness, his gentle regard, his . . . *charity* as genuine affection. Was I so horribly wounded that I couldn't tell the difference between compassion and love?

He waited. I must say something. Pushing past the burning in my throat, I croaked, "And what if I am unable to make my way in America?"

He opened his mouth, shut it again, then slowly ground out, "Then we shall remain married."

A solemn gravity weighted his words. He didn't want this. Or was I misunderstanding the hard press of his lips?

He took a step closer and tightened his grip. "Avalina, I know this isn't ideal but I promise to protect, teach you, and care for you to the best of my ability."

And he would. I was certain of that. He was nothing if not a man of honor. "And what about your family?"

He frowned. "This is a decision between you and me, not my father or mother."

They would be disappointed in his choice. The answer was written as clear as water across his face. And what would they do if they ever learned I was a slave? My stomach knotted.

He attempted a cajoling smile. "Come now. Marriage to me won't be all bad." He leaned close and winked. "And if you say no, I fear the good captain will run me straight through with his cutlass."

There was no other choice, at least for now. Still, the idea rankled, though I couldn't explain why.

Despite my whirling emotions, I nodded slowly. His shoulders relaxed and he lifted my hands, pressing a soft kiss to both before releasing me. "I'll tell the captain straightaway."

As he closed the door behind him, I pressed a hand to my quivering stomach.

Today was my wedding day.

CHAPTER 27

"I now pronounce you man and wife."

Josiah fought for breath. For rational thought. For, well, anything to ground him in reality. His nerves were spun in knots, a tangled mess of foggy emotions and frayed pieces of words. He had grasped only a snippet of Captain Blackthorne's clipped monologue during the short ceremony. *Promise, death, vows ...* It was as if Josiah was floating outside his body, watching the entire affair with numb shock.

But he was not so disengaged as to miss the shaking in Avalina's slim fingers when she tentatively grasped his. Or the words that so heavily slipped past his own lips.

"I do ... "

She stared up at him then, her eyes beguilingly wide with trust. Admiration warred with a sudden qualm in his belly.

I have a wife. A wife. Wife. His brain muttered the single word over and over until it no longer made sense.

And now what? His dream of leaving home, of becoming a lawyer, of fleeing the destiny his father was determined to thrust upon him ... all of it scattered like dust in the wind.

Or had it?

You know nothing of the real world, boy. He could already hear his father's garlicky mock when he finally told him the news. *A wife? You have no idea how to care for anyone without me.*

That's what really bothered Josiah. He'd never been responsible for another soul besides his own. The weight of it settled around his shoulders like an oppressive cloak. No wonder society spoke of wedding jitters.

Yet as something indefinable filled her face, his tumultuous heart stilled. Blackthorne was correct. Josiah had been the one to whisk her from the only life she'd ever known. It was his job now to see her into independence, living the way the Almighty intended … free.

He need only treat her with kindness and see her settled. Then all could go on as he'd planned with freedom for himself. Freedom from his father's oppression. Freedom to do more, be more, than he'd ever imagined.

"You may now kiss your bride."

Josiah's gaze darted to the captain's, who smiled merrily. *Kiss her.* Josiah swallowed down a knot. It wasn't as if he hadn't already done so once before. But now, with Blackthorne looking on, he balked. Avalina's stormy blue eyes stared into his, uncertain. A hesitant bite of her lower lip turned him on end.

Letting his eyes slide closed, he leaned in and brushed her lips with his own. Fire flared. His chest constricted and he pulled away, the tender touch far too fleeting. But he couldn't allow himself to feel anymore. He would never maintain his vow to stay away if he didn't embrace the rigid inflexibility of self-control.

He turned to the captain and shook his hand. "Thank you, Captain."

"My pleasure, and a hearty congratulations to the both of you." The crusty fellow lifted Avalina's fingers to his lips and pressed a genteel kiss across the back, as if she were a well-bred lady and he, a suave courtier. "May God Himself look down on ye with favor and abundant blessings."

A blush dusted her cheeks a becoming shade of pink as Josiah cleared his throat. "I'll see her to her, er, *our* quarters."

The captain chuckled. "Take yer time. We won't be in Charleston for another week, at least."

A week. Josiah shuddered at the yawning expanse of time. Instead of dwelling on the thought, he held out his hand to her and she silently slipped her fingers into his as he led her below deck.

I'm not sure what I expected. Embarrassment, perhaps. Awkward laughter. But not this. This man who had so tenderly shown me compassion and kindness in Barbados, the strapping fellow who had gifted my parched heart with a compass and unlocked the mystery of language, now stood staring absently at nothing. Avoiding my gaze with his stony presence.

The eerie silence clamped my stomach as I waited for him to say something. Do something. Instead, I witnessed only the rigid set of his shoulders as he shuffled, angling his body away from me.

Was I so wretched he already regretted the hasty ceremony?

Stubborn seconds ticked by as I cast about for words—any thought or semblance of sentences—but my tongue remained unyielding.

Anticipation reared up and mocked me. Why? I had no idea. I had witnessed so few marriages in my days— just a handful of slaves anxious to find some shred of hope in their lives— but I'd always pictured it as a fulfilling kind of existence. A sweet camaraderie. Foolishness on my part.

I smoothed the skirt of my lavender gown and knotted my fingers together as sailors thumped down the corridor. We were preparing to set sail. Leave Slocum and his threats behind. And for that, at least, I was grateful.

Finally, he spoke. "Sounds like we're setting sail."

I nodded, swallowed up in misery.

"Look, Avalina"—he finally turned, his chocolate eyes apologetic—"nothing has changed. I'll guard the door each night. Sleep on the floor."

I frowned. He sounded resigned. Almost…unhappy. Anger flared from somewhere in my chest.

He paced the length of the small room. "Make sure your needs are met. I—" He opened his mouth and shut it again before heaving a thick breath. "I have no idea what I'm doing, truth be told."

Compassion tugged but I steeled my heart. He was acting as if I had dragged him in front of a firing squad. And why should it matter to me? It didn't. It shouldn't.

Rubbing the skin of my temple, I nodded and eased my weight onto the edge of the berth. He stopped pacing and stared at me for a long moment, rubbing his jaw a second before his eyes brightened.

"There is no reason this change must be so awkward. Why don't we share three things about each other we didn't know before?"

Yes. Conversation. Surely that would smooth my tangled emotions. I nodded. "You go first."

"All right…" He paced for a second, then stopped and tilted his head. "Favorite color?"

I thought of the sapphire-tipped feather Matias had only recently brought me, his smile wide as he held out the plume for my inspection. "Blue."

"Mine too." A smile creased the handsome planes of Josiah's face. "Your turn."

What to ask? "You've spoken little of your family. Do you have brothers or sisters?"

He nodded and settled on the edge of the mattress, expression thoughtful. "I haven't told you anything about them, have I? You, of course, know of my father. I have a mother as well and a younger sister. Her name is Isabelle."

"No other siblings?"

TARA JOHNSON

"No." He looked down at his fingers, absently smoothing the skin near his nail beds. "There were others—two before me—but they both died in infancy. Boys."

"I'm sorry." His poor mother must have been devastated by the losses. "How did your parents cope?"

He offered a wry smile, yet it was devoid of humor. "By focusing their sole attention, hopes, dreams, and aspirations on me. I was tutored as a child, and then sent to boarding school for years to receive a quality education. I'm expected to take over the running of Father's estate one day. Expected to care for my mother and sister when he passes on." A frown tugged his mouth, and a sharp line marred the skin between his brows. "It's ... overwhelming."

And he was taking me across the ocean to meet them? My nerves spun into knots. I had been ignorant of much tucked away at Azaka Mede, but not so foolish as to be unaware of how things worked among the elite. Marriages were arranged, chosen. If Josiah's father had survived the ordeal in Barbados, would he not want to arrange a wife for Josiah? The elder Holland would be displeased when we arrived on his doorstep. I studied Josiah carefully. Or had he agreed to the captain's wishes as a way to spite his family's plans?

Josiah opened his mouth to ask another question when a boom rocked the ship. I gasped as the room canted sharply to the right. I stumbled backward while Josiah fought to keep upright, hurtling toward me like a rag doll tossed carelessly through the air. My back slammed into the wall. Josiah collided against me with a grunt. His arms wrapped around me, whether for grounding himself or protecting me, I couldn't say.

"What's going on?"

Another boom. The walls reverberated against my back. The lantern hanging from the wall clattered. Its glass globe would be naught but shards if the barrage continued. Josiah tucked me into the shelter of his arms, but every muscle was hard, tense as we struggled to stand upright. "That sounded like cannon fire." His voice was low near my ear, tight as a yanked string.

"Why? Who?" I willed my clattering teeth to still, but an eerie foreboding slithered through my chest. Josiah clenched his jaw and closed his hand around my own.

"We're going to find out."

We raced through the corridor, and even before we climbed the deck, shouts and stampeding feet pounded through the ship. Captain Blackthorne barked instructions, spittle flying from his lips, his dark eyes wide.

"Bones, unfurl all sails! Erasmus and Flapjack, man the cannons!"

Cannons? I hitched a breath. Josiah propelled us toward Blackthorne. "What's going on?"

Blackthorne growled, stomping toward a group of sailors, urging them to hasten. "A ship docked just outside of San Juan is firing on us." Pointing to the sails above us, he bellowed, "Move, move! Unless ye have a hankerin' to be blown to bits!"

Josiah snagged the captain's coat lapel, forcing him to look us in the eye. "Why would anyone be firing at us?"

Blackthorne shrugged away from his hold and glared. "Smugglers have enemies, young Holland."

Josiah huffed. "Are you sure this isn't a bit of violence from Slocum?"

Blackthorne shook his head. "There would be no time for him to have gathered a crew."

"Unless he told the authorities in Puerto Rico about your smuggling."

I held my breath, gaze flicking between Josiah and Blackthorne. After a long moment, Blackthorne cursed and yanked his hat from his head, slapping it against his leg.

"By Zeus, I bet yer right! That low-down, yellow snake!" Black-thorne's face paled. "We cannot fire upon that ship, lest they overtake us and we hang for damaging government property."

"What's to be done, then?"

The captain's face steeled into hard lines. "We outrun them."

CHAPTER 28

Josiah's pulse thumped erratically in his ears as Captain Blackthorne pointed below deck. "The two of you get down there and gather up what's stowed below. Keep the coffee, tea, silk, and sugar, but toss the books and spirits overboard."

A sailor standing to the captain's left muttered, "The spirits? All of them? Why, those barrels must weigh a ton!"

Blackthorne whirled to him with a glare. "All the more reason to get rid of them. *Neptune's Tide* is not called the fastest ship in the Atlantic for nothin', but we must give her a fightin' chance. You and you!" He pointed to two other sailors scurrying past. "Help them."

"Aye, sir!" Josiah turned to follow but paused, studying Avalina's wide eyes. She would not have the strength to haul barrels of whiskey, ale, and rum, but there was something she could do.

"I need you to find Esco and tell him what's going on. He's hidden in a small room within the stores. Farthest corner to the right, behind a stack of crates. The latch is near the bottom of the wall and the door slides open. You'll have to crouch to enter." No doubt, Esco was alarmed at the sudden fracas. "You need only tell him what you've heard from the captain." Josiah placed his hands on her slim shoulders. "Do you think you can do that?"

She winced ever so slightly and swallowed. Was her hesitation over how to find the hidden door, or speaking to Esco? Never before had her affliction aggravated him, yet with cannons bearing down upon them, threatening to tear the ship apart, she still couldn't speak? Couldn't shout a warning? Heavens above, there were lives at stake.

Unleashing his frustration on her would serve no good purpose. Inhaling a fortifying breath, he fastened his gaze upon hers. "Will you try, at least?"

She nodded. It would do for now.

They scurried to the storeroom, where a handful of sailors were already rolling stout barrels across the floor. Offering one last look, Josiah nodded to Avalina and joined them. She would melt into the shadows and chaos to find Esco.

She wouldn't let him down.

I couldn't bear to watch the men gathering up books, pitching them carelessly in crates only to be heaved overboard. I had searched all my life for the mysteries contained in their pages, and now, after having tasted the nectar of the world within, it felt as if something precious were being slaughtered before my eyes.

Another boom as *Neptune's Tide* canted sharply to the left. Men shouted, tumbling over each other to hasten their task. The tumult provided a perfect distraction.

Slipping behind the crates and barrels in the farthest corner, I crouched low, brushing my fingertips along the wall, searching for the concealed panel. Any farther and I would run out of wall.

There! I fumbled with the small lock hidden in the shadows before flipping the bolt and sliding the secret door open. I slithered inside the small space and pushed it shut.

Squinting against the onslaught of light from a nearby lantern, I held up a single hand to shield myself as my eyes adjusted. Blinking once—twice—images slowly sharpened into focus. A cot with tangled blankets, a small stack of books, an empty tin that bore a remnant of crumbs, and a man staring at me in silence, his dark eyes sharp.

My breath escaped as I wiped my clammy hands against my skirt. I sensed his fear but was helpless to reassure him I meant no ill will. My tongue stuck to the roof of my mouth. Why, now of all times, must the words disappear?

"Who are you?"

The man's voice was low, but not unkind. I opened my mouth, then pressed my lips shut again. If only I could say something, make some kind of noise... even a squeak would suffice.

A crack of cannon fire jolted me to the right as the ship shuddered. I fell on my hip and sucked in a breath at the pain. Overhead, thumps sounded as masculine voices shouted. Still, the smuggled man remained quiet, waiting.

What had he asked? Oh, my name. With his gaze focused so squarely upon me, heat rushed up my spine and bloomed hot in my cheeks. If only he would look away. I couldn't stand the stare, the pregnant pause, waiting in anticipation.

It would be so much easier if he couldn't see me.

My gaze shifted to the flickering light in the lantern. With a rush, I reached for it.

"Hey!"

The man barked the reprisal as I turned the lantern knob, extinguishing the flame. We were plunged into inky darkness. The abyss was like a mask, allowing me to hide as words trembled from my lips.

"My—my name is Avalina. Josiah Holland sent me here to you."

"Why? What's going on?"

This man must think me daft, plunging him into shadows and sputtering like a simpleton. Perhaps I was. What kind of person

216

couldn't speak until no one was looking? The workers at Azaka Mede were right. I must be cursed. "*Neptune's Tide* is under attack."

"By whom?" Esco's voice tightened like the strings on a *guitarra.*

"We don't know, but the captain believes someone left the ship and reported the crew's activities to the authorities in San Juan."

In the dark obscurity, I heard him sigh. "Because of me." His voice thickened with defeat.

I knew nothing about this man, but the urge to protect him tightened my chest. "No, at least I don't think so. I think it has more to do with the smuggled goods aboard ship."

He chuckled. "Am I not a smuggled good?"

"No. You are a man."

Another boom but this one sounded farther away. Perhaps the crew had managed to put some distance between us and the port. I cleared my throat.

"That's all I needed to say."

"Thank you for telling me."

I nodded, then realized how foolish the action was, shrouded in nothingness like we were. Leaning forward, my fingers bumped the lantern and slid it closer to him, scraping it across the floor. "Your lantern is near."

I scooted backward and groped once again for the door. Esco's deep baritone stilled my movements.

"You have nothing to fear from me ... Avalina."

He remembered my name. Odd how much it pleased me that he'd cared enough to cling to that small detail. The only others who had dared to see me, really see me, were Molly and Josiah.

Or maybe conditions at Azaka Mede were much more dire than I'd imagined. The people cold and calloused.

Or perhaps one soul in pain could hear the cry of another.

I escaped from his view just as a sizzle of a match flared behind me.

CHAPTER 29

May 2, 1816
Charleston, South Carolina

The evening was foggy and dank. A perfect night to escape.

An itch burrowed between Josiah's shoulder blades. The voyage and the strained silence between him and Avalina during the past few days had grated, stretching his nerves into taut ropes, ready to snap at a moment's notice. They had done little more than avoid each other, the awkwardness looming like an impenetrable wall.

And then there was the worry over delivering Esco to Edward Pickering as they approached Charleston harbor. What if he failed? What if they were caught? The letter from Najaf burned Josiah's pocket. Finding Edward Pickering was the first obstacle. Delivering Esco Pence into his hands, the second. The third would approach on the morrow... introducing Avalina to his family. Even now she was preparing, enjoying a bath provided by a large washtub the captain had provided.

Josiah squinted in the darkness, the ship beneath his feet creaking as it bobbed slowly in port. The slight snap of sails, the squeak of timber—each noise popping like gunshot in his ears.

Footsteps thumped behind him on deck. Josiah turned to see Captain Blackthorne approaching, his gait unhurried. Stopping at

Josiah's side, he crossed his arms and studied the lights twinkling along the Charleston harbor.

"You ready, Holland?"

"As ready as I can be, sir." He studied the grizzled captain's profile. "Thank you for watching over Avalina tonight until we depart in the morning. And if anything happens to me ... "

Blackthorne nodded, his face drawing tight. "Aye. I'll see to her. Help her get settled. But ye have nothin' to fear. You'll return and she'll be safe, tucked aboard ship in the meantime."

It did Josiah's heart good to know he could trust the captain. The way he'd led them all away from Puerto Rico with little more than a small mast broken and dumped cargo was nothing short of a miracle.

He inhaled and peered into the foggy night sky. No. It was more than the captain's instincts. The Almighty Himself had led them to safety.

Please do so again, Father God.

With every nautical mile they had drawn closer to Charleston, the tighter the knot in Josiah's middle had grown. Too many people were counting on him ... Najaf, Captain Blackthorne, Esco, Avalina, and even his family.

Where was Father anyway? Still stuck on the island with a revolt unfolding around him? How would Josiah ever explain his absence to Mother? If George Holland failed to return, all the responsibility would fall on his shoulders, a burden he no longer wanted.

The noose around his neck tightened with each passing day.

"Here." The captain shoved a slip of paper into his hand. Josiah squinted at the smudged ink. "What's this?"

"Bones did some investigating once we docked." The captain nodded at the missive. "That's Pickering's address."

55 South Battery. He knew the location, right next to Mr. Osborne's grand home along the same street. If he remembered correctly, the houses were lined with an abundance of palmettos and shrubs. Between that and the murky fog, perhaps this venture would prove successful.

More footfalls approached. Turning, Josiah spied Esco standing behind him. The wane light illuminated little, but the solemn concern etched in Esco's expression was evident. A knapsack hung from his shoulder.

"You ready?"

Esco nodded and shifted his gaze to Blackthorne. "Thank you again, sir, for carrying me here."

"Aye. May Providence speed your journey." Blackthorne offered his hand and the two men shook, their postures straight. Mutual respect. Josiah bowed his head. He could not fail them.

Blowing out a breath, he reached for the bundle of fabrics resting near his feet and tossed them to Esco. "Here. Don these. If we stumble across anyone's path, you will look like an elderly woman being assisted by a gentleman. Oh, and slow your gait. Shuffle a bit. Better it take longer to arrive at Pickering's than be caught in haste."

A wry smile tilted Esco's mouth as he fumbled to unfurl the clothes. "You've thought this through, I see."

After Esco slid the dark fabric over his head and hunched his posture, Josiah led him down the gangplank of *Neptune's Tide* and into the shroud of night.

From the cover of large palmettos and elms, Josiah and Esco stared up at the two-story house with its wide verandah and sculpted-iron trim. Esco had made nary a peep since leaving the ship, but his hunched stroll had made the passing minutes agony. Even pressing into the shadows along Battery Street, Josiah's heart had thrummed like a hive of angry bees when a carriage approached, the clop of horse hooves clattering against the cobblestone. Not until the vehicle passed could he think again.

Indecision rolled through his brain. What would be the best way to smuggle Esco inside? If they approached the back, a servant would question their arrival, nor was it feasible to walk up to the front door and usher themselves into the presence of the man's family. If Pickering commonly engaged in clandestine activities, he likely worked in silence and obscurity, even away from his family's knowledge. And who could say who might be watching his house even now?

Pulling the scrap of paper bearing the address from his pocket, Josiah whispered to Esco, "Stay here until I return."

Josiah emerged from the shadows and strolled up the path to the front door, folding the paper into a square and tucking it between his fingers. Knocking on the door, he straightened and braced himself for whatever lay ahead.

The door squeaked open, revealing a tall Negro with graying curls. "May I help you, sir?"

"I have a message for an Edward Pickering."

"Ah. Let me fetch him for you."

The door closed again and Josiah prayed. *Be favorable, O Lord.*

The door reopened and a fellow with a jovial face, thinning gray hair, and a paunch born of middle age greeted him. Josiah held the parchment aloft in the air.

"Mr. Pickering? A message for you, sir."

Pickering's brows lifted as he took the missive, reading it swiftly, and then he looked up, spearing Josiah with sharp eyes. Josiah lifted his chin, waiting.

Breathe in, breathe out.

After a long moment, Pickering waved him inside. "Come in, good man, and let me write a response so you can deliver it post-haste."

Josiah's breath left him in a rush. Pickering understood, and good thing too, considering all that was scratched on the bit of paper was his own address.

He followed Pickering through an ornate foyer and homey parlor into a dark paneled library. Pickering shut the door behind him before pointing to an upholstered chair across from his mahogany desk. "Please sit."

Josiah settled into the chair, his nerves loosening by measures. Pickering tugged at his vest, smoothing it into order, before easing into his own chair. He leaned forward, settling the weight of his upper body on his elbows, gray brows lowered.

"Who sent you?"

"A Captain Blackthorne, sir. And another man named Najaf. I believe he's an acquaintance of yours from Barbados."

Pickering's eyes widened. "Ah. I see." He offered a lopsided smile. "Two good men. And how is it both of them deigned to send you my way?"

He swallowed. How much information should he divulge? "My father and I were visiting a plantation in Barbados. A revolt arose all over the island between the slaves and plantation owners. I helped a girl escape and, in the process, ran into Najaf, who agreed to help us, provided I bring this message to you." Holding out the wrinkled envelope, he passed it into Pickering's stout fingers. A trickle of relief siphoned through his middle. That burden, at least, was removed from his shoulders. "Najaf rowed us to *Neptune's Tide* and Captain Blackthorne agreed to carry us to the States."

Pickering smoothed the edge of the envelope. "Quite an adventure you've been on, I'd say."

An understatement, to be sure. "There's more."

"More?" Pickering's brows lifted. "Explain."

Josiah leaned in, dropping his voice lower. "I have a man outside, a fugitive named Esco Pence, who is needing refuge. Captain Blackthorne insisted I bring him to your door."

"Is he seeking his freedom?"

"From what I gathered."

Pickering grunted. "I will see to his needs." Tucking Najaf's letter into his vest pocket, he said, "The best way to sneak Esco inside would be through the cellar door. If you lead him to the back of the house, you'll see the cellar door underneath a set of double windows." A smile tipped Pickering's mouth. "If you glance at the door handles, you'll see a lock, but it's of no concern." A twinkle lightened his blue eyes. "The lock is for appearance only. It slides open easily enough."

"Thank you, sir." Josiah rose to hasten to the task, but Pickering motioned for him to sit as he toyed with a pen near his fingers, lips pursed in thought.

"Is this your first time to arrange such a—" he searched for the word—"transfer?"

Josiah swallowed. "Yes, sir."

"What is your name?"

He considered lying, but it would serve no purpose. Najaf and Captain Blackthorne already knew his name. Pickering could inquire of them easily enough. "Josiah Holland."

"Holland." Pickering tapped the pen against the desk. *Tick, tick, tick.* "And where do you hail from?"

"Right here in Charleston, sir."

"Mm." Pickering leaned against the chair. It squeaked in protest. "Have you ever considered making such work permanent?"

Josiah frowned. What was the man saying? "I'm afraid I don't understand."

Pickering leaned forward and fixed Josiah with a probing stare. "I'm in need of good men. Men who can skillfully lead fugitives like Esco to freedom."

Freedom. How the word tugged at Josiah's heart. Freedom for the enslaved. Freedom for himself. But was such a thing possible?

"There is a multitude of us, you see. Men just like you and me who yearn to see the blight of slavery abolished. And while our nation seems content to let this vile institution flourish, many of us believe God has called us to do more."

Something in his chest constricted at Pickering's fervent plea. "How is such a thing arranged?"

Pickering chuckled. "Discreetly. Once an enslaved man or woman escapes, there is a line of us ready to assist them north from here to Philadelphia. We need wise men to lead them from one location to another, as well as families ready to give shelter to those fleeing."

Philadelphia. Wasn't that where Benjamin Magee was determined to arrive? Understanding dawned.

This collection of people had created a train of freedom stretching from one ocean to another.

As quickly as excitement buzzed through his veins, disappointment nipped at its heels.

His father. George Holland would never agree to such a thing.

"I'm sorry, sir, but despite my own desire to see slavery wiped away from our country, my father has no such proclivity. He owns a large plantation on the outskirts of Charleston. If he were to learn of my involvement—"

"Then I suggest we not tell him." Pickering's brows lowered. "Discretion is of utmost importance in these matters." He sighed. "Please consider it, at the very least."

"I shall."

Satisfied, the older man nodded. "I shall summon you within a fortnight for your answer."

"But how will you find me?"

Pickering smiled. "I have my ways."

CHAPTER 30

May 3, 1816
Charleston, South Carolina

What terrible torment was this?

I stood pressed to Josiah's side, my hand lightly resting in the crook of his elbow as I stared up at his family's white-columned plantation home. It boasted a sweeping verandah, potted plants and flowers of every color and variety, massive windows, and an intricately carved front door, yet I found no comfort in its beauty. The sheer enormity of it left me feeling, by comparison, no bigger than a pesky ant. An ant that needed to be squished beneath a boot.

I swatted away a mosquito buzzing near my nose. Offering me a lopsided smile, Josiah inhaled a fortifying breath, but his walnut eyes held traces of unease. I used my free hand to smooth the folds of my sky-blue skirt. At least I was not meeting his family dressed in rags. Josiah had seen to that ... yet was it for my benefit, or his own?

Before he could open the door, a thick-waisted woman with skin the color of creamed coffee burst through the opening. Her round face creased into a wreath of joy when her gaze sharpened upon Josiah.

"Master Holland! Good to see you, sir. Land sakes, everyone 'round here been worried sick 'bout you ... especially since your father returned home three days ago."

Josiah stiffened ever so slightly but kept his smile fixed in place. "Good to see you too, Hattie. So Father arrived home?"

"Yes, sir, and laws, but he looked flat weary." She pressed chubby fingers to her face. "Mercy! Here I am a-squawkin' and gawkin' and you jest arrived yourself. Come on in here."

Hattie shot me a wary smile and shooed us both into the foyer. I swallowed as I stepped inside, taking in the ornate chandelier overhead with its hundreds of dazzling crystals, and the wide, curved staircase to the right that led to the second story. My slippered feet sank into a thick Turkish carpet runner. If only I could vanish into its fibers and disappear.

The sound of a rustling skirt grew louder and I heard a cry from somewhere behind me. I whirled to see a woman with a voluminous green gown rushing toward Josiah.

"My son! Oh, how glad I am to see you."

Josiah pulled away from my touch and reached to embrace her. With silver threads weaving through her brown curls, and faint lines around her eyes and mouth, this must be his mother. My tongue dried to the roof of my mouth as I watched her teary welcome.

After long moments, she pulled away, cradling his face in her hands. "When your father arrived home without you, my heart plummeted to my feet, especially when he told me of the revolt in that dreadful island."

Josiah forced a smile and eased away from her touch. "What did he say?"

His mother shuddered. "That those violent slaves all over Barbados rose up to defy God-ordained authority."

I stiffened at her words. The derision in her tone was difficult to miss.

She continued on. "Your father learned some horrible fellow named Bussa started the whole thing. Martial law was declared and the whole awful debacle was squelched by local militia and British imperial troops. They were the ones who helped your father leave with haste." Twisting her fingers together, she fixed Josiah with a quizzical stare. "But how did the two of you come to be separated?"

Josiah cleared his throat. "Because I was helping Avalina secure passage to leave. Everything happened quickly."

As Josiah motioned for me, his mother's gaze darted to mine and held fast. Curiosity, concern … I couldn't label all the emotions that crossed her expression.

"Oh?" The older woman pasted on a pleasant smile and shifted to greet me with a bob of her head. "You must be, uh, Avalina, I presume?"

I nodded and mimicked her behavior, unsure if I was greeting her correctly. Josiah slipped his arm around my waist and straightened. "Mother, Avalina is my wife."

All the color drained from her features as her brown eyes widened. "Your—wife?"

"Josiah!" A girlish squeal punctuated the tension like a jab of a sharp knife. I startled and whirled to see a young girl of no more than fourteen or fifteen flying across the foyer before tackling Josiah in a bear hug. He released me to brace for the girl's impact. Long brown curls flew behind her and he was quickly swallowed up in a tangle of arms, pink fabric, and frilly white lace.

"Isabelle." He laughed and set her lightly on her feet. "You haven't changed a bit."

"Much to Mother's dismay." Isabelle offered her mother a cheeky grin and beamed. "I feared the worst when Father arrived home without you."

Josiah chuckled. "You know me. Always up for adventure."

Isabelle's cheeks glowed pink with health and as she saw me for the first time, merriment danced in her eyes. "Hello! I'm Isabelle, Josiah's sister." She moved to my side and squeezed my hands. "And you are?"

I fumbled for any semblance of thought, but Josiah's mother clipped the conversation short with a scowl. "Really, Isabelle! Have I taught you nothing? You must be introduced to someone before conversing with them." She sniffed and glared at her daughter.

Isabelle released my hands with a sigh, enthusiasm deflating. "Yes, Mother."

The older woman smiled stiffly, though the pleasant expression never reached her eyes. "This is Miss Avalina, your brother's w-w-wife." At the word, her nose crinkled.

Isabelle gasped. "Josiah's wife?" A grin burst across Isabelle's pretty features and, before I could brace myself, she squeezed me into a rib-crushing hug. "Oh, I've always wanted a sister!"

I laughed lightly and returned her embrace, catching Josiah's gaze over Isabelle's shoulder. The richness of his stare flickered with some undefined emotion. What was it? Had I done something wrong?

Isabelle released me and bit her lip, her eyes dancing. "Oh, we shall have the best of times! We can shop together and I'll show you everything there is to see in Charleston."

Josiah slipped his arm back around my waist. "Mercy, Isabelle, give my bride time to breathe."

"My bride." The simple claim kindled a fire in my heart, but perhaps he was only acting the part of a doting husband in front of his family. He'd paid me little mind over the past few days. My emotions tumbled like rippling water over rocks.

His mother cleared her throat softly and I startled, realizing she had been watching me carefully. Warmth bloomed in my cheeks at her sharp perusal.

"And I am Virginia Holland, my dear. Josiah's mother." Her chin lifted a notch, mouth stretching into a smile, but her eyes remained cold. I bobbed another slight curtsy and dropped my gaze to the floor. Silence stretched.

"What's wrong, child? Do they not speak where you're from when being introduced?"

I swallowed hard and Josiah's hand tightened around my waist.

"Mother, Avalina canno—"

"What's all this caterwauling?"

A tall man with thinning gray hair, a salt-and-pepper beard, and a rounded stomach marched into the foyer, scowling. I sucked in a breath. Josiah's father. I had seen him several times during their stay at Azaka Mede. An exacting man, who brooked no nonsense.

This was a mistake. I should never have come.

Josiah straightened. "Father, I am glad to see you well and safe."

George Holland frowned, mouth puckering. "Humph! You didn't seem overly concerned when you left me to fend for myself in that rabble."

Josiah frowned. "I protected you from being beaten to death outside. My ribs still pain me. I gave you an option and you chose to stay."

"You left me on the island!" His father narrowed his green eyes. "If it weren't for the British troops, I would be there still."

"George, please." Virginia shot him a reproving look. "Josiah only just arrived. He is well and that is what matters. And look." She gestured toward me and I resisted the urge to shrink backward. "He has brought us a ... surprise."

George frowned, his gaze fixing upon me.

"Father, this is my wife." A muscle ticked in Josiah's jaw.

George's eyes bulged in a grotesque fashion. "Your—wife?"

"Indeed."

His father's gaze darted from Josiah to me and back again. Crimson streaks flushed his neck. "Might I have a word with you, son? In my study?" But it was not a request. It was a command spoken through gritted teeth.

Josiah's hold tightened around me. "I must first see to my wife. She needs to settle in. We've had an exhausting journey."

George's eyes narrowed. "Isabelle, see to your new *sister-in-law*." The words were spoken as if he'd sucked on a pickle. His gaze never left Josiah's face.

"Yes, Father." Isabelle stepped close and gently tugged my hand, pulling me away from Josiah. I swallowed and searched his face but his gaze was locked on his father's. Cold, unyielding, and hard.

I allowed Isabelle to pull me through the sprawling house. My attention was no longer on the elaborate furnishings but lingered with the man I'd left behind.

"I suppose I should take you to Josiah's room, but goodness, that seems strange." Isabelle laughed lightly and squeezed my hand, leading me to a wide, curving staircase. "I can't tell you how pleased I am that you're here." She smiled sweetly at me, and my chest squeezed in response. If only the rest of his family were as kind as his sister.

Guiding me to the second door on the left, she pushed it open and let me step inside. Josiah's room was decorated as the man himself... strong and dependable. Tones of blue and red were complemented with wood furnishings. Cedar, if my nose guessed correctly. I stared at the large bed. Would I be expected to share it with him?

Heat flushed up my neck and bloomed hot in my cheeks. Of course I was. We were married, after all. My stomach flipped and I pressed a hand to my middle.

Isabelle turned to me then, tilting her head to study me carefully. "Here you are. Home sweet home." Leaning close, she whispered, "Don't mind Mother and Father. They will come around. They depend too much on Josiah to let your union get in the way. A union that pleases me to no end. My brother deserves happiness and I'm happy he has you." With a smile, she winked and released my hands. "I'll have Cook bring you some refreshments."

With a tiny wave, she closed the door behind her. Only then did I realize I'd never spoken a word. And Isabelle hadn't seemed to mind.

Josiah followed his father into his study, his skin buzzing with irritation as George Holland stomped to his desk and whirled to face him.

"How dare you!"

Stiffening at the outburst, Josiah's nostrils flared. "How dare I what? Leave Barbados when you refused to come with me, or is this about marrying without your knowledge?"

"Both!" Father slapped his hand on the desk, the crack reverberating through the still room. "Dash it all, Josiah, I only just secured your marriage to Louise Abernathy. Her father and I signed the agreement this morning."

Josiah's eyes slid closed. Louisa was a vain, pampered debutante who had not a thought in her head other than the latest Parisian fashions or the necessity of parasols. Father's color deepened to scarlet and he coughed loudly into his fist. Josiah waited. George Holland was not done berating him.

Wiping his mouth with a handkerchief he'd pulled from his pocket, he crumpled the scrap of fabric in his fist and heaved a thick breath, eyes narrowing. "Don't you understand what's at stake here? The future of our family, our fortune ... everything I've worked for and what do you do? You toss it aside like a worn boot."

"I don't see how marrying a woman of my choice is going to bring destitution to our door."

Father stepped closer, so close his breath hit Josiah's cheek. "I know who she is. That meek little scullery maid from Azaka Mede."

Josiah's pulse ricocheted, pounding in his ears. "I will not tolerate you speaking ill of her. Not one whit." His jaw hurt from clenching his teeth so tightly.

A sudden calm draped his father's features as he offered a single shoulder shrug and eased into his chair with a squeak of leather. "It is of no consequence. You will annul your marriage to her immediately and wed Louisa. It is arranged. No one in Charleston need know of your foolishness."

Josiah placed his fists on the desk and leaned forward. "Hear me now, Father. I will never, ever do such a thing. Avalina is my wife. You will inform Mr. Abernathy of my nuptials. He cannot hold you to a contract that is clearly null and void."

"Abernathy is a wealthy man. With your union to Louisa, our family's fortunes will be secured."

Josiah pushed away and scrubbed the back of his neck. "Why are you so insistent on this? We have more than we need." Pulling his hand from his neck, he fisted his fingers, aching to smash something. Anything. "Why insist on a union that cannot be?"

His father dropped his gaze to his mahogany desk. The clock behind him ticked with all the force of a war drum.

"Because"—he looked up, all the fight gone from his eyes—"I'm dying."

CHAPTER 31

Josiah stared at his father. George Holland's shoulders slumped as he toyed with a pencil, rolling it end over end between his hands, his lips pursed, lines creasing his forehead. Dying? George Holland seemed too big and stubborn to ever succumb to something as inconsequential as death.

Reasonable thought fled. "But how? Why?"

He frowned. "Dr. Morris says it's consumption."

The dreaded killer. Josiah assessed his father with a critical eye. True, he had lost weight of late, but traveling on a ship for weeks on end was without an abundance of fattening delicacies. "I don't understand." Josiah shook his head, trying to wrap his mind around the confounding news. "You've never said a word."

As if on cue, a coughing spasm rattled his father's chest. Yanking the handkerchief from his pocket, he barked a cough into the linen and waited to catch his breath.

"I've tried to hide it as best I can. I've done well enough here over the winter, but our time in Barbados was vexing, to say the least. The high humidity made breathing at night nearly impossible."

"I heard nothing."

His father arched a brow. "Nor would you, not with how soundly you sleep. You always have, even when you were naught but a babe." Reaching into his vest pocket, he pulled out a dark green leaf and popped it in his mouth, chewing slowly. "Peppermint. It eases the ache in my lungs."

Come to think of it, Josiah had noticed his father smelling of peppermint more often, but he had assumed Mother was weary of the constant aroma of tobacco that always surrounded him.

Father leaned against the back of his chair. "Do you now understand why your cooperation is of utmost importance? When I'm gone, your mother and sister will solely depend on you."

Josiah's own chest constricted as the noose of responsibility settled around his neck. "But why not attempt to extend your life? Summer here in Charleston will only worsen your condition. Why not sell the plantation? Move somewhere with a milder climate? Rest and enjoy your family in your declining years?"

Father's face mottled red once again. "And toss away everything my father, and grandfather, and his grandfather before him have achieved?" His breath heaved raggedly as he rose to his feet. "Does your own family's legacy mean so little to you?"

"People matter to me, Father. Not property or possessions."

Father's jaw clenched. "Then you have failed all of us."

A slap would have hurt far less than that damning assessment. Father stalked to the window and pushed aside the thick red and gold curtains, staring vacantly across the lawn. "Your mother would rather die than leave our home. Do you not care for her wellbeing? Or Isabelle's?" His lips pinched. "She is a mere two years away from coming out to society. Would you cut her off from an advantageous match simply because you don't see the value in what you have been given?"

Josiah pinched his eyes closed. Father was mustering all his manipulative tactics to bend him to his will.

"I would rather see her marry a God-fearing man and be happy than reap profits to line my own pockets."

Father whirled, causing the heavy draperies to swish with his movement. "I will not tolerate this addled thinking any longer! You will do as I say, and you will prepare yourself to take on the mantle of this plantation. Do I make myself clear?"

Josiah was caught between two impossibilities. Walk away from his duty, from his loved ones, those who had nurtured and raised him, or embrace a legacy fraught with ideals he could no longer espouse. *Honor thy father and thy mother…*

The scripture bit like a viper. What was one to do when his parents cared little for God's law?

Bowing his head, Josiah released a tight breath. There was no way around it. "I will acquiesce on one condition."

"And that is?"

"You drop all nonsense of an annulment and cancel the contract you made with Mr. Abernathy. If you do so, I will stay here and care for Mother and Isabelle."

Father lifted his chin. Was that a gleam of triumph in his eyes? "We have an accord."

I sat on the edge of Josiah's bed, running my fingers along the floral etching of the compass he had given me. Could it only have been weeks ago? It seemed a lifetime. Someone had seen our possessions safely delivered to the room while I napped.

Pinching the clasp, I opened the compass and tugged the slip of paper he had pressed into my palm the night he intended to say goodbye at Azaka Mede. Thanks to his tutoring, I could now read the words for myself. Well, most of them anyway.

In the beginning, God created the heavens and the earth.

I still fumbled to read many words, but Josiah had gently, patiently taught me letters, my name, and this bit of verse. The mysteries that had beckoned me for years were a hair's breadth away from being answered.

The door creaked opened softly and I looked up. Josiah. His handsome face was etched with fatigue. Or was it resignation?

There was still so much I didn't know or understand about my new husband.

His face softened upon seeing the compass in my hand.

"You treasure such a simple token?" He shut the door behind him and moved to stand beside me.

"Of course." I smiled and heat warmed my cheeks, feeling strangely shy now that we were alone. "It was the one thing I would not leave Azaka Mede without."

Easing down beside me, his weight caused the bed to squeak. Weariness radiated from his body in waves. I looked up and held his gaze with my own.

"I'm sorry for the trouble I have caused with your family."

Reaching out, he toyed with one of the curls dangling below my temple. "You caused no trouble. Their own rigidity and convoluted expectations did that."

His fingers dropped to skim the skin of my jaw. I shivered with delight at his touch. If only he would kiss me again. Somehow let me know that I was more than just a burden.

Sighing deeply, he pulled away and stood, pacing the room slowly.

"I don't know what to do, Avalina. My father is dying and is requesting, no, demanding, I take up the responsibility of running this plantation." He faced me, stuffing his hands in his pockets. "It's not what I want. What I planned. I abhor slavery. You and Benjamin Magee showed me the evil it is." He lowered himself to one knee before me, clasping my fingers in his own warm palms. "But I cannot abandon my mother or sister." He shook his head. "If you want no part of this, I—I free you. I'll see you settled somewhere new, just like we talked about. Give you money. I have the coinage Captain Blackthorne gave me for delivering Esco to Pickering. I can settle you somewhere north, and—"

I shushed him, pressing my finger to his lips. "No. I don't want to be settled somewhere north. You were the one who saw me at Azaka Mede. You were the one who offered me kindness when few others did." Emotion clogged my throat. Words long trapped inside bubbled for release. My chin trembled. "If I choose to be chained to anyone, if I give my life to another in humble submission, it will only be to the one I trust. I give myself to you. You may not want me, but I want you."

He drew close, achingly slow, nuzzling his face against mine. I flushed hot, then cold as his lashes, his lips traced the contours of my face.

"Avalina." He breathed my name like a sacred benediction. "I've tried to stay away. Tried to give you freedom with no expectations." His lips brushed the hollow of my throat. "Tried to let you go." His voice was husky as he pulled away ever so slightly, studying my face with tenderness. "But I can't. Don't you know it is your smile that forms my own? Your face that fills my dreams? The touch of your hand that begs mine to forever remain entwined with yours—body, mind, and soul?"

Reaching out, he touched me then, tentatively at first, as his fingertips grazed my wrists, moving slowly upward. Then my upper arms, the curve of my hip, the small of my back. My heart stammered in my chest as heady sensations flooded my body. Dare I speak?

I stroked his stubbled jaw with my fingers and stared into his eyes, those fathomless pools of cinnamon and chocolate that watched my every movement, my very breath.

"You've taught me how to read, how to dance, to step beyond the only life I'd known." I swallowed, mustering all the courage I had inside. "Teach me more."

Leaning forward, he brushed his lips against my chin, my cheeks, teasing me with ecstasy I didn't know existed. "Teach you what?" he murmured as his lips caressed my temple.

My breath shuddered. "Teach me the ways between a man and a woman."

He stilled, and pulled back, staring into my eyes. "You're sure?"

I nodded. "Teach me, Josiah."

The world exploded with color and light as his lips met mine. I was falling like a feather through the sky. Tumbling, riotous, free.

And all our troubles were forgotten.

CHAPTER 32

Heaven. Bliss. There were no other words to describe it as Josiah stretched out on the bed, watching his wife sleep. The pale light of dawn drifted lazily through the window. A sigh escaped her lips as she slumbered, the sound as soft as the down of a dandelion.

He curled a tendril of fiery hair around his finger and smiled, admiring the pink tinge of her cheeks, the long sweep of lashes, her lush lips. She was perfect.

And perfectly unaware of how much she'd turned his life upside down.

His smile vanished. Spiriting her away from Barbados was the first impulsive thing he'd ever done in his life, and he'd not fully calculated the consequences of such a rash decision. Yet, remembering her ardent fervor last night in his arms, her whole-hearted trust, her gentle spirit and curiosity, he would not undo anything if given a million lifetimes. He extended his forefinger and skimmed it down the curve of her cheek. How had he ever thought he could just walk away and let her go?

Protective instincts burst in his chest, spreading through his middle and flooding his whole body with warmth, with longing. Was this love? Perhaps he'd loved her the first moment they'd met. She knew little of God, nothing of the way the world worked. He winced. Charleston society would eat her alive. He couldn't let them crush her spirit. He wouldn't.

And Mother...she would try to force Avalina into a mold he did not wish her to be. Why was each decision fraught with difficulty?

Sighing, he moved to lie on his back and stare at the intricate design etched into the white ceiling. Since seeing the dead slaves tossed overboard on the ship, his foundation had shifted. The world that once upon a time seemed black and white now morphed into hues of gray. Scriptures and admonitions warred in his mind. All of them contradictory to each other.

Honor thy father and mother. Disavow the cruel and inhumane institution of slavery. Protect Avalina. Fight to give freedom to others. Find freedom for himself. Be obedient to God. *Be ye not unequally yoked...* It all muddled in his mind like a tangled ball of yarn.

He wasn't sure he even knew what was right anymore.

Avalina inhaled and stretched lazily, curling against his side. Her warm palm slid against his bare stomach. Desire pooled in his middle as he pressed a kiss against her hair.

"Good morning." He could hear the early morning growl deepening his own voice.

"Hmm?" She blinked prettily, her stormy blue-gray eyes widening as she awakened. A shy smile curled her lips. "Good morning."

"Did you sleep well?"

Her cheeks pinked even more. "Yes. And you?"

"No." He chuckled and kissed her forehead. "I was awake most of the night admiring my wife."

She bit her lower lip and stared into his eyes. "It seems like a dream. But here I am."

He smiled. "And here you shall stay."

Lowering his head, he brushed her lips with his and pulled her close. He ran his hand up and down her arm, relishing the soft feel of her skin. When his fingertips brushed raised welts, he frowned and pulled away to study her upper arm. Deep red scars formed bold uppercase letters on her skin, as if branded there by a hot iron. *A~M.*

His gut tightened. "What is this?"

Seeing how his attention latched onto her arm, she tugged the sheet over her skin. "I—it's nothing."

"Avalina, stop." He kept his voice gentle, even though a fire raged inside. He slowly pulled the covers back to expose her arm. She shivered. Who had marked her in such a way?

Her gaze dropped to the bed, studiously avoiding his stare. "It's the branding mark of Azaka Mede."

His jaw tightened. "Harding did this to you?"

"Yes." She swallowed. "To all the slaves. He branded me after the first beating."

His eyes slid shut. The *first* beating. That meant there were many more. "How old were you?"

"I'm not sure." Her eyes took on a faraway look as she lifted her gaze from the bed. "Five? Six? I don't know. No one truly knows my age."

His throat clogged with emotion. What other horrors had she endured? "Why did he beat you?"

She inhaled a tremulous breath. "Baara heard me sing one day and told Master. Afterward, he insisted it would be my job to entertain his guests. When I failed to perform, he whipped me mercilessly. I couldn't rise for weeks." Her muscles tightened, eyes growing hard. "After that, words wouldn't come. I tried." Her eyelids fluttered rapidly, moisture glistening in her eyes. "Oh, how I tried. But the only one they would appear for is Molly."

"And then me."

"Yes. And you." A solitary tear slipped down her cheek. "I hate the letters on my arm. If I could wash them away, I would. Even now, away from Master Cyrene, he marks me. Holds me. It's as if I can never escape him."

Reverently, tenderly, Josiah skimmed his thumb over the puckered skin, tracing the letters. "No. Harding has no control over you. Not anymore. These scars tell a story. Nothing else. It shows you endured. You survived." He whispered, "They are beautiful. *You* are beautiful."

Leaning forward, he slowly kissed each raised, red mark before pulling her close once again.

As they melted into each other, he lifted a prayer heavenward.

Don't let me hurt her, Father. I could not bear it. Anything but that.

I tucked a wayward curl back into the pins jabbing my scalp as I descended the stairs on Josiah's arm. After the debacle of yesterday, I must make a good impression on his family.

Sensing his gaze upon me, I lifted my face to his and grinned. He winked as if sharing a secret. My stomach flipped in response. Indeed, we had shared many secrets the past few hours.

The clink of dainty spoons against porcelain cups, the morning grumble of slow chatter, and the rustling of skirts echoed loudly as we approached the dining room. Hattie scurried around the table to refill Mr. Holland's coffee. Josiah's mother looked up from her food. Isabelle beamed upon seeing us enter, but Mrs. Holland stiffened. George Holland never tore his gaze from the newsprint held in his fingers.

"Good morning." Josiah forced a cheery tone into his voice before moving to assist me into a chair at Isabelle's left. I offered him a grateful smile and he winked again. Warmth skidded up my neck.

"My, my, aren't we a bit late for breaking the fast?" Virginia arched a reprimanding brow but primly reached for her own cup, clasping it daintily between her thumb and forefinger. "I pray you've not adopted native habits while on that island, Josiah."

"Of course not, Mother." Easing into his own chair, he opened his napkin, spreading it across his lap slowly. I swallowed and did the same. He was intentionally giving me clues for proper etiquette and I loved him for it. Reaching for the eggs, he filled my plate before spooning a healthy portion onto his own. "Our journey was quite arduous. It was good to sleep in a real bed for a change. Travel aboard ship is treacherous, to say the least."

Isabelle's dark eyes sparkled. "Did anything exciting happen?"

I nearly choked on my first spoonful but managed to keep myself from spluttering eggs all over the lace-covered table.

Josiah smiled. "As a matter of fact, we had quite an adventure. Didn't we, darling?"

I nodded and reached for a cup of water with shaking hands. If Isabelle noticed, she had the good grace not to comment.

"Well, what was it?" His sister leaned forward, excitement palpable. "Pirates?"

"No." *Yes.*

"Warfare?" *Only guns and cannon fire.*

He chuckled. "Of course not."

She frowned, her lips puckering. "What, then?"

"A massive storm." He waggled his eyebrows. "A storm so treacherous we were nearly swept overboard."

I arched a single eyebrow. I *had* been swept out to sea until he rescued me from death. Despite that niggling bit of fact, he was spreading it on a bit thick, and his sister gasped with delight.

"How romantic!"

"Romantic?" Josiah laughed and shook his head, reaching for the salt. "Nothing romantic about slogging through torrents of rain and heaving sails into submission. And our captain was a gruff fellow. Why, when the gale swept in, our captain said—"

"Enough of this horrid talk. Isabelle needs no help in fanning her overactive imagination." Virginia turned her cool gaze to me, her focus dipping to my plate and then lifting to study my eyes. "And how is your meal, my dear?"

Oh no. The words. They wouldn't come. I opened my mouth but they stalled, thick and heavy. I nearly strangled over the knot bobbing in my throat. Josiah slid his warm hand over mine and squeezed.

"Avalina cannot speak, Mother."

She gasped and tingles raced up my spine. George Holland lowered his newsprint, frowning over the top of the paper. "What's this?"

"She's a mute. Oh, my heavens!" Virginia fanned her face with a hankie, a blotch of crimson dotting each cheek. "You brought home a mute as your bride? What will people say?"

"That I picked the most beautiful woman in Barbados."

Shame burned my face as I stared at the table, each intricate swirl of lace staring back.

"You cannot be serious."

The derision in George Holland's biting tone was a lash. To my right, Isabelle shot me a sidelong glance and lifted her chin.

"I don't think it so very disadvantageous. What a wonderful gift to be able to observe the interactions of others without the obligation of making silly prattle." Reaching between us, she squeezed my hand. "I'm sure you're quite astute."

I attempted to force a smile but it felt more like a grimace.

"Indeed, my wife is extremely intelligent." Josiah's voice was calming, like a balm. I could not have borne their scowls without him.

The conversation lapsed into awkward silence. My appetite fled. After long moments, his father slapped the newsprint against the table and grunted, motioning Hattie to clear his plate. "Josiah, I'd like you to visit the south field with me in a few minutes."

Josiah wiped his mouth with his napkin and frowned. "Any particular reason?"

"I planted a new crop this year—corn—besides tobacco and cotton, and I want you to see how it's progressing."

"I thought to show Avalina the plantation first."

His father coughed loudly into his linen napkin. Josiah blanched but nodded curtly when the spasms ended. "Very well."

George arched a graying brow. "Isabelle, you can show your new sister-in-law the premises until your tutor arrives for afternoon lessons."

"Yes, Father." She glanced my way and smiled. "I'll show you the gardens first, Avalina. You will adore them."

I nodded and pushed away from the table after his sister did the same. As I rose, I sensed Virginia's cold stare boring into me. A knot fisted my middle.

"You endured. You survived."

Josiah's ardent words whispered through my mind. He was right. I was a survivor.

I met Virginia's hard stare and held her gaze, unflinching. Her eyes narrowed to slits.

Isabelle, oblivious to the silent battle being waged between us, tugged my arm. "Come. Let me show you the jasmine and roses."

I broke the hold between his mother and myself. For now, it was enough.

After Isabelle led me through the maze of gardens—the fragrant jasmine, roses of every color, and the silky magnolias dotting the lush lawn—we explored the house. Isabelle rattled off facts about the oil paintings, expensive vases, carpets, and the expansive home's history. Apparently, I had married into a family of import, though Josiah had never boasted of such. My head ached from all the information, but Isabelle was cheerful company, never seeming to mind that I could not respond in kind, though I communicated as best I could with smiles and gestures. There was something so winsome about her ... a wonder, considering the sour dispositions of her parents.

Now we sat in the room reserved for her schooling. Isabelle hunched over the desk, scribbling Latin, whatever that was, on parchment while her dour schoolmaster, a spindly fellow named Lucius Igiby, stood nearby, his nose perpetually wrinkled. I held needlepoint in my lap, making a pitiful mess of the embroidery, so consumed was I with their lesson.

"No, no, no!" Igiby heaved a thick sigh and pushed his glasses farther up his nose. "John 1 is in *principio erat Verbum et Verbum erat apud Deum et Deus. Et*, not *ut*! You must learn to pay attention, Miss Holland."

Isabelle's lips pinched, and the scarlet blots on her cheeks were hard to miss. Even though I was the only spectator, the scolding embarrassed me, just as it did her. I had disliked the scowling schoolmaster upon his entrance into the room, and his behavior only reinforced my opinion. Matias always said a bit of syrup worked better to attract hummingbirds and ants than a splash of vinegar. Perhaps those of us on the island were more civilized than Americans had led us to believe.

"Never mind, never mind." Igiby pinched the bridge of his nose in a longsuffering air and swatted his hand toward her work. "Enough Latin. Put it away. I have a new book for you to begin."

"Is it *Pride and Prejudice*? I have been longing to read it."

"I will not stuff your head full of sentimentality. Austen's work is nothing short of a trifle, although–" his scowl mellowed as he winked—"I do confess to enjoying her work from time to time." He plunked a massive tome in front of her. "Instead, we will begin *A Tale of Two Cities* by Dickens. Read aloud, please, until I instruct you to stop."

Isabelle flipped it open and cleared her throat. "'It was the best of times, it was the worst of times, it was the age of wisdom, it was the age of foolishness, it was the epoch of belief, it was the epoch of incredulity, it was the season of Light, it was the season of Darkness, it was the spring of hope, it was the winter of despair ... '"

My imagination took flight as I listened, needlework forgotten. My heart hummed as I drank in the story spilling from Isabelle's lips: a place called France where a mad shoemaker lived, a fellow named Charles accused of treason to the English crown, an orphan, and an evil aristocrat. Though many of the words were foreign to me, I puzzled out their meaning quickly enough. I leaned forward in rapt attention and listened.

When Master Igiby rapped his knuckles on the table and told Isabelle she had read enough for one day, I startled as if awakened from a dream. How much time had passed? An hour? Two? My mind was lodged in the streets of Paris, where the wealthy and the poor battled for their future.

Igiby pulled a shiny pocket watch from his vest and peered down his nose at the face. "Time for a respite, I believe. Return in an hour's time."

Isabelle nodded but he swept from the room with his rigid posture, never acknowledging her acquiescence. She turned to me and blew out a loud breath.

"I'm sorry. This is not very exhilarating for you."

I shook my head and pointed at the book before smiling. She glanced between the story and me. "Are you saying you enjoyed it?"

I nodded and she laughed.

"That makes one of us, then." She fell back against her chair and studied me for a moment before waggling her eyebrows. "Wanna know a secret?"

I nodded.

Isabelle peeked over her shoulder to make sure no one had entered the room. "I have a smuggled copy of *Pride and Prejudice* in my bedroom." She flashed a wicked grin. "I knew Igiby would say no, so I had Hattie find me a copy in town."

A giggle slipped out and I pressed my fingers to my mouth. Isabelle grinned.

"Listen to that! You laughed. And it's a pretty laugh too." She squeezed my arm affectionately. "Would you like to read it when I'm done?"

I bit my lip. How to tell her? My reading was still rudimentary, and barely that. I flipped the book back open and pointed to a line of letters before shaking my head. She frowned, not understanding.

"You don't like to read?"

I shook my head again and shrugged. Understanding dawned in her expression.

"You can't read?"

I pinched my thumb and forefinger close together.

"Only a little?"

I nodded.

Wrinkling her nose, she thought for a moment and shrugged. "It's of no consequence. I shall just teach you. Does that suit?"

How I wished I could push the unyielding words past my throat. Isabelle had shown me nothing but kindness and I couldn't even answer the most basic question. Instead, I nodded yet again.

She squealed and tugged me through the schoolroom door, making a beeline for her bedroom. I was helpless to resist.

Father tucked his hands behind his back, surveying his kingdom. Stalks of green corn sprouted thick and lush, stretching as far as Josiah could see. Father nodded toward the field.

"Already talked to Carruthers. If the crop is as good as I predict, he'll buy all his corn exclusively from us."

Josiah whistled low. "That's quite a feat. From what I've heard, Carruthers rarely contracts with a single plantation."

"Well, I have a way of talking him into the seemingly impossible."

Josiah ground his teeth against the grating sound of his father's bragging. Instead, he smiled when he saw Fountain approaching, sweat staining his shirt across the chest and armpits. Tugging his straw hat from his head, he clutched it in his hands and nodded respectfully.

"Sirs."

Josiah clapped Fountain on the back. "How are you today, my friend?"

White teeth flashed. "Good, sir. Mighty good."

Father pursed his lips and continued to study the field. "Need something, boy?"

Josiah's shoulder blades itched with mounting fury. Why had he never noticed the way his father spoke to Fountain?

"Yes, sir." Fountain swallowed. "Granny Chloe, she powerful sick with rheumatism. Wants to know if she has your permission to rest."

George Holland scoffed. "Does Granny Chloe not realize I'm the one who puts shelter over her head and food in her mouth? She can tend to her work like all the others."

"But, Father, she's an old woman. Surely you don't expect her to work like the men and women in their prime? Heavens, she must be near eighty."

"Toil is good for the soul. Keeps a body young." He jutted out his chin. "If I gave a day off to every slave who complained, we would have no food to eat." He shooed Fountain away. "Get back to work."

"Yes, sir."

A billowing fire flamed in Josiah's chest as he watched the strapping man, his childhood playmate, turn away and submit without a word of disagreement. He whirled to his father, acid pooling in his mouth. "Was that necessary? What good can Granny be to you or anyone else if you work her to death?"

Father sneered. "Really, son, you sound like a whimpering milksop."

"But I—"

His father coughed loudly, doubling over, face reddening with the effort.

Honor your father and mother. Josiah clamped his mouth shut.

That simple command was getting harder to obey with every passing moment.

"Mister Holland!"

Amos, the aged groomsman, crossed the yard with an uneven gait, a letter clutched in his hands. Both Josiah and George turned but he fixed his gaze on Josiah.

"This just came for you, sir. Thought I'd give it to you now since I'm on my way to rub down the horses."

"Thank you, Amos." He took the envelope, careful not to open it until his father had moved away to chat with the overseer.

When he was alone, he tore the seal and read the contents, pulse hammering.

Package is ready to be delivered to you anytime. Please contact me to receive transport instructions.

Pickering

A *package* could only mean one thing ... another fugitive seeking freedom just like Esco and countless others had done. Pickering had been all too serious in his request for Josiah's help.

But how to hide him without George Holland finding out?

CHAPTER 33

I did not care for the way Josiah's mother stared at me over breakfast the following morning.

Josiah had been called away from my arms in the early morning hours—something about an issue with a sickly woman on Slave Row—leaving me alone in the too-cool sheets. Was this love? This aching to be with Josiah every moment? To seek the comfort of his touch, his kiss, his caresses each evening?

Instead, venomous darts and poisoned glances were flung my way with alarming frequency during the meal. At least Isabelle remained faithfully at my side. Her mere presence bolstered my trembling confidence.

"So, Avalina…" Virginia lifted her chin a notch, her mouth creasing into a stiff semblance of a smile. "You managed to turn my son's head, a feat no other woman in our area seemed able to do." She raised her teacup to her lips and daintily sipped the steaming brew. "Charleston's elite are dying to meet you. Though I know your, uh, condition contains it challenges, I wondered if it might be too forward to plan a party in your honor. Introduce you to society, if you will."

Isabelle gasped in delight at my side, but the fluffy eggs I'd just swallowed turned to lead in my stomach. A party? In my honor? Such a thing could not be. I had only ever watched such occasions from behind cracked doors and open windows, too busy serving food and drinks to understand the intricate dance steps, the flow of conversation, or the political implications of such an event. And South Carolina was not Barbados ... not by a small stretch. The customs and manners would be altogether different than anything I'd known ... wouldn't they?

Virginia must have witnessed the dismay on my face, but instead of pity, her lips tightened into a smile of what I could only assume was triumph.

"There, there, my dear, fear not. Isabelle and I will do all we can to prepare you. Won't we, Isabelle?"

"Of course, Mother!" Biting her lip, she turned to me, her dark eyes shining. "Oh, it shall be such a lark, Avalina! Please say yes. Why, we can fill the house with flowers and fine food. And we shall both receive new gowns." Isabelle turned to Virginia, brows lifted. "Won't we, Mother?"

"But of course."

I opened my mouth to beg them to reconsider, but snapped my lips shut instead. A new gown? Food and flowers? I had no money, no way to pay for such finery.

"And don't worry about the cost." Virginia offered a simpering smile. "Mr. Holland will be happy to provide everything we desire. Having Josiah here is recompense enough. Why, someday you'll be the lady of the house, won't you?"

I startled. Such a thought had never occurred to me. Virginia's presence was so very ... big. The intimidating way she could command the trembling staff with a twitch of her mouth was a power I could never wield. Nor would I want to.

But they knew I would not, could not protest. Virginia dabbed her lips with her napkin and pushed away from the table. "I called Mrs. Durand. She is coming this morning to select the perfect pattern and fabric for you." Moving to my side in a rustle of voluminous skirts, Virginia placed a single finger under my chin, tilting my head up to meet her probing stare. "Mm. Green. No, perhaps something blue."

Heat seared my neck and crept into my cheeks. I had the strangest sensation the older woman was trying to compliment me, yet the simple assessment left me feeling bereft.

"What about me, Mother?"

Virginia turned to her daughter and her smile stretched, lifting the corners of her eyes. "What would you like, darling? Perhaps a modest frock of sage?"

Isabelle wrinkled her nose. "My gown for the McNab's ball was sage green. Perhaps something pink?"

Cupping her daughter's cheek, Virginia nodded. "Pink will look lovely with your complexion." She released her daughter and straightened to her full height. "Mrs. Durand will arrive within the hour. Will that suit?"

What could I possibly do to stop such an event? Virginia must have sensed my apprehension, for she moved a step closer, her voice dropping to a steely-soft command.

"I know this is important to Josiah. You want to please him, don't you, Avalina?"

Breath snagged in my chest. My deepest fear was embarrassing my new husband. Which option was worse ... making a fool of myself, or hiding away from strangers' quizzical stares?

I nodded slowly. His mother offered a curt nod.

"Very good. This will be a wonderful thing for you. I promise."

Never had I been so thoroughly dizzy from activity. Even now, hours later, my mind spun.

From the moment Mrs. Durand had set foot in the Holland plantation, her nasally French accent filled the space. Her rapid instructions to her assistants as she fawned and fussed over me left me turning in helpless circles.

"Nannette! Bring me the blue taffeta." Reaching for the fabric with an impatient huff, Mrs. Durand held it up against my face, tsking under her breath as she stared at me with pursed lips.

"Good, but not there yet. Louisa! The soft green silk. And bring me the silver as well."

Swatches of silks, satins, and lace were flung in my direction with military precision. I was fussed at, scolded, praised, measured, cinched, and admonished. In the midst of the tumult, a thought flitted through my mind that caused me to giggle.

Mrs. Durand would be a formidable foe against Captain Blackthorne.

As the chuckle erupted, the sassy French woman turned to me with a scowl. "And what is so funny, Mademoiselle Holland?"

I pressed my lips together. Virginia, who had been watching the process from the corner of the room, arched a single brow.

"Never mind her, Mrs. Durand. She is young and in love."

Mrs. Durand's stern expression melted. "Ah, how well I remember my first days with my husband. I acted just the same." The soft edges of her face tightened. "And now what do I have? A man who eats too much sweet cake and does nothing but smoke cigars in my parlor."

Another giggle threatened to break forth but at Virginia's warning glance, I kept the mirth to myself.

When the torturous session was over, and Mrs. Durand had turned her fussing to Isabelle, I slipped from the room with a sigh of relief. Where was Josiah? He'd been gone since dawn. All his mother had shared was that an elderly slave by the name of Chloe had taken a sudden turn for the worse.

I was tired of rattling around the too-large house. Tired of Virginia's chiding looks and barbed insults. Weary of being poked and prodded and stared at like a stray animal no one was sure what to do with. I wanted to feel useful. No, I needed it.

Creeping into the kitchen, I heaved a tense breath. Empty. I opened one cabinet then another. None of them contained what I sought. Slipping into a backroom that boasted a large table and shelves of canned goods, I scoured through the collection. Aha! Herbs.

I gathered a pouch of dried lavender, some ground ginger, cinnamon, thyme, and a container of canned garlic. I eased the herbs into a cheesecloth and tied it all together by knotting the corners of the cloth before clutching it in my hand and easing out the back door. Amos, the groomsman, waved a greeting when I passed the livery, but everyone else kept to themselves, intent on their chores.

Gingerly lifting the hem of my skirt, I crossed the expansive lawn and hastened toward a row of ramshackle buildings that beckoned beyond the green fields of crops.

I would not rest until I found Chloe among those housed on Slave Row.

Josiah pulled the reins, urging the sleek black horses to a stop before setting the wagon brake. Father had not understood a whit when he'd insisted on fetching the doctor himself. After all, that was why Father kept men like Amos around. But something in Josiah's chest rebelled at the idea of sending the old man to do what he was more than capable of handling on his own.

Strange how that thought had never entered his mind until the transformative trip to Barbados.

He could yet see the fire blazing in Benjamin Magee's blue eyes. He could yet hear the lilt to his brogue as he chastised any who would listen about the evils of slavery, the sin of the apostates. What would his friend think now, seeing Josiah firmly ensconced in the very institution he had sworn to disavow?

Guilt tasted thick on his tongue as he jumped from the wagon seat. At least he was doing something, however small, to ease his own conscience.

He turned to offer aid to the physician but Dr. Morris had already climbed down from his side of the wagon, swiping dust from his black coat as he clutched his medical bag. The older man frowned, lines tightening around his thin lips.

"And where is this afflicted woman?"

Josiah pointed to the fourth cabin. "There. Granny Chloe should be inside. She complains often of rheumatism but is significantly worse today, so much so that Fountain sought me early this morn, saying she could no longer rise from bed." He only hoped the runaway slave was still safely hidden in Granny's backroom. Hers was the only cabin that was built with a small addition. All the rest of the slaves had a shelter of only a single room with a fireplace, table, and cots.

Pickering had led the emaciated fugitive to Slave Row in the morning hours while the rest of the plantation slept. Granny had been only too happy to shelter the man under Josiah's supervision. After all, who would assume a sickly, elderly woman guilty of conspiring with the master's son to aid a runaway?

"Mm." Dr. Morris stepped around the remnants of a cold fire pit and narrowed his eyes. "How old is she?"

Josiah shrugged. "Hard to say. She's lived here as long as I can remember. Eighty. Eighty-five perhaps."

"And you're certain she's not merely attempting to shirk her duties?"

Josiah ground his jaw at the implication. Dr. Morris and his father seemed to be cut from the same cloth.

Approaching the door, he pushed it open and murmured, "I shall let you examine her for yourself to make that determination."

But as he stepped over the threshold, he froze. The physician, unprepared for the sudden stop, slammed into Josiah's back.

Granny Chloe lay on her lumpy bed as Avalina stood over her, wrapping some sort of poultice around the old woman's feet. The aroma of spice permeated the air . . . cinnamon and something floral. Josiah sniffed. And was that . . . garlic?

"Who is this?"

Dr. Morris's voice was gruff as he stared at the two women. Avalina flushed and stepped away from Granny, her cheeks reddening. Josiah swallowed, unsure what it all meant, but he did not like the accusation in the man's tone.

"This is Granny Chloe, as she's affectionately called around here." Josiah moved to the old woman's side and placed a gentle squeeze on her shoulder. He met Avalina's gaze as she shrank away from the physician's glare. Josiah offered her a smile and turned to Morris with a stern look. "And this is my wife."

The older man stiffened but nodded curtly. "It's a pleasure, ma'am."

Avalina bobbed a small bow and moved away. Granny chuckled lightly.

"Laws, Master Holland, I didn't know this pretty young thing was your missus. She came not an hour ago with a mess of herbs and has been busy making poultices for my old bones. Like a breath of fresh air, she is."

Josiah winked at Avalina and stooped to grasp Granny's gnarled fingers. "She's a wonder, that's for sure. How are you feeling?"

"The garlic is helping a mite and your girl found a mess of cherries just a while ago in the big house. She pointed at my feet and urged me to swallow a heap of 'em." She wrinkled her nose. "Not a speck of sugar in them but she acted like it would help."

His gaze darted to his wife, who blushed again and took a sudden interest in her shoes. His heart tugged. Avalina likely knew more about healing than ten physicians combined.

"Cherries? Nonsense." Dr. Morris frowned and examined Granny with all the care of a team of oxen stomping through a field. "What this woman needs is my own personal tonic. Cures anything and everything." The physician pulled a brown bottle from inside his bag. "You take a swallow of this three times a day, you hear?"

"Yes, sir." Suspicion lined the old woman's face but she took the bottle in her warped fingers, too compliant to outwardly disagree. Anger flared in Josiah's chest. The man had spent all of one minute with Granny and done nothing more than shove a snake oil remedy at her? Poppycock.

Tugging a gold pocket watch from his vest, the physician clicked the face open as his brows knit into a pucker. "I'm due at the Honeycutt's within the hour. I'll send my bill to your father."

Josiah's ire rose. The man had done nothing yet was only too happy to charge an inordinate sum for his so-called "services." Just as he always had over the years.

"Amos can drive you to the Honeycutt's."

"Much obliged." With that, the physician turned on his heel and left, as if afraid remaining in the small hut would somehow contaminate him. Josiah sighed and shook his head before turning his attention to Granny Chloe.

"You don't need to take his tonic if you don't wish."

She shrugged against her woolen blanket. "Might do good. Might not." Her dark eyes danced. "If you don't mind me sayin' so, I've got a heap more confidence in your missus than old Doc Morris."

Josiah laughed. "I do too."

He lifted his gaze to Avalina's and smiled. She bit her lower lip, then grinned in return.

"Is there anything else you need to do for Granny?"

She nodded and turned back to the table, then set to work crushing another cutting of dried herbs. He watched her work, her movements methodical, graceful. After long moments, she straightened and wiped her hands on a ratty towel. She glanced around the sparse space, searching for something.

"Can I help you?"

She shook her head and moved to open the door at the back of the cabin. Panic burst in his chest.

"No, don't go in there—"

But he was too late. She opened the door, froze, and started to scream.

CHAPTER 34

I backed up a step, unable to fathom what I saw. I had merely sought a kettle or a pot of some kind to brew Granny a tea. Instead, a skeleton of a man stared at me from the shadowy corner of the tiny room. He wore no shirt and his right foot was a mangled, bloody mess. A pile of rags and a pot filled with dirty water rested nearby.

As a scream scraped my chest, Josiah slipped around me, pressing his hand to my mouth as he tugged me against the wall, whispering soft words meant to comfort and silence.

"Shh! It's all right. I know this man. So does Granny. Don't scream. If you do, others will hear and this poor man will have no chance for freedom."

My heart thudded against my ribs but my terror eased by measures as Josiah's warm palm moved, freeing my lips. He watched me as if fearing I might flee the room and run bellowing across the plantation.

My gaze shifted to the stick-thin man in the corner. He stared at me with wide eyes, his body still as a tomb. No movement. No shifting. Was he frozen from fear or too weak to respond?

I turned to Josiah and whispered, "You brought him here?"

Josiah swallowed and nodded. My husband's dark eyes stared at this man with a strange mix of sadness and regret. "Though I loathe this new role I must play in the family, I can at least do something small to amend for our sins."

"But how did you find him?"

"Pickering. He asked me to help transport him to a safe place."

I slid my fingers to Josiah's arm, my greatest fear finding voice. "But what if your father finds out?"

A muscle twitched in his jaw. "He never comes to Slave Row. I'm sorry I didn't tell you."

"You were attempting to keep me safe."

He nodded as his shoulders sagged ever so slightly.

"Let me help you."

Josiah's head shot up and he met my gaze with a slow, ever-widening grin. I returned his smile and released his arm. I focused my attention on the injured man watching us with wary eyes. Strange. I had spoken in front of him and hadn't even realized it. I knelt by the fugitive's injured foot and studied it carefully, trying not to cringe at the damage. I opened my mouth to ask him how it was injured but only a squeak emerged. I pointed at his foot.

"Ma'am?"

His own voice was raspy and dry. Taking a deep breath, I pointed again and whispered, "How?"

"Animal trap. Caught me as I was running." Each word caused his chest to rise and fall with effort. Not only was he badly hurt, but he needed water and sustenance quickly.

"Pickering managed to get the trap off his foot but he was afraid he was being watched and needed Saul here moved quickly."

So that's where Josiah was this morning. Not checking on Granny but moving Saul to Granny's cabin.

I rose. "I need lots of clean water, salt, clove if the kitchen has some, and clean bandages, along with food for both Saul and Granny Chloe."

Josiah nodded and moved to the door. "Don't worry. Granny knows everything and is one of the few I completely trust. And her current illness provides the perfect cover to let Saul recuperate. I'll gather what you need. I may even tell the others that Granny has a nasty infection and everyone should stay clear of this cabin until she's well."

A solid idea. Saul tried to shift and sucked air through his teeth—and no wonder. That foot was an angry mass of blood and dirt.

One thing was for certain ... if infection set in, Saul's attempt to be free would end here, in a cabin on Slave Row.

As Josiah lugged the things Avalina had requested across the plantation in the direction of Slave Row, the jingle of harnesses and the clopping trot of a team of horses drifted from the front of the house. Turning, he peered at the arrival and frowned. What was Dr. Morris doing back so soon? Amos waited patiently from the driver's seat as the older man emerged from the buggy and stepped down.

The doctor hadn't forgotten something at Chloe's cabin, had he? If he barged in and found Saul sprawled out in the front room with Avalina tending his wounds ...

His heart hammered. Dropping the basket in the yard, Josiah half-walked, half-ran back to the house, anxious to intercept the fellow before he knocked on the door.

"Dr. Morris!" He shouted the greeting and raised his hand in welcome. "Back so soon?"

Dr. Morris released a sigh and shook his head. "My memory's been awful of late. Your family asked me to bring some pain powders on my next trip and I clean forgot when I was here earlier." Opening his bag, he tugged out five small envelopes and offered them to Josiah. "There you go."

"Much obliged. For Father, I assume?"

The doctor's mouth turned down and lines appeared in his forehead. "Your father? No, no. It was your mother who requested them. Something about her afternoon headaches."

That was a relief. "I'm glad. Considering his recent health, I feared pain was already plaguing him."

Tilting his head to the side, Dr. Morris squinted. "Your father's health? Why, what's wrong?"

Perhaps the old physician's memory was indeed fading. And rapidly. "His diagnosis. Remember? You told him he has consumption."

Rearing back, Dr. Morris widened his eyes. "I did no such thing!"

What? Impossible. Father had told him with certainty. And the coughing. The pleas for Josiah to step into the mantle of familial responsibility.

"Father told me himself just a few days ago. Said you diagnosed him less than a fortnight ago."

The physician bristled like a riled cat. "Indeed, your family summoned me less than a fortnight ago, but I diagnosed your father with catarrh, likely caught from being aboard ship for so long. Not severe and certainly not fatal."

With a huff of annoyance, Dr. Morris marched away from Josiah and slid back into the carriage, instructing Amos to get the team moving.

As the carriage rolled away, Josiah stared after it in dumbfounded silence.

His father had been lying about his condition.

I stepped lightly away from Slave Row, smoothing my hands down my skirt. Though I had washed my hands repeatedly with the lye soap and clean water Josiah provided, I yet sensed Saul's blood beneath my fingernails. Stitching his foot back together had not been easy. I pressed a hand to my rolling stomach. Bile had climbed in my throat, the task made all the harder as the fugitive sucked in harsh breaths at the pain, though he made no outcry. That had unnerved me far more than cleaning his mangled flesh.

Who was I to undertake such a task? I was naught but a simple girl, shipwrecked, enslaved, and now bound in marriage to a man whose family loathed me. The only thing I could boast was a rudimentary knowledge of herbs and a kind husband.

I pushed my own inadequacies from my mind as I walked back to the big house, lest my absence be noticed by Josiah's family. Cool wind whipped my skirts around my ankles. It was summer, or so Josiah had said, but the air was much cooler than on the island.

I had done the best I could with both Granny and Saul, and there was little more I could do but fret. What would it be like to be a real nurse? To know about disease and healing and step into such horrors with confidence . . . not trembling like a frightened rabbit?

Such dreaming was useless. I skirted around an ant hill and brooded. At Azaka Mede, I'd never wrestled with such thoughts. I was a slave and would remain a slave. But now? Wild thoughts beckoned me, fruitless dreams and imaginings. Perhaps this was what Master Cyrene had meant when he said education was dangerous. It gave people ideas.

I shivered at the thought of my old master clawing at me, his eyes filled with rage. The explosion of the gun. The way his body had collapsed to the floor with a wet *thunk*. Wrapping my arms around my middle, I made haste toward the house. Thankfully, Cyrene Harding could no longer hurt me. Or could he? The memories had filled my dreams with nightmarish visions. My only solace was the comforting presence of Josiah never farther away than a touch through each night.

I had never told him what I'd done.

And I never would.

A lonely cry rose from the western field. A man's voice, deep-held notes that rose and fell in soothing cadences.

"Go down, Moses, way down to Egypt land. Tell old Pharaoh to let my people go ... "

The song of the slave toiling the earth was a strange kind of reassurance. It reminded me of the island, though the song was far different from anything that had been sung at Azaka Mede. Their songs boasted of the glory of the gods, the harsh load that burdened them. I paused mid-step, listening.

"So the Lord said, go down!"

A cacophony of voices echoed the leader's, drifting lazily through the warm air.

"Go down!"

"Moses." The leader's voice boomed out strong.

"Moses."

"Way down in Egypt land ... "

The melody fell into low tones I could no longer hear distinctly. I frowned. Who was Moses? Pharaoh? Another fabled story like Yarico? The song made no sense. I would ask Josiah about it later when he returned.

Despite the longing melody, there was a strange thread of hope weaving the words together. Odd.

No sooner had I stepped into the shelter of the house than Virginia turned the corner, her eyes widening at the sight of me. Her wide skirts swooshed as she came to a sudden stop in the foyer.

"Where have you been?" She marched forward and leaned down, tugging the hem of my skirt in her slim fingers. "And what is this? Blood?" She released the fabric and snapped to her full height, eyeing me like a wayward child. "What trouble have you gotten into?"

Drat! I let my eyes slide closed. I thought I'd been so careful, but clearly I hadn't been successful. For once, I was thankful I could not speak in her presence. Instead, I merely shrugged.

Virginia heaved an exasperated sigh and motioned me toward my room. "You must change immediately. I have invited my dearest friends to tea this afternoon and you are to meet them. Despite your lack of … *abilities*"—a slight sneer twisted her lips at the word—"you must make a good impression. These women control Charleston, my dear. Do not let me down."

Properly chastised, I scurried up the stairs and slid into the bedroom, shutting the door behind me firmly, my breath coming in shallow pants.

For the first time since leaving, I longed to be back in Barbados.

I trembled as I sat in the parlor, my head spinning. Madam Blanchet, as she introduced herself to me with her strange, nasaled intonations, had been a strict taskmaster throughout the early afternoon—teaching me everything from pouring tea, to walking properly, posture, and making small talk—all while staring at me with pinched lips and a lifted chin. Isabelle had stood silently to the side, her expression filled with compassion.

Unfortunately, Virginia had insisted I meet her vulturous friends without my own ally. Isabelle was unhappily ensconced upstairs with her tutor, conjugating Latin verbs. Again.

I took a small sip of the steaming orange tea, careful to keep my face a blank mask. I despised oranges but would not dare risk Virginia's wrath by anything other than perfect compliance. The last thing I wanted to do was lose Josiah's love by angering his family. He'd done too much for me already.

TO SPEAK HIS NAME

Despite my best efforts, my cup clinked noisily against the plate when I returned it to its place. Virginia arched a single brow in my direction but returned her attention to a buxom woman with coal-black hair streaked with silver along the sides, who pattered on and on.

"My Grover doesn't know what will happen if the weather doesn't warm soon. Our cotton and rice look pitiful. Barely sprouting and here it is at the beginning of summer." The matron sniffed. "Personally, I blame President Madison."

"Oh, come now, Beatrice." A reed-thin woman with tiny, springy curls arranged delicately atop her head laughed lightly. A practiced laugh. Nothing sincere about the sound. "How could President Madison possibly have any control over the weather and crops?"

Beatrice scowled darkly. "All I know is we never had these issues under President Jefferson. And I never did hold to those Federalist ideals of Washington and Adams, say what you will."

"Heavens, why must you always bring politics into our conversation?" An older woman with a plethora of wrinkles shook her head and nibbled on a cookie. "My own dear husband believes women discussing politics is a waste of time. After all, we have no say in elections, finances, or the weather."

The group tittered nervous laughter and fell silent. Virginia cleared her throat softly and turned a thin smile toward me. "I'm so thankful Josiah's bride is here to enjoy the afternoon."

All eyes swung to me and warmth flooded my face. None of the expressions were hostile, but curious, if a bit skeptical.

Virginia tsked under her breath. "I'm afraid the poor thing has not the ability to speak, but her manners are impeccable."

Soft gasps peppered the room and I resisted the urge to slouch. Madam Blanchet made it clear that infraction was a sin on par with immorality. I had no idea what that entailed but she made it sound most horrific.

The thin woman with curls offered a gentle smile. "And where do you hail from, dear?" When she realized I could not answer, she blushed pink and turned to Virginia.

Josiah's mother stiffened but forced another smile. "Barbados."

More gasps. Beatrice pressed her pudgy fingers against her cheek. "Why, she's a heathen!"

Virginia's expression darkened ever so slightly. "My Josiah would never marry a heathen. Why, her character is flawless and George and I gave our full blessing."

Silence stretched thick as molasses. No one dared challenge the woman. When would this horrid afternoon end?

Virginia continued as if unaware of the tension. "In fact, we are throwing her a grand reception on Saturday. I pray you can all attend. The invitations are in the post." Her dark eyes glistened like jewels in sunlight. "It will be *the* social event of the season."

Excited murmurs rippled through the parlor as the women bent their heads together, smiling and chattering about gowns, music, and food. No one acknowledged me, and for that, I was thankful ... for the angst-filled crease of my brow was no doubt there for all to see.

I was barely making it through an hour of tea. How would I ever make it through an entire *grand* evening?

CHAPTER 35

May 27, 1816
Charleston, South Carolina

Josiah stooped and ran his hand through the fine Carolina soil, letting it trickle through his fingers. All the crops had stopped growing during the past week. Corn. Tobacco. Rice. Cotton. All of it.

Sighing, he rose and studied the sky. Pewter clouds had rolled in, eclipsing the warmth of the sun. Never did he remember Charleston being so cool in the summer. Usually, sultry heat dogged each day from May until September. Plants grew thick and hale. Mosquitos buzzed and bees swarmed hives. Not this year. Insects were conspicuously absent. The leafy green tops dotting the fields in orderly rows were stunted, unable to mature.

If the cold snap lingered into June, there would be no crop this year. No crop meant no money. He pinched the bridge of his nose. He must speak to his father immediately... and about more than the failing harvest.

His gut twisted. Surely Dr. Morris had been wrong. Father had always been difficult, a cranky sort in general, but amiable when things were going his way. But Josiah had never seen him being less than honest, even brutally so. His own flesh and blood would never stoop to such foul tactics as lying just to bend Josiah to his will... would he?

Rushing to judgment would be foolish but he could no longer ignore the unease nagging his chest. Things at the Holland plantation were not what they seemed.

And Father was not all of his trouble. He must move Saul tonight. It could wait no longer. Granny's health was improving and as her routine returned to normal, Saul's presence would surely be discovered. Only yesterday Fountain had delivered a tin of hot food and had nearly opened the door to where the fugitive was hiding. Only Granny's quick wit had spared him as she feigned a fit of coughing to distract him. So busy was he with fetching her a cup of water, he forgot about all else.

Josiah clenched his fists. Nor was he willing to risk Avalina traveling back and forth to Granny's cabin anymore. She had checked on both Saul and Granny for the past three days and had somehow managed to evade his family's perusal, but it would not last forever. Not only that, he was now certain his mother was up to something.

Isabelle had told him of Virginia's plans to hold a dance in Avalina's honor and how she had kept her hopping with dress fittings, tea, etiquette lessons, and more. His chest tightened. What was she doing? Planning to parade Avalina in front of Charleston society like a bird in a cage? He suspected it was less about welcoming his new wife and more about mortifying her in front of the elite, yet that didn't make sense either. If Avalina did not perform well, it would reflect on the entire family, not just her. The last thing his mother would want was a fall from grace in the eyes of her friends.

He flexed his fingers. Indeed, something at the Holland plantation was not as it should be.

Blowing out a long breath, he strolled toward the eastern field. Dust stirred in little puffs with each step. Regardless of the schemes his mother might be hatching, his first goal must be to transport Saul. Pickering had sent another ambiguous message only this morning and as soon as Josiah had committed it to memory, he'd burned the missive in the fireplace. He must lead Saul to the home of Matthew Holmes. Tonight.

On the morrow was the dance, and though the commotion provided the perfect cover to evade his family, there was no way he would leave his wife alone in the sharp-tongued mob that made up the societal elite.

He smiled thinking of the stolen moments he and Avalina had shared over the past days. Feverish kisses and embraces in the night hours, while waking each morn to study the Bible together. He encouraged her to read as many words as she could aloud, and although the going was slow, she was making remarkable progress. She peppered him with questions, proving that her intellect was as sharp as any scholar's.

"Why did your God create man and woman with instructions not to touch the fruit of the tree? Why not resist creating the temptation in the first place?"

"How did Abram seek your God if all he had known were the ways of his fathers?"

"Who are Moses and Pharaoh?"

The last question had given him pause. They hadn't yet read Exodus yet she knew of Moses?

With his arm lazily draped around her as they studied the Scriptures from the solace of the bed, he'd turned to her with surprise. "How do you know of Moses? Did Matias teach you?"

She shook her head. "No. I heard your slaves singing a song about Moses and Pharaoh several days ago. What does it mean?"

He'd carefully explained the lineage of Abraham, Isaac, and Jacob. How Joseph had been abused and sold by his brothers and had later saved the entire family during a time of famine. How Jacob's children had filled the land and how an evil Egyptian king enslaved the lot of them until God saw fit to send Moses, the one chosen to lead them from bondage.

Her eyes took on a faraway glaze as he ended the tale. "Odd, isn't it, how one corrupt man can rule an entire land and affect generations?"

He'd have wagered a hundred dollars she was thinking of Cyrene Harding and all those she'd left behind in Barbados. Pulling her closer, he murmured into her hair as he kissed her temple. "Stranger still how the God of the universe sees the suffering, stoops down, and frees us from captivity."

She stiffened at his words, her nostrils flaring. "But he hasn't! What of Matias and Tabia and Molly and the thousands of others yet in chains or killed without one taste of freedom?"

"There is more than one type of captivity, Avalina." He kept his voice gentle, soothing.

"I don't understand."

"There is captivity of the body. Men like Harding, and Pharaoh, and even my father see slavery as a necessity. Someday when my father is gone and the Holland plantation is mine, I will free every single person on this piece of land." She lifted his hand and pressed a kiss to his fingers. His chest tightened in response. "But far worse is captivity of the soul. Those who reject God's Son, Jesus. Who insist on being their own saviors." He stared into her smoky eyes and lifted his hand to stroke her cheek. "Men like Matias might be physically chained, but they are freer than Harding or my father will ever be."

She had grown quiet then, and he'd let her ponder all they had discussed. He would not see his mother undo all the care both he and Isabelle had poured into her. Her future was at stake, in all the ways that mattered.

He kicked at a clod of dirt and eyed the darkening sky. Rain was coming. Cold rain.

The moon was hidden behind the dark clouds that refused to budge over Charleston. From the shroud of shadows, Josiah supported Saul's weight, taking care as they stepped from the shelter of Granny's cabin. The thin man leaned heavily against Josiah's side as they skirted the edges of the small building. Emerging from the shack carried its own risk, but the greater threat was taking Saul to new location. Between here and the Holmes house was an abundance of forest, broken by wide fields with little shelter. If anyone were to see them ...

When he'd shared the plan with Avalina, cold fear washed over her face. How he hated to worry her but there was no help for it. Saul would never make it to Holmes on his own, not with his foot yet bearing the pain of the animal trap.

Protect us, Lord.

Was it wrong to ask the Almighty for His blessing while doing something illegal? He had no idea.

The two men had barely walked thirty paces into the woods behind Slave Row when something rustled in the bramble. Josiah froze, Saul's arm still slung around his neck as they waited, their breathing thick. More rustling, this time accompanied by the faint snap of a twig. Josiah's heart leapt from his chest when the wan light illuminated Avalina's silhouette as she approached clutching leather reins, a mare plodding behind her.

"Avalina!" Josiah winced, the sound of his voice carrying farther than he'd intended. He dropped his voice to the faintest whisper. "Why are you here?"

Her gaze shot to Saul's but she stepped close and brushed her lips against his ear.

"To help, of course."

Josiah reared back, anger billowing in his chest. "Go back. This is too dangerous."

"I agree." She whispered again, her breath tickling his skin. "Which is why you ought not go it alone. You forget, I've checked on Saul every day since he arrived. I knew he couldn't make the journey without help."

Josiah's nostrils flared. "*I* am his help."

"We'll make faster time with the mare." She leaned away and tugged the horse close, rubbing its nose with a slim hand.

Josiah shook his head. "A horse will be too loud. Hoof beats travel like buckshot through the night."

She simply smiled and pointed to the mare's hooves. Squinting, he stooped down as far as he dared while bearing part of Saul's weight and blinked. Why, she had wrapped burlap around the horse's hooves and tied it off with strips of leather.

When his head jerked up, he and the fugitive nearly slammed into each other. "How did you come up with that?"

She grinned saucily. "Matias. He taught me a lot. On occasion, he would sneak from Azaka Mede to search for soursop and Bajan cherries. He would take a horse to make the journey faster."

This woman never ceased to surprise him. He pursed his lips. In truth, they did need the mare. Saul was far weaker than Josiah had anticipated. He looked at his wife. "Do you mind walking?"

"Not at all."

With a nod, he helped Saul mount the sleepy mare and grabbed the reins, silently leading the trio through the woods toward the Holmes house. The scurrying of squirrels, the hoot of an owl, every sound of the night tangled Josiah's nerves into a frayed knot.

After nearly two hours of plodding over fallen limbs, ducking the thorny grip of brambles, and the snorts of the horse, a modest cabin appeared. A small creek gurgled sleepily behind it, masking their footfalls. Handing the reins to Avalina, he whispered, "Stay here until I know it's safe."

She nodded and he crept along the tree line. Pickering said a storm cellar was directly behind the cabin, nothing more than an earth dugout with a door. The thin moonlight glinted off the handle. With a prayer for protection, Josiah plunged from the shelter of the woods and tugged the heavy wooden door open. The old hinge didn't so much as squeak.

He descended the steps slowly, darkness closing in around him.

"You looking for me?" A masculine murmur lifted the hair on the back of his neck.

"Matthew Holmes?"

"One and the same."

Josiah heaved a breath of relief as a match flared to life in the cellar, the sizzle illuminating a middle-aged man with a shock of dark hair and a beard so thick, he resembled a bear. Even his eyes were dark and piercing.

Lighting a lantern, Holmes blew out the remnants of the match and tossed it on the dirt floor before grounding it out with the toe of his boot.

"I'm surprised you came. No offense, but when Pickering told me the son of George Holland would be delivering a fugitive to my door, I could scarcely believe it." He shook his head. "If your father finds out, there'll be hell to pay."

Josiah snorted softly. "I see my father's reputation precedes him."

Holmes's lips puckered, moving his bushy beard with the expression. "Again, I mean no disrespect."

"None taken."

"I suppose it's a good lesson for all of us." He set the lantern on top of an old crate and straightened to study Josiah, his face somber. "If the Lord can call the son of a man like George Holland, nothing is too hard for Him."

Josiah frowned. There was a world of meaning behind the man's words, but he didn't fully understand the implications. "Surely it's not so odd to have abolitionists among the relatives of slave owners. This is South Carolina, after all. Most of the men I know own at least a couple slaves."

Matthew's brows shot into his hairline. "It's not the owning of slaves that surprises most about your father, my friend. It's his reputation."

"What reputation?"

Matthew blinked rapidly and crossed his arms, his brows knitting ever so slightly. "Why, that your father sired such a large number of his slaves."

A punch to the face would have been less shocking. Josiah stepped back, the wind rushing from his lungs. "Wh-what?"

Matthew's eyes widened. "Didn't you know?"

"I—I . . . " What could he say? The possibility had never even crossed his mind. Josiah leaned against the earthen wall of the cellar, his legs strangely gelatinous. If Holmes was correct, how many children had his father sired?

A surge of fire pillared through his chest. All this time, George Holland had played on Josiah's fear, his sense of obligation, of duty, even his obedience through Holy Scripture. And all the while, the same man had broken countless commandments, turning a blind eye to his own sin. And for what? Lust? Power?

Clenching his teeth, Josiah pushed away from the wall. "I have the fugitive outside. He's badly injured. My wife has been caring for him."

Matthew nodded. "We'll see to his comfort and move him again as soon as the Lord provides opportunity."

Josiah nodded curtly and turned away, every movement as brittle as a dead leaf facing a winter wind. He didn't know what to do with such anger, such betrayal.

After leaving Saul in Matthew's capable hands, he and Avalina silently returned to the Holland plantation. Not even his wife could coax him from his morbid thoughts. Something had to be done about his father's lies and deceit. But what?

How much of Josiah's life had been shrouded in deception?

CHAPTER 36

Josiah looked over his shoulder for the tenth time, ensuring no one had followed him into Father's study. This was a sacred place... or so George Holland had always claimed. Despite the frequent reminder that Josiah was his predecessor and heir, he'd never once been allowed the privilege of perusing the ledgers or documents held inside the dark room. It had always been an imposing sanctuary, even as Josiah had grown and matured. The dark paneled wood, the musky scent of cigar smoke that perpetually hung in the air, the aroma of aged parchment and old books... entering had often felt like intruding upon a dragon's lair.

Make that a lying dragon.

He snorted to himself as he opened another drawer.

Yanking out a handful of folded documents, he studied the lot quickly. Bills of sale for the many slaves Father had purchased over the years. Zeke, Big Tom, Charley, Annie...

Josiah cast the lot of them atop the desk, as if touching them somehow stained his fingers. What price could be put on a human life? Yet there it was, scratched in ink—450 dollars, 500 dollars, 850...

His nose wrinkled as he turned his attention from the papers and looked deeper into the drawer. Ah, finally. A ledger marked with the current year.

Tugging it free, he opened the worn pages and flipped through them with haste. Tallies, accounts, deposits, money going in and going out. All seemed to be in order.

He flipped to the last page and found a note. *Prospero.*

He set the ledger on the desk and frowned. Prospero? What did that mean? He riffled through the rest of the drawer but saw nothing of import. After replacing the ledger and bills of sale, he tugged open the last drawer. More of the same.

Josiah leaned back in the chair and frowned, absently running his forefinger over his lips. This was a fruitless endeavor. He didn't even know what he was looking for. But if his father had indeed lied about his own health, what other secrets were buried at Holland plantation?

And Prospero . . . why was the word so familiar?

Of course!

Josiah pushed up from the chair and hastened to the shelves holding endless rows of books. He knew what he needed. Shakespeare.

He skimmed the titles quickly. Prospero was a character in the playwright's classic *The Tempest.* It had been years since he'd read the story, but he remembered enough after his tutor had droned on and on about the story for over a fortnight. Prospero was a magician, and an exiled duke as well, who had spun lies to hide his true history. What had the iniquitous Prospero told Ariel? *I have done nothing but in care of thee.* He had claimed his deceit was intended to protect. An admission of pure motive surrounded by lies. When Josiah had asked Mr. Combs his tutor, if God forgave lies in order to seek a greater good, the older man had peered over the top of his spectacles and offered Josiah a dismissive smile.

"Machiavelli asked the same," the tutor had said.

As a child, Josiah hadn't understood the veiled retort, but now the meaning was all too clear.

He ran his finger across the books as he found the collection of Shakespeare. *Romeo and Juliet, MacBeth, Othello…*

Finally, *The Tempest.* Josiah tugged the large tome free and flipped through the pages, looking for anything significant. A scribbled note, a letter, but there was nothing.

With a sigh, he stepped forward to place it back on the shelf when his eye caught a slip of paper sticking out where the back of the wood met the corner. He tugged at the parchment but it wouldn't give. There was a seam along the bottom of the wood and it moved when Josiah picked at it with his fingernail.

Spine tingling, he removed the row of Shakespeare tales and tugged at the bottom of the shelf's back. The dark wood panel pulled free. A ledger and a handful of yellowed letters spilled out from the hidden compartment.

His mouth turned to cotton. Why would his father have installed a false shelf back? Clearly, he wanted no one to see this particular cache of documents.

Breath quickening, he replaced the piece of wood and arranged the volumes of Shakespeare so nothing would appear amiss. Satisfied with his work, he scooped up the ledger and letters and scurried from the room. If his father caught him with them, his wrath would know no bounds. Josiah needed time. Time to read, to figure it all out.

He could take them to the bedroom, but no. Avalina was preparing for tonight's dance, and Mother would be in and out all day, overseeing her preparations like a bee buzzing around a hive. The livery? The greenhouse? Too risky. Too many people underfoot.

Fountain. His old playmate would keep the documents secure until he could sort them all out and find a safe hiding place. And none of the slaves could read, so there was no danger in spilling sensitive information.

He hurried from the house, one destination in mind: Fountain's cabin.

I was going to cast up my accounts.

Pressing a hand to my middle, I sat in front of the vanity mirror as maids fretted around me, dabbing powder to my nose and neck. Another tugged locks of my hair and twisted it around curling tongs, long pieces of metal heated over a candle flame. I wrinkled my nose at the acrid stench. Why did Americans torture themselves so? I never remembered such devices on the island.

Still, despite the smell, glossy red ringlets cascaded down my back and shoulders. The warmth skimmed my bare skin where the chemise rested. I shivered at the sensation. My gown, I learned from Virginia, was to be of blue silk and would expose my shoulders, neck, and part of my chest.

My cheeks heated and I wrapped my arms around my middle. Never had I worn anything so elegant ... or so revealing.

I looked for Isabelle to distract me from my own tortured thoughts but she was absent. Of course. She was making preparations in her own room.

How would I ever survive this night? Nameless faces, stares, questions ... a tumult of people intent on judging me. Josiah was too good for me and I knew it. Why rub lemon juice into a cut? My breeding, education, and social standing were nonexistent. Why play the ruse of a lady of worth?

Unless this entire event was orchestrated by Virginia ... not to parade, but expose.

A knot tightened my middle. I couldn't shake my unease at the thought. Josiah's mother had no particular fondness for me. That much was certain. But would the woman stoop to humiliating me in front of Charleston's elite? I bit my lip, forcing the tears away by sheer force of will.

"Hairpins, miss?"

The young maid, Eliza, stood at my side, hand extended. I startled back to the present. She needed hairpins. My gaze scanned the vanity but saw nothing.

Yanking open the left drawer, I spied a jumble of the small metal pieces and placed them in her palm.

Wait...what was this? As Eliza busied herself arranging my curls, I blinked and tugged small cream-colored envelopes from the drawer. Bold font was stamped across the top. What did it say?

I sounded out the letters silently in my mind. *H ... hh ... eh ... deh.* Head ah ... *ch*. I wrinkled my nose. That didn't make sense. Wait, Josiah had told me sometimes '*ch*' made a '*k*' sound. *K ...* ee. Hedackee?

Headache! The second word was easier. *Powders.* I frowned. Why were envelopes of headache powders in my dresser?

Perhaps they were Josiah's. But I'd never seen him take any medicine like this. I shrugged and handed them to Eliza.

Eliza frowned and released one of my curls, reaching instead for the medicine. "That's exactly like the medicinal powders Miss Virginia gets from the doctor." Eliza pursed her lips. "Powerful stuff. Makes a sick person sleep all day. Queasy too." The maid studied me in the mirror. "You found 'em in the vanity?"

I nodded.

"You sure you don't want them? Might come in handy if you get to feelin' poorly."

I shook my head and the little maid slipped them into her apron pocket. The last thing my fluttering stomach needed was something to turn it end over end. No, I needed all my wits about me tonight.

Now, more than ever.

Josiah lowered the papers, mind reeling at the words scratched onto the parchment in black ink.

His father was deeply in debt. The papers showed a running list of people he owed money to, as well as investment schemes, gambling debts, and men he'd worked with to bleed investors dry. Running columns of numbers marked what he claimed was in his office ledgers versus the truth of what his accounts actually contained.

Worse still was the final page that outlined his will. As Josiah expected, George Holland intended to leave the land, the house, and his holdings to Josiah ... though how much would remain after his debts were paid, no one could say. What he *didn't* expect was the list of names with modest sums next to them. Most of them Josiah didn't recognize but one stood out with shocking clarity. Fountain. And the words at the top of the column? *Additional Sons Sired.*

George Holland was Fountain's father.

Josiah's former playmate, his earliest friend, was actually his brother. Bile curdled up his throat. Not only did his father hold men and women in chains, he had abused the women in the vilest way possible and then sought to ease his own warped conscience by leaving them a handful of coins.

He let his eyes slide shut and blew out a breath from the shade of Fountain's cabin. It couldn't be true. It couldn't. He didn't want to believe his own flesh and blood was capable of such horror but deep in his heart, he knew it to be true. Hadn't Matthew Holmes said George Holland's reputation was well known? How had Josiah been so blind?

The crunch of shoes on rocks snapped his senses alert. Fountain rounded the corner, sweat staining his chest and armpits. Even though Father had moved him from the fields years ago to work in the stable with Amos, the man still found a way to work up a sweat each day. He stopped upon seeing Josiah near the cabin.

"Sir." He nodded respectfully.

Josiah forced a stiff smile. "Good to see you, Fountain. I have a favor to ask you. I need a safe place to temporarily keep these papers." He held up the stack of yellowed pages and struck a relaxed pose, praying the man couldn't see his heart hammering out of his chest. "Do you mind if I leave them here for a few hours?"

Fountain shook his head slowly, but his brows knit. "What you needing them papers for? Something for the overseer?"

"No, nothing like that." Fountain was smart. Always had been. Josiah exhaled heavily and glanced toward the big house. "They are just some personal documents that need to be kept safe from prying eyes." Not exactly a lie, but still, his conscience niggled.

Pursing his lips, Fountain pointed to the door. "Put them anywhere you like, sir. I'll keep them safe for you."

"Much obliged." Josiah pushed the door open and set the papers on Fountain's thin cot, resisting the urge to stuff them under the straw-tick mattress. He straightened and studied his half-brother as the man swallowed a ladleful of water from the pail in the corner.

"Who was your father, Fountain?"

He froze, water dripping on the floor from the ladle. After a long pause, he dropped the dipper back into the pail with a plop and wiped his mouth with the back of his sleeve. "Don't know, sir. Momma never did say."

"Your mother was Ruby, correct?"

"Yes, sir. Gone ten years now."

"Mm. I'm sorry. She was always kind. Smart too."

"Yes, sir. I agree."

"She never said if your father was another slave who lived here?"

Fountain shifted his weight from foot to foot. Silence stretched tight as a fiddle string. "She didn't say, sir."

He knew more than he was letting on. With a terse nod, Josiah stepped past the big man and clapped him on the shoulder as he passed. "Thank you, Fountain. I appreciate your discretion."

Their gazes met and held. Two pairs of brown eyes, searching. After a long moment, Fountain lifted his chin.

"Your secret is safe with me, Mr. Holland. I promise."

"Josiah. Call me Josiah."

He left, his heart and mind in turmoil.

CHAPTER 37

"Take courage, my love."

I swallowed the ash in my mouth and fortified my heart with the murmur Josiah had whispered in my ear as he led me down the stairs of the bustling plantation home. Women tittered behind brightly colored fans and chattered with graceful ease, the lot of them parading their high-waisted silk gowns as they cast coy smiles at men dressed in black coattails. Before Josiah had claimed me, Isabelle had peeked at the assembly from the second floor. She had whispered something about Cossack trousers being all the rage this year but I had no idea to what she referred. Virginia had swept into my room minutes before ushering me out the door, studying me with a caustic eye.

"No time to teach you the nuances of fan etiquette." She sighed. "We must muddle through as best we can."

She thrust a shimmering silver fan in my hand and ushered Josiah to my side so we could descend the stairs together. I stared blankly at the fan. What did she mean by "fan etiquette"? Didn't one simply wave it back and forth if overheated?

Nothing in this new world made sense. All I could hear in my mind was Virginia's nonstop litany of terse instructions.

Never slurp your soup.

Never substitute your oyster fork for your dessert fork.

Can't something be done about your freckles?

Avoid looking into the faces of strangers whom you meet, especially of ladies.

It is a mark of good breeding to suppress undue emotion. This regards laughter. Such behavior is uncouth.

I patted my nose and winced. Despite Virginia's insistence that I dab lemon juice on my freckles each night, the blemishes remained. All the admonitions tangled in my mind like knotted yarn. I had no idea where to look, how to react, or how to eat.

Yet when Josiah's eyes met mine, joy and desire radiated from their depths, and my heart calmed. I could brave anything with him by my side. Strange that the thought both thrilled and disheartened me. What I dreaded most was disappointing him. I could not fail.

As I slipped my hand into the crook of his arm, I silently repeated all I had been taught.

A lady never runs, but floats on the arm of her escort as if weightless.

Never rub your eyes.

A lady never raises her voice.

Despite my trepidation, a smile tugged at my mouth. At least I would not disappoint on that score.

At our arrival, the strain of violins ceased and every eye in the room turned to us. Nameless faces, the men's bold stares, whispers behind fans... their open curiosity was nearly my undoing. Bile bubbled up my throat.

Josiah's father, with Virginia at his side, lifted his hands and flashed a winsome smile.

"Ladies and gentlemen, we thank you for joining us tonight as we celebrate. May I present my son and his lovely bride ... Mr. and Mrs. Josiah Holland!"

Applause rose and heat scorched my cheeks. Josiah slid his free hand to cover mine and the warmth of his touch caused me to lift my eyes to his. He was smiling. My stomach flipped and I could do nothing but respond in kind.

Back straight. Be demure. Do not respond with excessive emotion.

How could I do anything but warm to his affection? I allowed my smile to stretch wide and Josiah lifted his hand to stroke my cheek.

Virginia cleared her throat as the applause died away. Mr. Holland turned to the musicians and offered them a nod. "And now, we dance!"

The strings launched into a rollicking tune and cheers rose as men and women parted into two rows to dance what Josiah told me was a reel. I swallowed the lump in my throat. I had been given no instructions on this dance.

Josiah must have sensed my angst, for he chuckled and whispered, "Don't worry. We will be busy greeting guests for some time. No need to fret over the steps just yet."

Biting my lip, I took a deep breath and moved to smile at the first couple to congratulate us. For days I had been tormented by nightmares of my tongue frozen as guests glared at me with contempt, but my fears had been for naught. With the raucous laughter flooding the room, the cacophony of instruments and dancers, I had little more to do than smile sweetly, curtsy, and offer my hand to any gentlemen who pressed chaste kisses against my skin. Josiah introduced me to countless guests, his chest expanded in pride.

From time to time, I caught Virginia staring at me through the throng with narrowed eyes, but as quickly as I observed the subtle hostility, her expression smoothed into a polite smile. A few others, mostly preening ladies my age, glared at me. No doubt they had set their cap for Josiah and were disappointed to find him taken. As the evening progressed, and the wine flowed freely, the knot in my stomach eased by measures. My spirits were high as my husband turned to me, a twinkle in his eyes.

"I think it's long past time to claim my bride for a waltz. Don't you agree?"

I giggled and offered him my hand as he swept me into the clamber of spinning dancers. I no longer worried about the steps, or the gentle one, two, three, one, two, three of the minuet. All I knew was this moment, trapped in Josiah's arms, basking in his adoration. Surely no queen could ever feel as blessed. Master Cyrene, and the misery of my past were far behind.

When the song ended, he tugged me free of the crowd and led us to a table of refreshments. "Would you care for some punch?"

I nodded, already anticipating the cold sweetness that would soothe my parched throat.

Before he could fetch the refreshment, a woman sidled close, her blond hair piled in ringlets atop her head. Her emerald gown complemented the sharpness of her green eyes. Her chin lifted ever so slightly, as if she were peering down on me from a perch somewhere above.

Shifting her gaze to Josiah, she batted her lashes prettily and offered him her hand. "Josiah, how lovely to see you again."

He stiffened but bowed slightly over her extended hand as he gently grasped the tips of her fingers. "Miss Pembroke. We are glad to have you in attendance."

Her full lips puckered into a childlike pout. "And here I thought you would ask me to a dance, as you have so many times before." One brow arched high as she shot me a smug smile.

Crimson crept up his neck. "I find the only lady whose attention I long for is my beautiful wife's." A tight smile curved his lips as he placed his hand on the small of my back. "May I introduce you to my bride? Miss Rose Pembroke, this is my wife, Avalina Holland."

Her nose crinkled ever so slightly on one side but she bobbed her head quickly and I returned the gesture, a stiff smile on my lips.

"Avalina, is it? How do you find Charleston? I've heard you're not even from South Carolina." She tittered a laugh. "I can't imagine such a thing."

How I longed to wipe the gloating sneer from her too-perfect face, but my tongue stilled. I nearly choked over the words begging to burst forth.

Josiah straightened. "My wife cannot speak, Miss Pembroke, but I assure you, she has been on the most exhilarating adventure in the past few months."

Miss Pembroke's snide grin slipped a notch. "A mute? How … quaint. Why, however did the two of you meet?"

My gaze shot to Josiah, silently pleading with him to keep my past a secret. What would this horrid woman, or the entire crowd for that matter, think if they knew I had been enslaved?

But my husband showed no such trepidation. He smiled down at me and tightened his hold on my waist. "I saw Avalina dancing and lost my heart to her."

The dance at Azaka Mede? The night I had been laughing with the children, dancing with a broom? The cold shame in my middle evaporated at his warm perusal. But he had intended to leave the island without me. Hadn't he given me his compass as a farewell present?

Or perhaps he had cared for me as more than a poor slave longer than I'd imagined.

The realization freed something trapped in my soul. Josiah had seen me at my worst and chose to love me anyway. Nothing in my past could hurt me any longer. I was free.

I beamed and Miss Pembroke cleared her throat, talking lightly of mundane things before excusing herself. I breathed a sigh of relief. If she was the worst this night would offer, all would be well.

Josiah plucked a cup from the table and pressed it into my hand. The pink punch shimmered in the light of a thousand candles. I jumped ever so slightly when his baritone boomed over the room. "Attention, please!"

Couples turned in our direction. Chatter died. Every eye in the house was trained on my husband as he smiled.

"I would like to offer a toast to my lovely bride, Avalina." He lifted another glass of punch high in the air. "To friendships, hope, and laughter. To love."

"To love!" The entire ballroom echoed the sentiment. Warmth bloomed in my cheeks as guests cheered and sipped, but it was a delicious heat ... like snuggling down in a thick quilt during a thunderstorm.

A commotion sounded from somewhere beyond the yawning space. Masculine shouts erupted. I heard Hattie shrieking. "You can't go in there! You have not been invited!"

A mob of stern-faced men pushed inside. The lot of them wore black jackets with long rows of buttons down their fronts. Revolvers were strapped to their hips. One particularly sour fellow pushed to the front. A silver star was affixed to his lapel. Gasps peppered the room.

Josiah's father stomped forward, his eyes blazing daggers. "Sheriff Edwards! What is the meaning of this?"

Josiah stepped in front of me, shielding me from view. I trembled, clutching his arm. Had patrollers learned of his activities with Pickering? Had they come to arrest him?

Edwards pursed his lips beneath his bristly mustache. "I have come with a posse of patrollers. We have reports of a person in attendance who has broken the law. I come seeking only justice. We want no trouble."

George scoffed and puffed out his chest like a banty rooster. "You'll find no law breakers here."

I sensed Josiah's muscles tense underneath my touch.

"Be that as it may"—Sheriff Edwards scoured the room through narrowed eyes—"I am looking for a young woman. Her name is Avalina."

Spots danced before my eyes as the entire assemblage shifted their focus to me. Josiah took a step forward, his fists clenched.

"My wife has done nothing wrong."

A muscle twitched in the sheriff's cheek. "That is for the law to decide." He motioned the group of men forward as I stepped back. This couldn't be happening. It couldn't. The room spun.

"Avalina ... Holland?" The sheriff approached, his steps measured. "You are under arrest for fleeing your master and attempted murder."

Shouts rose into a tumult. "Murder?" Josiah's eyes widened as he whirled to me. "What is he talking about?"

I shook my head. How? How had they found out? A tall, broad-shouldered figure stepped across the threshold. My knees buckled.

Master Cyrene stood in the doorway, his jaw clenched. His dark eyes glittered with triumph.

"Did you think you'd won, Avalina? As you can see, I am decidedly alive."

My mind screamed as the world went black.

CHAPTER 38

"I knew that girl was trouble! Didn't I try to convince you to annul your marriage?"

His father ranted and raved inside the small parlor where he paced. Virginia, Isabelle, and Josiah sat in stunned silence. Upon Avalina's arrest, guests had filed out quickly, the evening's celebration dissolving into scandal. Virginia wailed from time to time into her handkerchief. Hattie came in and out with smelling salts, but Josiah was numb to it all. Isabelle sat beside Mother, absently patting her hand.

Josiah slumped in the chair, elbows on his knees, his head in his hands, digging his fingers into his scalp. Why? How? His wife was no murderer. Yet, when she finally regained consciousness and the sheriff led her away in shackles, one emotion painted her lovely face. Guilt.

None of this made sense. He had witnessed Cyrene Harding face-down in a pool of blood. Yet the events of the rebellion were fuzzy...too much had happened to pay close attention. Between the shattering glass, booming gun blasts, blood, and violence, his only goal had been to grab Avalina and rush away. Had she played him for a fool?

After all, his own father had been lying and cheating for years...a fact Josiah had yet to confront him with. Who could he really trust? Was there anyone?

Benjamin Magee. The name popped into his brain like a beacon. The diminutive preacher was honest to a fault. He had a way of cutting through façades to expose the raw truth beneath the charade. Heaving a thick sigh, he dropped his hands from his head. Benjamin was miles away, likely in Philadelphia by now.

After another of Virginia's wails, Isabelle frowned. "I still don't believe it. Avalina is no murderer."

Father whirled, pinning her with a scathing glare. "The girl can't speak! How do we know what she is? Or who?" His acidic gaze shifted to Josiah. "And you marry her without even questioning her morals or breeding. A fool! That's what you are."

"She speaks to me." Josiah uttered the rebuttal void of emotion. He was numb. Tired. He could not reconcile the woman who had so enriched his life, who had lain in his arms, with a cold-blooded killer.

Ignoring her parents, Isabelle rose and crossed the room before kneeling at Josiah's feet, imploring him with a hopeful gaze.

"You must go to her, Josiah. Hear the truth from her own lips. What if all this is a huge mistake? What if she is being mistreated?" Tears glassed her brown eyes. "Please don't give up on her. She's innocent. I know it."

The flicker of an ember burned in his chest. Isabelle was right. For better or worse, richer or poorer, Avalina was his wife. He owed her that much. Guilt niggled, shame that his baby sister had to spur him into action. He was so ... confused. There had been too many lies. Too much deception.

He nodded and rose. "I'll go now."

Father huffed. "I forbid it! It's bad enough that our family has become a laughingstock in front of every important family in Charleston tonight. Now you want to snivel around the jail? I won't have it, Josiah. Do you hear me?"

But Josiah had already stalked to the door, opening it with a grunt and letting it slam behind him with a deafening crack.

When I stared up at the imposing fortress that constituted the Charleston jail, my knees knocked so loudly, I feared the dour lawman would accuse me of smuggling rattles in my skirts. The gray building with its octagonal towers and narrow windows was meant to intimidate. No, terrify. And it did.

Yanking me unceremoniously from the black carriage, the stern man with his thick mustache kept a relentless grip on my arm. The irons clanked around my wrists as he tugged me ever closer to the fortress.

Looking back at me, he sneered. "Cheer up, miss. You'll have loads of company inside. Why, the warden might even house you with Lavinia Fisher. Heard of her?"

I shook my head as he jerked me up the single stone step.

His white teeth flashed. "We apprehended her not long ago. She's a thief. Murderer. You two should be quite the chums."

Icy dread snaked through my belly. Chuckling, he opened the creaking door and shoved me toward a cranky fellow sitting behind a rickety table in the hall. His paunchy gut hung over his belt. A tin plate filled with gnawed bones rested near his elbow. Sucking the fat from a chicken leg, he wiped his greasy lips along the back of his hand and plopped the remains into the tin with a clunk.

"Who ya got, Harvey? The Queen of England?" The pudgy man laughed at his own pitiful joke.

"Avalina Holland."

The robust man eyed me with displeasure and scratched my name into a ledger. "Second floor. South tower." His gaze scraped mine as the corner of his nose curled. "Enjoy your stay … princess."

Harvey nodded curtly and pushed me toward a shadowed stairwell. I still wore my beautiful blue gown and I stumbled over the long skirt brushing the grimy stone floor. I nearly wept at the thought of the dirt that would soon stain the exquisite dress. Foolish to cry over fabric, but in some odd way, it seemed symbolic of my life. I never should have fled Barbados. Never should have listened to Josiah. I was a poor slave girl and always would be. Ribbons and lace would not change my destiny... or who I was.

As I climbed the stairs, the air grew stale, fetid. I gagged at the odor of unwashed bodies and urine. Once we reached the landing, Harvey shifted to lead me down the narrow hallway. Iron bars could scarcely conceal the horrific smells... or the misery contained behind them.

Somewhere to my left, an inmate moaned softly, his weak cries resembling the haunts Tabia always claimed were real. I never knew whether to believe her tales or not. After all, she'd accused me of being a witch on more than one occasion. And though I'd always scoffed at the notion, now, trembling in this abode of torment, I had no doubt I was cursed.

A voice drifted from a cell on my right. "Look at her. Hair as red as blood."

I backed away from the door, bumping into Harvey, who uttered a curse under his breath. A bony woman with stringy gray hair and yellowed teeth peered at me through the cell barrier, her dark eyes narrowed to slits.

"Come here and let me pet you, lamb."

Harvey kicked at her door. "Back away, Maude. Keep your foolish blatherings to yourself."

The woman slunk back into the darkness, resembling a rat. The metal around my wrists clanked noisily as my shivering increased. The lawman stopped before a cell and, yanking a ring of keys from his belt, shoved one into the lock. The hinges squealed as he tugged the door open. "In."

I swallowed and held up my bound hands. Rolling his eyes, he withdrew another key and pulled them from my wrists before shoving me inside. I tripped on the hem of my skirt and landed on the slick floor with an explosion of pain. Wincing, I scrambled into the corner. Why were the stones beneath my feet damp? Revulsion skittered up my spine.

Harvey slammed the door and the reverberation echoed in my heart. There was no escaping.

Quaking tremored through my gut and quickly traveled to each limb, each finger, each toe. I was alone. Soon to be forgotten.

And it was nothing more than I deserved.

Somewhere in the distance, metal clanged and echoed. Footfalls. Masculine murmurs. I blinked and pushed up from the floor, swiping grit from my cheek. I must have fallen asleep. I braved a glance at the lumpy cot in the corner. I had not the courage to rest on it. Judging by the holes bursting from its seams, and the straw carelessly littered around it, rats had long ago claimed it for their nest.

Edging against the wall, I clenched my jaw and tucked my knees under my chin. How long would they leave me here? Weeks? Months? Perhaps my punishment had already been given. Death in this damp, filthy cell.

Heavy footfalls scraped down the hallway. Two men approached my cell and stood, watching me. Harvey and …

Josiah.

My heart hammered.

"Avalina." His voice was hoarse. A knot welled in my throat as I looked away, eyes burning. He should not have come.

Turning to the guard, he murmured, "May we have a moment?"

Harvey glared in my direction. "Five minutes."

Once the scowling man left, Josiah wrapped his hands around the bars and pressed close. "Avalina, come to me. We need to talk."

I shook my head.

"Please. I can't help you if I don't know what happened."

I blinked, tears pooling. He would choose to help me, after all he'd endured on my behalf?

Pushing from the floor, I approached, letting my cold fingers curl around the iron. He covered my hands with his own, infusing them with warmth. I allowed the scant pleasure of his touch, my eyes sliding closed. Would this be the last time I would see him?

He ran his thumbs over my knuckles. "Talk to me."

I ran my tongue over my dry lips. "What do you want to know?"

He inhaled a deep breath. "Did you attempt to murder Cyrene Harding?"

"Yes. No." I sucked in a breath and opened my eyes. "I—I don't know. It all happened so quickly."

"What did?"

My mind replayed the images of that horrid night. The glowing red of the sky. The smoke and ash. Screams. The chaos. "It was the evening of the rebellion. Master had shouted for all hands to form a bucket line to quench the approaching fire. But when I attempted to follow, he grabbed me, and—"

Josiah's jaw clenched. "And what?"

My stomach cramped. "He attacked me."

Josiah looked away, blanching white. I forged ahead.

"He'd never done such a thing. It was in his library and something wild rose up in me. I—I had to fight. So I clawed and kicked . . . but he was too strong." I began to shake at the memory of his hands bruising, punishing me. "When I saw the gun, I don't know, I just grabbed it, and—and fired."

Josiah's steely gaze met mine. "I'll kill him."

"You'll—?" I sucked in a breath. "Wait . . . you're not angry with me?"

299

His eyes glassed. "What? How could I be angry with you?" He shook his head as a tear escaped, skimming down his tanned cheek. "Listen to me, Avalina... you were innocent. Merely trying to defend yourself."

My chin trembled as he reached up to cup my jaw. "He told me as his slave, I was his property and he could do whatever he liked."

Josiah's nostrils flared. "The ravings of a monster. Nothing more." He sighed, expression pained. "Why didn't you tell me?"

"I thought I'd killed him. He was face-down in a pool of blood."

"I remember. We spied his body as we fled. I thought he was dead too, only I assumed he had been killed during the uprising." Josiah's jaw twitched and he dropped his hand from my cheek. "And now he's back, seeking vengeance."

"What will happen to me?" I hated the fear I heard in my own voice. Despised every quaking part of myself.

His lips thinned into a hard line. "We fight back."

"But how?"

Josiah stepped away from the bars and paced. "No doubt Harding chose to have you arrested here because South Carolina is a slave-holding state. He could have demanded to bring you back to Barbados, but he didn't. He wanted the sympathy and the audience a public trial would produce." He paused, eyebrows knit. "He knows the spectacle will whip every slaveholder in the area into a frenzy."

Understanding dawned. I swallowed. "It's not enough to punish me. He wants to humiliate me."

Josiah nodded. "And me as well."

I grimaced, letting my head fall against the cold metal. Harding had power and money. Two things I woefully lacked.

With a wide smile, Josiah reached through the bars, pulled me close, and claimed my lips. He broke away after a long moment. "Stay strong, my love. Help is on the way."

The guard swaggered back down the corridor. "Time is up, Mr. Holland."

I clutched a fistful of Josiah's shirt, pressing another kiss to his lips. "I love you." Warmth crept into my cheeks. I'd never uttered the words before but I felt every ounce of the declaration down to my soul.

His smile turned tender. "And I love you."

Then he was gone.

I slid back down to the unforgiving floor. Josiah loved me. And he believed me.

That was enough.

CHAPTER 39

Josiah refused to be discouraged. He could not. Would not. Too much was at stake.

Tugging the collar of his shirt with one hand, he swiped the back of the other across his sweaty forehead. He'd spent all morning scouring Charleston for a lawyer empathetic to Avalina's plight. Most turned him away before he'd finished explaining her situation. A few laughed. The rest merely shrugged, saying there was nothing they could do for her.

Glancing up at the too-bright noonday sun, he expelled a thick breath as Amos turned the carriage onto Broad Street. Once Josiah realized no one would give him a moment's time, he'd turned to his last ally . . . Edward Pickering.

Inside the older man's office, the fellow listened quietly before scribbling a single name and address on a piece of parchment. "This is the only lawyer I know who might be able to help."

Josiah turned his bleary gaze to Pickering's slanted script. "Bartholomew Lewis." He murmured the name and scanned the address. "I don't know him."

"Most don't." Pickering leaned back in his chair and grabbed a cigar from his humidor, absently rolling it between his fingers. "He hails from Darby Boroughs, Pennsylvania. Long line of Quakers in his family." Pickering offered a lopsided smile. "You know them. They breed nothing but farmers and abolitionists."

No, Josiah didn't know, but he forced his attention to remain on his friend.

"Good man, Bartholomew. Underestimated by most, because of his quiet nature, but he's a brilliant lawyer. His stance on slavery has made him less than popular in these parts."

"No doubt." Josiah jiggled his leg. All he could think of was his wife, alone and scared in a foul prison cell. Had they mistreated her? Fed her this morning? He felt as if his efforts to find her legal help were nothing more than attempting to scratch his nails through mortar. Seeing her in the grimy building only added to his frustration. Haste was of the utmost importance.

"Tell Bartholomew I sent you." Pickering rose and offered his hand. Josiah sprang from the chair and clasped his friend's thick fingers, grateful for the fellow who had so quickly become his lifeline.

And now, with the midday heat swelling to suffocating proportions, Amos drew the sagging horses to a stop in front of a small building at the farthest end of Broad Street. The white law office with green trim was in desperate need of paint.

Josiah jumped from the carriage and straightened his rumpled coat. If this Lewis fellow turned him away, he had no idea what he would do.

Clenching his jaw, he pushed the door open and winced when the bells announcing visitors bobbed and hit him on the head. He rubbed the offended spot and peered in the small office. Bookcases filled every available wall, each of them crammed full of thick volumes. A long wooden table held stacks of more references, and piles of papers were scattered haphazardly across its top. To the right, a thin man with sandy blond hair and spectacles sat behind a desk filled with ledgers and opened tomes. He ran his finger down a particularly fat book and muttered, "Be with you in a moment."

Josiah cleared his throat and shifted his weight. A cuckoo clock mounted on the space behind the desk ticked the seconds loudly. *Tick, tick, tick, tick…*

"There." The wiry fellow looked up, blinking as if trying to find his bearings before pushing the large book away and rising. "Bartholomew Lewis, at your service."

Josiah pumped his hand and offered a smile, although he was hard-pressed to feel any elation. "Josiah Holland."

Lewis pointed to the empty chair across from the desk. "Please sit. How can I help you?"

Easing his weight into the rickety spindle-backed chair, Josiah sighed and leaned forward, resting his elbows on his knees. "You can agree to represent my wife in court."

The tilt of the man's head was his only response. "Please go on."

Josiah spilled the entire story… the scant details of Avalina's arrival on the island, her life under Cyrene Harding, the night of the revolt and their escape to the States, their hasty marriage, and now Harding's accusations. Bartholomew listened carefully, asking a question on occasion and scribbling on a piece of parchment.

Josiah resisted the urge to wipe his hands down his trousers. "Will you help us, Mr. Lewis? Edward Pickering told me you are the only one he would trust with such a case."

Pursing his lips, Lewis rolled a pencil between his fingers, brows lowered. "This certainly is interesting. First, your wife's childhood, her unknown origins, and a man who enslaved her. Don't many of the white Irish work as indentured servants in Barbados?"

"Many, yes, but I was told there are a few remaining, quite elderly in fact, who were brought over and remembered being forced from their homes as young children."

"Hmm. So if Harding's plantation is in Barbados, why have Avalina tried here?"

Josiah leaned back, fatigue tugging on every muscle. "I believe he means to punish me and my family for taking her away from the island. He wants a spectacle. See our names dragged through the mud."

Lewis grunted. "And he picked a prime place to do so. He knows the sentiments of the South. I'm afraid to say, either way, your family will not escape this unscathed." He blinked several times. "From where does Harding hail?"

"I don't know."

Lewis grunted and scratched another note on his paper. "And then there are the legal issues surrounding your departure from the island. Combine that with your nuptials and your situation is messy indeed."

Josiah's hope deflated. Lewis seemed extremely intelligent. Thoughtful. "Thank you for your time." He could hear the dejection in his own voice.

The lawyer's gray-green eyes widened. "Whoa! No need to assume the worst. I'm merely sorting through the information." He tapped the pencil tip absently against the desk. "As I'm sure you are aware, I have no fondness for the institution of slavery and long to see it wiped from the face of the earth."

"Despite my own family's holdings, I quite agree."

Lewis leaned forward, pinning Josiah with a hard stare. "Are there any surprises you need to inform me of? Secrets?"

Josiah's shook his head slowly. "No, sir. You already know Avalina fired the revolver and believed Harding to be dead. She acted in her own defense."

Lewis's eyes narrowed. "Anything else? Any reason why your wife should not be on the witness stand?"

Josiah nearly winced, dreading the next admission. "There is one more thing, Mr. Lewis."

"Yes?"

"My wife, Avalina ... she's mute."

"Mute?" Lewis's blond brows lifted.

"Well, mostly." Josiah did cringe then. He knew how unbelievable it sounded, but it was truth. Some unknown fear kept Avalina trapped, unable to speak at the most pointed times.

"Mostly mute." The lawyer echoed Josiah, but instead of the anger Josiah expected, or a scoffing rebuke, Lewis leaned forward, gray-green eyes alight.

"Yes, indeed, this is a *very* interesting case. I'll take it."

Thank You, Lord. A whoosh of relief burst through Josiah's chest. "Thank you. I cannot express my gratitude."

Lewis grinned and pushed his spectacles into place. "Come, Mr. Holland. We have much work to do."

Hunger gnawed my middle but I had trouble choking down the coarse bread, even after the third day in jail. When the guards noticed my uneaten food on the first day, they merely shrugged and walked away. I soon learned why. If I chose not to partake, the rats would appear by nightfall, squeaking and scurrying past my feet to fight over the morsels. By the evening of my second day, I could take it no more. I would rather choke down the stale, hard biscuit than shiver from the dreaded rodents.

Each morning I was given bread and water. In the evening, a small cooked potato and water. Nothing more. Even with the scant diet, my middle cramped. Where was Josiah? Why had he not returned? Were the authorities even now sentencing me to death? As I stared at the thin light streaming through the high window above, I supposed there was mercy in knowing I hadn't killed Cyrene Harding. That particular sin had haunted my waking moments and taunted my dreams at night.

Of course, a corpse would not have appeared suddenly and so thoroughly upended my life. I allowed my eyes to slide shut. Whatever meager sympathy I had garnered from Josiah's parents, I had now assuredly smashed to bits. And what of Isabelle? What did she think? The thought of disappointing my new sister stung like the bite of a scorpion.

Footsteps scuffled down the corridor. A door squeaked open and the guard cursed before banging a cell door closed. "Enjoy your stay, preacher. Maybe you will learn your lesson. Ain't no place for a man who teaches slaves to read."

There was more scuffling as the guard's steps thudded down the corridor. The new prisoner was a preacher? I wondered if he worshiped the same God as Matias and Josiah. Though I still couldn't fully grasp what I had read from the Bible with Josiah, there was a strange comfort in knowing a man who adored the same God as my husband was only a few steps away.

I huffed and allowed my head to fall back against the grimy stone wall. The space between us might as well be five hundred feet.

Glancing at my soiled gown, I picked absently at the stained skirt. If Madam Durand could see her marvelous creation now, the poor dressmaker would faint. Who could have imagined the hours of sewing and pain-staking decisions would not result in the delicate trappings of a woman embraced by Charleston, but the mocking dress of a criminal?

As the heat of afternoon climbed inside the stuffy cell, the muggy warmth lulled me into a drowsy sleep. I lay upon the slick stone floor and fought restless dreams... cheerful Molly, Baara with her perpetual frown, Naomi's venomous glares, and Josiah extending his hand to mine. I stared at Josiah's warm, tanned fingers, his palms open, beseeching me.

"*Trust me . . .*"

I place my callused fingers in his and, after a thick moment, pull away. My own sleeve cuffs are dirty and frayed, a stark contrast to his clean shirt and warm smile. We don't belong together, he and I.

And then he calls me, as his face fades away, his voice growing dim, murky.

"Avalina ... "

I startled awake and shuddered, my breath hot against the cool floor. Sweat soaked my bodice. A deep-throated chuckle skittered down my spine as I blinked, trying to make sense of my surroundings.

"How do you like your accommodations, my dear?"

I knew that voice. Gasping, I pushed up and scampered back, pressing my body against the far wall.

Cyrene Harding stood on the other side of my cell, smiling like the wicked jackal he was. I was both terrified of him and despised him, longing to lunge at him in rage and cower at the same time. Thus it had always been between us ... since that horrible day so long ago when I had been unable to sing.

He stepped forward and wrapped his fingers around the bars. "You thought you could escape? Kill me? Be free?" He snorted with derision. "Bewitch young Holland into believing you are more than dirt?" His gloating grin dimmed, morphing into a sneer. "You are nothing, Avalina. Do you hear me? You mean nothing."

My pulse galloped as heat billowed in my chest. Years of fear, pain, and fury roiled like a tempest in my soul. My nostrils flared. If only I could shout, scream my frustration, but my tongue turned to stone. He arched a single dark brow.

"Ah, you're angry, I see. Did you so despise me, Avalina? Enough to put a bullet through my chest?" He patted his ribs on his right side. "Fortunately for me, you missed my heart. What a pity."

His mocking tone grated but I refused to let him goad me further. I looked away.

"And now look at you. Publicly disgraced and awaiting trial for attempted murder." He clucked his tongue, tsking like nails tapping a desk. "Too bad you took so many down with your foolishness."

Ignore him. Don't let him manipulate you. Josiah loves me, Josiah loves me...

"Your *husband*, for one." He uttered the sentence as if tasting something bitter. Harding pushed away from the bars and laughed low. "You always obeyed me, didn't you, Avalina? But I never could break that foolish streak of spirit in you. A pity." He thrust his chin forward and glared. "And now I get to enjoy watching others break you instead."

He disappeared, leaving me alone in silence.

Always silence.

CHAPTER 40

September 3, 1816
Charleston, South Carolina

Turned away again.

Josiah clenched his teeth, biting back an oath of frustration as he stood before the Charleston jail, the sneering guard as unyielding as a wall.

For weeks he had come to the jail each morning to check on his wife, her welfare, and to inform her of the progress Lewis was making on her case. Each time they turned him away, citing various reasons, none of which made sense. Compressing his lips, he stomped toward the waiting carriage. Something fishy was afoot. The guards had been bribed ... he was certain of it.

As he climbed in, he thanked Amos for waiting before the elderly groomsman clicked his tongue, urging the sleek black Morgans into a trot. Their hooves clacked loudly against the cobblestone, the echoes reverberating through Josiah's mind as his thoughts clambered.

Only three more days before Avalina's trial. He needed to see her. His nerves were stretched taut, nearly fraying with the need to assure himself she was well. Mr. Lewis needed to speak with her, educate her on what was going to happen during the trial. At this point, Josiah had no idea how she would respond to the scrutiny or pressure.

As the carriage bounced beneath him, he rubbed his temples. His parents had certainly been no help. His mother stayed confined to her room, languishing between fits of weeping and sullen anger. Isabelle had been sent to visit their aunt Dorothea in Savannah for an indefinite period of time, no doubt to keep her reputation from being sullied by Charleston's opinion of the Holland family. His mother had railed at him one particular evening, insisting Avalina had destroyed Isabelle's chances for a good match, and therefore, her happiness and future.

And then there was Father. When Josiah returned from seeing Avalina on the first day of her imprisonment, he had fully intended to confront him over his ledgers and enormous debts ... not to mention the list of names tucked in the volume of Shakespeare. He didn't want to believe the worst of his own flesh and blood, but the evidence of his sins was stacked to the heavens.

Yet, instead of the accounting Josiah longed to see, he had been informed by Amos that George Holland had left that morning on "urgent business" and was not expected to return for some time. Did he suspect Josiah had discovered his treachery, or was he merely fleeing the public humiliation from his son's scandalous wife?

Josiah fisted his hands as he watched the teeming streets slowly pass by. Either way, his father was a coward. He had fled Charleston when Mother needed him most. And though Josiah would never regret marrying Avalina, he did hate the pain inflicted on those who had raised him.

Shoulders slumping, he heaved a thick sigh. What a mess he'd made of everything. He couldn't even aid Pickering and the fugitives in need because the Holland plantation was constantly being watched by the authorities. He was useless to everyone. If he had his way, he would emancipate every human on his family's property and leave, never to return. But God's Word also instructed him to honor and obey his parents. Where was the line? For months, he had been walking on the edge of a precipice and one wrong move would send him spiraling.

Who was he fooling? He'd stepped off the edge months ago.

Was it better to stay in an oppressive situation and effect change from the inside? Or was it wiser to flee when the obstacles were too numerous to conquer?

He had no idea. At this moment, all he could think of was his wife. He would not leave without her by his side.

Amos drove the carriage up the lonesome lane toward home. Home. What a strange word. The plantation was merely a residence now. His real home was locked inside a cramped cell in the Charleston jail.

A meeting was scheduled with Mr. Lewis later in the afternoon, and in the meantime, he would occupy his hands—and his mind—in the fields. Harvest was in full swing and he longed to be helpful, despite the overseer constantly complaining that his involvement was highly irregular. He shrugged away the concern. Work kept him sane while fretting over Avalina.

His plans soon changed upon stepping down from the carriage. Hattie burst through the front door, eyes wide, flapping her arms like a scared chicken.

"Mr. Josiah, your daddy done returned while you was gone. He in a mighty big temper too." The older woman's round cheeks glistened with tears. "I ain't never seen him like this."

He wrapped his hands around Hattie's plump arms, trying to soothe her agitation. "Why? What has he done?"

She hesitated and Josiah forced himself to speak calmly. "You'll not be punished for speaking the truth. Take heart."

She nodded and let her eyes slide closed before reopening them and fixing him with a beseeching plea. "Master Holland out back right now, whippin' Fountain."

Fountain? No, it couldn't be. The man had never done anything, never would do anything to merit such harshness.

He released the crying woman and raced to the closest field. His heart plunged to the pit of his stomach with what he saw ... Fountain, stripped to his breeches, his hands tied to a post, while the overseer raised a whip over his head and released it with a sickening crack. Fountain reared back, screaming with the pain. The other workers stood around him in a circle, silent. Some watched with forlorn expressions. Others stared at the ground, mute with shock. Father planted his feet like a conquering hero, his face a storm.

Rage coiled Josiah's middle as he stomped forward. The overseer raised the whip over his head again, but his arm jerked back when Josiah grabbed the whip from behind and hurled it away.

"Stop this instant!"

His breath was a ragged pant. He glared at the sweating overseer before his gaze swung to Fountain's mutilated back. Bleeding, cruel lines marred his once-smooth skin. Before he could think, Josiah stalked his way toward the pole, putting himself between Fountain and his oppressors. Anger shook his hands as he faced his father.

"This man has done nothing! And you beat him like a dog?"

Father glared, a muscle twitching near his eye, his skin mottling red. "Don't you talk to me like that! He was caught trying to escape. Wasn't he, Seamus?"

The overseer nodded, wiping the sweat from his forehead with the back of his sleeve.

Josiah shook his head. "I don't believe it."

Fountain wheezed and mumbled, "It's true."

313

Josiah turned to his long-ago playmate and knelt beside him, sinking to the ground slowly, staring into his stricken face and swollen eyes. "It's true?"

Fountain nodded, his body convulsing with pain. "I tried to run. Figured if I'm Master's son ... I got a right to be free ... " Sweat streamed off his face. "Just like you."

"But how—"

He winced. "I read them papers you brought to my cabin."

Josiah groaned. Fountain could read? Who had taught him? How?

It didn't matter. The damage was done.

The shard of truth stabbed Josiah's heart afresh. Whatever cords had kept him tied to this place were now severed. His soul flooded with light. In a flash he knew he would never change the situation on his own. Fitting in was not the same as belonging, and that's what he'd been trying to do ... hold on to both sides. But he no longer belonged here.

His father would never listen to him. It would take a force much greater to transform George Holland. It would take God Himself. And Josiah could no longer obey his father *and* follow the Almighty. He must choose.

"Get away!" Father spat at Josiah, his eyes bulging. He turned to Seamus, his face filled with ire. "Find that whip, and finish what I told you to do!"

There was a sharp cry from somewhere behind them. Josiah turned to see his mother watching on the back porch, her skin ashen, eyes wide as she slowly lifted her hand to her mouth in horror.

"Virginia, enough of your caterwauling!"

She choked on her cries, and Josiah knew then—watching the stubborn set of his father's jaw, the hard lines framing his mouth, the large hand that quivered with suppressed rage as his mother clutched her dressing gown to her chest—he wanted to be nothing like him. For so many years he had tried to please him, tried to earn his favor. No longer.

Slowly, Josiah rose and slid off his jacket, tossing it onto the grass. He stared at George Holland, stuck somewhere between pity and horror. "Your business trip didn't go as planned, did it? Your debts and business schemes are failing."

Father's steely eyes narrowed. "What do you mean?"

"I found the ledgers. The secret ledgers. I know you've lost almost everything, and you're trying to stay afloat with schemes that have yielded nothing. Does Mother know? Does she know about your gambling debts and financial subterfuge?"

If George Holland was red before, he was purple with fury now. Josiah squared his shoulders and slowly unbuttoned his shirt.

"Does she know our family will have nothing in a short matter of years?" He laughed harshly and unhooked the last button before tossing his shirt to the ground with his jacket. "Some might say we have nothing *now*. Nothing but lies and deceit." His nostrils flared. "And I want no part of it."

Father took a menacing step forward. "Rest assured, you'll have no part of it! You've never been anything but a disappointment. You have no stomach for what it takes to be a man. To run this land." He sneered. "And then you marry a murderer, dragging our family down with you into the muck."

The accusation did not sting as he expected. Instead, he felt ... peace.

"Does Mother know of all the others here you have fathered?" Josiah leveled him with a hard stare. "Does she know you just ordered Seamus to whip your own son?"

Father paled and stepped backward. "Wha— How—?"

"I figure one son is as good as another." Josiah whirled and gently released Fountain from his bonds. The bleeding man fell into a heap near Josiah's feet, groaning. Josiah met the faces surrounding him ... Mother, with her white lips and trembling hands, Father with his seething fury, the scowling overseer, the heartbroken men and women forced to work against their will.

If he couldn't take away their pain, he would at least share it.

He stared at Father. "Whip me instead."

"No!" Virginia raced to George's side, clawing at his arms, his hands. "No, please no, George! Don't hurt him! Please!"

Josiah turned away and wrapped his arms around the pole, waiting. Breathing. *God, You are my rock and fortress, my deliverer ...*

A whooshing rent the air a second before fire sliced across his back. He gasped at the white-hot pain of it, his knees buckling.

"No!" His mother's voice again but it was followed by murmurs of shock. Through his bleary gaze, Josiah peeked over his shoulder. Mother's hand gripped a revolver, leveled at Father's heart.

"Do not touch my son."

Josiah pressed his head against the pole, wincing against the pain as silence stretched, thick as taffy. No one moved. No one dared breathe.

Finally, his father took measured steps across the yard, scooped up Josiah's shirt and coat and threw them down before him. Josiah met his hard glare, panting against the pain ripping through his muscles.

"Get out."

Virginia's strength faded as she dropped the revolver in the grass and collapsed to her knees, her sobs harsh in the quiet. Despite her scheming and manipulation, she was in pain and Josiah could feel nothing but pity. He winced and turned, offering her what little solace he could.

"I'm sorry, Mother."

Tears streaked down her face as he stooped to pick up his clothes. His back screamed with each flicker of movement. Before he could take a step past his father, Fountain called his name.

"Mister Josiah."

He turned and faced his childhood friend and brother. Looking up from his prostrate position, Fountain whispered, "Thank you."

Josiah nodded and walked stiffly past his father as he went inside to pack his and Avalina's necessary belongings.

Less than an hour later, he carried two bags filled with their clothes, his Bible, the compass he had given Avalina, and the gold he'd acquired from Captain Blackthorne.

As he walked the road back into the heart of Charleston, a solitary verse came to mind.

And the truth shall set you free.

How long since I had seen Josiah? Days? Weeks? Months? Time was elusive in this place of torment, my only bearings the meticulous dawn through my window followed by the sweltering heat of midday and then nighttime when I was plunged into darkness.

I no longer felt hunger, each meal a dreary repeat of the day before: bread, water, potato, water.

My sweat-slicked skin had long ago soiled my gown's loveliness, it's glory now reduced to filthy rags. My teeth felt loose and foggy images tortured my mind both day and night. I found myself reaching for Josiah in the night, for Molly, for any source of comfort, but I was alone. All my life I had been grasping at ghosts and capturing nothing. They always slipped through my fingers.

I was going mad. Perhaps I already was.

On occasion I could hear the wail of another prisoner, begging for food. A woman down the way mumbled incoherently, babbling about long-ago friends and family. At times I heard men curse the guards and this abode of misery. But the only voice that intrigued me belonged to the preacher.

Since his arrival, mere days after my own, his voice lifted in song from his cell.

"Come, Thou Fount of every blessing, tune my heart to sing Thy grace. Streams of mercy, never ceasing, call for songs of loudest praise ... "

Praise? In this place of death and disease? I didn't understand. I scooted closer to the bars and listened.

"Jesus sought me when a stranger, wandering from the fold of God. He to rescue me from danger interposed His precious blood."

I certainly was in danger, never more so, but as the preacher sang the name *Jesus*, a sweet reverence colored his voice. A hushed benediction ... a sacred lullaby. Did he find such comfort, even in the midst of this suffering?

Leaning against the bars, I pondered the thought. Josiah had oft mentioned this Jesus, his God's Son. And Matias had spoken his name with the same kind of awe and devotion. Why couldn't I understand what these men possessed?

I longed to brave a question to the preacher, ask him what he meant by his song, ask him why this Jesus was so worthy of his love while he languished in prison, but my tongue would not obey.

Instead, I lifted my eyes to the dark, moldy ceiling.

God? Josiah's God? If You are real, show me. I promise to listen and wait.

No voice answered as I cried myself to sleep.

CHAPTER 41

Thanks to Edward Pickering, Josiah had a roof over his head that night, but he tossed and turned with restless energy in the spare room bed, his thoughts ricocheting between his mother's wails, Fountain's screams, and Father's fury. The pain yet lacing his back. Yanking the tangled blanket into submission, he gingerly eased once more on his side, staring into the dark. That bridge was now burned. His inheritance gone. His dream of becoming a lawyer, vanished. How could he without his family as benefactor? Yet he did not regret his decision. It was impossible to live in two opposing worlds. Avalina was all that mattered now.

And truth.

Long into the wee morning hours, he finally fell into a dreamless, fitful sleep.

The next morning, Pickering looked over the top of his newspaper when Josiah entered the dining room and eased himself into an empty chair.

"You look frightful."

"Good morning to you too." Josiah attempted to keep the grouchiness from his voice but failed. Pickering took no offense and chuckled while folding the newsprint in half. "My wife will have breakfast ready in a moment. Some coffee will help you, I imagine."

"Thank you. I confess, I slept little."

"Replaying the events of yesterday, or because of pain?"

Josiah shrugged. "Both. Right now, I'm more worried about my wife than anything."

Pickering grunted. "Think the jail will let you in today?"

Funneling his hands through his hair, Josiah sighed. "I don't see how they can turn us away, not if Mr. Lewis accompanies me. Her trial begins tomorrow."

Mrs. Pickering scurried in, bearing a tray filled with a carafe of coffee. She was a sweet thing, plump, with dancing green eyes and silver-streaked brown hair. "Coffee's ready." She plunked the tray in the middle of the table and set to work pouring, while offering cream and sugar. "Now, Mr. Holland, you need to eat a good break-fast, what with all you have to do today."

He smiled at her motherly scolding. "Yes, ma'am. I want to thank you and your husband again for taking me in."

She tsked and waved her hand in dismissal. "I'm happy to have the company. Since our children have homes of their own now, it gets mighty quiet around here. You are welcome anytime. Now"— she clapped her hands together—"would you like eggs?"

"Yes, ma'am."

"Grits with cheese and bacon? Toast with blackberry jam? Sausage? Hot cakes?"

Josiah laughed, despite his fatigue. "My goodness, I'm going to leave as fat as a toad."

She giggled and stooped to brush her husband's cheek with a light peck. "Now you know why my Edward is such a happy man."

Edward shook his head, grinning. "That has nothing to do with your cooking, and everything to do with your pretty face."

"Pshaw!" She scurried back into the kitchen as he chuckled. Josiah's gaze swung between the two of them. Had he ever seen his own parents act so kind? So carefree?

Not any time he could recollect. This was the type of marriage he wanted for himself and Avalina. His admiration melted into worry.

If she survived the trial, that is.

A cloud swept in, once again darkening his mood. What if Lewis failed? What if Harding turned the judge and jury against her? Surely he would try. If the court found her guilty, at best she would languish in prison for the rest of her life. At worst, death. He needed a distraction. He reached for Pickering's discarded paper but stopped when the man shook his head.

"Don't look, Josiah."

He blinked. "At what?"

Pickering winced. "Avalina's impending trial is splashed across the front page."

No, no, no! He snatched the newsprint, devouring the headline. He winced when bold letters announced: WOMAN ON TRIAL FOR ATTEMPTED MURDER.

Hastily, he scanned the article. The reporter thoroughly dragged Avalina's name through the mud, practically declaring her guilty while, at the same time, denouncing the Holland family for their ties.

"Blast!" He threw the newspaper on the table and pushed away from his seat, pacing the length of the dining room, ignoring the pain in his back and stopping only for short moments to stare out the lace-draped windows. Cyrene Harding must have spoken to the press. Pickering tapped his fingers on the tabletop, glowering.

"This isn't good, is it?" On Josiah's part, it was more statement than question.

"No, it's not ideal," Pickering conceded. "But never forget you have truth on your side. That accounts for much. God fights for His children. He's going to war for you even now. And who knows? With Avalina being a white woman, public opinion may sway her way."

Josiah stopped and stared at his friend, longing to be as confident. "But what if Harding tries to corrupt the decision?"

Pickering fixed him with a level stare. "He will, but God is still greater than any scheme man can devise."

Josiah nodded and lifted a prayer heavenward.

If I ever needed You to show Yourself strong, Lord, this is it.

I lay on the gritty cell floor, softly humming to myself. The melody and words the preacher had sung yesterday refused to leave me be. *Come Thou fount of every blessing, tune my heart to sing Thy grace...*

Something about it was oddly comforting, as if returning from a long trip to find belonging. Familiarity. Love.

A guard barked through my cell bars. "Mrs. Holland, come with me."

I stared dumbly at his large form as he inserted the key in the lock, scraping open the door and swinging it wide.

Streams of mercy, never ceasing...

"Did you hear me? Get up!"

Slowly, I pushed my face away from the floor, swiping at the dirt that marred my once-smooth skin. No longer. My hair was a tangled mass. My dress hung loosely from my frame. Worse still, I didn't care. All I wanted was to hear that song again.

Call for songs of loudest praise...

"Move!"

The guard lurched forward and yanked me to my feet, his fist wrapping around my arm like a vise, bruising and cruel. The room spun in circles. I tilted to one side and he cursed, pulling me upright before shoving me forward.

He offered no explanations. Just pushed me down the dark corridor. I peered to the left, looking for the preacher. A lone man with a blond beard stared at me through his prison cell. Kindness radiated from his eyes. I knew it was him instinctively.

Instead of lingering to hear more of the preacher's melodies, the guard unceremoniously led me farther down the damp hallway to a lone room. My knees nearly collapsed when I saw Josiah sitting at a table with a guest.

"Avalina." He breathed my name and hurried to enfold me in his strong embrace. At his touch, tears pooled in my eyes. We pulled away after long moments and he lifted my face to his, wiping away my tears with the pads of his thumbs. "I feared you dead. I've been trying to see you every day for weeks but they turned me away."

All that mattered was he was here now. After pressing a kiss to my lips, he turned and introduced me to a middle-aged man slight of stature with spectacles and a serious demeanor.

"This is Mr. Bartholomew Lewis. He has agreed to represent you in court."

Represent me in court? I could see Josiah's mouth moving but the words made little sense. The room tilted to one side.

Mr. Lewis smiled gently and offered his hand. "Mrs. Holland, I'm delighted to make your acquaintance, and I promise to do everything in my power to see you released."

I nodded and my knees gave way again. Josiah caught me before lowering me into a chair. "Guard!" He turned to the scowling man just outside the door. "We need water, please."

"This isn't an eating establishment."

Mr. Lewis rose, his eyes flashing fire. "My client requires water immediately. It would be a shame to see Mrs. Holland expire before her trial and see the blame shifted to your shoulders. I don't imagine that would go very well for you, would it?"

The guard hesitated a moment but then stomped away to see to the request. He returned moments later, a tin of cold water in hand.

"Thank you." Mr. Lewis pressed the cup into my hand and I lifted it to my lips. Cold. Clean. After a small sip, I gulped the lot of it, coughing against the rush as it flowed down my throat.

"Easy." Josiah rubbed my back and glanced at the lawyer. "What have they been doing? Attempting to starve her?"

Lewis sighed. "It appears so. Giving the prisoners just enough food and water to exist keeps them docile. I will file a complaint with the judge. For now"—he pulled out a pencil and a sheet of paper—"we must prepare your wife for the morrow."

Prepare? For what? I licked my lips, pushing past the fogginess in my head. Why was Josiah staring at me with such worry?

"Mrs. Holland." Mr. Lewis cleared his throat. "I fear this trial will take several days. Mr. Harding will do his utmost to discredit you, falsify facts and outright lie. At times you may be furious, scared, or sad. I need you to do your best to remain composed. Do you think you can manage that?"

I nodded, but his voice was like the low buzz of a bee in my ear. *Come Thou fount of every—*

"—understand Harding was able to arrange the trial here because he was born in Georgia."

Master Cyrene Harding was born in the States? I didn't know that. I stared at the scarred wooden table, trying to focus.

"—clear he wants to publicly disgrace both Avalina and me."

"Of course." Mr. Lewis rolled the pencil between his fingers absently. I sensed him staring at me, but I was suddenly tired. So horribly tired.

He leaned forward. "Mrs. Holland, your husband tells me you have a condition that makes you unable to speak most times, correct?"

Mute. That's what I was. Mostly. The words never came when I wanted or needed. Naomi called me a witch, Tabia declared me cursed, but the first time Molly heard them say such, she blistered her tongue, fussing so much no one dared speak the accusations in her presence again.

Sweet Molly. How she would grieve to see me now.

"Mrs. Holland? Did you hear me?"

I blinked and lifted my gaze to his. He stared, his brows knit.

"I said, are you sure you cannot testify on your own behalf?"

I shook my head. No, my tongue would be useless with the entire court watching.

Pursing his lips, he told me what he expected Harding's lawyer might do. Tactics, plans, words like *judicial process*, and *arbitration*, and *exemption*. Josiah leaned forward, engrossed in tomorrow's proceedings but I barely held my head upright. My head was thick. Or perhaps I was dying.

He to rescue me from danger, interposed His precious blood…

I didn't realize I had nodded off until Josiah slipped his arm around me.

"Avalina, are you ill?"

Was I? I had no idea.

Josiah glanced at Mr. Lewis. "Will they not allow her fresh clothes before the trial begins? A bath?"

Lewis's lips pursed. "Knowing the way they run things, I doubt they will concede to a bath, but I'm quite sure I can convince them to let her change in the morning, provided you bring her a gown."

"Mrs. Pickering will assist me. I'm certain of it."

Mr. Lewis shifted to give me a smile of sympathy. "I will do everything in my power to see you set free."

Free. I didn't even know what the word meant. Not truly. All my life I had been subject to the whims of others. Their rules, demands. Perhaps that was why I had never felt peace, always grasping for an elusive truth. I thought I would find it when Josiah taught me to read, but it hadn't spared me from Master Cyrene. It hadn't saved me from the uprising on the island. If anything, it only made me long for more.

I swallowed. I didn't want freedom. I wanted peace.

Before I could blink again, Josiah wrapped me in his arms, whispering words of comfort into my ear. I was led back to my cell, the door clanging behind me. I sank to the floor as the preacher sang softly.

"Nearer, my God, to Thee. Nearer to Thee. Though like the wanderer, the sun gone down. Darkness be over me, my rest a stone. Yet in my dreams I'd be nearer, my God, to Thee. Nearer to Thee … "

I succumbed to the blessedness of sleep, the song my lullaby.

My feet sank into the soft sand, mud squishing between my toes as I knelt, running my fingers over the bumpy ridges of a starfish tucked into the shore. The air was ripe with the scent of the sea—fish, salt, brine— as water lapped my toes. I looked up, glancing down the length of beach. Matias was smiling, laughing at the antics of a school of fish, the deep lines around his eyes crinkling. Molly was spreading a blanket over the stray clumps of grass. A veritable feast spread out as she chattered.

In a flash, the sun was eclipsed by pewter clouds. A drop pelted my skin, then another and another. Thunder crashed as my hair whipped around me like a lash, my skirt slapping against my legs. Lightning flashed its liquid silver as Matias and Molly disappeared, their voices shouting my name.

"Avalina!"

I turned to the left and the right but I was alone in the chaos. I clamped my hands against my ears in the roar, the rain now an assault. Somewhere in the churning sea, I could see a figure. A woman with red hair, walking toward me, her melody lifting over the cracks of thunder.

"Here's my heart, O take and seal it. Seal it for Thy courts above … "

She held her hands out to me, smiling as she sang. My heart pounded against my ribs.

"Mother!" I screamed into the storm. "Mother! I'm here!"

I ran toward her, water rising to my ankles, my knees, my middle, but as I fumbled in the seething foam, her eyes widened with shock, her body slipping below the waves. Her song evaporating into silence.

"Mother! No!"

I sobbed, rain mingling with tears as they ran down my face in rivulets, my heart ripping open. Sobs scraped for release and I fell to my knees in the waves' fury.

"Child, you are not alone."

A masculine voice pierced the night. Gasping, I looked up as more lightning streaked through the black mass of clouds. A man was walking on the water. Light hovered around him, illuminating his silhouette. His dark eyes bore into mine and he held out a hand.

A hand bearing a bold, raised scar.

"Come to Me, my child. I am both father and mother to the orphan. I am truth. I am peace."

I trembled, somehow exposed to this mysterious figure. I reached for him, saltwater foaming around me in the tumult, filling my mouth with salt.

"Save me!"

I gasped and sat upright, the vision melting away as the walls of my cell stared back at me. I was not in a storm, not slipping below the ocean's fury, but trapped in a filthy abode to await punishment.

Tucking myself into a ball, I shook, trembling starting from my middle and radiating through each limb. The dream had been so real. *My mother . . . I saw my mother.* Tears welled and slipped down my cheeks. And who was the mysterious man?

"I am both father and mother to the orphan."

I pinched my eyes shut, trying to envision his pleading eyes once again.

A violent shudder wracked my body. I had asked God to reveal Himself to me and He had. I was undone, naked . . . my sins laid bare for Him to see.

As I cried, I yanked at the sleeve of my gown, breathing relief when the seam tore. I touched the raised scars branded into my upper right arm, a cruel mark meant to display Harding's power over me. But what if it wasn't?

My fingers traced the letters. *AM*. Azaka Mede.

I AM truth.

I AM peace.

I was not branded to be a slave. I was branded to belong to the Great God. Josiah's God. My God.

My throat thickened as I whispered into the quiet.

"God, I am nothing. I have nothing. I am naught but woman lost. Make me Yours. I give You all I am. My heart is bound to Yours forever."

Words could not describe the sensation flooding through my chest. I was light. Buoyant. My chin quivered with a flood of joy as I eased back to the floor and succumbed to sleep.

Peace.

CHAPTER 42

September 9, 1816
Charleston, South Carolina

"All rise! The honorable Judge Hargrave Calhoun presiding."

Josiah cleared his throat and pushed to his feet while watching Avalina rise near Mr. Lewis's side. The weight she'd lost in the past weeks was shocking. Her blue eyes were much too large, cheekbones more pronounced. What bothered him most was the way her focus drifted into vacant stares.

Lord, help her this day.

A sour-faced man with sagging jowls and frizzy white hair, wearing a black robe, entered and plopped into his chair while motioning for those in attendance to sit.

As Avalina eased shakily into her seat, Josiah perched on the edge of his. His chest pinched as if in a vise as he stole another glance at his wife. Despite her weakened condition, she sat calmly, her face serene, hands folded in her lap. It was almost as if she was ... peaceful. How? His own belly was a riot of moths.

They'd had little time to speak when the guards brought her in mere minutes before the trial was to begin. After Mr. Lewis had provided her with a fresh gown and brush, she had been led to a chamber to change and then emerged resembling the shadow of who she was before. Beautiful yet frail.

The judge frowned as he picked up a piece of parchment and perused the details of the case. After long moments, he cleared his throat and peered over the top of his spectacles, his jowls bunching under his chin. "If the defendant will please rise."

Mr. Lewis assisted Avalina once again to stand as they faced the stern judge.

"Avalina Holland, you are accused of attempting to murder a Mr. Cyrene Harding of Fort Hawkins, Georgia. How do you plead?"

Avalina glanced to Mr. Lewis, who lifted his chin. "The defendant pleads not guilty, Your Honor."

The judge grunted, motioning them to sit. Josiah glanced at the emotionless faces lined up along the far wall of the courtroom. The jury, all men, held his wife's fate in their hands. The breakfast he'd eaten that morning threatened to revolt.

Judge Calhoun peered at Harding's lawyer, a tall man with russet hair and a too-confident sneer on his face. "Is the prosecution prepared to address the jury with an opening statement?"

The lawyer rose. "Yes, sir."

"Proceed."

The ruddy man slowly paced back and forth before the jury. "Gentlemen, we are here to reveal truth. The truth of what happened on April fourteenth of this year. It was a day of extraordinary measure. An uprising on the island of Barbados, slaves striking down masters. Rebellion and looting and killing on a mass scale that would make every man and woman in this room shudder. I'm sure many of you read about it in the newspapers."

Whispers rippled through the crowd but quieted when the judge scowled.

"And in the middle of that dark, unfathomable day, Mrs. Holland attempted to murder Cyrene Harding in cold blood."

Josiah bit the inside of his mouth, tasting the metallic tang of blood as it seeped across his tongue.

The lawyer waved his hands melodramatically. "A girl my client had taken in as an orphaned child and reared as his own. A girl he had doted on and lavished kindness upon day after day. And how does she repay him?" The lawyer whirled to Avalina, narrowed his eyes, and pointed. "She put a bullet through his chest."

Josiah's fists clenched. He glanced at Mr. Lewis, who was scribbling furiously on paper.

The condescending man turned his attention back to the jury. "Not only did she attempt to murder my client, she fled that very night with a man who was staying as a guest in my client's home, indicating that this was no mere whim, but a calculated, premeditated plan by both of them." The lawyer turned and fixed Josiah with a smirk. "You see, unbeknownst to Mr. Harding, these two had fallen in love and were overwhelmed by their lascivious desires. But my client did not wish to see them together. After shooting Mr. Harding"—he motioned to the odious man sitting at the prosecution's table—"they ran away, stealing two of his horses, and joined up with a crew of pirates. Smugglers, if that word makes this sordid tale any more palatable." The lawyer flashed white teeth at Josiah but his gaze was icy. "They claim to be married, but without witnesses, how do we know?" He arched a single brow. "It is my belief that Josiah Holland and Avalina Holland were not married at all, but living in sin, and murdering my client was a way to be rid of the one man who stood between them."

More gasps and chatter flooded the room. The judge banged his gavel. "Quiet in the court!" His jowls sagged with displeasure. "Continue, Mr. Abernathy."

Harding's lawyer, Abernathy, resumed pacing, his voice rising and falling like an adept storyteller, meant to entertain.

"But running away was not enough. Mr. and Mrs. Holland, if she indeed can be called that, fled to find sanctuary here, in our beloved state." He stopped, nostrils flaring. "But South Carolina will not be a refuge to murderers and fornicators!"

"Hear, hear!" a man shouted from the balcony.

The judge banged his gavel once more. "Quiet, or I will clear this courtroom."

After the crowd settled, Mr. Abernathy addressed the jury. "My friends, my client and I only want to see justice meted out, and our beloved state free from those who attempt to morally decay it from the inside out. Thank you." He strolled back to the table with a swagger and sat.

Josiah shook with suppressed anger. Lies! Sham! The slithering snake was flinging innuendo as a way to sway the public against them.

Judge Calhoun fixed his sour stare on Mr. Lewis. "Defense, you may give your opening statement."

Mr. Lewis rose slowly and moved to the jury box, fixing each juror with a small smile. "Thank you, gentlemen, for sacrificing your time and commitments to be here for this trial." Lewis's smile dimmed. "In the short time I have known Mrs. Holland, I have found her to be a woman of abject gentility, kindness, and strength. Her husband and his family are pillars within Charleston society, beacons of virtue." Lewis scanned each juror, gentling his tone. "Most remarkable of all is how Mrs. Holland is able to communicate on a daily basis. You see, she is mute."

Josiah was certain he could hear the slightest shuffle of a shoe, the mere rustle of a skirt, so silent was the room.

"My client arrived on the shores of Barbados as a small child, her origins unknown. Orphaned and alone. Instead of taking her in as a father, as Mr. Harding claimed"—Lewis shot the prosecution a fleeting glance—"my client was abused. Held as a slave and imprisoned, just as thousands of others are in the Caribbean, without a single way to defend herself. Her entire life, she has been trapped in silence, unable to give voice to her pain and subject to the whims of a vengeful oppressor ... Cyrene Harding. And I promise you, we can prove it."

I watched Mr. Lewis share pieces of my story with the jury, but it was Master Cyrene's presence that unnerved me. He was the silent, snarling monster, waiting to devour me.

I AM love. I AM peace. I AM hope.

The quiet reassurance sustained me from Mr. Abernathy's glare, the judge's scowling demeanor, the blank stares from the jury box, and the malicious whispers at my back.

I startled when Mr. Lewis eased into his chair beside me. I had missed the last bit of his opening statement. When I had first witnessed his slight size and scholarly look, I feared he would be unable to stand against Harding. I didn't fear that now. My attorney did not speak with meekness. He roared like a lion.

Judge Calhoun tapped his fingers impatiently against his podium. "Prosecution, you may call your first witness."

Mr. Abernathy rose. "We call Josiah Holland to the stand."

My eyes slid shut. Josiah would be exposed to these lecherous men because of me.

My handsome husband walked to the stand to the judge's left, lifted his hand, and swore an oath on the Bible provided by a guard. I blinked. Was this what happened in the States? Men and women swearing on God's Word while turning a blind eye to the horrors of enslavement all around them?

I did not understand this place, and I doubted I ever would.

Mr. Abernathy's lips pinched. "State your name, sir."

"Josiah Holland."

"From where do you hail, Mr. Holland?"

"Charleston, South Carolina."

Mr. Abernathy's demeanor shifted, charging the room with an unseen force. "How long in advance did you help Mrs. Holland plan the murder of Cyrene Harding?"

Air fled my lungs.

"Objection!" Mr. Lewis shot to his feet. "Unsubstantiated. Leading."

"Sustained." The judge skewered Abernathy with a withering look. "Remember your place, sir."

"Yes, Your Honor."

I clenched my hands in my lap as I sat, helpless, watching my husband be picked apart by a vulture. All of the words nothing but lies. The imaginings of a deranged man. Was it Master or his lawyer who had concocted such accusations? I looked down, staring at my tight fingers with their white knuckles. A memory of Matias drifted through my mind.

It was a warm summer day and I was no more than half a score, picking my way through the foliage, Matias at my side, as I gathered a basket of fruit for Molly—mangoes, soursop, and ackees—when I spied a flurry of butterflies scampering around lush blossoms. Setting the basket on the ground, I tiptoed close to the fluttering insects, admiring their bright colors, and tried to trap one in my hands. Over and over, I attempted to catch the whimsical creatures, but each time they escaped. Matias had laughed, shook his head, and sidled close.

"Ach, Redbird, you're going about it all wrong. The fliers, they know you want to trap them, so they scatter. You must rest. Be at peace. Love and wonder cannot be forced." He cupped my pale hands in his and turned my hands so they were lifted with palms up. His gruff voice whispered near my ear. *"Surrender your desire to chase them and let them come to you. Palms up."*

I waited for what seemed to be an eternity, sweat dripping down my back and seeping into my dress, but I held still. Breathing. Waiting.

And finally, it happened.

An orange and black butterfly winged closer, hovering over my head in circles before gingerly easing itself down to perch on the edge of my thumb.

I gasped in delight and studied the miraculous butterfly, entranced.

Matias laughed low. *"See there, Redbird? Good things happen when you keep your heart pure and your palms up."*

Palms up. I unclenched my fingers, Mr. Abernathy's voice droning like the hum of a hive. The white skin receded into hues of pink as I turned my palms up and rested them in my lap.

Surrender.

Great God, come to my husband's aid. Do not let evil triumph.

CHAPTER 43

Josiah raked his hand through his hair as he stared blankly out Mr. Lewis's office window. The trial had been unraveling for four days—four long, miserable days of testimony. Abernathy had called a variety of people to take the stand against Avalina, each one more damning than the last. It wasn't enough that Harding's attorney had tried to rip Josiah apart—he most certainly had—but he had called a litany of witnesses against them. Multiple guests who had attended their engagement party, some Puerto Rican official who had been bribed to make up lies about the crew of *Neptune's Tide*, and worse still, Cyrene Harding himself.

From the moment the man had taken the stand, Josiah's ire raged.

Gone was Harding's pompous grandiosity. Instead, he'd portrayed himself as a humble benefactor, a generous father figure who wanted nothing more than to see Avalina cared for and cherished. He even managed a rather convincing show of emotion when his lawyer asked him about the gun blast.

"I was shocked. Absolutely devastated. The girl I had spoiled and pampered turned on me in a snap of the fingers." His eyes glassed. "I'll never forget how she pointed the revolver at my heart. My only thought before the bullet knocked me backward was, 'No, not my precious daughter.'"

Women sniffled. Men shook their heads. Mr. Lewis, however, fired back with a blistering cross-examination that tore Harding's testimony to pieces.

"You claim Mrs. Holland was happy with you."

"She was." He smiled gently in Avalina's direction but she kept her gaze focused on her lap.

Lewis frowned. "How do you know she was happy since she is unable to speak?"

Harding shrugged. "Smiles. Gestures. The way her eyes lit up when I brought her some small trinket or gift."

"And where are these gifts?"

"Back in Barbados, I imagine." Harding's dark brows pinched. "The night she ran, she took nothing with her. Nothing but my heart."

Josiah clenched his teeth so hard, they nearly cracked. Judging by the jury's sympathetic gazes, they gobbled up his story like meat for a starving man.

Worse still, the prosecution declared they needed to question one more witness. But who was it? Josiah had racked his brain as to who they might call, but came up empty.

Now, Josiah's gaze focused on the blur of people passing Lewis's window. "I just don't know, Bartholomew. Harding packed that room so full of lies, it will take a week to sort through them all."

Lewis offered a wry smile. "That's my job, remember? And if it takes a week, I'll do it. You did a remarkable job holding up under Abernathy's questioning. Direct, honest, succinct, and you didn't waver."

Josiah shrugged and crossed his arms as he brooded. "Truth is truth. It's easy enough to maintain if a body isn't worried about remembering a litany of lies."

"I agree." Lewis leaned back in his chair and rolled the tension from his shoulders. "We need only get through tomorrow and then I can begin calling our own witnesses." Lewis looked up, expression grim. "Are you sure your wife will not testify? Is there no way to change her mind?"

Josiah shook his head. "It's not a matter of unwillingness. It's inability. There's something about her condition ... a kind of nervousness that prevents her from saying what she longs to say. I've seen her desperately struggling to cooperate, but the more stress, the worse it becomes. Perhaps a physician could explain it better."

"That's a thought." Lewis scribbled again. "I made a note to speak with a few doctors in Charleston. See what they know of this peculiar phenomenon." He pursed his lips and tapped his pencil absently against the desk. "Harding is taking a gamble, in my opinion. He is counting on her being unable to speak against his lies."

Josiah winced and rubbed the back of his neck. "Then it merely becomes a matter of Harding's word against mine. He's painted himself as a compassionate father. A heap of hogwash is what it is."

Lewis rubbed his finger across his chin thoughtfully. "Truth needs no defender. If we don't allow him to rattle us, God will provide a way. He always does."

Josiah walked to the rows of law books tucked into the shelves and frowned. "In many ways, I feel our hands are tied. Everyone who can speak to the evil at Azaka Mede is either dead or too far away to be of use."

Lewis arched a single brow. "Your father was there."

Josiah paused, then cast the possibility away. "My father is so angry with me, he'll never testify in her defense. He's more likely to aid Harding ... especially after the way I exposed his sins. And honestly, Father sees what he wants to see."

"A pity." *Tap, tap, tap.* Lewis stopped and gripped his pencil, eyes brightening, and hastened to write a note. When he finished, he stuffed it into an envelope and scrawled an address across the front.

"What's that?"

"I'm calling on a friend of mine. An associate, if you will. He's a man who can get things done, and quickly."

"Like an investigator?"

"Among other things." Lewis straightened his tie and tucked the envelope into his suit coat. "Come. We need to find Meyers as quickly as possible. I have a job for him."

"And that is?"

Lines around the lawyer's eyes tightened. "To unearth anything and everything about Cyrene Harding's past in Fort Hawkins, Georgia."

How many days had I been on trial now? Four? Five . . . six?

Everything blurred together and my mind grew fuzzier with every passing day. I sensed Josiah's strong presence behind me in court, a steadying force against Mr. Abernathy's accusations. Mr. Lewis had been kind, patting my hand, murmuring advice, or explaining the legal terms that swam through my ears, but I was starved. Starved for my husband's touch, starved for food, longing for any scrap of hope I could snatch.

At least I had been given ample cups of water. I drank greedily each day, knowing what awaited me in my cell every night.

Mr. Abernathy swaggered like a rooster across the room, tugging the bottom of his blue silk vest and snagging the jury's attention with his flamboyant theatrics.

"Gentlemen, the prosecution would like to call one more witness." His gaze swung to me and the corner of his mouth tilted up on one side. "Avalina Holland."

No! I sucked in a breath.

Mr. Lewis shot to his feet. "Objection, Your Honor. My client is mute!"

"Overruled." The judge crossed his arms and leaned back in his chair. "The prosecution has a right to call whoever they choose as witness, just as it is Mrs. Holland's right to plead the fifth."

"But, Your Honor, pleading the fifth is different from inability to—"

"Overruled!" Judge Calhoun glared and Lewis clamped his lips shut, body rigid before sitting back down.

He turned to me and squeezed my hand. "If you can speak, speak truth. If you cannot, do not fret. I will handle it."

A wad of cotton lodged in my throat, limbs quaking.

The judge cleared his throat. "The court is waiting, Mrs. Holland."

I felt the stares of hundreds of eyes boring into my body as I rose and shuffled to the witness stand. My knees turned to water and the room spun in dizzying circles. A frowning guard moved to my side and assisted me up the steps. When he held a crisp black Bible in front of me, I slid my left hand on top and raised my right.

"Do you solemnly swear to tell the truth, the whole truth, and nothing but the truth, so help you God?"

I nodded, which must have sufficed, for the judge shooed him away from the stand. The chair was a straight-backed spindle that offered no comfort. *Courage, Avalina.* I lifted my chin and stared at the attorney, who was studying me carefully, his head tilted to the side.

"Please state your name for the record."

My heart raced. I opened my mouth but only a squeak emerged.

His brows lifted. "Pardon? What was that?"

Cold sweat rolled down my back, as my mouth opened and shut again.

"We're waiting, Mrs. Holland."

I fixed him with a long look, and I understood what he was doing. It was not enough to create malicious lies and smear my name through the papers. Mr. Abernathy—no, Cyrene Harding—intended to humiliate me completely. My shame melted away as white-hot anger took its place.

Mr. Abernathy sneered and resumed his strutting. "It is of no concern. Enough people have identified you in this room already. Tell me, Mrs. Holland, do you know how old you were when you found my client's plantation?"

I shook my head.

"Mr. Harding claims you couldn't have been more than five. Is that a fair statement?"

Offering a curt nod, I narrowed my eyes. This vile man was up to something.

"Little enough that you were looking for protection. Nourishment. Shelter. And you found it in Cyrene Harding, yes?"

I shook my head no, nostrils flaring. From behind the lawyer, people bent their heads together, whispering. But Mr. Abernathy plunged ahead, expression morphing into rage.

"And after all he'd done, you shot him! Watched his life blood spill as you ran away to chase your carnal desires! Didn't you? Answer me!"

I allowed my eyes to slide closed, to block out the words, but they were true. I *had* fired the gun. Indeed, I *had* watched his blood pooling on the Turkish carpet. But Abernathy was wrong... I took no delight in it. I had merely tried to survive.

I popped my eyes open and shook my head vehemently.

Spittle flew from the man's mouth. "Where did you get the revolver? Was it Josiah Holland's? How long had you been planning to murder my client?"

My stomach clenched but the words refused to leave my mouth. I stuttered. "N—n—"

"Enough!" Mr. Lewis stood again, his face mottled red. "Objection! Harassing the witness."

"Sustained." The judge speared Abernathy with a irritated glare. "I don't see what you hope to gain from this charade, sir. Considering the witness's, ah, condition, I request you ask her questions that can be answered with a nod or a shake of her head."

"Yes, Your Honor." Abernathy feigned acquiescence to the judge but I was not fooled. A glimmer yet lingered in his eyes.

"In all the years you were at my client's abode, Azaka Mede, did he provide you with shelter?"

I paused. Without a way to explain, the answer would seem as if I was grateful for his benevolence. But he *had* given me a place to live.

I AM truth.

I nodded.

"I see. And food? Did Mr. Harding give you food to eat each day?"

Again, I offered a curt nod.

"Clothing as well, I presume?"

Though it pained me, I nodded and looked down at my hands, clenching a fistful of skirt fabric.

Abernathy smiled and turned to the jury. "You see? Mrs. Holland was well loved and cared for by Mr. Harding." He whirled back to me and stepped close, the color of his ruddy skin rising. "One more question, Mrs. Holland. Did you pull the trigger on the revolver that nearly killed Cyrene Harding?"

The fabric twisted in my hands. Bile choked my throat. *Truth. I AM truth.* Pushing down a sob, I nodded, dropping my gaze to the floor. The courtroom burst into wild chatter.

"Silence!" Judge Calhoun banged the wooden gavel, his expression thunderous.

Mr. Abernathy grinned, much like a fox attempting to hide a stolen egg from a henhouse. "No further questions."

Tears pricked my eyes. I would not cry, not in front of Master Cyrene, but I had already lost without saying a word. The facts spoke for themselves. The truth had not set me free. I was condemned by my own answers and deeds.

I AM peace.

Mr. Lewis rose and approached me, his hands tucked behind his back. "Thank you, Mrs. Holland, for sharing what I can only imagine to be a very painful experience. Mr. Abernathy has already revealed that Cyrene Harding provided you with food, shelter, and clothing. I wonder, did he give you love?"

I shook my head.

"Did he force you to work like the other slaves at Azaka Mede?"

I nodded.

More whispers followed my response.

"Objection!" Mr. Abernathy stood, his jaw rigid. "There is no way to prove such a statement."

Mr. Lewis arched an eyebrow. "Is there not?" He turned to the judge. "Sir, if you'll allow me to pursue my line of questioning, the proof will be revealed."

Judge Calhoun nodded, his lips pinched. "All right then. Over-ruled."

He glanced once more at the judge. "Your Honor, may I ask Josiah Holland to assist me?"

The judge sighed. "This is highly irregular."

"I promise he will not address the jury or answer any questions on Mrs. Holland's behalf."

"Fine." The judge waved his hand dismissively. "Be quick about it."

What was Mr. Lewis doing? My gaze locked with Josiah's as he walked up and whispered in Lewis's ear. A thin blanket of some kind was tucked under his arm. Lewis patted him lightly on the back and straightened. His attention shifted to the jury of confused men.

"Gentlemen, I can prove Mrs. Holland was not the cherished daughter Mr. Harding claims. In fact, I can prove she was held against her will, abused, and mistreated." He turned to Josiah and nodded. "Go ahead."

Josiah approached me, his eyes tender as he offered me a small smile. Setting the thin blanket on the floor, he reached and clasped my hand, his warmth enveloping my cold fingers. Before I could protest, he flipped my wrist over and began unbuttoning the cuff of my sleeve.

Abernathy scowled and stood. "Now, see here! I protest this vulgar display!"

"Vulgar?" Lewis's eyes rounded with feigned surprise. "You consider exposing a wrist vulgar? What about branding another human being with a hot iron? Burning their flesh until permanent marks are seared into their skin? Treating them no better than cattle or pigs?" Shocked whispers rippled through the air. The judge leaned over in his seat above me, eyes wide.

With an apologetic look, Josiah yanked the length of sleeve away, exposing the *A-M* scarring my upper arm. He stepped back and let Mr. Lewis take over.

"You see?" The small man pointed to my arm. Heat flushed the back of my neck and bloomed into my cheeks at the stares and shocked expressions. "*A.M.* The letters, and brand, of Azaka Mede, Mr. Harding's plantation." Lewis wheeled to stare Harding down. "Do you have other sons or daughters, Mr. Harding? Is it your habit to burn the skin of all those you love and cherish, or was that a special gift solely for Mrs. Holland?"

Harding's neck dappled purple as he shot Lewis a murderous glance.

I longed to cover the brand with my free hand but forced my fingers to unclench. To open.

Palms up.

Mr. Lewis swallowed and approached, softening his tone. "I'm going to ask you a question, Mrs. Holland, but I want you to focus on your husband."

344

Swallowing, I nodded and turned to drink in the handsome planes of Josiah's face. His brown eyes that resembled the richest coffee. The stubble lining his angular jaw. There was no condemnation. Only love.

Lewis raised his voice. "Did you shoot Cyrene Harding?"

I nodded, keeping my eyes trained on Josiah's. He mouthed, "Don't be afraid."

"Did you do so maliciously?"

Palms up.

Josiah whispered, "No matter what happens, I love you." I shook my head, lips curving ever so slightly when Josiah smiled.

Take courage.

"Why did you shoot Cyrene Harding?"

My heart wobbled. My gaze flicked away from my husband's. All the people. All the faces and whispers and shame. Master glared at me from his seat. I would be executed if I could not come to my own defense.

Witch. Cursed. I hated this condition. Hated that I could never break past my own weakness.

Josiah leaned in, murmuring, "Look at me, sweetheart. Truth. That is all you need."

I AM truth. I AM peace. I AM forever.

Truth.

The room was still as death. I whispered, my pulse tripping, the word of the One Who saw me eternally branded on my heart, spilling past my lips. "Jesus."

The judge leaned forward. "What did you say?"

Lewis raised his voice. "Why did you shoot Cyrene Harding?"

I licked my lips and stared into Josiah's eyes, drinking in his strength. *I AM…*

"Because he attacked me!"

CHAPTER 44

The courtroom exploded at Avalina's shout. Josiah smiled in wonder, staring at the emotion glassing her eyes. She had done it. She had pushed past the strangling fear and spoken truth.

His chest squeezed.

Abernathy shouted, "You said she was mute!"

Josiah whirled around. "She is! She speaks for no one but me." He swallowed and reached for her hand as the tumult rose. "Or, should I say, she speaks at the name of Jesus."

Despite her trembling, a smile tilted her lips.

Judge Calhoun banged his gavel repeatedly, shouting over the din. "Quiet! I demand silence!" When his screams finally quelled the shouts of exclamation, he threw down the gavel with a reverberating *thunk* and glared. "This court has no tolerance for these kinds of theatrics." He pointed at Avalina and speared Lewis with a murderous expression. "You claimed your client is mute."

Mr. Lewis shrugged, his face yet flooded with amazement. "And so she is."

The judge's eyes bulged. "And how are we expected to believe any word of her testimony?"

Lewis stiffened. "You saw the branding marks on her arm." He hesitated. "And there are ... other ways."

Judge Calhoun's eyes narrowed. "Then you best be getting to it, Mr. Lewis."

Lewis sighed but nodded at Josiah, who gathered the discarded blanket from the floor. "Mr. Holland, will you prepare your wife?"

Josiah released a breath. This would scandalize Charleston society, but he could see no other way to prove the claims against Harding. Catching Avalina's wide-eyed gaze, he whispered, "Trust me."

She bit her lip and nodded as he bunched the fabric in his fists, waiting for Lewis to lay the groundwork. The slight man pierced Harding with a hard stare before turning to Avalina.

"Mrs. Holland, Mr. Harding claims you were shipwrecked upon the island as a young girl of no more than five, is that correct?"

She nodded.

"Would it be fair to say you've lived the majority of your life in Barbados with Cyrene Harding?"

Again, she confirmed his words. Lewis arched a brow. "Do you have any memories of your life before you arrived?"

She shook her head.

"Other than the shipwreck, no moments of trauma or difficulties that would leave you physically wounded before arriving at Azaka Mede?"

Her brows knit but again, she shook her head.

"Very well." His gaze connected with Josiah's. "Mrs. Holland, I need you to rise and turn around."

Confused, Avalina tilted her head but did as he requested. Josiah stepped to her side and murmured, "Here. Use this fabric to cover your front. I will protect you. I promise."

Her eyes widened. As he made haste to unbutton the top buttons lining her back, gasps of shock reverberated through the air. Crimson crept up her neck.

"Mr. Holland, we need only reveal the top half of your wife's back."

Josiah nodded, his jaw tight as he worked quickly. Avalina clutched the fabric to her chest, her eyes squeezed against the humiliation. Gasps turned to shouts when Josiah lowered the back of her dress.

Puffy red scars crisscrossed the tender flesh. He swallowed when one fellow declared, "That's the mark of a whip. I'd know it anywhere."

The judge ordered silence again but it did little to quell the soft hisses of whispered horror. Lewis pointed to the scars. "Sometime while Mrs. Holland was living on Cyrene Harding's plantation, she was whipped. You see the proof before your very eyes."

Josiah's throat welled with emotion. She had endured much. He would spend the rest of his life giving her all she had missed, if the Lord saw fit to free her. Glancing around the packed room, he witnessed the stricken expressions on women's faces, the curl of noses from some of the men, and pity in nearly every person present.

If only they saw those held in bonds on their own plantations with the same heart of compassion.

A welling rush of realization swept through Josiah, starting in his head and sweeping into the broken shards of his heart. This was what he was made to do … to fight for those trapped in chains. God had positioned him to see the horror of slavery firsthand. He knew that way of life inside and out. God had gifted him with a wife who understood it better than himself. The Almighty had even birthed a desire for law into his heart. None of it had been by chance. His life, his mind, even his dreams were like squares in a patchwork quilt, being stitched together in the hands of the Creator … the same One who longed to give every man, woman, and child freedom.

Lord, I ask You to set my wife free. May we have a long life together, working, loving, serving. But even if You don't, I vow my future to You. I'm clay in Your hands. I'll fight for the oppressed, strive for compassion for the hurting. Give voice to those unable to speak.

His focus returned to Avalina's scarred back and he startled. A voice for those who couldn't speak. All this time, the Almighty was using her brokenness to teach Josiah about Himself.

Sucking in a breath, he worked to refasten her buttons. When the job was complete, he gently turned her around as she eased back into the chair, the fabric intended to cover her still gripped in her fingers.

Mr. Lewis nodded curtly in his direction. "Thank you for your help, Mr. Holland. You may be seated."

Josiah moved to reclaim his seat behind the defense's table, but his heart was strangely light. As if the sentence had already been given.

Bartholomew Lewis clasped his hands behind his back. "Mrs. Holland, were you attacked the night of the rebellion in Barbados?"

She nodded and he pursed his lips. "Can you identify your attacker?"

I glanced up, unable to stop a hot tear escaping my lashes as it dripped down my face. *Lord, give me courage.* My eyes fastened on my former master. The man I'd feared but never respected. Black hair streaked with silver, onyx eyes, the slight sneer that tilted his mouth—a fearsome mask to hide the monster inside.

I pointed at Cyrene Harding, my finger an accusation, a spear to his heart.

The room was eerily quiet as I lowered my hand and placed my fingers in my lap.

In the back of the courtroom, the door swung open and banged against the wall. Judge Calhoun scowled as two figures stood silhouetted in the doorway. A large man I had never seen before with massive forearms and a drooping mustache, and a woman with beautiful skin the color of cocoa, high cheekbones, and dark hair tucked under a rust-colored bonnet. Her dress was clean but plain, but the way she held herself—stately, serene—made her appear more like a queen. Sunlight spilled onto the courtroom floor as the man's gaze swept right, then left. When he spotted Mr. Lewis, he walked to him with wide strides and whispered in his ear.

"Now see here," the judge groused. "This is a court of law."

I watched my lawyer's face light with hope as the burly fellow muttered something quietly. Lewis nodded and turned to the judge. "Your Honor, I have no further questions for Mrs. Holland."

My insides quivered. I had done all I could do. With my legs shaking, I moved to ease into my seat next to Mr. Lewis. The man looked my way and winked. What was he up to?

The judge shuffled a few papers on his desk. "The defense may call their first witness."

Lewis smiled. "The defense calls Mary Harding to the stand."

Harding? The same last name as Master? I blinked, my head thick as the woman framed in the doorway walked slowly down the aisle and took her place behind the witness stand. After swearing her oath, she settled into the chair, her dark-eyed gaze fixed resolutely on Mr. Lewis.

"Please state your name."

"Mary Harding." Her voice was lush, like smoke and honey.

"Where are you from?"

"I hail from Fort Hawkins, Georgia." Her delicate chin lifted. "I am part of the Creek people."

"And what is your relationship to the prosecution?" Mr. Lewis folded his arms and stilled, as if knowing the moment was filled with import.

A fleeting expression of grief and anger skittered across her face. "I am the wife of Cyrene Harding. He attacked my sister and killed her more than twenty-five years ago. I have come to see him brought to justice."

Shouts buzzed in my ears. The room tilted on its side as I succumbed to nothingness.

CHAPTER 45

"Avalina, wake up."

Strong fingers stroked my cheek and I blinked. Colors and images sharpened. Josiah's face swam in my vision, his eyes shadowed with concern. Somewhere above him, a guard frowned down at me. I licked my dry lips.

"Wh—what happened?"

"You fainted. Likely from malnourishment or shock. Here." His arm was under my head and he lifted me gently while placing a cup of cold water against my lips. "Drink."

After a few sips, my head cleared ever so slightly. His mouth twisted into a wry smile.

"Well, my dear, you missed quite a show. After you fainted, the judge ordered you to be carried to the hallway while Mrs. Harding gave her testimony." His brows lifted. "Apparently, the Creek people have been searching for Cyrene Harding for years. Mary and two other witnesses saw him attack and stab her sister Lily before escaping to Barbados. The judge ordered a recess and wants to speak with the jury."

I couldn't wrap my mind around the chain of events that had unfolded. What did it all mean? To my left, a door opened and closed. My lawyer approached, his eyes bright.

"Mrs. Holland, are you feeling well?"

I nodded but Mr. Lewis faced the guard. "I request food for my client. Bread and cheese if it is available."

The guard hesitated a moment but moved to do as he'd asked. Cheese? It had been so long since I'd eaten anything other than moldy bread and cold potatoes. The treat sounded heavenly.

Josiah lifted me into a sitting position and shifted to study Mr. Lewis. "Where do things stand?"

"Considering the change in circumstances, Judge Calhoun advised both the prosecution and defense to make our closing arguments as quickly as possible, but I imagine Mr. Abernathy will bellow and rage, drawing out the miserable process. When we've both spoken, the jury will deliberate and reach a verdict. And good news." He grinned, lines crinkling around his eyes. "Mary Harding said her two witnesses are willing to testify against Cyrene when he is brought to trial for the murder of her sister."

Josiah released a breath. "Do you think we've done enough?"

Lewis pursed his lips but nodded slowly. "Yes. We've spoken truth and spared nothing." His gaze shifted to me and his face softened. "You have been exceedingly brave, Mrs. Holland."

Heat warmed my skin and I could do nothing but stare at my lap. Would the truth be enough?

Instead of doing as the judge advised, Mr. Abernathy spoke on and on during his closing statement, berating me, Josiah, Mr. Lewis, Mary Harding, the entire Holland family, and all those who had spoken a word against Harding. I, of course, knew the truth, but I sensed the desperation in the man's voice as he pleaded with the jury to do the "right" thing and condemn me. After a while, his voice became dull, a listless rant that left me numb as I stared at the table. I thought of Matias, Molly, Josiah, Captain Blackthorne, Najaf, the nameless preacher held in the jail, and all those who had sacrificed to see me live.

Not just live. Flourish.

Strangely, I now believed I could, even if the jury found me guilty. I was free in all the ways that mattered. Free from death, free from captivity, free from guilt and shame, free from myself. God had scrubbed my soul clean and there was nothing but utter peace inside.

Come thou fount of every blessing, tune my heart to sing thy praise...

Mr. Lewis covered my hand with his and patted it gently. Heat crept up my neck. I didn't realize I had begun humming.

Wild thought, that. I was on trial for attempted murder but my heart had never been lighter.

After Mr. Lewis spoke briefly, the jury left to deliberate and I sat in the hallway with Josiah, my head resting on his shoulder as I dozed. Before I realized I had drifted away, he was shaking me awake.

The jury had reached their decision.

I stood as they entered, each of the men as solemn and stoic as stone. Sweat dampened my palms and I smoothed the skin against my skirt.

"Have you reached a verdict in the case of Harding versus Holland?"

A stocky juror with enormous sideburns stood. "We have, Your Honor."

"And what say you?"

Streams of mercy, never ceasing, call for songs of loudest praise...

"We find the defendant, Avalina Holland, not guilty."

My knees turned to water as I plopped into my chair, stunned. Mr. Lewis squeezed my shoulders as the courtroom burst into a frenzy, everyone chattering at once.

Judge Calhoun called for order, his ferocious stare turning to me, but for the first time, his voice was gentle.

"Mrs. Holland, you are free to go." His face morphed back into the fierce lion I knew. "Guards, take Cyrene Harding into custody for the murder of Lily Snow."

My last view of Master Cyrene was of a man trembling with rage as irons were clapped around his wrists. He turned, glaring venom at me before being pulled from the room.

But he could hurt me no longer.

November 9, 1816
Philadelphia, Pennsylvania

Two months later

Josiah clasped Avalina's hand in his own as the carriage jostled them left to right and back again. Despite the never-ending ride north, the past few weeks had been idyllic, a time to mend from their wounds and embrace hope.

"And how have you enjoyed our honeymoon?"

Avalina shook her head, the curls she had loosely pinned into a chignon dancing against her smooth neck. "It's a dream. I never knew so much of the world existed." She smiled. "At Azaka Mede, each day was the same. But here?" She glanced once again out the window. "It changes each day."

"And we've only seen a small portion of the country." He sobered. "I'm sorry we've had to spend so much time in the carriage."

Turning to face him, she smiled prettily. "I haven't minded."

He grinned wickedly. "There are advantages. Such as kissing you whenever I like."

He claimed her lips and drank in her exquisite taste. He would never tire of this woman. Everything about her was intoxicating, from the way she touched him to her insatiable curiosity. Each morning, they read the Scriptures together and her questions never ended. Each evening, she read, each text more complex than the last. Within a year, she might surpass his own abilities, so sharp was her mind.

But it was her spirit—gentle, pure, and passionate—that left his heart ever aching for more.

The country roads had long ago melted into city streets, the buildings larger and closer together than any he had ever seen in Charleston. Carriages, wagons, and horses crowded every square inch of road. Hawkers shouted their wares and fish trucks loaded with heaping catches of crabs, clams, oysters, and cod were driven to market. A far cry from the sprawling plantations of home.

His throat clamped. No, Charleston was no longer his home. After the trial, his father had been unrelenting, banishing Josiah from the plantation, but not before his mother pressed a wad of bills into his hand with a teary kiss goodbye. She had even asked Josiah for forgiveness—she had stashed headache powders in their room and had urged the maid to slip them into Avalina's drink to make her appear a drunkard at the engagement party, but the maid had not the heart to do it. It grieved Josiah's heart to witness the lengths his family was willing to go to have their way, but it was over and done now.

The only two people who still haunted his thoughts were his sister Isabelle and Fountain. What would become of them?

Pickering had given them shelter until Avalina was well enough to travel, and Mr. Lewis had used the skills of his detective to locate the very man they sought now.

Thanks to Captain Blackthorne, Pickering, and his mother's generosity, he and Avalina had just enough to begin life anew here. He would attend law school and aid the abolitionist cause.

The carriage hit a bump and she pressed her hand against her middle when it swayed to the side.

"Are you well? How is the baby?"

She laughed and shook her head. "I never should have told you. You worry incessantly."

He lifted his brow. "Don't you think I would have eventually noticed?"

Avalina grinned and bit her lip. "Not for a while. You'll be too excited to begin your law classes than to worry about me and this little one."

Shaking his head, he lifted her hand and pressed a kiss to her soft skin. "Never."

And he would be a father. A greater calling, he could not fathom.

A drizzle shimmered from the pewter clouds as the driver turned onto Second Street. When the carriage stopped before a plain, two-story building, Josiah opened the door and held out his hand for his wife.

As they stepped onto the muddy road, she looked at the building, nerves deepening the lines between her brows. Josiah squeezed her hand.

"Don't worry. He'll love you."

After asking the driver to wait before unloading the trunk, Josiah tugged Avalina's hand as they climbed the short flight of stairs to knock on the dark green door.

Long moments ticked by, but finally, it swung open. Benjamin Magee stared at him through one eye, the other squinted as he stroked his long white beard. "Well, hello, young Holland. I told ye I'd be seeing ye again. And good timing, too. I have work for ye to undertake."

Josiah grinned.

And so, another adventure began.

AUTHOR'S NOTES

The Irish slave trade is not an easy topic in our world's dark past, but I believe it is relevant to discuss even today as more information is coming to light about human trafficking and its cruel reach.

History notes the Irish slave trade began when King James I made the Proclamation of 1625, which required Irish political prisoners be sent overseas and sold to settlers in the West Indies. From 1641 to 1652, over 300,000 Irish were sold as slaves. Ireland's population dipped from roughly 1.5 million to 600,000 in the span of a generation. When Irish fathers were not allowed to take their wives or children with them, it left a huge fatherless population filling the streets. In time, Britain's solution was to auction them as well to rid the streets of the "poor rabble".

In the century following King James I's edict, some reports say as many as 52,000 Irish women and children were sold to Barbados, Jamaica and neighboring islands. Groups of the "Redlegs", so called because of the scorching effects the Caribbean sun had on their fair skin, still live in Barbados today.

When I learned of this horrifying event, my imagination took flight. Although *To Speak His Name* is based on historical events, the people in this story are completely fictious.

The character of Benjamin Magee is based completely on inspiration from real-life abolitionist Benajmin Lay. The real Benjamin was just as I described in this story: a Quaker, abolitionist, vegetarian, diminutive and feisty. After witnessing the horror of slavery in Barbados, Lay traveled to Philadelphia and worked to free as many people as possible. And yes, to make his point in a rather dramatic way, he actually filled an artificial bladder with pokeberry juice, tucked it inside a Bible, and stabbed it to "catch the attention of those who needed to be awakened".

This story has stretched me to my utmost and none of it more difficult to write than a character who is unable to speak. I based Avalina's condition on the present-day diagnosis of selective mutism, which is a type of peculiar anxiety disorder. A person affected by selective mutism is capable of speech, but becomes unable to speak when exposed to specific situations, specific places, specific people, or multiple triggers. The result is a freeze response and the sensation that the words are 'stuck'. This condition is near and dear to my heart since a much-loved family member struggles with this on a daily basis. Of course, in 1816, no such official diagnosis existed, and I have often wondered how those with this condition handled everyday life when so little was known about it. It is a widely misunderstood issue, but there is tremendous help available for those seeking to learn more. I took a smidge of liberty with Avalina's issue, since the majority of selective mutism is not trauma-based. More information can be found at www.selectivemutism.org.

$\mathcal{A}$CKNOWLEDGEMENTS

I'm not sure this story would exist without the unfailing confidence and encouragement of Michelle Griep and Ane Mulligan. So many times I tried to give up—I wanted to give up— but you wouldn't let me. From the bottom of my heart, thank you.

To the Golden Arrows (Michelle Griep, Ane Mulligan, and Elizabeth Ludwig), thank you for pushing me to be my best. My writing has grown leaps and bounds because of you.

To Laura Frantz, Tricia Goyer, Jill Osborne, Shadia Hrichi, and Jocelyn Green, your friendship and encouragement has meant the world.

To the Golden Sausage Award Nominees—Sarah Bennett, Linda Howard, Leann Barna, and Hannah Prewitt—there is no one I would rather laugh with that you. You're more than friends … you're my sisters. In Jesus Name.

To Charlene Patterson, you made my rough and tumble story sparkle and shine. Thank you for being an amazing editor who elevated Avalina's story into places I was afraid to go.

To Christina Suzann Nelson, thank you for sharing Charlene. Lol! You are a treasure.

To my earliest readers and dear friends who were willing to give me honest feedback and let their iron sharpen mine: Leslie Moore, Savannah Kaiser, Cara Grandle, Amy Earls, Casey Patterson, and Holly Varni. You are all precious to me.

To Janet Grant, amazing agent ... thank you for allowing me to pursue my heart.

To the Classical Conversations of Saline County Community: I love you deeply. Thank you for embracing our family with open hearts and arms.

To Todd, Bethany, Dylan, Callie, Carson, Nate, Paisley, Sadie, Hudson, my parents, brother, in-loves, outlaws and everyone in between ... I love you all!

To Jesus, to You be all the glory, the honor, and praise. There is no greater joy that living and dancing in the shadow of Your wings. You are my everything.

ABOUT THE AUTHOR

Tara Johnson is an author and speaker, and loves to write stories that help people break free from the lies they believe about themselves.

Tara's debut novel *Engraved on the Heart* (Tyndale) earned a starred review from Publishers Weekly, and was a finalist in the Carol and

Christy awards. Tara has been published by Tyndale House, Annie's, and Guideposts. In addition to being published in a variety of digital and print magazines, she is a certified body language expert and has been on radio, television and podcasts. She is a history nerd, especially the Civil War, and adores making people laugh. She, her husband, and children live in Arkansas.

You can connect with Tara, and keep up with all the latest news, by visiting www.TaraJohnsonStories.com

$\mathcal{T}$ARA'S PUBLISHED WORKS

Engraved on the Heart (Tyndale)

Where Dandelions Bloom (Tyndale)

All Through the Night (Tyndale)

Every Trick in the Book (Annie's)

A Novel Approach (Annie's)

Contributor to *50 Life Lessons for Grads* (Worthy Inspired)

Contributor to *Angels All Around Us* (Guideposts)

Contributor to *Pray a Word a Day* (Guideposts)

Coming Soon: *A Woman of Little Consequence*

www.ingramcontent.com/pod-product-compliance
Lightning Source LLC
Chambersburg PA
CBHW051941240626
47153CB00005B/1583